Praise for *Falling Star*

"You'll never watch local TV news programs the same way after reading *Falling Star*. Diana Dempsey has poured her experience as a news anchor into a fast-paced novel about television, big business, and the reality of growing old in a youth-obsessed culture."

—Jane Heller, author of *Female Intelligence*

"What a fabulous read! Like the TV news business, *Falling Star* made me laugh and made me cry. It's funny, fast, and full of great one-liners. You'll have a hard time putting it down."

—Sue Herera, CNBC anchor of *Business Center* and *Marketwrap*

"An absorbing, fast-paced story that rips the false eyelashes off TV news. If you've ever wanted to throttle your husband, torpedo your rotten boss, or derail an undeserving rival, this book is for you."

—Ciji Ware, author of *A Light on the Veranda*

"Diana Dempsey does a great job taking you inside the real world of television news. So many people think this is a glamorous business, but Diana captures the true cost of the passion the job demands. . . . All this while crafting a page-turner of a story."

—Daryn Kagan, anchor, CNN News

ued . . .

"A laugh-out-loud experience, this book has you rooting for the heroine all the way. . . . A fun read with lots of twists and turns."

—Laurie Jacoby, agent, Napoli Management Group

"A fast-paced and engaging look into the intriguing world of TV news—behind the camera. Dempsey . . . has turned her real-life experiences into a story you can't put down."

—Soledad O'Brien, coanchor,
Today Show Weekend Edition

FALLING STAR

Diana Dempsey

AN ONYX BOOK

ONYX
Published by New American Library, a division of
Penguin Putnam Inc., 375 Hudson Street,
New York, New York 10014, U.S.A.
Penguin Books Ltd, 80 Strand,
London WC2R 0RL, England
Penguin Books Australia Ltd, Ringwood,
Victoria, Australia
Penguin Books Canada Ltd, 10 Alcorn Avenue,
Toronto, Ontario, Canada M4V 3B2
Penguin Books (N.Z.) Ltd, 182–190 Wairau Road,
Auckland 10, New Zealand

Penguin Books Ltd, Registered Offices:
Harmondsworth, Middlesex, England

First published by Onyx, an imprint of New American Library,
a division of Penguin Putnam Inc.

First Printing, August 2002
10 9 8 7 6 5 4 3 2 1

Printed in the United States of America

To my father, who is looking down on this and smiling

JUNE

CHAPTER ONE

Monday, June 17, 2:19 P.M.

Natalie Daniels stood apart from the other mourners in the rear of Our Lady Victory Catholic Church, clutching a damp balled tissue. Brilliant sunshine streamed through stained-glass windows far overhead, dappling the spray of white lilies on Evie's casket with iridescent color. Beside her in the hushed nave Natalie could hear the soft whir of videotape rolling as her cameraman recorded the eulogy for posterity. And for that night's edition of *The KXLA Primetime News*.

"We all knew Evelyn as a woman who grabbed life with both hands," the elderly priest said, "whether she was winning ballroom dance competitions or skewering politicians for *The Downey Eagle*."

The assemblage chuckled knowingly at the description but Natalie shook her head with a surge of bitterness. Evie *had* to write for *The Eagle*, its circulation all of thirty thousand, because she got fired from KXLA.

"Evelyn was a rule breaker," the priest went on. "And not only when she played bridge or golf or tennis." The mourners' chuckle grew into a laugh. "She broke the rules when she became the first woman reporter on Los Angeles television. She broke the rules when she used the men's rest room because her station had no facilities for women. And she broke the rules when for two decades she won countless Emmy awards and put her news department on the map."

And still *I had to fight to bring a camera here!* Natalie shook her head in disbelief, angry tears stinging her eyes. Evie did so much for KXLA but what did the station do for her? Fire her when she hit forty-five and ignore her death a dozen years later. Natalie practically had to hijack a cameraman to cover her funeral.

"Evelyn also cheated death.We were friends for forty years but she did not share her burden until she could no longer hide cancer's ravages. I am filled with admiration for her courage." The priest's voice caught. "She was a great lady, our Evelyn Parker. And now she rests with God. Let us pray."

He began a lulling, singsong prayer and Natalie allowed her mind to drift. How could Evie be gone? Mentor, friend, relentless booster. The person most responsible for launching Natalie as an anchor, the person who taught her the ins and outs of television news. Natalie fought to control a sob that rose in her throat, her compulsion to maintain professional composure battling her grief. *I never thanked her enough. And now it's too late.*

Flanked by altar boys, the priest moved toward the casket, framed at both ends by standing floral arrangements. He sprinkled the coffin with holy water, all the while praying in a low monotone. The warm air, laden with incense, seemed to thicken.

Natalie heard a rumble in the distance. She cocked her head, puzzled. A thunderstorm? In Los Angeles? In June?

The rumble intensified, grew closer. Natalie felt the earth shudder far beneath the church's stone flags. One of the floral arrangements swayed like a drunken sailor, then toppled, clattering to the floor. Involuntarily Natalie's hand flew to her throat. *No. It can't be. Not now.*

Her cameraman, Julio, turned to her, his dark eyes wide. Both mouthed the dreaded word. *Earthquake!* The next moment the ground shifted with such force that Natalie was thrown off her feet. She dropped to her knees, powerless as she fell to keep her head from banging into a pew. As pain ricocheted through her skull she was aware of people screaming and shouting, Julio beside her on his knees struggling to keep taping.

And the noise! Deafening, like a train pounding through her brain, or a 747 taking off right overhead.

Seconds passed, the unreal undulation growing in intensity. Suddenly the earth gave a particularly ugly lurch. Seventy feet overhead, the church's masonry vaulting groaned. Then a stained-glass window burst from its frame, the sound a shotgun blast. Shards of multicolored glass sprayed the congregation like so much deadly confetti, the screaming around Natalie growing frenzied and animal.

She crawled under a pew, cramming her body into the smallest possible ball. A vision of a man's intense dark eyes rose in her mind. *Where is Miles now? My God, I hope he's safe.*

The image vanished in the next shock wave, as all at once the church was rocked by one apocalyptic spasm of noise and motion. Votive candles rolled crazily across the flagstones, the sickly sweet smells of beeswax and incense mingling with acrid dust. All Natalie could do was cling to the seesawing ground, her head banging repeatedly against the pew, the pain numbing.

Then, as quickly as it started, the shaking stopped.

For a moment she was immobilized, too dazed to do anything but remain in her crouch. Seconds passed. Around her she could hear people clambering to their feet, the priest appealing loudly for calm. Slowly she began to believe that indeed, for the moment at least, the earth had settled grudgingly back into place.

Natalie rose to her full height, struggling to think despite the pounding in her head. The church had taken an unholy beating. Now sunshine slanted through three gaping holes high in the nave, lighting the shards of stained glass strewn across the flagstones like crystals in a kaleidoscope. Votive candles and prayer books lay in piles like abandoned toys, alongside chunks of gold-painted plaster. But the heavens had worked their magic: she and Julio and their fellow mourners were intact. Slowly her instincts as a newswoman scrabbled to the surface: *Call the station.*

Natalie groped to find her cell phone. Briefly she shut her eyes. *Oh, Evie. Even your funeral got overshadowed by a news event. Now you won't make air.* She conducted a quick personal inventory. Her head throbbed as though she'd been attacked with a sledgehammer. Her blond hair was wrenched free of the neat French twist into which she habitually knotted it for air; dust streaked her black suit; somewhere she'd lost one of her pumps.

But she was the beneficiary of a miracle, she soon discovered. Her cell phone worked.

Natalie jabbed the QUICKDIAL button for the Assignment Desk and picked her way unsteadily toward the central door, trying not to cut her unshod foot on the broken glass. She'd just wrenched the door open when a female intern answered her call.

"My God," Natalie breathed into the phone, momentarily forgetting herself, mesmerized by the spectacle across the street. A concrete hulk that used to be a portion of the 210 freeway now pitched at a crazy angle. Bloodied commuters stood dazedly next to their vehicles. Cars that hadn't already skidded earthward teetered on the buckled concrete like Tinkertoys. "It's Natalie—" she began.

The intern cut her off. "Hold for Tony Scoppio."

Natalie clenched her jaw. Her new news director, whom she would gladly return to whatever hole he'd slithered out of.

He came on a second later. "Get your ass back here, Daniels. Pronto."

"If you've got juice back at the station I want to go live from here." Natalie raised her voice above his instant protest. "I'm at Our Lady Victory in Pasadena and we can see from here that the 210 at Sierra Madre Boulevard collapsed."

"No way. We took a power hit but can get on faster from the studio than from the field."

"No. We shouldn't pass on these pictures and we're the only crew here!"

Luckily they'd driven to the church in an ENG, or electronic news gathering, truck, which gave them live capability. Julio edged closer, holding a handkerchief to his forehead. He pulled it away to reveal a jagged gash. Natalie arched her brow questioningly and without missing a beat he gave her a thumbs-up. She returned her attention to the phone, over which she could hear Tony yelling at someone about power hits and generator breakdowns.

He came back to her. "Okay, Daniels, but if you're not ready to go live when we're back up, we're taking it from here without you. Got it?"

Natalie bit her tongue. "Got it."

"And don't say another word to me about that goddamn funeral." He hung up.

Tony Scoppio leaned back in his chair and checked his digital stopwatch, which he'd started the moment he and Natalie Daniels had gotten off the phone. Nine minutes, nine seconds, and counting. The power was still intermittent, and they still weren't on the air.

He focused his eyes on the six television monitors that sat across from his desk, set to Channels 3, 6, 8, 10, 14, and his own, Channel 12. It was his responsibility as KXLA's news director to keep an eye on the competition all day, every day, news emergency or not. The early signs were that, apart from the collapsed portion of the 210 and a widespread power outage, the temblor hadn't wreaked much havoc on quake-hardened Los Angeles. But a 6.2 on the Richter scale still qualified as an emergency.

He did a quick scan. Four of his five competitors were live on the air with quake coverage. Meaning he got lumped with the perennial also-ran in L.A. TV news, Channel 14, the only other station in town incompetent enough still to be running a full-screen PLEASE STAND BY billboard.

Shit.

He threw down the remote with disgust and wiped his hands on the stained expanse of his yellow button-down shirt. What a shop he'd inherited. The backup system had gone on the fritz and he had a bunch of union hires who didn't know a generator from Santa Claus. And a princess anchor talent whining about going live from the field.

Tony ran an impatient hand through what was left of his graying hair and pushed up the half glasses that stubbornly refused to park on the bridge of his nose. Sure, Natalie Daniels was good. But not only did she cost him seven hundred fifty big ones a year—she had a body that a decade earlier had ceased screaming babe-alicious. What with the blond hair and the blue eyes, she looked good, but she looked good *for a woman of forty*. That didn't cut it in an era when "mature" for a local TV female started at thirty-five. And the viewers of choice—the young guns who fit the demographic profile advertisers had wet dreams over—thought any local anchorwoman more than a decade removed from prom night was a prime candidate for retirement.

Well, he'd been around KXLA two months now. Long enough to get the lay of the land. Long enough to start the ass kicking.

His eyes darted back to his own programming, drawn by the sudden onslaught of KXLA's pulsating news theme. *Finally* those bozos had the generator going. So who was gonna show up on the air? Ken in the studio? Or Princess from the field?

Tony hiked the volume until the glass walls of his office vibrated. In the newsroom heads swiveled but he didn't give a good goddamn. He was boss and he liked news loud. He pulled a yellow legal pad closer, poising a pen over its pale blue lines. If Princess screwed up, he'd catch it. And remember. Because he needed ratings, and he sure as hell wasn't going to get them with an aging diva on his air.

At that moment several miles west of KXLA's Hollywood lot, Geoff Marner rocked back in his ergonomically correct chair to gaze out his huge office windows, which traversed the entire wall and reached from Persian carpet to twelve-foot-high ceiling. From the thirty-eighth-floor penthouse of the Century City skyscraper where powerhouse entertainment law firm Dewey, Climer, Fipton and Marner practiced, the windows gave off onto a stunning view of the Santa Monica Mountains, baking in garish California sunlight. Long lines of cars snaked through the streets around his office tower, filled with people who apparently thought a moderate quake was good enough reason to quit work early.

To Geoff Marner, that was a foreign concept. His workaholism put paid to the stereotype of Australians as lazy, beach-loving party animals. Oh, he loved the beach, *and* parties, putting in at least one appearance at each in any given week. But those weren't the arenas in which he passed the lion's share of his time, not since he'd turned twenty-one and bid farewell to Sydney, the city he still considered the most beautiful in the world.

He spun around to face the television across his mammoth office, his attention arrested by a pompous-sounding male announcer. "This is a *KXLA News* Special Report. Natalie Daniels reporting." Geoff hoisted his long legs atop his mahogany desk and clasped his hands behind his head to watch.

Suddenly she appeared, his A-1 client, in front of what looked to be a buckled freeway. *Good for you, Nats. Terrific backdrop.* His face cracked the kind of smile typically induced by high surf and free time. But then his grin faded. She looked a tad the worse for wear. He spied dust on her black suit and tendrils sprung loose from her hairdo. Not to mention a bruise on her neck, which apparently she hadn't even tried to hide with makeup.

But then again, he realized, this was Natalie Daniels. Her appearance was no doubt deliberate. She was heightening the drama, as desirable in TV news as it was in entertainment.

He raked a hand through his light brown hair and listened to her voice over the live pictures. There was a great rawness to it, what with the camera handheld and the word LIVE superimposed on the screen in can't-miss red letters. But not one word she spoke was out of place, not even as she guided viewers around the debris. He grinned, relieved he'd thought to tape the segment. An agent never knew when he'd need fresh material for a client's résumé reel.

Minutes passed. Natalie conducted a few man-on-the-street interviews. *She's a great ad-libber,* he thought for the umpteenth time. *Hell, she's great reading from TelePrompTer.* Agents died for clients like her. He grinned again. *That's my girl.*

"If you're just joining us, at 2:25 P.M. seismologists registered a magnitude six point two earthquake, the epicenter in Paramount, twelve miles south of downtown Los Angeles."

Natalie repeated what she knew, which wasn't much. She was about five minutes into her live shot and so far had run through what basics she'd gleaned from the wire-service reports and done a few quick-and-dirty interviews with petrified commuters who'd been on the freeway when it plummeted to earth.

But it was good. Nothing in TV news was grabbier than strong emotion and good pictures, and she had both.

"The collapse here appears to be the only substantial damage suffered in the Southland," she reported. Out of the corner of her eye she could see the monitor Julio had set up, tuned to KXLA. The screen was filled with a graphic map of the area instead of with her, which meant she had the luxury of reading from her notes.

"Go to Kelly in Santa Monica," the director's voice suddenly demanded in her earpiece. "Tony wants you to go to Kelly. Now," he added.

Her mouth kept moving but her mind raced. *To Kelly in Santa Monica?* Why would Scoppio want to go there? Was there damage there she hadn't heard about?

She finished her thought, then segued smoothly into a toss. "For another perspective we go now to reporter Kelly Devlin in Santa Monica. Kelly, what do you see from your vantage point?"

In the monitor she watched Kelly appear—Kelly in all of her fresh-faced glory, dressed in an aviator jacket that managed to look at once battle-scarred and fashionable. Kelly began to talk and gesture animatedly, then pulled someone next to her to interview, standing so close to him that she remained fully on-screen.

Natalie rolled her eyes. *It's the interview they want to see, not you,* she thought, then forced herself to review her notes, scrawled in a slim, spiral-bound reporter's notebook. A minute later she again raised her eyes to the monitor. Kelly was waxing on, dark-eyed, full-lipped Kelly, standing in front of a grocery store. But what damage? Some Ragu jars fell off the shelves?

Natalie frowned and laid a precautionary hand over her mike, though she knew it wasn't hot. "There's nothing going on there," she hissed at Julio. "Do we have a line to Cal Tech?"

He nodded. He looked in pain. The gash in his forehead had darkened from red to purple.

Another thirty seconds ticked off. Natalie glanced again at the monitor. Kelly was on a tight shot, still chattering. *It's my own damn fault,* she thought, irritated. *I'm the one who taught her it's all about airtime.*

That was the name of the game, no question. The more airtime a talent got, the more recognizable she became. The higher her star rose. The more money she made. All of which in turn translated into still more airtime, and the happy continuation of the cycle.

Another half minute. Kelly's brow was furrowed with concern, her chocolate-brown hair blowing lightly back from her forehead. Who was it who said Kelly had the best TV-news hair? Miles.

Miles. Natalie hadn't let herself think about him, but now his image resurfaced in her brain like a life preserver on water. *I wonder if he's watching.*

She snapped to attention. *If he is, he's seeing Kelly.* Knowing the director could see her from the control booth she stared meaningfully into the lens and motioned for her audio to be brought up.

Nothing.

She frowned and motioned again. But it wasn't the hum of her own mike she heard next, but the director's voice. "Tony wants to stay with Kelly."

Natalie shook her head vigorously, mouthing the word no. They should be going to Cal Tech! This was ridiculous! Why should viewers be held hostage to a report from a site with no damage?

Half a minute later she detected a slight hum and knew that *finally* her mike was hot. "Thank you, Kelly," she interjected in a commanding tone, not bothering to wait for a pause in the blather. She noted with satisfaction the uplift of Kelly's perfectly arched brows as, surprised, she stopped speaking midsentence. A moment later Natalie could see in the monitor that she'd replaced Kelly full screen.

Good! She did a quick recap, ready to toss to seismologists standing by at Cal Tech.

"Wrap," the director ordered in her ear. "Tony wants you off. All the latest at ten, blah blah—you know the drill."

What? Natalie struggled not to lose her train of thought.

"Now," the director snapped. "Ten seconds."

She felt a surge of frustration. But there was no way to fight the edict, so she shifted gears into good-bye mode. "Please join Ken Oro and me tonight at ten on *The KXLA Primetime News*"—Julio had five fingers up—"with all the latest on the quake and the other news." Three fingers. "Thank you for joining us."

She stared into the lens until the director's voice, now returned to some semblance of calm, filled her ear. "Stellar as always, Natalie. But get back ASAP. Tony wants you in his office."

Julio grinned. He'd heard the same directive via headset. "He probably wants to be first in line to offer congrats."

Natalie pulled out her earpiece. Right.

Kelly Devlin stared at her gray-haired cameraman, her lower lip curling with distaste. Why did the Desk always send her out with a geriatric shooter? This one was so ancient it was a wonder she got even one decent frame of video out of him.

"For the last time, *Harry*," she spat the name, "we are going to use the dashboard in the next live shot." She pointed at the Honda Civic still wrapped around a light pole, its driver just spirited away by ambulance.

"It's a goddamn coup that I found this. It's the only thing in Santa Monica that's got any blood on it! What are you afraid of?" she taunted. "You'd rather stay at the grocery store and shoot broken bottles?"

Harry just stared at the ground and shook his head. He looked fed up. Well, so was she.

Kelly abandoned her cameraman and stalked across Pico Boulevard toward the ENG truck, its mast high in the air. *Forget Harry*, she ordered herself. *Worry about something important. Like checking your makeup before the next live shot.*

She had to look *perfect*. What everybody said about TV news was true: If it bleeds, it leads. And *she* would lead *The KXLA Primetime News* tonight! She was damn smart to have found an idiot who'd slammed into a light pole when the quake hit.

Tugging at her eighteen inches of black lycra skirt, Kelly climbed through the truck's open sliding door and perched on one of the Naugahyde swivel chairs that faced the wall of knobs and monitors. She pulled her makeup bag out of her satchel and dumped the contents onto the other swivel chair. Swiftly she went through her routine, which in her two years as a reporter she'd honed to perfection: concealer for any imperfections (rare), base to even out her skin tone (olive), powder to keep the shine down (her one beauty cross to bear), three shades of brown shadow (the darkest at the outer corners to add drama), eyeliner (thick), mascara (thicker), lip liner and lipstick (dark and matte), and blush to highlight her cheekbones (high).

Now for hair. Kelly spread her knees and threw her head down between them, brushing from the nape the thick brunette mane she had cut every four weeks at seventy bucks a pop. Every other week she trimmed the bangs herself to keep them at their sexiest (just above her brows). At least that was what the photog told her when she posed for *Playboy*'s "California Collegiate" issue, and he must've been right because she was the only girl to get a full-page spread. Kelly pumped the hair spray, then jerked her head back. When her last boyfriend had seen that maneuver he'd told her she looked like a girl in a commercial.

Commercial, my ass. Kelly snorted and held her compact's mirror close up to her face. What *she* looked like was a prime-time anchorwoman.

"Why did you cut Kelly off?" Tony demanded.

Trying hard not to let her jaw drop, Natalie stood in front of her news director's desk and listened to him hurl the question like an accusation. She'd just hauled ass to anchor a brilliant interrupt and what did Tony Scoppio do? Demand to know why she'd cut off a cub reporter?

"Kelly was in Santa Monica." Natalie kept her tone level, sensible. "Miles away from the action. We, on the other hand, were in front of a freeway collapse. We—"

"There was a helluva lot going on in Santa Monica."

"Broken windows and jars off grocery store shelves!"

"Car accidents," Tony shot back. "Collapsed walls."

"*One* car accident! *One* collapsed wall!"

"I don't know who you worked for before but let me tell you how *I* run my shop." Tony jabbed his thumb at his chest. "*I* decide who goes on the air, and for how long. *I* decide. Not producers, not directors." He paused. "And certainly not talent."

Natalie narrowed her eyes at Tony, enthroned behind his desk like a news director buddha. Anybody else would applaud her but *he* was attacking, using a pretext as thin as script paper. "May I remind you that thanks to *me* we were the first station to air pictures of—"

"We were the *last* station on the air!"

"That is a function of technical problems that *you* haven't fixed." More than any other news director she'd ever had, this guy made her blood boil. "I honestly do not understand this. This is not how this newsroom used to be run. You—"

He cut her off. "You got that right, Daniels."

She stared at him, momentarily silenced.

"The way this newsroom used to be run," he went on,

"it lost money. And ratings were heading south. Well, no more. It's a whole new world and you better get with the program. Or I'll tell you what."

He stopped and she waited, for what she couldn't imagine.

"You'll be off the program."

"Oh, come on." She scoffed at him. "Kelly was doing a monologue on a nonevent. I made a judgment that it was time to—"

"That's not your judgment to make."

"As an anchor it *is* my job to make editorial decisions—"

"No. It is *your* job to listen to *my* editorial decisions."

Her arms flew up in exasperation. "Tony, I am not some brainless mouthpiece out there! Of *course* I have to make judgments about what's news and what isn't, particularly in a breaking—"

"Did it ever occur to you that maybe your judgment isn't what it used to be?" He arched his brows. "Maybe you're out of touch. Maybe you've gotten soft from all those years behind the anchor desk."

"That is the most asinine thing I ever heard." Natalie spoke with as much dismissiveness as she could muster but felt as if the earth beneath her feet were again shifting. She tried to maintain control by focusing on the weave in the industrial-strength carpet. It was the color of television static.

"Now is as good a time as any to tell you." Tony paused and something changed in the stale office air. "As of right now I'm not planning to pick up the option on your contract."

Natalie felt as if a truck had careened into her lane of traffic and hit her head-on. *He wants to get rid of me?* She had to force herself not to reach for a seat.

"The ratings aren't what they should be," he went on, his tone now so conversational they might have been discussing the weather. "You've seen the numbers for the May sweep?"

As if through a fog Natalie watched him grab a manila folder and slap it open. *Just happened to have it handy,* she thought dazedly. Then he tossed in her direction a sheet of paper with those don't-lie columns under the heading NIELSEN. But she didn't take it.

"Of course I've seen them," she managed. "But the drop-off has a lot more to do with the stories you're putting on the air than with how I'm anchoring."

"That's funny, Daniels." He grabbed the top folder from another pile. "When I was news director at KBTT in Dallas, before I came here, the stories I put on the air got us into first place." He held up a chart and grinned broadly. "Want to try another explanation?"

Her mind raced. There were all sorts of reasons ratings dropped. Ratings ebbed and flowed like seawater. No newscast stayed number one forever.

"I'm as frustrated as you are with the numbers," she told him. "But mark my words, they'll rebound with the quake coverage."

"Right." Now his tone was dismissive.

Natalie watched as the man who held her fate in his hands slapped his pile of manila folders shut.

"Let's just see what happens with the numbers, Daniels." He smiled at her. "Let's just wait and see."

CHAPTER TWO

Monday, June 17, 5:25 P.M.

Bastard! Natalie cut her way across the newsroom, then out through the security door, striding past the darkened studio, hair and makeup departments. Her goal was the ladies' room at the far end of the production wing, just before the swinging double doors that demarcated KXLA's executive suites. It was the only place she might get some privacy.

She pushed open the battered door with the black-and-gold paste-on letters spelling W MEN that led into the tiny pastel anteroom, its lone piece of furniture a moth-bitten pink couch left over from some long-canceled talk show. Frantically she paced the minuscule space, her rage threatening to burst out of her like a volcanic blast. How she'd maintained any semblance of calm in that meeting with Tony was beyond her.

My God, he's trying to get rid of me. Just like Miles.

She shook her head vigorously. *No. No Miles now. Concentrate on one bastard at a time.*

All those years! *Fourteen years* of working all hours, just to be drop-kicked like some worn-out pigskin? And all those awards . . . how many? She halted and tried to think. Three Emmys, four Golden Mikes, too many Women in Journalism awards to count. Periodic ratings domination for *The KXLA Primetime News*, though Tony was right that hadn't been the case for some time. But still, the suits should give her a medal! Not only had she outlasted a parade of news directors but an army of coanchors, too. Now she was on her fifth: a vapid Nordic stripling Tony had imported from some Minnesota backwater. All too appropriately named Ken, he looked straight out of Mattel.

But if there was one constant at KXLA, it was Natalie Daniels. She was the L.A. TV-news equivalent of death and taxes. Or *had* been, back when she'd seemed an eternal star in L.A.'s glittering firmament. Now she felt herself falling, plummeting back to earth from her heavenly perch.

Maybe you're out of touch. Maybe you've gotten soft from all those years behind the anchor desk . . .

Her anger fled as rapidly as it had risen, leaving her deflated like a day-old party balloon. She moved slowly toward the mirror and splayed her hands on the narrow shelf below the glass, vaguely aware of the diamond on her engagement ring scratching the Formica. These days, she kept the stone turned inside toward her palm. It seemed somehow better than removing the ring entirely.

Miles.

She looked up and stared into her own eyes. Big blue pools stared back. Stranger's eyes. The eyes of someone she'd never met. Someone named Natalie Daniels who wasn't a television anchorwoman. Who was nobody's wife. Nobody's mother. Who was *nobody.*

Tony's been around only a few months and already he's trying to get rid of me. She blinked as the realization sank in. In some still-functioning part of her brain she realized that long before today he'd spoken with the Legal Department. Other people knew—people she passed in the halls. The bastard had *planned* it.

Footsteps. Approaching from down the hall. Natalie spun on her heels and dashed into one of the stalls, pulling the door shut behind her with a metallic clang.

The outer door to the ladies' room groaned open. "Natalie?"

It was Ruth.

Natalie listened, hardly breathing, as the older woman hesitated, then slammed the door open, the hinges protesting mightily as the door hit the wall. She could envision thick-legged Ruth in her sensible shoes striding inside, almost sniffing the air trying to find her, like a loyal dog.

Ruth pushed open the door to the first stall, two down from Natalie. "I know you're in here. I saw you leave Tony's office. Like a bat out of hell, I might add. Come on out."

Natalie stayed put, stupidly, even though all Ruth had to do to find her was push all the stall doors and realize she was behind one of them. Or look down and see . . .

"Jig's up." She heard Ruth grunt as she bent at the waist to peer under the stall doors. "Nobody else in this joint can afford Manolo Blahnik pumps. Come on, give up the ghost and come out."

Sheepishly Natalie slid back the latch and walked out, eyes averted from Ruth's probing gaze. The woman didn't miss a thing. It wasn't for nothing she was the executive producer of a prime-time newscast, a top-level position rarely attained by a woman.

Natalie leaned her fists on a sink, staring down into the white porcelain. Up to her nostrils wafted the bleachy scent of some industrial-strength bathroom cleanser. "Don't say a thing. Just don't say a thing."

Ruth sighed. "What did that dirtbag do this time?"

Natalie shook her head.

"What'd he do? It must've been a doozy. I don't think I've ever seen you this upset." Ruth folded her arms across her bosom and leaned against a sink, her flesh settling in rolls beneath her suit du jour—a matronly royal blue polyester. Natalie raised her head to look into Ruth's keen no-nonsense blue eyes, shining bright with intelligence and kindness below her mop of perennially unkempt dark blond hair.

"You're right. It was a doozy," she heard herself say. To her surprise, Natalie felt herself wanting to tell the story, felt the words gather in her throat like horses straining behind the gates to begin a race. "He said he isn't planning to pick up the option on my contract."

The words started spewing out then, careening wildly,

rolling out and over one another like a verbal wash over a just-crested dam. "He said the ratings aren't what they should be. He said I've lost touch and gotten soft." The tears that had been gathering spilled out, but for once Natalie was oblivious of how she looked, conscious only of Ruth's comforting bulk beside her, Ruth's plump hand rubbing her back.

"Come on." Ruth was gruff. "This is bullshit. He's not going to fire you. He needs you."

"That's not what he says."

"He's posturing. Probably wants to cut your salary when your contract's up. Which is soon, right?"

"Early October," Natalie admitted.

"See?"

They stood for a while in silence, listening to a mournful drip from one of the faucets. *Plop. Plop.* Glistening wet drops that fell like tears onto the porcelain, then rolled down the drain. Uselessly.

Finally Ruth shook her head. "Hell, I half wish it were me on the hot seat. If *I* got cut loose I'd drive down to Long Beach and hop on the first cruise ship I could find, bound for who the hell cares where so long as there's a reasonable selection of still-breathing men on board." Ruth screwed up her face as though imagining the scene. "Not like that's so easy to find these days."

Natalie frowned at Ruth. "What are you saying?"

"Just that when it comes right down to it," Ruth continued in that same bewildering commonsense tone, "would it be all that bad to be beached? I mean, it happened to Evie and she went on to do something else. It happens to all of us eventually."

"It does not!" Natalie reared back from the sink. "What in the world are you talking about?"

"Face it, Natalie. This is TV news! The women they're hiring to go on-air are getting younger by the nanosecond." Ruth faced the mirror, gave herself a narrow-eyed appraisal, then shrugged her shoulders. "What do you think Scoppio's getting at? We're warhorses compared to the nymphets they're bringing on these days. Doesn't matter they can barely read. Plus all they want is T&A

news and you and I do the real stuff. I'm surprised we've lasted *this* long."

Natalie gaped at Ruth, not believing what she'd just heard. Was this *Ruth* talking? The woman who'd produced her newscast every weeknight for the last decade? The only other woman on God's earth who loved the news as much as she did? Natalie rubbed her forehead, as confused as if she'd suddenly been pitched into a topsy-turvy, Alice-in-Wonderland world where nothing was what it seemed to be.

"You've got money in the bank, right?" Ruth peered at Natalie quizzically. "That's not it, is it? You can afford to retire?"

"*Retire?* Ruth, I just turned forty!"

"Right. Ready for social security in TV-news terms. At least in local. At least for a woman."

"I cannot believe I'm hearing this." Natalie lowered her voice almost to a whisper. "Not from you."

"You don't think I'm in the same boat? You don't think I cost Scoppio more than some smart-ass grad from U.C.L.A.'s Writers' Program?"

"Yes, but what about—"

"Listen, pumpkin," Ruth interrupted. "You haven't asked for it but I'm gonna give you a piece of advice." The veteran news producer pursed her lips and gazed into the distance. She looked wise at that moment, like a matriarchal elder who doled out her hard-won knowledge to the younger tribal females only on momentous occasions. "You've had a good run. Hell, a *great* run. It's not only been better but it's lasted longer than it does for most people, male *or* female."

She paused and the women looked at each other.

"You don't need this crap," Ruth continued more lightly. "Go to the beach. Do something else. Do *nothing* else. Shit, I'd quit in a heartbeat if I didn't have to work for a living."

"But wouldn't you *miss* it?"

"I'd miss it," Ruth allowed, "for, like, a *day*. And believe me, my day will come. Now they need me to train all these babies they're hiring. They still need people who know how to do the work. But I'm saving my pennies, because one of these days some shit-for-brains news director will call me into his office and tell me he wants to take a 'fresh approach.' And I'll be on the street."

"And you'll be all right about that?"

"Have to be. What I don't get is why you're not."

Natalie felt Ruth fix her laser gaze on her again. Quickly she looked down into the porcelain, but knew she hadn't been fast enough.

"So," Ruth said quietly, "how much does this have to do with Miles?" Natalie felt Ruth's hand on her back. "Maybe even crusty old Ruth can figure out this is pretty tough coming on the heels of Miles leaving."

There it was. Out. Natalie remained silent. Despite how closely they'd worked together, cheek by jowl for years, she'd never spoken to Ruth about Miles walking out. She hadn't spoken to anybody. It was too private, too humiliating. But word of his abrupt departure from the home they'd shared for a dozen years—*for a bimbo from his sitcom!*—had of course made the gossip rounds in Hollywood, and KXLA, too. And one night Ruth had simply bent over Natalie's desk while she was gathering her things to leave after the newscast and asked quietly if there was anything she could do. Natalie's eyes had misted over. She'd just shaken her head, mutely, not even able to muster the courage to look up. But Ruth had just rubbed her back and asked her over for dinner the next night, a Saturday. She'd already written her address on a Post-it note, and left it on Natalie's desk with instructions that she come at seven. Natalie had forced herself to go. But then she surprised herself by having a good time, laughing at Ruth's offbeat humor, at the array of hippie-era tchotchkes that cluttered Ruth's modest ranch-style house. She'd drunk too much chardonnay and eaten mountains of garlic bread and fettuccine Alfredo—so much that her stomach stuck out in a bloated mound for the next two days. It turned out that Ruth was a terrific, though hardly health-conscious, cook and a wonderful companion. While she gave Natalie plenty of opportunity to talk about Miles, she never forced it. And Natalie had stayed mum. Later she was startled to realize she'd actually forgotten about him for a while. It was the most relaxed she'd felt since he'd left. To this day, months later, she was grateful.

"I can see you don't want to talk about it now. But I'm here if you change your mind." Ruth's voice was back to gruff. She raised her wrist to look at her watch, an oval mother-of-pearl face on a slim gold band that looked incongruously delicate on her fleshy wrist. "Damn, look at the hour. I've got to go round up the reporter kidlette scripts so no major fuckups make it on air tonight." Ruth plodded into the anteroom, then turned around, hands on blue polyestered hips. "By the way, have you told your agent about the Tony thing yet?"

"No. Geoff's out of the office."

Ruth nodded. "Chin up, kiddo." Then she was gone.

Once again the ladies' room fell silent, save for the steady drip from the faucet and the ticking of the round white-faced clock that hung above the anteroom couch. Natalie looked in the mirror. In the harsh fluorescent lights she saw a tall, slim blonde in a severe black suit—a woman who, if you didn't examine too closely, looked as if she had everything under control.

It was only a mirage.

But what happened next was very real—a powerful aftershock that rattled KXLA from studio floor to satellite dish.

"Natalie, we need you on set. Pronto."

The stage manager caught her by the elbow as she raced past the tall studio doors on her way to the newsroom. He was sinewy, outfitted in denim like most techies, his fingers strong. They dug painfully into her skin. His ice-blue eyes, circled by fine lines, darted nervously under the bill of his Dodgers cap.

"That was a big aftershock." He made a move to pull her inside the studio, where the lights were already on. The anchor desk stood center stage, awash in the klieg lights like the star of a Broadway show. "Tony wants us back on the air within two minutes."

Natalie hesitated. The adrenaline that usually pumped at the mere mention of going live failed to flow, stopped up as though dammed. A vision of a smug Tony Scoppio danced before her eyes. *Maybe you've been at this too long.* She glanced down at her suit, still streaked with dust from the church. "I have to clean up."

He shook his head. "No can do."

"I have to go to the newsroom to get wire copy."

"The intern'll bring it out." The stage manager made a stronger move to pull her inside the studio and this time it worked. He propelled her to the anchor desk, even pulling out her chair and attaching her mike, which normally she did herself. The studio was a beehive. Crew members raced around recalibrating the monitors and stage lights that had been thrown out of whack by the aftershock. Somebody brought her a Styrofoam cup of lukewarm water.

Natalie fumbled to insert her earpiece. It took a few tries to plug the endpiece into the correct jack under the console. Her fingers felt bloated and awkward, like on a hot day. Even in the studio's frigid air she felt a bead of sweat shiver down her back.

How can I be so nervous? She struggled to slow her breathing. *This is insane! I've done this a million times!*

"Thirty seconds," the stage manager announced loudly. He stood sentry next to Camera One, talking on his headset.

Natalie clutched the anchor desk's cool laminated surface. Her clammy fingers left damp marks, telltale smudges of panic.

In her mind's eye she saw Tony arch his brows. *Maybe your judgment isn't what it used to be.*

"Ten."

No! Natalie banished the image. A female intern, tee-shirted and ponytailed and breathless, ran in to dump a pile of just-ripped wires on the desk. The girl pulled her hand back too fast and knocked into the cup of water, sending the liquid in a fast-moving river across the anchor desk. The girl's hands flew to her horrified face. "Oh, Miss Daniels, I am *so sorry*—"

"Five, four, three—"

Someone grabbed the girl out of the way. Time tunneled into slow motion. Mesmerized, Natalie watched the stage manager's fingers count down the seconds to airtime. As though it were happening to someone else she saw the water soak the print on her wires into illegible blobs of bluish ink, then cascade in a stained rivulet onto her lap.

That was the only information I had, she realized, settling into an odd, surreal calm. *I don't know a damn thing about the aftershock.* Going live without the shred of a fact to rely on was so catastrophic she'd zoomed right past fear into a bemused acceptance.

The studio filled with a booming male announcer's voice. *"This is a* KXLA News *Special Report. Now from our studios in Hollywood, Natalie Daniels."*

The bright light above Camera One bloomed fire-engine red. She was live.

Natalie took a deep breath, her heart pounding a staccato rhythm. "Good evening. At 2:25 this afternoon Cal Tech seismologists registered a magnitude six point two earthquake, the epicenter in Paramount, twelve miles southeast of downtown Los Angeles."

She paused. The lens stared back, all-seeing.

"Just a few minutes ago," she went on, "the Southland was shaken by a sizable aftershock—"

Was it an aftershock? Maybe it was an unrelated quake?

"—We do not yet know the magnitude of that temblor—"

At least I don't. I haven't read the wires.

"—but it appeared to be considerably weaker than the initial jolt."

At least to me. But what do I know?

She struggled to remember what she could about the first quake. Somebody would bring in new wires any second—they *had* to. Anxiety congealed into a solid mass in her stomach. Gooseflesh rose on her thighs from the spilled water, which had by now soaked not only her legs but her upholstered anchor chair.

"The earlier temblor brought down a portion of the 210 freeway at Sierra Madre Boulevard," she added desperately.

Old news! People want to hear about the aftershock!

She glanced down at the sodden wires, trying to pull one off the top without looking obvious. She was still on a tight shot. Why didn't the director go to video? Why didn't somebody bring in new wire copy?

Then she broke one of her cardinal rules, one she hadn't broken in almost two decades of television news. She simply stopped speaking and looked down from the lens. In the odd silence that gripped the studio, her eyes flew across the blurred wires, searching frenziedly for anything faintly legible.

Then to her immense relief she saw a number she could make out. Immediately she began speaking. "Seismologists report the aftershock to have registered eight point three on the Richter scale," she reported, then stopped.

Eight point three? She became aware of the sudden puzzled stillness of the stage manager, of the hot glare of the klieg lights, of the oversize red numbers relentlessly reading out the time on the digital clock below Camera One. Desperately, she looked back down at the wire. Was that number an eight or a three?

"I'm sorry," she said, thinking fast, and managed a weak smile. "That was a three point three. The aftershock that struck only minutes ago was a three point three on the Richter scale."

"Natalie." The director's urgent voice filled her ear. "It was a *four* point three! *Four* point three!"

"I'm sorry," she repeated. She could feel her cheeks begin to burn. "That was a *four* point three on the Richter scale. I apologize for the confusion."

"Toss to break!" the director yelled in her ear.

She managed a smile. "We'll be back in just a moment." She forced herself to stare at the lens until she saw an SUV commercial roll. Never in her entire career had she been forced to toss to commercial to save her ass. It was something other anchors did. Never her.

It hit her full force, like a bomb detonating mere feet away.

That was the worst on-air mistake she'd ever made. In eighteen years. This throbbing humiliation racking her body was the aftershock of screwing up, badly, on air.

She looked at the stage manager, but he was fiddling with the bill of his Dodgers cap and didn't meet her eyes. No one did. No one spoke. In the silent studio, a cocky male voice pounded in her ears.

Maybe you've been at this too long.

Three hours later, Harry stood outside the ENG truck's open sliding door, hands on denimed hips, staring inside at Kelly. "You gonna call the hospital again?"

Kelly threw down her compact and swiveled on the rotating chair to glare at her cameraman. "I already called!"

"That was a while ago. And the guy's in critical condition, right?" Harry jutted out his chin. "Don't you think you should—"

"Lay off!" Kelly suddenly launched out of the truck, landing on Harry's cowboy boot. He winced. "What do *you* know about anything editorial? Don't bug me! You're ruining my concentration before I have to go live again." She grabbed her compact, earpiece, and script and headed back across Pico Boulevard, kicking at a squished beer can. Forget the hospital! Who had time for that? She should probably be nicer to her cameraman, if only for P.R. reasons, but Harry was an idiot if he thought TV news was about checking every last detail. She knew it was about looks and sass and determination.

Kelly arranged herself in front of the camera and pulled out her script, scrawled in her reporter's notebook in a large girlish hand. She'd written a live toss and tag and about a minute ten of pure drama in between. It might be for local news but it was good enough for a national tabloid like *Hard Line.*

DARRYL MANN WAS ALMOST HOME FROM A LONG WEEKEND PLAYING THE CRAP TA-

BLES IN VEGAS, BUT HE SURE DIDN'T BET ON THIS! POLICE SAY MANN WAS DRIVING THESE RESIDENTIAL STREETS AT FIFTY LIGHTNING MILES AN HOUR WHEN THE QUAKE STRUCK. HE LOST CONTROL OF HIS HONDA CIVIC AND SLAMMED INTO THIS LIGHT POLE AT FOURTH AND PICO, NEARLY GOING THROUGH THE WINDSHIELD. YOU CAN BE SURE NO VEGAS GAMBLER WOULD LAY ODDS ON HIS CHANCES OF RECOVERY!

Kelly giggled. She loved that line! She hadn't sent in her script for approval, which she was supposed to do, because no way would stick-up-her-butt Ruth let her get away with saying what she wanted. Not to mention airing the video of the victim she'd made Harry shoot.

Kelly plumped her hair, grinning to herself. Getting those shots before the ambulance came had been a brainstorm. Ruth would freak but so what? Tony was the real boss and Kelly bet *he'd* like it. Realistic video was hot these days. Tony liked hot. And she liked giving the news director what he wanted.

Kelly ran her eyes down her live tag.

AS DARRYL MANN LIES IN A SANTA MONICA HOSPITAL FIGHTING FOR HIS LIFE, HE MUST BE WONDERING WHY A FREAK ACCIDENT WOULD DEAL HIM SUCH A CRUEL HAND. WE CAN ONLY HOPE HE HAD BETTER LUCK AT VEGAS'S GAMING TABLES. KEN AND NATALIE, BACK TO YOU.

Silently, over and over, Kelly mouthed her toss and tag, memorizing them so she wouldn't have to look at her notes. She needed to make love to the lens.

"Here's the—"

"I told you not to interrupt!" Kelly grabbed the mike from Harry's hand. "I'm memorizing!"

Harry shook his head and loped back to the camera. "A minute back," he reported. "Give me a level."

Kelly counted to ten and Harry tweaked the volume. "Thirty."

Her heart started really pumping. She did live shots all the time but for some reason it felt like this one really counted.

"Ten."

Kelly launched into her breathing exercises and checked the monitor that Harry had put left of his tripod. It was set to KXLA, the volume muted. But she could hear the audio in her earpiece.

On came the open for *The KXLA Primetime News*, over it Natalie's voice:

> *"TONIGHT, OUR FIRST COMPLETE LOOK AT THE DAMAGE SUFFERED ACROSS THE SOUTHLAND FROM TODAY'S QUAKE. KELLY DEVLIN IS LIVE IN SANTA MONICA WITH A FULL REPORT. ALSO COMING UP—"*

Kelly closed her eyes, her heart racing. Her damp palm slipped on the KXLA microphone. *Keep it punchy! Work the lens!* Again she glanced at her notes.

Out of one eye she saw Natalie and Ken appear on the monitor. Natalie looked even tighter than usual. Kelly forced herself to focus. Showtime.

Then, as if by magic, she saw herself materialize on screen. *Damn, I look hot!* Then Natalie's voice.

> *"KELLY DEVLIN IS LIVE WITH THE DETAILS. KELLY?"*

Kelly took a deep breath.

> *"NATALIE, I MUST WARN OUR VIEWERS THAT THIS VIDEO IS GRAPHIC. DARRYL MANN WAS ALMOST—"*

Perfect! Kelly got through her live toss and watched on the monitor as her package rolled. She wiped her palms on her skirt. Damn, did it look good! Quickly she reviewed her tag. The second before she came back Kelly dropped her chin and lifted her eyes, which the *Playboy* photog said made her look even more dramatic.

"AS DARRYL MANN LIES IN A SANTA MONICA HOSPITAL—"

She kept a serious expression on her face and her eyes trained on the lens until Ken started to intro the next story.

"That was a real piece of work," she heard Ruth snarl in her earpiece. "That video of the victim was completely unacceptable, Kelly. I notice you didn't bother to get script approval. *Did* you bother to check with the hospital?"

That fat bitch. Kelly pretended she hadn't heard and sashayed out of frame, pulling out her earpiece.

Whew! She threw back her head and grinned at the sky, bright with stars. She'd done it! That was a kick-ass live shot and she had a strong instinct it had been noticed.

By somebody who counted. Not never-been-fucked Ruth Sperry.

"Break down fast, Harry," Kelly ordered, tossing the mike in his general direction. It scraped hard on the asphalt. "Let's blow this pop stand." It would take half an hour minimum to get back to the station and then she'd have to cut at least one piece for the morning shows. She *should* do two. After all, what had Natalie taught her, back when Kelly was playing eager beaver? *Get airtime. Period.*

Kelly grinned. Thanks for sharing!

Harry unplugged cords and stowed gear, grunting all the while. Restlessly Kelly paced, her heels clicking on the pavement.

They were just back in the ENG truck's cab when its phone rang. Harry answered, then after a second raised his eyebrows and wordlessly handed the receiver to Kelly.

She frowned. Why would anybody at the station be calling? They knew she'd be back. "This is Kelly."

"And this is Ruth. You've got a serious problem this time, missy."

Kelly tensed.

"I just got a call from the hospital where Darryl Mann is being cared for. Or *was* being cared for, more to the point."

"What?" Kelly clutched the phone.

"Suffice it to say everyone there was very upset. Not only because of the video of him, Kelly, which was *appalling* and goes expressly against policy—"

That hog and her "policies." Kelly rammed her pen through the spirals on her reporter's notebook. She'd have fewer restrictions if she'd gone into the goddamn military!

"Once and for all," Ruth demanded, "*did* you call the hospital before you went live?"

"I couldn't get through," she lied.

"Don't even *try* shitting me, Kelly. I can see right through you. And mark my words, if Darryl Mann's family finds out about this, your ass'll be in a sling. You'll be staring at a lawsuit—we all will be."

Kelly froze. Lawsuit?

"You were on the air at 10:03, right?" Ruth growled. "At 9:24, Darryl Mann was pronounced dead."

Natalie jammed her newscast script into the trash can in the matchbox-size yellow office she'd called her own for fourteen years. Its only adornments were the seven Emmy and Golden Mike statuettes perched on the gunmetal-gray steel cabinets.

Finally it was over. She collapsed in her chair and laid her head on her desk blotter. She couldn't remember the last time she'd been so drained. Everything ached. What didn't ache pounded.

The evening had been an extraordinary humiliation. By sheer force of will she'd gotten through *The KXLA Primetime News* without a blemish. There was no way she would allow herself to screw up more than once in a day. She didn't allow herself to screw up more than once in a *year*, and never on so grand a scale.

She winced. Calling the aftershock an eight point three? What an asinine mistake.

For the first time in her television life, she prayed the ratings had been low. And that one person in particular had missed her performance. Miles. There was no hope in hell Tony Scoppio had.

Which reminded her that she had one more chore to accomplish that hellacious evening. Telling her agent that her news director was threatening to can her. Not the sort of thing an agent likes to hear.

Natalie forced herself to pick up her phone and punch in his cell phone number. Two rings, then a muffled "Yes?" on the other end.

"Geoff? It's Natalie."

There was a pause. She heard traffic noise, the blaring of a horn. She'd caught him in his car. She could just imagine him in the navy Jaguar convertible with the top down, yellow tie slapping like a flag in the breeze, sunglasses on at eleven at night to protect his contacts from dust. At times like that Geoff Marner did a good imitation of a Hollywood mogul. Not that that was much of a stretch.

Geoff swore faintly under his breath. Then, louder, he said, "Whoa, Nellie, are you all right? Those eight point threes can really getcha!"

"You sicko!" But she had to laugh. "I can't believe you caught that."

"What? You don't think my eyes would be trained on KXLA while the ground rocks beneath my feet? Searching desperately for reassurance from L.A.'s premier anchor?" Another horn. He swore again. "You know, we Aussies aren't used to quakes of that magnitude."

"All right, already."

He paused and his voice took on a solemn tone. "Actually, Nats, it's really not all that bad. Maybe I can get you on *America's Funniest Bloopers*."

"Shut up!"

Another horn, then a more somber tone. "Seriously,

I wouldn't worry about one mistake. You were gangbusters today. So lunch tomorrow? But remember, I still want to take you out for your birthday and lunch doesn't count. The usual?" The blare of a car radio. Another softly uttered expletive.

"12:30," she agreed. "I'll bring sandwiches."

"Not that crazy health stuff you keep pushing on me. One sprout and I'm gone."

She nodded, thinking swiftly, *Maybe I can put off telling him about my conversation with Tony? Just till tomorrow?*

"Agreed?" he asked.

"Fine!"

"Good! One for the Aussie. Thank God I'm a patient man."

At that, she rolled her eyes. "Patient" was the last adjective she'd ever use to describe Geoff Marner. Wild man, yes. Smartest man she'd ever met, yes. Shark of an agent, yes. Least lawyerly lawyer on planet Earth? That, too. But "patient?" Never.

"Till tomorrow then," he said; then he was gone.

Natalie hung up and stared down at the date on her desk blotter. June 17. A day that would live in infamy. She grabbed a black marker, drew a thick annulling X across the square, and grabbed her things to leave.

Once out of KXLA's gated compound she drove her butterscotch Mercedes 320E west on Sunset Boulevard, the smarmy stretch bordering the station crowded with bail bondsmen, pawnshops, and sex stores. At Highland Avenue she turned right to head north into the Hollywood Hills, the commercial district slowly giving way to residential streets. At a red light at Franklin, as she gazed absently at a middle-aged couple entering the crosswalk, the woman gasped and threw her hand to her mouth in a telltale gesture of recognition.

"You're Natalie Daniels!" the woman sputtered, abandoning her companion to approach the car. "I love you! I watch you all the time!"

Natalie nodded, as she always did, and smiled, as she always did.

The woman's voice turned reverent, which never failed to amaze Natalie. It was as if she were a demigod in anchor's clothing. "Will you sign an autograph?"

"Of course, I'd be delighted," Natalie replied, as she always did. The light turned green but she ignored it, as did the woman standing in the street fumbling in her purse for a scrap of paper.

The transaction accomplished, the couple scurried away, the woman clutching her companion's arm and jabbering excitedly. Natalie smiled indulgently and rolled through the intersection toward home.

But she had to admit she did feel better. It was a cheap fix but certainly the one big thing she'd miss if she weren't an anchor. Who then would she be? Her husband had walked out on her. She'd never had a child. Her parents were dead. It was all she had, at the end of the day.

She drove swiftly the short distance to Nichols Canyon Road, then hung a right. The narrow road, heading ever upward, was well illuminated by a waxing moon. After all these years its hairpin curves were nearly as familiar to her as her own skin. Near the crest she slowed to turn left into the gated driveway of an imposing Mediterranean-style home. Nestled in a wooded enclave, it was all white stucco and terra-cotta tiled roof, with San Diego red bougainvillea climbing up the exterior and geraniums cascading from window boxes. She'd loved it the moment she and Miles had seen it, a decade before.

Natalie parked and eased her aching body out of the soft leather seat, walking around to the passenger side to retrieve her briefcase. Then she heard a rustle and a shadow fell across the driveway. She spun around, her heart pounding. There was someone there.

A man.

CHAPTER THREE

Monday, June 17, 11:46 P.M.

"Miles?"

"Natalie." He stepped forward on the stone path that curved to the front door.

She could see him clearly now that he had moved out of the shadows cast by the palm trees. The same Miles as ever, dressed in shades of gray: charcoal trousers, smoke-colored cashmere turtleneck. Same dark eyes, same thick black hair flecked with silver. He looked solid, dignified, respectable: like a well-to-do professor.

"What are you doing here? And at this hour?" She busied herself with gathering up her briefcase. She hadn't seen him since he'd left, four months before. *Maybe he wants to come back?* She slammed shut the Mercedes' door. *You don't want him back.* Carefully she locked it. *Are you sure?*

"I've been waiting for you," he said. He motioned up the walk to the house. "I was hoping we could talk."

Wordlessly she brushed past him. She fumbled for her key, and as usual when she wanted it quickly, it had buried itself deep in the nether regions of her purse.

"Here. Let me." He relieved her of her briefcase. "I notice you changed the locks."

She recoiled. "You tried to get in?"

He laughed. "It's chilly out here!"

She felt a flicker of annoyance. Same old Miles. He'd dumped her but still considered the house *his*. Finally she located her key and inserted it in the lock, pushing open the thick oak door and setting off an insistent beeping from the alarm system. Miles followed her into the beamed two-story foyer, their heels clicking on the terra-cotta Spanish tile.

She punched in the security code, then flicked a switch on a separate panel. A heavy iron chandelier flooded the foyer with light. Strong light, but she preferred that to standing with her husband in the dark.

She turned to face him. Space and silence yawned between them. *Like the nights I've spent alone.*

"It looks the same," he said finally.

Her voice came out in a snap. "Of course it looks the same."

"I half expected you to call in exterminators to wipe out every trace of me."

"If there were people who did that, I probably would have."

To that, he said nothing. She walked into the adjacent study and switched on a table lamp, needlessly. How could he have anything to say that she wanted to hear? Maybe she should just shut the door and leave him out in the foyer. Eventually he'd go.

She heard his voice behind her. Resentful. Petulant. "I'm sorry you're still so angry."

"Oh, Miles!" She threw up her hands and turned to face him. "What the hell do you expect? You walked out on me. For some *bimbo* from your sitcom! If that's not the tritest, most pathetic—"

"It's over."

"What?"

"It's over. It was a mistake and it's over."

She eyed him closely under the chandelier's harsh glare. Could it be true? He looked tired, hardly happy, she realized. And now his black hair was more than flecked with gray. It was streaked.

She felt a stab of pity. For the first time Miles actually looked his age. He looked like a fifty-five-year-old man.

Well, she wasn't exactly a youngster, either.

Her body felt leaden with fatigue. She didn't have the energy to know what to feel, what was right, what to do.

She certainly didn't have the wherewithal to fight. All she wanted was for the blasted day to end.

She stalked into the living room without turning on a lamp. Moonlight gleamed through the beveled panes to illuminate all she needed to see. Two crystal snifters stood in their usual place and she sloshed brandy into each, then held one out in his direction. He'd drink, he'd talk, he'd leave. "All right already, Miles. Spill it. Why did you come by tonight?"

He moved forward to take the drink. "I told you. I want to talk."

"And you picked *me* out of all the people you know?"

"It was you I wanted to talk to."

The brandy burned down her throat. She laughed. A mirthless sound, high-pitched and forced. "There's something ironic about that but I'm too tired to pin down what it is."

"Natalie, please." He sounded exasperated. "Can't we be civil to one another?"

She hoisted her snifter high in the air. "What could be more civil than this? I've got news for you, Miles. Couples who break up don't get more civil than this."

She couldn't quite bring herself to say "couples who divorce." She didn't know whether it would come to that, whether she wanted it to. Even now, seeing him here, she didn't know what she wanted.

She returned to the carafe to refresh her brandy. It was being kind to her, this amber liquid, coursing through her tired veins, making everything seem that much less important.

She collapsed onto the plump white sofa and leaned back, closing her eyes. Her limbs began to relax.

He sat down next to her, then spoke, his voice soft. "You look lovely."

"I look like hell." But she had to admit it was pleasant, like the old days, him next to her on the sofa, relaxed, nursing a brandy. She smelled the old familiar smells, his skin, his musky cologne.

He was silent for a moment. "Do you ever wish you could turn back the clock?"

She opened her eyes. "What do you mean?"

"You know, take back some of the things you've done."

His eyes were on her face. *Is he talking about leaving me? Does he want to come back?* She felt a crazy lurch of hope, even as she castigated herself for the reaction. *The guy leaves you for a bimbo, but the minute he wants to come back, you're there with open arms?* She spoke carefully. "I have to say, I have no major regrets."

He gave a quiet laugh. "That's one of the wonderful things about you, Natalie." His hand reached out to brush her cheek, his touch light, gentle. "You're always so upbeat, so positive." His hand dropped to his lap. "You probably never feel unappreciated."

At that, a bitter laugh gurgled in her throat. After the day she'd had. After he'd walked out on her. "Who isn't appreciating you, Miles?"

"Oh, the network, mostly. The executives, the suits." He shook his head, as though it were all more than he should have to bear. "It never changes. They just don't understand the creative side."

"Are you having problems with the show?" *Forget Maui*, the sitcom was called. Miles had told her it'd taken him years to write the pilot script. His baby, he'd called it.

The irony was that, not long after he'd walked out on her, he'd sold the script in an enormous deal that had gotten massive coverage in the trades. It had been huge, inescapable news: *Miles Lambert to Helm New Series of His Own Creation.* Of course she'd read all about it. And every word had felt like a slap in her own face. All of a sudden the man who'd just unloaded her was at the pinnacle of his career.

"No, no problems with the show," Miles said. "But still, everybody wants to put their own stamp on it." He snorted.

She regarded him silently. It was a good twenty years since Miles's first success—a humungous blockbuster of a success—one that had catapulted him and his writing partner into the top echelon of sitcom producers. It was while he was still riding that wave that they'd met and married. Everything about Miles had been intoxicating then, and yet reassuring, because he'd seemed so solid, so dependable.

But afterward had come the drought. Miles unable to write, unable to "find his muse," he told her. Or writing pilot scripts that never sold. Or that sold but never got made. Never earning more than a tiny fraction of what he'd made in the past. Natalie had been his constant cheerleader, not to mention financial support. When he broke off with his writing partner. When he was hurt and angry after his partner scored a second hit, on his own, while Miles continued to languish.

She was jolted back to the present by Miles's fingers on the engagement ring he had given her years before, twisting it so the stone would face the correct way, diamond up.

"Your ring," he said. His eyes were so dark she couldn't see the pupils. "You're still wearing it."

Yes. But backward. Because I can't quite take it off.

"You remember the day I gave it to you?" he asked.

How could any woman forget? They'd been walking on the beach in Malibu. It was late afternoon, in June, exactly a dozen years ago. A chill off the ocean was making her shiver. He'd taken off his jacket and laid it over her shoulders, then hugged her close. *Will you make me the happiest man in the world?* he'd whispered. *Will you be my wife?* She'd burst into tears and he'd pulled the ring from his pocket, an exquisite pear-shaped stone on a platinum band.

Natalie stared down at her ring. Then up at her husband. "I do remember."

"I miss you," he whispered. He leaned forward and kissed her.

She didn't back away, though part of her screamed to. Another part, warmed by his lips, felt the old familiar tug, as though he were on one end of an invisible string and she on the other. *Is this real? Can I trust you?*

Then he leaned back against the sofa cushions, slowly thumping one with his hand. "Remember Frank?" He raised his eyes to meet her own. "My roommate from college?"

She nodded, her lips still tingling from his kiss. Frank, from Haverford. Became a tax lawyer. Yes.

"He died last week." Miles shook his head. "Heart attack. He was younger than me."

"I'm sorry." She was puzzled. It was years since Miles had spoken to Frank, let alone seen him.

"Made me think, Natalie." Again he met her eyes. "About the mistakes I've made. About what little time I may have to make up for them."

Slowly, without looking away, he removed the brandy snifter from her hand. Again he kissed her, gently, his mouth covering hers with the warm possessiveness she remembered so well. He felt so good, so familiar. Again she felt that crazy hope lurch in her heart and this time didn't fight it. *Maybe he* has *learned something. Maybe now he understands how much we had.*

How wonderful it would be to have the nightmare just end, almost as if it had never happened. No longer to have to suffer everyone's pitying looks, to be a cast-aside wife, to come home every night to a shell of a house and a cold bed. Imagine if they could go on as before, *better* than before, because this time they would truly appreciate each other.

When she rose to go upstairs, he followed, as she knew he would. They moved slowly through their time-worn rituals, honed after twelve years of marriage into a familiar path that led to their bed.

He propped himself on his elbow. She stared into his eyes, and hesitated, still not completely certain what she saw there. "I don't know if we can make it right this time," she said.

He looked surprised. "But we're making it right, right now."

Could it be? She wanted to believe that all the pain of the last months could dissipate like smoke after a fire, leaving not the slightest trace.

The warm reassurance brought by that sudden hope made words cease, thoughts cease, everything cease but the heavenly feel of his hands on her body and the very wonder of being in his arms again. She'd been untouched for so long, her femininity squashed under layers of hurt and loss, that it was as though she'd ceased being a woman at all. But now he was being so thoughtful, so tender. And, oh, God, her chemise was off. Now his lips were on her breasts. He was arching over her in the dark, her nipples taut, his tongue teasing. *It's been so long.*

Then he came on top of her, and she was ready, his ministrations and her pent-up need making her body open like a bloom to the sun. Sweet, so sweet.

It had been so long and yet was so wonderfully, achingly familiar. His smell. The weight of him. The wonder of his chest pressing against her breasts, his neck craning above her, his mouth planting kisses along her forehead, her face, her throat.

When finally he made his final thrust within her, and her own body shuddered with release and happiness, tears rose in her eyes, hope rose in her throat, all the ache was banished in the awesome joy that they had found each other again.

They lay quietly, entwined, tears running down her face and disappearing into her hair. Tears for Evie, for time lost, for Miles, for everything that had been and might still be. She felt no need for words or promises. Only sleep. Happy, blessed sleep.

A few hours later Natalie stretched a languorous arm out from beneath the thick, downy duvet, thrusting it across the wide bed into the shaft of moonlight that sneaked beneath the draperies. She raised her head to read the digital clock: 3:13 A.M. She fell back against the pillow and let her gaze drift around the shadowy bedroom: pine beams crossing the ceiling, gracefully hewn dressers and side tables stained a luminous teal, the green iron bars of the bed's footboard wrought into an intricate web of vines and leaves. The sheets were thoroughly rumpled and gave off a decadently musky scent of sensual pleasures shared. She felt Miles's side of the bed. It was cool.

He was probably downstairs reading. Like always. Like the old days.

She smiled and rose from the bed, her muscles pleasantly sore, and pulled on a robe. Her bare feet slapped on the hardwood. She stepped into the hallway. "Miles?"

Silence. She frowned, arrested by the odd quietness. Slowly she made her way downstairs and peered into the pitch-black living room. Two brandy snifters stood on the coffee table. The cushions of the plump white sofa were askew, a pillow knocked to the floor.

An ugly thought crossed her mind. "Miles?"

Silence.

It simply wasn't possible.

"Miles?" She was moving swiftly now, running across the cold Spanish tile to the front door. She pulled it open and ran down the curving stone path to the street.

Gone. His Porsche was gone.

Miles was gone.

She stood in the street, looking both ways, disbelieving. A yellow-eyed cat looked at her warily from a nearby driveway. Why had Miles come, if all he was going to do was leave? To sleep with her, to prove he could? Because on some level he missed her? Why?

Dazedly, she returned to the house. In an odd penitential rite, she forced herself to conduct a thorough search, first of the main floor, then of the rooms upstairs. All to confirm what she already knew.

There was no sign of Miles anywhere. Nothing. Nowhere.

It wasn't until she was again standing on the cold tile of the foyer that she realized he had never once asked how she was. Never asked how she had managed, what was new. *Oh, by the way, Natalie, there's a bruise on your neck. Did that happen in the earthquake?*

She was struggling to take it all in when the next jolt came. He'd never mentioned her birthday. Her fortieth. He didn't care. Or much the same, he simply hadn't remembered.

Damn. Tony gulped his morning coffee and stared at the in-house computer message from Ruth Sperry that scrolled across the top of his screen. Just what he needed.

(r-sperry) Got a call from the hospital where Darryl Mann died that his family has *seen a tape of Kelly's crash piece and is meeting with a lawyer. I suggest a strategy session this afternoon and again I urge you to suspend Kelly. I've spoken with Elaine in Legal about the required grounds and Kelly's behavior certainly meets the threshold.*

Tony jabbed at the DELETE key, then sat back in his chair and crossed his arms over his chest.

No question, Kelly sure was a wild card. Airing that video of Darryl Mann all banged up in his mangled car was a big-time TV-news no-no. The phone banks lit up like goddamn Times Square after her spot aired. And not getting script approval? That was downright insubordinate.

Still . . . Tony wondered. He bet that lots of the folks at home were secretly fascinated by the video and that the ones who called in were mostly crazies. He couldn't let his news department be dictated to by *them.*

He'd seen a lot of talent. He trusted his ability to judge talent. And in his estimation Kelly Devlin had serious potential. He *knew* it. What he had to do was get her to exercise some judgment, without losing her edge.

His direct line rang. He picked it up. "Scoppio."

"Tony, it's Willa."

From Promotions. Boring. "Yeah?" He stared across his office at his far-left monitor, which he always kept tuned to CNN, his attention caught by spectacular video of a train burning.

"I need you to make the final call on the photos of Ken and Natalie for the billboard campaign," Willa said.

Tony watched the flames lick the silver chassis. Amtrak crashed *again*? "What photos?"

"For the billboard campaign for *The KXLA Primetime News*?"

"Oh." He forced himself to look away from the fire video. "Those." He frowned. Did he really want to do a billboard campaign?

"We had blowups done of the shots you liked, remember?" She was sounding irritated now. "But we need to get down to your one or two favorites if we want the billboards up by the July book."

He cleared his throat. Did he want to promote *The KXLA Primetime News*? With Ken and Natalie? Now? "Uh, put a hold on that."

"What?" Willa sounded stunned. "We've been gearing up ever since you got here! I—"

"I said put a hold on it." He hung up.

That was what he liked about being boss. He could start things. And he could stop them.

He returned his attention to the CNN monitor, on which the train was still burning. Grabby. That was what he needed. Grabby. Grabby stories. Grabby talent.

His eyes drifted to the middle monitor, which he kept set to his own Channel 12. On air was Kelly's taped teaser of her piece for that night's *KXLA Primetime News*. Something about school violence—he didn't know what the hell it was about, but she had the collar up on her leather jacket and was on a real tight shot. Tony narrowed his eyes appraisingly and decided, not for the first time, that she looked good.

Suite 3800. Natalie stepped off the elevator directly into the reception area for Dewey, Climer, Fipton and Marner. She had the same reaction she always did when she stopped by Geoff's firm: it made her think of an exclusive men's club. Persian carpets. Cherrywood paneling. Tapestries hung from bronze bars. She half expected to see aging British gentlemen in wing chairs poring over *The Financial Times,* port and cigars by their side. It was a jarring counterpoint to the rest of crass, vulgar Los Angeles thirty-eight floors below.

"Good afternoon, Ms. Daniels." The receptionist was a tiny Japanese woman, impeccably turned out, who'd fronted Dewey, Climer for more than thirty years. "I'll tell Mr. Marner that you're here." A moment later, she said, "Please follow me."

Natalie allowed herself to be led down a hall lined by offices, doors ajar to reveal men and women suited in navy and gray wool, the only obvious variation solid or pinstripe. To a person they were bent over desks piled high with documents and outsize leather-bound tomes, no noise save for the murmur of conversation and the tap of computer keys.

"Whoa! Another hit! Yes!" A shouting male voice suddenly shattered the quiet, a voice raised in the sort of delirious frenzy produced in males by only two activities, though Natalie could hardly imagine either sex or sport ever occurring in these rarefied chambers. Unperturbed, the receptionist deposited Natalie inside Geoff's plush corner office and glided away.

Natalie shook her head. Her agent, the only person besides herself on whom she depended to manage her career, was perched on a stool in front of a mammoth television screen, video-game joystick gyrating in his hand, shirtsleeves rolled to his elbows, red paisley tie loose around his neck.

"Give me a second, Nats," he demanded, his eyes never leaving the screen. "I'm closing in on my all-time best score."

Which did look in serious danger of toppling. Bemused, Natalie watched this paragon of legal skill make pinpoint hit after pinpoint hit on alien spaceships, huge blobs of orange and yellow light exploding repetitiously on the screen. His score ratcheted ever higher until, suddenly, the screen shimmered with a blinding silver flash as his own vessel, *Surfboy*, got sideswiped by an alien module and peremptorily dispatched.

"Shit!" His voice raised in a paroxysm of glee and anger, Geoff let go of the joystick and swiveled around on his stool. "I hate it when I lose!" He leaped to his feet, towering over Natalie with a grin spreading across his face. "But I already had one huge victory today so I'll let this slide."

Seeing her agent this way reminded Natalie of meeting Geoff Marner years before. Her initial reaction to the brash Australian three years her junior had not been good. He'd seemed like a New Yorker in Aussie camouflage: loud-voiced, prone to big movements, somehow managing to take up a great deal of space. He was very tall—she guessed about six foot four—and lean, with light brown hair and bright hazel eyes.

But over time she'd come to trust him completely. Whoever her news director of the moment, Geoff's ability to manage him was spot on. He was, she realized, the only person besides Ruth she could always count on.

"So what was the victory?" she asked.

He loped over to his desk. "Sorry." He began unknotting his tie. "I'm too sweaty to keep wearing this shirt." Geoff stripped it off and tossed it in a desk drawer, talking all the while. "Finally settled with one of the studios. Got my client the share of the gross they'd promised, then reneged on when his movie was a hit. Twenty mil."

Which no doubt more than justified the enormous retainer the client was paying Dewey, Climer. Natalie conducted a careful study of Geoff as he stood half naked at his desk, rummaging in another drawer for a laundered shirt. *He's a real stud,* she decided, at that moment more admiring of his well-muscled, lightly haired chest than of his legal prowess. *The man actually has pecs.* Unlike Miles, for example, who'd gone more than a little soft. Of course, Miles was almost twenty years older.

Which realization reminded her just how thoroughly she'd explored her husband's body the prior night. Briefly she shut her eyes. What an idiot she'd been to sleep with him. In the hours since his disappearance, she hadn't heard a peep out of him.

"So what's up?" Geoff asked suddenly. She felt his eyes on her, keen, appraising. "Were you awake half the night worrying about that little eight point three mishap?"

Natalie grimaced. *You're partly right. I* was *up half the night.*

Geoff, returned to proper office attire, relieved her of the bag of sandwiches she'd brought, then steered her to an upholstered wing chair, seating himself in its mate. He poked his nose in the bag. "Really, Nats, don't give it another thought." He handed her a mountain of a sandwich wrapped in waxed paper. "But clearly something's up. Talk to me."

Natalie surveyed her sandwich, then dropped it on a side table. She threw up her hands. "Tony told me he's not planning to pick up the option on my contract." She still couldn't quite believe it, even as she said it aloud.

Geoff frowned and let his own sandwich drop onto his lap. "What did he say exactly?"

"Exactly that. That the ratings aren't what they should be. He cited the May sweep." She couldn't bring herself to tell Geoff the rest of what Tony had said, which on some primal level she'd found even more disturbing. *Did it ever occur to you that maybe your judgment isn't what it used to be? Maybe you've gotten a little soft from all those years behind the anchor desk.* After all, agents made judgment calls on clients, too. What if Geoff agreed she was too old to be marketable and wanted to dump her as well?

"Remind me when your contract's up?"

"October fourth."

Geoff was silent for a time, squinting into the middle distance. "Well," he said eventually, "it's not what I like to hear, but my bet is he's only trying to scare us. He used the same tactic in Dallas with the main male anchor, who's still there, mind you."

Natalie felt a surge of reassurance. "Really?" Then, as quickly, her optimism faded. "But did the guy have to take a cut?"

Geoff nodded. "He's down by a third."

Great. "So this comes down to money?"

"At least in part. I'm fairly sure Scoppio has an incentive deal. If he gets the ratings up and the budget down within some set period, he gets a bonus. He had a similar deal in Dallas."

"And he *did* get the Dallas station to number one."

"He's gotten every news department he's ever headed to number one."

Natalie knew that. Tony's reputation was legendary, or notorious, depending on point of view. "And he's done it the same way everywhere. By doing outrageous news. And cutting heads."

"Only the most *expensive* heads." Geoff smiled. "Like yours." He bit into his pickle. "The bottom line is Tony's new to KXLA and wants to make his mark. And the easiest way to do that is to change who's on the air."

"Standard procedure."

"Two can play at that game. It's clear what we have to do." Geoff leaned back in his chair and crossed his ankle over his knee. "Show Scoppio how highly you're regarded in this town."

"By getting me another offer?"

"He won't want you going across the street and taking viewers with you."

Natalie pondered anchoring at another station. After fourteen years at KXLA, she regarded every other shop in town as the competition. She couldn't imagine working at any of them.

"Even if you want to stay at KXLA," Geoff continued, "another offer puts you in a stronger bargaining position."

"And what if I don't get any other offers?"

"Unlikely. But then of course it would be tougher."

Geoff bent forward and went seriously to work on his mound of sourdough bread, salami, and swiss cheese, while Natalie mulled over an idea that had taken root in her brain since her meeting with Tony. "I've been thinking I'd like to do more anchoring from the field," she told Geoff. "You know, next Monday I could anchor the show from the collapsed part of the 210. 'Where are we one week later' kind of thing. It's always good for the numbers."

"Terrific." He grabbed a paper napkin and wiped his mouth. "But, Nats, don't let yourself get caught up in every tenth of a ratings point."

She threw back her head and stared at the ceiling. "It's hard not to."

"Granted." He eyed her keenly. "So are you really all right?"

"I'm fine." Which was a lie but she'd never discussed her personal life with Geoff before and she wasn't going to start when it was at such a humiliating ebb. It was all part of maintaining the facade of competence and success, in front of agents as well as news directors.

And viewers. And almost everyone else she could think of.

He nodded, then crumpled his sandwich wrapping and tossed it basketball style into a trash bin across his office. "There is something else," he said, and the unexpected somberness of his tone arrested her attention. "I wasn't going to mention it, but now I want to give you a heads-up." He paused and met her eyes. "I spoke with Berta this morning. Just after she hung up from Miles's attorney."

Natalie stared at Geoff, the air around her seeming to still. Berta Powers, her personal attorney, also from Dewey, Climer, would handle the divorce. If there was one. "Miles's attorney called Berta *this morning*?"

Just hours after Miles left our bed?

Geoff stared down at his hands. "Natalie, Miles is going to file."

"What?"

"He's going to file." He paused. "For divorce."

Odd, miscellaneous things snapped into focus. Dust motes in the air. A slice of tomato poking out of her untouched sandwich. Geoff leaning closer to look into her face.

Miles was filing for divorce. She was getting divorced.

"Are you all right?"

"I'm fine." She struggled to gather her wits. "It's just . . . I know I should have expected this, but—"

Miles was still warm from our bed when he gave his attorney the nod. Let's move. Full speed ahead. I'm ready to dump her now.

"There's more." Geoff paused. "He's going for half the community property."

"What?"

Geoff just shook his head, his mouth set in a grim line.

She was stupefied. "What about the prenup?"

Geoff frowned. "This is the first I've heard of a prenup."

"Well, there is one." Of course there was a prenuptial agreement. Natalie's attorney at the time had insisted.

"There's no copy in Berta's file," Geoff said.

"I have one in my safe-deposit box."

"Good. Then get a copy to Berta and she'll take it from there."

"I can't believe Miles is claiming there's no prenup." The gall of him. Concocting bald-faced lies. How did he think that would ever stand up? All she had to do was get the document out of the bank.

Then another thought leaped to mind. A terrifying notion she couldn't believe was true. Yet . . . Miles was claiming there was no prenup? She sprang up, knocking her sandwich to the Persian carpet, bread and sprouts and tomatoes collecting in a soggy pile. "I've got to go." She grabbed her purse and strode out of Geoff's office, then began running when she hit the hall. She glanced back once to see Geoff in his doorway staring after her, concern and bewilderment on his face.

It didn't take her long to get to the bank, or to fill out the paperwork to get inside her safe-deposit box. The clerk buzzed Natalie into the sanctum sanctorum where the boxes were located, a maze of narrow alleys that seemed to double back on themselves.

"Here we are," the clerk said cheerfully. She selected a key from a massive ring and poked it into one box's master keyhole. Natalie entered its mate, and the door swung open.

Inside the box was a jumble of documents, licenses, bonds, records: all the paperwork paraphernalia that defined a modern life. Natalie didn't find the prenup on her first hasty pass, so carried the box to an empty room and dumped its contents on the table.

Ten minutes passed.

It's not here.

By this time she was flat-out scared. She forced herself to do another, more methodical search, then returned the box to its metallic slot and went looking for the clerk.

"All done, Miss Daniels?"

"Actually, no. I can't find what I'm looking for." Natalie kept her voice steady. "Will you check my file? I'm trying to remember whether my husband has access to—"

"Oh, yes, he does." The clerk nodded cheerily. "In fact, it's so funny you're here now because he was here this morning. Of course I remember because he's sort of"—she giggled—"Mr. Natalie Daniels."

Natalie felt as though the wind had been knocked out of her. "He was here this morning?"

"Oh, yes. He was very charming."

"He had a key to the box?"

"Yes. On his key ring. He . . . Miss Daniels?"

Natalie was out the door and on the street. The enormity of Miles's perfidy struck her like a physical blow.

That's why he came to the house last night. Not to talk. Not to see me. But to get the key to the safe-deposit box, the one he knows I keep in the study. So he could steal the prenup.

She threw herself in the Mercedes and tore off in the direction of Wilshire Boulevard.

He used me. He used me to get inside the house. It didn't mean a damn thing to him that we made love. He just wanted me to fall asleep so he could get the key, and figured, "Hell, may as well get laid while I'm here."

She drove like a woman possessed, dodging and weaving through the midday traffic, fuming at all the people going shopping and to school and back to their offices after lunch, living normal lives.

I won't let him get away with it . . .

At Barrington she turned right and sped north, racing like a bullet through a just-red light at San Vicente Boulevard. A woman wheeling a stroller did a fast backward step to the curb, and Natalie had a fleeting image of the woman's face contorted in shock and anger. Left on Sunset, faster still, making very good time as she headed toward the coast, careening right around the corner at Pacific Coast Highway, tires screeching on asphalt. Other drivers honked their horns and screamed at her out their windows.

I don't give a flyer! Natalie silently screamed back. *I can't let him lie and cheat. And now steal!*

Pacific Coast Highway was a blur, the side that fronted the ocean lined with deceptively simple multimillion-dollar houses that ran together in hazy pastel as she whirred past. From the road she was actually seeing the backs of the properties; their grander facades fronted the beach, one of the most exclusive stretches of sand in the world.

How in the world did Miles get the money to buy here?

Then, she remembered. Of course. No doubt after selling the pilot for *Forget Maui*, he leveraged himself up the wazoo to get his hands on a Malibu beach house. That was just like Miles. He believed in living large. He believed he deserved it.

And he thinks he deserves even more of mine. Even after I supported him for twelve years while he wrote the damn thing!

She located the beige clapboard house and made an angry left onto the gravelly driveway on its south side, parking behind a brand-spanking-new red Porsche. So the bastard was home.

She jabbed at the doorbell till her finger stung. Nothing. "Miles!" She kicked at the door, leaving scuff marks on the fresh navy blue paint. "I know you're in there, you lousy scum! Open up!"

Still nothing. He was skulking around inside, no doubt, pretending not to hear her. So what else was new?

She stood, panting. Then she went back to the driveway and surveyed the house. Beige clapboard, one story, lots of windows. She snorted. Typical three-million-dollar Malibu beach house.

Still being remodeled, she could tell from the debris abandoned on the beachfront deck. Apparently the work crew hadn't finished the fireplace yet. They'd left a mound of gray stones, cut into rectangular chunks.

She walked over and picked one up. It felt good in her hand. Heavy. Slowly she returned to the driveway and studied the house.

There were four big windows, two for what looked to be the dining room. She looked down at the stone in her hand, then back at the first window on the left.

Then she threw it, fast and hard.

Right in the kisser. The rock sliced through the window as if it were made for the job, then skidded along the hardwood floor inside. The impact set off a shrill alarm.

"You coming out yet, Miles?" she screamed. Then she raced back to the rock pile and selected the next stone for its greater heft. That one she smashed through the window just right of the one she'd already broken. This time all the glass in the frame fell to the hardwood with a satisfying crash. The third she aimed at a smaller window in opaque glass, probably the window for a half bath.

After that, she lost count, lost all track of sense and time, until she paused, panting, her shoulder sore from hurling rocks the size of canteloupes. Trembling she raised her left hand to stare at her ring finger, winking with her platinum wedding band and diamond engagement ring. Without a second thought she wrenched them over her knuckle and flung them through the largest broken window, exulting in the tinny clatter they made as they skipped along the hardwood. "Pawn them, why don't you, you bastard!" she screamed. It was then that she noticed a thick middle-aged Hispanic woman standing at the other end of the driveway, a white plastic grocery bag dangling from each hand, calmly watching her.

The women stared at each other for a moment. Then the Hispanic woman shrugged. "I think he'll get the message, missus."

CHAPTER FOUR

Tuesday, June 18, 7:52 P.M.

Kelly pushed out her breath for her final sit-up. Two hundred. She grunted and sank back against the rust-colored shag carpet in her shoe box of an apartment.

It was almost eight, so Howard would be by shortly. Great. She'd have two workouts that day: the usual plus an extra to placate her shit-for-brains managing editor.

But it had to be done. He was mad at her and she had to get him over it. After all, as managing editor Howard had a lot to say about assignments. And assignments dictated airtime.

Reluctantly she heaved herself to her feet and over to the fridge. She pulled out a Gatorade and propped the door open with her hip, enjoying the deliciously cold air as it wafted over her flushed skin. Absently she looked around. From the kitchen she could see almost all of her one-bedroom unit, housed in a mammoth West Los Angeles complex. Her apartment was on the sixth floor of Number Four Tower, all of them vying for Most Nondescript. Even the interior screamed generic. Almost everybody who lived there was single: hordes of newly divorced men prowled the laundry and workout rooms all hours of the day and night. She felt like she should be living in a snazzier place—shouldn't a TV reporter be living in a snazzier place?—but in L.A. housing prices were sky-high. It just had to do until she could get a house, and who knew when that would be. She wasn't exactly good at saving for a down payment.

Kelly twisted the cap back on the Gatorade and jammed the almost empty bottle back on a shelf crowded with diet sodas, abruptly deciding she wouldn't shower. Why bother? Howard liked her sweaty and no doubt he'd get a rise out of her current getup: short shorts and a strappy midriff-baring tee. And who needed a bra? Not a twenty-four-year-old with implants.

Kelly loosed her brunette hair from its rubber band and plumped it with her fingers, reviewing the day's events. Not good. Susan and Eric Mann, the parents of Darryl-the-car-crash-victim, somehow had seen her piece. Meaning they'd seen the blood-and-guts video. Meaning they knew she hadn't mentioned that their kid had died.

Just her luck! Tony and Ruth and Howard had some big powwow about what they'd do if the Manns sued the station but Kelly had managed to dodge it, which was what had pissed Howard off. She snorted. Like the Manns had a leg to stand on anyway!

The doorbell buzzed. Showtime.

She opened the door a strategic crack, just enough to let Howard see her. He looked his usual preppy self, pin-striped shirt and khakis, both creased after the day's labors, and Topsiders sans socks. Like almost every other ambitious thirty-something who passed through local television, Howard Bjorkman was using it as a stepping-stone to bigger things. Read: network. But Ivy Leaguer though he might be, he wasn't quite well-bred enough to stop his eyes from flickering down Kelly's body as she stood enticingly at her door. She noticed, trying not to giggle, that his slicked-back hair was newly combed and that he smelled of fresh cologne. How many other employees did he get so spruced up for? She opened the door wider. "Come in," she invited huskily, laughing softly as he brushed by. He was a goner.

She felt his eyes on her ass when she angled past him to get some beers, bending over real far to give him a nice long look at her rump, perhaps his favorite part of her anatomy. She closed the door with a bump of her hip and, nipples hard from the blast of cold air, sashayed toward him. She stopped herself from smiling as she handed him a beer and reached out to ruffle his ash-brown hair. He swatted her away.

"Ooh, you wanna play rough." She giggled, leaned forward, and licked his ear.

"Quit it, Kelly." He rose and slammed his beer on the glass coffee table with such force that a few drops flew out and splattered the *People* magazines. "You're not getting away with it this time."

"You're the one who's trying to get away." She pouted and moved closer to grab his belt buckle.

"Where the hell have you been?" He twisted away. "I must've paged you fifteen times! You knew you were supposed to be in that meeting, so where were you?"

"I never got the message," she lied.

"Oh, I suppose your pager is broken?"

"It's a little hit and miss."

"Right." He clenched his jaw.

Kelly had the sudden thought that the hardness in his face made him fairly attractive. Again she grabbed for his buckle, but again he batted her away.

"You shouldn't be taking this so lightly," he muttered. "Ruth is pretty pissed."

Kelly rolled her eyes. So what else was new? Ruth Sperry suffered from terminal PMS. "What about Tony?"

"It's hard to tell. But believe me, there's no news director around who wants his station to get sued."

Kelly sank onto the black Naugahyde couch and crossed her long bare legs, rhythmically kicking one in the air. "You think the Manns'll sue?"

He threw out his hands. "They've got every right to! That video before the ambulance came? And not reporting that Darryl Mann was dead? That's *huge*!"

"So I didn't do a double and triple check." Kelly rose and reached languorously for his belt.

"You failed to report that a man was *dead*. And checking is a key part of being a reporter, perhaps *the* most important part."

She waved her hand dismissively. Yeah, right. Like the real careful reporters were the ones getting all the airtime.

She watched Howard pace in front of the bar that separated the kitchen from the living room. He was wiping his brow, looking straight out of an ad for some Wall Street investment product. Serious and kind of cute, at least for the extreme short term. She approached him and draped her arms around his neck. "So even though I'm such a naughty reporter," she whispered, pushing her pelvis into him, "you still like me?"

"Stop screwing around, Kelly." But now his voice was strangled. "I'm telling you, this is the last time."

"Then let's make it good." Slowly she licked his mouth, aware of his growing erection. Right on time.

She locked his gaze as she pulled off her top. She knew her breasts were magnificent and, to men with far more self-control than Howard Bjorkman, irresistible. His eyes glazed, and slowly, a little roughly, she pushed down on his shoulders until his mouth was at her nipples. "Do me, Howard," she ordered, certain he'd oblige.

Kelly lay against the couch, the Naugahyde now sticky against her skin. Howard was in the shower singing "Desperado," his favorite postfuck refrain. She chuckled softly. That man was never in tune, in or out of bed.

Maybe she should have become an actress. Lazily Kelly reached for Howard's khakis, in a heap next to the glass coffee table with the jockeys still inside. TV news and acting were a lot alike, but the payoff to succeeding as an actress was bigger. The competition, though, was hell. Kelly shook out the khakis and pulled the wallet from the back pocket. Those girls were to-die-for beautiful and there were so damn many of them. There were a lot of good-looking girls in TV news but few true babes. In that group she was a clear ten.

Howard had a twenty, two tens and four ones. She lifted the tens and two of the ones and returned the wallet, idly poaching a cigarette from the crumpled pack in the other pocket. Howard's voice carried from the shower. "Why don't you come to your senses? You been out ridin' fences for so long now." He was happy as a pig in shit. She lit the cigarette. Morons always were. It was like that news director in Bakersfield who told her everybody in his newsroom had an IQ of a hundred fifty plus. Then what were they doing in California's armpit?

The water stopped. Howard must be clean enough now to go home to Sally, or whatever her name was, who was apparently so stupid she couldn't tell her boyfriend had just done the nasty with his favorite coworker. Kelly fingered the khakis again, pondering taking the twenty before he came out. She could sure use it.

"So you'll be more careful from now on?" Startled, she pulled her hand back when Howard emerged from the bathroom wrapped in a towel, his legs sticking out from the thick white fleece like hairy tree trunks.

"I'll be careful." Shit, that was close.

"I can count on you to get script approval in the future? Show up to meetings? And do your level best not to get the station sued?" He bent to towel his feet. "I don't want to have to cover for you again."

Kelly ground out her cigarette. He hadn't minded covering her twenty minutes ago. "Will you do something for me?"

"Again?" He tossed the towel in the general direction of the bathroom. It landed in a heap in the hall. "What?"

"Will you tell Tony you think I should do some fill-in anchoring?"

"You mean for Natalie?" He laughed and pulled on his jockeys. "Get in line."

"But I never get a chance." She shimmied closer. "It's not fair."

"Life's not fair." He stepped into his khakis.

"I hope you're not telling me you won't talk to Tony." She couldn't stop an angry note from creeping into her voice.

"I'm not saying that." He pushed her away and reached for his shirt, finally glancing up to meet her eyes. "It'd be great for you to do some anchoring, Kell," he demurred, "but I can't just *make* it happen."

She arranged her full lips into a pout. "Couldn't you

just help me, Howard? I do so much to help *you.*" She batted her long lashes at him. "And I *could* do even more." She brought her mouth close to his ear. "Didn't you tell me you have a fantasy about two girls at one time? Who could pull that off better than me?"

He blinked.

"You do for me," she whispered, "and I do for you."

Slowly Kelly turned and strolled back to the couch, chuckling softly. *That* should keep him on good behavior through the July sweep! She flipped open a *People*, the face of the actress on the cover stained a light amber by the spilled beer. Out of one eye she watched Howard make three attempts before he finally succeeded in attaching his watch to his wrist. She gave him a coy wave from the couch when he let himself out.

Geoff switched off the speaker phone, his brow creased with worry. No way even he, the Aussie with the perennially sunny disposition, could put a positive spin on the afternoon's events.

He scanned his computer screen, reviewing the scrupulous record he'd kept of the dozen calls he'd placed. Four were to news directors in Los Angeles. Another eight were to their counterparts in other major television markets, selected for their superior news departments. But no matter how carefully Geoff chose his target, or how subtly he engaged him in conversation, he came back devoid of serious interest in Natalie Daniels.

It was going to be tougher than he'd thought getting Natalie another anchor offer.

Disgustedly Geoff shut down the computer file. Though it was couched in news directorese, the uninterest always boiled down to the same two things. She was too old. And too expensive. He'd hawked male clients who were high-priced geriatric patients compared to Natalie and never heard those complaints. He hardly considered himself a feminist, but on this particular afternoon, on behalf of this particular client, Geoff was pissed.

And worried.

To make matters worse, Scoppio was stonewalling him

by not returning phone calls. Geoff knew it was just another tactic to keep him off balance but still he found it irritating. This was the one aspect of agenting he disliked: at base he was a supplicant. He could cajole, he could reason, he could manipulate, but he couldn't *force* news directors to do what he wanted. Especially when he couldn't get them on the phone.

Restlessly, Geoff flicked a switch on the master remote that squatted on a corner of his expansive desk, one unit that controlled all three of his televisions, both his VCRs, the Nakamichi stereo, and for an added fillip of excitement, the sliding door on the adjacent wall that hid the forty-eight-inch Sony flat panel. He played with a few buttons on the remote, rewinding the tape in the left VCR and rerouting the connection so it would play on the Sony screen.

He rolled through the first section of Natalie's résumé reel, a video showcase of her best on-air work. If he was going to embark on a serious job hunt, Natalie should freshen the reel with new material, like the live shot from the collapsed 210 freeway. Nothing deadened news director interest like an antique résumé reel. The tape began with quick cuts of Natalie anchoring, in the studio and from the field. Geoff lingered over some segments, smiling, jotting down notes. A good bit of it he knew by heart. He also knew the reel was already as good as reels got.

Still, he made his way painstakingly through the second section, Natalie reporting. He smiled with recognition. There she was in front of the L.A. County Courthouse in a gray pin-striped suit, doing a stand-up amid shouting crowds just after the not-guilty verdict in the O. J. Simpson criminal trial. Ah, and there she was in Kobe, next to a collapsed Japanese-style house, reporting on the aftermath of the massive earthquake. Her blond hair wasn't in the elegant twist she maintained in studio, but blowing about her face. She looked lovely, he thought, but tired.

He remembered how she'd returned to L.A. from Kobe exhausted and promptly lost her voice. She was off the air for a few days and hating life. He'd gone to her house with a jar of honey and a few herbal teas and brewed her a sample of each and every one. She was in leggings and a flannel shirt, he remembered. It was the first time he'd ever seen her in anything but a suit.

He smiled at the recollection. Which tea had she liked best? Yes, Licorice Spice. He made a note. She could use a pick-me-up. He'd messenger a box to the station.

His intercom buzzed. "Janet on line one."

Janet. He hesitated before picking up the phone. "Hi." He cleared his throat. "Hi."

"Honey, are you okay? You sound a little under the weather."

"No, no, I'm fine." He kept his eyes trained on Natalie's flickering videotaped image but made an effort to enliven his voice. "So how was your day?"

"Fun! We took the summer schoolers to the zoo and they went wild, especially at the penguins. One wetting, one vomiting, only two crying fits. Not the penguins, the kids."

Janet laughed and Geoff listened absentmindedly as she continued to describe the outing. He could just imagine her tending to the ragtag band of six-year-olds. Wiping faces and behinds with equal equanimity, straight blond hair falling about her laughing face. She was one of the few blondes in southern California whose color didn't come out of a bottle.

"Geoff, are you still there?"

"Yup. Still here." He cleared his throat and forced himself to pause the VCR. "So what are you up to now?"

"I was thinking I might drop by your office, see if I could tempt you away from work for a little while. I packed a picnic basket." Her voice dipped to a lower register. "We don't even have to go out."

He grinned. Code language, though he knew it was more a tease than a true intention. "Why, Miss Janet Roswell, you have my full attention."

She giggled. "I hope to have more than *that* before long."

"How fast can you get here?"

"About an hour."

"See you then." He rang off. Janet. He slapped his mahogany desk firmly. Janet. She was perfect for him. He'd done the starlet thing, more times than he could count. He was over it.

But Janet? She was wonderful. Stunningly beautiful, athletic, from a great family. In a town of fakes, she was the real thing.

And it was time. For both of them. They'd been dating on and off for two years now and Janet was a few months' shy of her thirtieth birthday. Though she was far too well bred to start issuing ultimatums, he knew if he didn't act soon, he could lose her. And as for himself? He was thirty-seven, he'd made senior partner, and even his younger brother Russell had married and fathered a child. It was time.

He unlocked the narrowest of his desk drawers and extracted a small eggshell-blue Tiffany box. Inside was an even smaller black velvet box.

He opened it carefully.

Diamonds twinkled in the afternoon sunshine glinting through his windows. One large emerald-cut stone, encircled by smaller circular stones. All beautifully massed on a gold band.

He sat for a moment, thinking. Then he snapped shut the velvet lid and tucked the box away, carefully locking the drawer. He punched a button on the remote and out popped the tape from the VCR. What had she said her favorite restaurant was?

Recollection struck. *That's right. Four Oaks.*

He called directory assistance, then the restaurant, forgoing his habit of having his secretary make all the necessary arrangements. Yes, he told the maître d', it had to be eight on Saturday. Yes, he insisted on a corner table in the parlor. He preordered a bottle of La Grande Dame Veuve Clicquot 1990, his current favorite, which must be delivered chilled to their table the instant they arrived.

He rang off and smiled. He'd put on a wonderful birthday celebration. Natalie would love it.

* * *

Kelly decided the smart thing was to show up early at Tony's office for the meeting with the Manns and their attorney. The *smart* thing, since they were threatening to sue her butt to kingdom come, was to be on her best behavior. She knew she freaked everybody from KXLA out the minute she showed up because she sure wasn't dressed like usual. Instead of her normal work outfit of short skirt and chunky heels, she'd bought a boxy black two-piece suit that even Ruth might have plucked off the sales rack. With almost no makeup, flat heels, and opaque tights, Kelly knew she could pass for a Sunday school teacher.

That might be something Howard would enjoy, come to think of it.

She shot out of her chair the instant the Manns appeared at Tony's office, breaking the first rule he'd given her. She wasn't supposed to *do* anything, *say* anything, unless Tony asked her something straight out. But she'd thought about it and decided her way was better. So now, her features all serious, she held out her hand. "Good afternoon." She tried hard to sound sincere. "I'm Kelly Devlin."

She knew Susan and Eric Mann would have to shake her hand if she kept holding it out and sure enough they did. So did their attorney. Kelly gave him a once-over, though even if she hadn't seen his TV ads she'd know right off he was an ambulance chaser. Talk about a cheap suit. She went back to her chair, but not before directing all three to Tony's plaid couch, the best seat in the house.

Tony, Howard, Ruth, and Elaine Nance, KXLA's senior attorney, went through the same greeting ritual she had. They barely sat back down again before Kelly started her prepared speech.

"Please allow me to offer the condolences of all of us here at KXLA on the tragic loss of your son," she said, as though she were leading the meeting. She felt everybody's eyes on her, Tony's probably ready to bust out of their sockets.

"Well said, Kelly." That came from Tony, who then gave her a look that said, plain as day, *Shut the fuck up*!

But both Manns got all teary and Kelly noticed that the missus looked like any second she might crack. She had on a navy-blue polyester pants suit and a gold cross at her throat, and was clutching a balled-up tissue in her wrinkled right hand like it was a life preserver. Eric looked like a foreman a few years away from his pension. She'd heard they lived in Loma Linda, which Kelly knew was a smoggy shithole somewhere east of L.A.

Tony cleared his throat. "Mr. and Mrs. Mann, first of all I would like to apologize for the poor judg—"

"Mr. Scoppio," Kelly interrupted. "Please let me."

Ruth scowled at her. "Kelly, this is not the—"

"Please, Ms. Sperry, Mr. Scoppio." She made her voice sound pleading and stared right at Susan and Eric Mann like they were the only people in the room.

"Yes, please," Eric Mann said. "My wife and I are very curious to hear what this young lady has to say for herself."

Kelly hesitated long enough to where it started to feel really dramatic. "I've done a great deal of . . . praying since the tragedy." She let her voice break. "And God Almighty has shown me the error of my ways!"

Even though nobody said a damn thing, Kelly could sense the emotions that coursed through her listeners: incredulity from Howard, astonishment from Ruth and Elaine, suspicion from the vulture attorney, curiosity from the bereaved pair.

And, she didn't think she got it wrong, admiration from Tony Scoppio.

She raised her eyes, which by now were brimming with tears. "I know now that I erred grievously in airing that video and in failing to report accurately on your son's tragic death. God showed me that I was caught up in television's perverted desire for high drama but that it came at your family's expense. I have been so terribly unfair." She made a choking sound and let a tear spill down her cheek. She'd practiced that for half an hour the night before. "Though I know I don't deserve it, I have begged for God's forgiveness. And now I plead for yours!"

"Now wait just a minute." The vulture attorney sprang to his feet. But by this time Kelly was on her knees, sobbing into the blue polyestered lap of Mrs. Susan Mann. The older woman was stroking Kelly's hair and shaking like she had palsy.

"I didn't know we were dealing here with a young woman who's found the grace of our Lord Jesus Christ," Eric Mann began hesitantly. "Maybe we *can* work this whole mess out without going to court."

Kelly took that opening to sob louder.

"I don't see—"

"I strongly agree with you, Eric." Tony cut off the Manns' attorney. "Maybe this'll do?"

Elaine passed over a sheet of paper that Kelly knew all about from the talk she'd had beforehand with Tony. Typed on it was a single four-digit number. Basically, the payoff. She knew the Manns' attorney would figure out his forty-percent commission PDQ.

Kelly reared up from Susan Mann's lap, on which her tears had left a huge wet spot. "I'd like us all to join hands in prayer!" She held out both arms like a preacher and raised her eyes to heaven. "Father above," she began, ad-libbing wildly. And it wasn't that easy a trick to keep from busting out laughing when everybody around her was forced to kneel down. She kept on winging it, thinking this had to be the first prayer group ever to meet in the news director's office at KXLA Channel 12 Los Angeles.

"Hey, Daniels," Tony said hours later when Natalie entered his office. He watched as she arranged herself on the chair in front of his desk. "What can I do for you this fine evening?" He was feeling expansive now that the Manns had been ushered off the lot. No way they'd file suit now. Kelly might be a real piece of work, she might break every rule, but she sure as hell came through in the clutch.

"You can agree to let me anchor Monday's newscast from a remote location," Natalie said. "The collapsed section of the 210."

"And why would I do that?"

"Because it's newsworthy. My sources tell me that the revised damage estimates are coming out Monday and they're going to be higher than anyone's expecting. And of course it's the one-week anniversary. Two strong hooks. And remotes, if they're well promoted, are good for the ratings."

"That's right." He dragged out "right" and rubbed his chin theatrically. "I vaguely recall you saying something about how you expect the numbers to go up."

"Give it a rest, Tony."

He eyed her. She was feistier than usual. Seemed pissed off, maybe. But he liked it. Made her more fun to joust with.

He consulted his watch. "It's now 7:15 P.M. on Friday. How do you propose to set this up for Monday?"

"I'll do it myself over the weekend."

"You won't get any overtime budget."

"I'm not asking for any. But I *do* expect extra free-lance crew Monday night. And reasonable promotion."

He rubbed his chin again. Who was to say what was "reasonable"? The boss. Tony Scoppio.

He grinned. "You must think the numbers need a real push—that's all I can figure. Our little chat the other day scare you, Daniels?"

She made a scoffing sound but it wasn't convincing. "Hardly. This is simply a case in which anchoring from a remote location is both newsworthy and good television. It's a combo I like."

It was also a combo that was damn hard to pull off on short notice. Over a weekend, no less. But hell, if he gave Princess enough rope, she just might hang herself. Save him the trouble.

"Fine," he said. "But Ken stays in studio. I want backup in case of technical problems."

"There won't be any technical problems." She stood up. "And promotion?"

"I'll call Willa."

She nodded and walked out.

Confident broad, wasn't she? Tony stroked his chin.

But hey—it was his favorite kind of situation. Somebody else did the work and he got the higher numbers.

Natalie sat at the rosewood desk in her study, the phone at her ear, dressed in her Saturday-at-home uniform of leggings and baggy sweatshirt. She gazed out the west-facing windows as the setting sun cast a pink glow over the Hollywood Hills and forced herself to listen one more time to the same no-can-do excuse she'd been hearing from TV techies all day.

"Sorry, I'm booked Monday."

"Thanks, anyway." The guy didn't sound sorry. She crossed his name off the list. Twenty-six down, two to go. And no question she'd need at least one more warm body to pull off the remote Monday night.

"Call me if something else comes up," he said.

"Right." Natalie hung up. Unbelievable. Clearly the best gig in town was TV techie. She sipped her rapidly cooling licorice tea and surveyed her list.

She was now down to truly obscure freelancers. People she'd never worked with before. People next to whose names Ruth had drawn little red question marks. People she didn't know from Adam on whom she'd have to rely to make the remote work.

And it *had* to work. She'd put herself squarely on the line, daring Scoppio to watch, like a diver executing a triple gainer from the three-meter board. She couldn't afford to hit concrete.

The grandfather clock on the landing struck the hour. Eight melodious Westminster chimes. Followed by the doorbell.

Geoff, right on time. Damn! She hadn't planned to get all dolled up but hardly intended to dine in sweats, either. Especially when her agent had gone out of his way to take her out for a celebratory birthday dinner on a Saturday night.

She headed downstairs in her bare feet. She didn't really want to go, which was why she hadn't changed yet. It was a pity dinner, she knew full well, for her husband dumping her just before she turned forty. No doubt Geoff didn't want to go either, but felt compelled. People got themselves into extraordinary binds trying to be civil.

She arrived at the front door and threw it open. "I'm sorry, I'm sorry, I'm sorry." She stepped back and swept Geoff inside with her arm. "I can be changed in three minutes."

Geoff eyed Natalie's sweat clothes dubiously. "If that's true, I'll get you on Sally Jessy doing 'Unbelievable Female Feats.' " No woman he had ever squired to dinner could go from sweat clothes to evening dress in less than a half hour. He handed her an enormous bouquet of yellow tulips. "Do I remember correctly?"

"You do. I love yellow in roses and tulips. I'm impressed."

He smiled and strolled into the living room adjacent to the foyer. Not even to Natalie would he admit that he kept such client preferences noted in his Palm Pilot.

He spun around to face her. "We're seriously late. We have an eight o'clock table at Four Oaks." He clapped his hands. "Chop chop."

"Four Oaks! I love it!"

She dashed out and he returned to the foyer to watch her bound up the stairs two at a time. Despite how this was essentially a get-points-with-the-client evening, he'd actually been looking forward to it. Natalie was lively and fun, and knew the ins and outs of a lot of things. Probably came from working in news, but wherever she got it, it was entertaining.

He ambled into the study and amused himself by trolling through the selections on the crammed built-in bookshelves. Lawrence. James. Hesse. Greene. *Serious reading,* he thought, immediately dismissing the notion that any of these classics belonged to Miles.

Low-life wally.

Shortly he heard a noise on the stairs and spun around.

"You like?" she asked.

Inadvertently he caught his breath. Little black dress. Strand of pearls. High heels. She was stunning, and as far from her anchor armor of suit and pancake makeup as he'd ever seen her. "Very much." He glanced at his watch. "And in twelve minutes."

"Eleven. I couldn't do much with my hair, though." She fussed with a tendril that cascaded from what looked to him to be a beautifully massed pile. "I was in such a rush."

"You accomplished in haste what most women can't pull off at leisure."

"There you go. Being charming again." She grabbed her keys from the narrow side table in the foyer just as the grandfather clock chimed the quarter hour. "Eight-fifteen already," she remarked, then turned to face him. "Geoff, before we go, let me tell you again how sweet it is of you to take me out for my birthday. It's really above and beyond."

He nodded, for some reason reluctant to tell her how much he'd been looking forward to it. "Shall we go?"

He drove the few miles to Four Oaks at his favorite pace of breakneck speed, making the rare concession of keeping the convertible top up in deference to Natalie's hairdo. As they arrived, he understood again why she liked the place so much. It was a rustic white clapboard retreat nestled in Beverly Glen, a winding canyon road a few miles west of Natalie's own. The simple exterior was almost hidden by a profusion of shrubbery and oak and eucalyptus trees. It had little of the glitz of L.A.'s preeminent eateries, but the heady aromas they encountered at the entrance gave it away as a diner's paradise.

As Geoff had arranged, and despite their tardiness, he and Natalie were seated in a cozy room decorated in French country style. He noted with satisfaction the stir Natalie created among their fellow diners. Perhaps he had an uphill battle convincing news directors of her star power. But the viewing public was clearly won over.

The sommelier appeared instantly with their chilled Veuve Clicquot. Geoff held up his flute, suddenly awkward. What was the proper toast?

"To Natalie," he said finally, raising his glass, "as we celebrate this notable birthday. May the road rise always to meet you. May the wind be at your back. May the sun shine warm upon your face, the rain fall soft upon your fields, and until we meet again, may God hold you in the hollow of His hand."

In silence they touched glasses and sipped. Natalie smiled. "That's lovely. You have to be the only man in L.A. who can recite an Irish blessing from memory."

"A product of my classical education. My parents insisted on it. My father, really." He sipped his champagne. "But once my father decides something, my mother can't go along fast enough."

Natalie nodded. "A traditional woman." She cocked her head and the errant curl again fell loose from its moorings. "There aren't many of those around anymore."

There's Janet, he thought, but remained mum.

"Didn't you tell me that your dad's an actor?" she asked.

"He is. Ian Marner?"

Natalie shook her head.

"I wouldn't expect you to know him." Geoff raised a finger to summon a waiter. "Most Aussies don't even know the name, though his face is highly recognizable. He's a character actor, not a star."

The waiter appeared, bearing menus.

Natalie laid hers down unopened. "Is it from your father that you get your love of the entertainment business?"

"I'm sure it is." Geoff ran his eyes down the menu. "But his career convinced me that the rewards are more dependable on the agenting side of the business."

"Why didn't you stay in Australia and become an agent there?"

He stared at the menu, torn between the pink dourade and the halibut. "I like being at the center of the action. And Sydney's a long way from Hollywood."

Natalie laughed. "Not for Australians!"

"Nats, you're not exactly on solid ground here." He laid down his menu. "Would you give up L.A. for Lubbock, Texas?"

"No way. Touché." She laughed and raised her flute to his.

The waiter reappeared to take their orders, then glided away.

"So," Geoff said, "let's turn the tables and probe *your* family history. I know almost none of it, despite how long I've known you." It was true. Natalie was an enigma to him. Unlike most of his clients, especially the women, she shared little of herself, as if she considered even minor revelations somehow threatening. "Come on." He topped off her champagne. "Tell me about your mother." And at that he watched her face soften.

"She was kind. Gentle. She smelled good. She laughed a lot. I can still hear her laugh." Natalie fell silent, then shook her head. "I remember her in faded pastel housedresses."

"She passed away?" he asked gently.

Natalie didn't meet his eyes. "She died when I was seven. Of cervical cancer."

He watched pain wash over her face as she seemed, for a moment, lost in the past. It was the first he'd ever thought of Natalie as a bit of a wounded bird. "Did your father remarry?"

She gave a bitter laugh. "Sure did. He moved fast. It took him no time at all."

"Did you eventually get close to your stepmom?"

"No, not really. In the beginning I hated her. Eventually I came to understand that she was just *young*." Natalie's eyes, clouded with hurt, met his. "She was twenty-one when she married my father. He was thirty-six. No wonder she didn't want to deal with a kid by his first wife." She shook her head. "*Her* I could probably forgive. But my father—" Her jaw tightened. "I never forgave him for the way he shunted me aside. Never."

Forgave him. Past tense. So her father was dead as well. Geoff frowned. No surviving parents. No siblings. And her husband had left her for another woman.

Geoff didn't see much of his family. But he could if he got to Australia more often, or flew them out. She didn't have that option.

For a moment Geoff ignored that Natalie was a client. He reached across the linen-draped table and took her hand. She met his eyes, her own big and blue and no doubt much as they had been when her father had seen fit to skip out on one family for the next.

He spoke carefully. "You've done wonders with your life, Natalie. You should be very proud of how far you've come, all on your own."

"Right." She pulled back her hand. "All on my own."

Geoff was parsing that remark when the waiter reappeared with their first course. He watched her observe the complex proceedings that for some reason surrounded the serving of pumpkin soup, seeming to use the interruption to regain the thirty-odd years that separated her girlhood from the present.

This probably explains why she married Miles, he thought. He'd never understood her attraction to such a poseur. But perhaps she'd simply found an older, ostensibly dependable man highly desirable. A father figure.

All at once Natalie paled, her eyes drawn to a commotion at the maître d's post. "Oh, my God." Her hand flew to her throat. "I don't believe it."

Geoff followed her gaze and his heart sank.

"Miles," Natalie whispered. "With that . . . *woman.*" Her face twisted as if she were in physical pain. "We used to come here all the time. And now he's coming here with that . . . *bimbo.*"

At that precise instant Miles's eyebrows flew up in surprise. He'd seen them. A beat later the blonde on Miles's arm turned in Geoff's direction. He winced in recognition. This evening was going downhill fast. What was her name? Liza? No, no. Suzy.

The restaurant seemed to hush as the pair neared their table, Miles guiding Suzy with a hand on her naked back.

"Miles." Geoff rose but desisted from offering his hand. He nodded at Suzy, then moved behind Natalie's chair, as if joining forces with her. She looked stricken.

Miles snarled at his wife. "I don't appreciate your vandalizing my home."

She flushed. "And *I* don't appreciate your lying about our prenup," she hissed, "then stealing my only copy!"

"That's one hell of an accusation." Miles raised his voice. "Where's your proof?"

"That's enough." Out of the corner of his eye Geoff saw the maître d' edge closer. By now they were the restaurant's main attraction. "This is neither the time nor the place."

Suzy tried to pull Miles away. "Please, honey, let's go," she whispered.

"Thank you, Suzy," Geoff said, only to have Natalie whirl on him, shock and anger in her eyes.

"You *know* her?"

The maître d' approached, clearly flummoxed. "Is everything quite all right here?"

Natalie stood and threw down her napkin. "No, it's not. I'm leaving." Without a backward glance she marched out, every eye fixed on her until she cleared the restaurant.

"I'd like the check, please," Geoff informed the maître d', who scuttled away at top speed.

Miles made a move to guide Suzy away. "You need your head examined to stay hooked up with her."

"Just know this, Miles." Geoff kept his voice low. "If you really did steal that prenup, there'll be hell to pay." He nodded at Suzy and strode out, adding a sizable tip to the bill at the door.

Natalie was already seated in the Jag when he emerged. All evidence of the softer woman he'd glimpsed earlier had vanished.

"Thank you for getting out here so quickly, Geoff," she said stiffly. "I'm sorry our dinner had to end this way. I know this isn't how you wanted to spend your evening."

Geoff said nothing as he made the left from the restaurant's gravel lot onto Beverly Glen. Natalie was right—he was disappointed. And angry at Miles for being such an ass.

He drove swiftly along the narrow canyon road, so closely bordered by shrubbery that it repeatedly slapped the car as they sped past. Eventually his curiosity won over. "So just what did you do to Miles's house when you found out he stole the prenup?"

"I broke the windows."

"You did *what*?"

"I broke the windows. Most of them, anyway. It's not much work when you're sufficiently inspired."

He was surprised. And slightly admiring. "How did you find out he stole it?"

"My only copy was missing from the safe-deposit box. He stole the key to that, too." She gave a brittle, mirthless laugh. "I have been such a goddamn idiot."

Geoff could hear the pain beneath the anger. There was a lot more story there, obviously. But now she was closed up and turned away, resolutely staring out the passenger window.

Moments later she surprised him by speaking again. "Geoff, I want to apologize for snapping at you over"—she paused—"*Suzy.*"

He smiled wryly. "Apology accepted." He'd met Suzy at a Hollywood party a few years back and taken her out. Slept with her, too, of course, then bid her as hasty a farewell as he'd been able to manage. He couldn't believe Miles had left Natalie for Suzy. There had to be more to that story, too.

Natalie's next words came in an acid murmur. "He lied about that, too, the bastard. He told me it was over."

They rode in silence the last mile to her home. Geoff pulled over beneath the towering palm trees that stood sentry along that stretch of the canyon and broke the awkward quiet. "If you want to talk—"

"I don't," she interrupted curtly, then hastily exited the car. He watched until she was safely inside.

CHAPTER FIVE

Monday, June 24, 12:24 P.M.

Tony leaned over his plate to take a big messy bite out of his Burrito Grande, the perfect Monday lunch. Everything at Las Casitas Mexican Grill was *grande*, everything but the tables and the bill. The former were tiny and round and red; the latter came in under fifteen bucks for two people. That was why it was his favorite place to play host.

He looked over the basket of tortilla chips at today's lucky lady: Bobbi Dominguez, his counterpart at KNBC, the NBC-owned station in Los Angeles. BD, as she was known, fit in at Las Casitas. Everything about her was big: her hair, her caftans, her ambition. At the moment she had her big mouth wrapped around a chimichanga, which had shut her up temporarily. He glugged his Coke. *Better enjoy the quiet. It won't last.*

"So." BD wiped her mouth, leaving a smear of bright red lipstick on the paper napkin. "Is it true you guys dodged a bullet with that car-accident lawsuit?"

"They were never gonna sue," he lied.

"That's not what I heard."

"BD, the grapevine doesn't always get it right. It's like a wire service reporter."

BD arched her brows but remained silent. They both bent over their plates at the same moment and nearly conked heads.

"That Kelly Devlin is a real pistol." BD got the words out even though her mouth was chock-full of food.

Tony chuckled. Even *he* had been amazed at her performance with the Manns. Her going religious on them was fucking brilliant. "She sure is spunky," he deadpanned.

"Kind of a loose cannon, though."

Tony jabbed a tortilla chip at what was left of the guacamole. Was Kelly getting a bad rep? Or was BD fishing because she was interested in hiring Kelly herself? "Who wants shy reporters?" he asked rhetorically. "Anyway, we consider her a real up-and-comer." He decided to throw out a flyer. "I'm thinking of having her host a prime-time special."

"Really?" BD's heavily mascaraed eyes flew open. "What about Natalie?"

"You know"—Tony leaned forward conspiratorially—"Natalie's doing a little bit of the prima-donna thing on me. 'Why do I have to do everything all the time,' blah blah blah. So I figure, might do her good to see somebody else on center stage for a change."

Tony watched BD digest that, along with the half pound of fried pork and tortilla she'd jammed down her gullet. He knew full well that little tidbit would make the rounds of L.A. news directors by dinner. It would help quash any interest any other station might have in his primary female anchor.

He didn't want Natalie getting rival offers. If by some chance he decided to keep her, competition would only drive up the price. And if he let her go, he didn't want viewers following her like lapdogs to some other station.

Tony gave his mouth one last swipe and tossed a few bucks on the table. BD clattered out of her chair.

"You know what'd really put Natalie in her place?" she asked when they emerged onto the street, baking in Hollywood's summer sun.

"What?" Tony unlocked the passenger door on his Honda.

"Having to coanchor with Kelly one of these nights."

Tony laughed out loud. He clapped BD on her caftaned shoulder. "That's why I like you. You think just like me."

* * *

"Goddamn beeper!"

Kelly stood in KXLA's makeup room, blinking hard from the mascara wand she'd just jabbed in her eye. When she'd left that stupid mayoral press conference, she'd forgotten to reset her beeper from buzz to tone. And then when it went off, it totally freaked her out.

She angled it away from her waistband. *212.555.8697.* A New York area code. Who the hell would page her from New York?

She punched the number into the makeup room phone. Too bad the makeup girl would get billed for the long-distance call.

"Hard Line," a female straight out of Brooklyn rasped.

"What?"

"You called me, remember? *Hard Line*!"

The national tabloid TV show? Kelly's heart began to pound. "Uh, hello. My name is Kelly Devlin, from KXLA Los Angeles. I was paged by—"

"Right. Hold on."

Kelly tapped her foot impatiently. Maybe they wanted to hire her. Her agent could get her out of her KXLA contract. Maybe . . .

"Kelly? Bruce Lightner, senior producer."

"Bruce," she purred. "It's a pleasure to meet you over the phone."

"Likewise. Listen, we saw the piece you did on the car accident the night of the quake. Very edgy."

"Thank you." She tried to sound modest but confident.

"We're doing a spot on killer natural disasters—you know, freaky shit that happens during twisters and earthquakes and volcanos and like that—and we might want to use some of your car-accident video. Can you arrange for us to see more of it?"

Damn, they didn't want to hire her.

But they *had* seen her stuff.

And they liked it enough to call her.

But what about the Manns? Kelly hesitated. She could

never win them over a second time. If that video of their kid aired again they'd be so pissed they'd definitely file suit.

But, she told herself, the Manns would never see it. They were too goddamn religious to watch a good show like *Hard Line.*

"I'll FedEx you a dub," she said. The opportunity to get in with these people was just too good to pass up.

Kelly got the address, then hung up and grinned at herself in the mirror. This call was proof positive she was doing something right. Who else at KXLA had ever gotten beeped by a national tabloid TV show?

Monday night as ten p.m. approached, a techie rapped on the grimy passenger-side window of ENG Truck 2, rousing Natalie's attention. "We need you out there," he shouted through the glass.

She looked up from reviewing her script for the newscast and cranked down the window. A blast of wind whipped inside, riffling her script pages and hurling dust in her eyes. She blinked, hard.

"We're about ten minutes back."

"Thanks." She rubbed her right eyelid, trying to resettle her contact lens without smearing her heavy on-air makeup. "Charlie, is it? You're the engineer I hired for tonight?" She didn't say, *The last guy on the list?*

The guy nodded. "Yeah, I was lookin' to get together with the buds, you know, pour a few back, but, hey, duty called." He cocked his head at the sky. "But the wind's making it tough to keep up the bird." He made quite a picture: shaggy blond hair hanging below a Dodgers cap, jeans that looked like they'd never seen the inside of a washing machine, mustache newly primed by greasy takeout. He didn't look like much, but then again, the best techies rarely did.

"Well, I appreciate your help."

"My pleasure, ma'am." He saluted and sauntered off.

She rolled the window back up and fiddled with her earpiece for the umpteenth time. She felt fairly calm. *Fairly* calm. But she'd hung this remote on a wing and a prayer. And anchoring from the field, even under the best of circumstances, was a thousand times harder than anchoring from the studio. There were so many variables. Cold. Heat. Wind. Dirt. Noise. Onlookers. Satellite problems.

And somehow she couldn't forget her recent flub. The damn thing sat in her memory like footprints in concrete.

It happened once—it can happen again.

No! She clamped her eyes shut. *It happened once in a million times. It's the exception, not the rule.*

Another knock on the window. This time from the freelance field producer, a young bespectacled woman in jeans and an oversize flannel shirt whose name Natalie couldn't remember.

Her pulse sped up. She could delay it no longer.

She secured her script on a weather-beaten clipboard and attached a Bic to the metal clasp. With a deep breath she pushed open the door, the wind gusting around her.

"Here's your mark." The producer girl pointed to two strips of red duct tape laid out in a stand-here X. Natalie set herself up, from habit angling her right shoulder toward the camera. Behind her rose the collapsed hulk of the freeway, now cordoned off by orange tape. And floodlit courtesy of KXLA.

Dave—big, burly, cheerful Dave, the only other person besides her who wasn't freelance—was working audio. He handed her the remote box for her earpiece, and as soon as she plugged in she heard program, the drama that on Mondays preceded *The KXLA Primetime News*. The bird was up.

"Level okay?" Dave asked.

She nodded.

"I don't want to use a hand mike 'cause of the wind and 'cause you'll need your hands free." He jerked his head at her clipboard. "Here."

She strung the lavalier up under her jacket and attached the mike to her lapel. At least she'd had the good sense to put on thick black trousers, boots, a cashmere turtleneck, and a tweed jacket. Even in summer it could be seriously chilly in L.A. at night. She stomped her feet, partly to stay warm, partly to stop the tremors of nervousness that coursed through her.

Dave eyed her closely as he clipped the mike box to her waistband.

She flushed. Apparently she wasn't the only one wondering whether Natalie Daniels would mess up again tonight.

Maybe you've gotten soft from all those years behind the anchor desk . . .

"All set," Dave pronounced. He ambled back behind the cameraman, a tall African-American Natalie had never met.

"Ninety seconds back," Dave intoned.

Again Natalie felt her heartbeat ratchet higher. She held up the clipboard to scan her script. The gusts were so strong, she had to grasp it with both hands. The producer girl still hadn't budged from the ENG truck, where she was locked in conversation with Charlie. He was shaking his head and pointing at the sky.

Natalie frowned. Was something wrong?

"Thirty," Dave announced.

A crowd had gathered. Natalie noticed their furtive nudges and pointings and whisperings. Was it just the spectacle of a live news shot? Or were they thinking about her mistake on the air? A tremor ran through her like a current. She glanced again at her notes. *I never used to get this nervous.*

You never used to fuck up.

"Ten."

She fixed her gaze on the lens and took a deep breath. *Forget everything. It's only you and the camera now.*

Seconds later the voice of her coanchor, Ken, filled her ear. The show had opened. News video appeared on the monitor set up at the base of the camera. "A chain reaction pile-up on the 405 in Redondo Beach leaves three dead and six injured."

The wind gusts were now so strong she had to plant her feet a foot apart on the asphalt just to stay in place. She clutched the clipboard tighter in her hand. *Steady, steady . . .*

"U.S. military forces in the Adriatic Sea are on high alert, reacting to yet another deadly clash in Montenegro."

She lifted her chin and stared defiantly into the lens, her eyes stinging from the wind. *I can do this.*

"And one week after a six point two earthquake rumbled across the Southland, authorities have substantially raised their estimate of the damage. Natalie Daniels is live with the latest."

Deep breath. "Ken, the damage estimate is now over half a billion dollars, and local authorities tell me—"

"Fuck!"

Natalie ignored the outburst, which had come from Charlie. "—they're asking for assistance from Sacramento—"

"We lost the bird!"

What? "—and plan to meet with the governor—"

"Stop! Stop, Natalie." The producer girl ran over, arms flailing, eyes panicked behind her lenses. The knot of onlookers started to chatter. "We lost the bird. Charlie says it's the wind."

"In the middle of my open?" It was true, Natalie realized. She was no longer hearing program, just a series of staccato clicks as Charlie struggled to reconnect with the satellite.

"Pretty much at the beginning. Wait." The girl pressed her headset tighter against her ear. "Right." She looked at Natalie again. "Ken's tossed to the Redondo Beach live shot. He'll come back to us after that, presuming we're up."

"We'd better be up."

"We're up!" Charlie yelled from the truck, giving a frenzied hand signal. And then there was program, loud and clear in her ear.

She got back on her mark. *Easy. Think. Lose page one,* she told herself and threw it on the ground. It whipped away in no time, carried off by a gust.

"Okay," the producer girl said. "Ken's tossing back to us . . . Wait." She paused. "Not the damage estimate piece, it's not cut yet. Toss to the Cal Tech package, page B5."

B5? How the hell could the damage piece not be cut yet? *Don't think about it. Focus.* She willed her fingers to stop shaking. *There's A6. Just put it in the bottom of the script pile and put B5 on top . . .*

"Back in ten," Dave pronounced.

Ten seconds? Where's B5? Is that the one about the new fault line? Natalie fumbled with the script, her fingers cold and damnably slow to cooperate.

"Five," she heard Dave say.

Where the hell is it? Then there it was. She ripped it out of the pack.

Ken's voice. "We go back now to Natalie Daniels, who is—"

And suddenly her fingers slipped, the clipboard slammed to the ground, and the pages went flying, flying, like a white rush of birds taking off.

Ignore it. Don't think. Talk. You practically know the script by heart anyway. "Ken, seismologists at Cal Tech are reporting that the fault line which caused the quake—"

Good, keep talking. Look, the producer girl's running after the script pages . . .

"—is an offshoot of the one—"

Charlie screamed. "Fuck! Again! I can't believe it!"

This can't be happening. "—which caused so much—"

"Stop! Stop!" The producer girl waved her hands frantically, again pressing her headset against her ear, again running toward Charlie. He'd resumed his stance half inside the ENG truck, only his denimed posterior protruding. By now the bystanders were laughing at these buffoons from KXLA, like they were a comedy team serving up the biggest joke of the season.

Only the joke's all on me.

Natalie stood, immobilized by the high-tech umbilical cords that attached her to the camera. She watched helplessly as her script pages took off like kites, or were plastered by the wind against cars and fences and tree trunks, or blew like crazy winged creatures down the street toward Our Lady Victory Catholic Church.

"We're back!" The producer girl pointed frantically at Natalie.

No. Oh, no. Out of the silence she heard clicks in her ear, then program, sputtering—was that Ken's voice?—then no program, then program again, then none . . .

Dave frowned. "They're telling me we're back in five."

"I am not hearing program!" The words spilled out of her, breaching the wall of her training, breaking the cardinal rule. *Be very careful what you say when you're miked and possibly on air . . .*

Dave held up a hand. "False alarm . . . Wait."

Does anybody have the slightest clue what the fuck they're doing?

It was all going to hell, all of it.

And Tony Scoppio and hundreds of thousands of Angelenos were watching.

"Goddammit!" she heard herself yell. "Are we up or not?"

All the frustration of the last days burst out of her like a volcanic flow, filling the air with her rage. The surreal scene around her suddenly went quiet and slow. People turned and stared, their faces a blur.

And then it wasn't quiet anymore because she heard her own voice in her ear—*oh, no*—she heard her own voice on program, and knew as she stood paralyzed on the little red duct-taped X that her irate voice was blaring from hundreds of thousands of television sets across southern California.

CHAPTER SIX

Tuesday, June 25, 12:08 P.M.

"At least you're above the fold." Ruth sat on the plump white sofa in Natalie's living room, bifocals sliding down her nose, inspecting the *Hollywood Insider*, an entertainment industry daily. "And they spelled your name right."

Natalie turned away from her morose reflection in the paned window to glare at Ruth. "Very funny."

"You've got to find humor at times like this. Otherwise—"

"Otherwise what? You slit your wrists? Or put your head in the oven? Or jump out the window?"

"Don't jump out the window. You won't kill yourself. You'll just land in the *Insider* again."

"I cannot believe this is happening." Natalie stared through the glass, the canyon dull and gray under an overcast sky. L.A.'s famed marine layer, the bane of summer, had set in with a vengeance, creating a scene of unrelieved dreariness. Probably the sun wouldn't break through all day. She sighed and let her head drop forward.

It was past noon and she was still in her bathrobe. Unshowered. Refusing to answer the phone, which had rung a few dozen times. Refusing to read the *Insider* piece, which she'd glanced at briefly, then flung aside. All morning, she'd ricocheted between fear and humiliation, her embarrassment ballooning from painful to grotesque.

Ruth fiddled with a loose thread dangling from her suit du jour, a collarless lime-green rayon blend with gold buttons set with military precision across the square-cut jacket. "You think the article's worse than it is because you won't read it." She shook out the paper noisily. "I'll read it to you. But you're going to have to look at the picture, and in my never-to-be-humble opinion, that's the worst part."

Natalie was silent. She hadn't let herself give the picture more than a cursory glance, but she couldn't fail to note that in it she was crying, and her features were contorted, and she was holding up her hand ineffectually to block her face.

"You know, this photo was pulled from the aircheck," Ruth observed. Airchecks were videotaped copies of programming that broadcasters were required by law to save. One was made of every newscast and stored in Archives. "I wonder how they got a copy of it. I'll check that out. Anyway, headline." Ruth cleared her throat. " 'KXLA Anchor Blunders On-Air.' "

Natalie girded herself. She could just imagine what glee Tony Scoppio must have felt reading the piece. He'd probably already ordered Maxine to post it on the newsroom notice board.

" 'Natalie Daniels, long-time anchor of *The KXLA Primetime News* (Channel 12, ten p.m. weeknights), made TV-news history last night by swearing and crying live on air during a report from the portion of the 210 freeway at Sierra Madre Boulevard that collapsed in last week's earthquake. The newscast had been marred, and Daniels's performance apparently affected, by problems with the satellite linkup. The incident followed a similar snafu last week, when Daniels repeatedly misreported the magnitude of the quake's most serious aftershock. A source at KXLA says that morale at the station has been sinking—' "

"*What?* What 'source within KXLA'?"

"The famous 'unnamed.' " Ruth peered at Natalie over her bifocals. "You cannot seriously expect not to have enemies, Natalie. Not in your position."

"I don't expect not to have enemies. But I *do* expect to know who they are." She frowned. "Of course I know who *one* is."

"Don't we all." Ruth returned her eyes to the paper. "Blah, blah . . . 'Morale has been sinking with Daniels's, quote, "lackluster" performance since the breakup of her twelve-year marriage to sitcom scribe Miles Lambert. Lambert is the creator and executive producer of the fall season's highly touted new comedy *Forget Maui.* KXLA News Director Tony Scoppio, brought in recently from top-rated KBTT in Dallas, also owned by KXLA parent Sunshine Broadcasting, would not comment beyond saying, "I anticipate making some long overdue changes, but it's too soon to say what they will be." ' " Ruth threw down the paper. "Wonder where I can get concrete galoshes for that guy."

Natalie stared out the glass. So it was war. And her news director was using every weapon in his arsenal. Undermining her psychologically. Jibing at her in the press. Even more appalling was that she was her own worst enemy. In the last week she'd flubbed both an in-studio interrupt and a remote newscast. The Natalie Daniels of old never made on-air mistakes. But now she was handing Tony exactly the ammunition he needed to shoot her down.

Ruth spoke up. "Have you spoken with Geoff?"

Natalie nodded. She'd called him. It had been awkward, the first time they'd spoken since their botched Saturday dinner. He'd reacted calmly, though both agent and client knew how seriously Natalie's reputation had been marred. "He put in another call to Tony. For all the good it'll do. Tony's been dodging him all week."

Ruth rose from the sofa. "I gotta get back to the salt mines. Can I do anything for you?"

"No, thanks."

"Are you sure?"

"I'm sure."

Natalie watched Ruth let herself out. Then she walked with deliberate steps out of the living room and across the foyer to the wood-paneled study, pulling open the big double doors to a storage cupboard filled with the only thing that could help her now.

Boxes. White and brown cardboard shipping boxes, battered and bruised from age and handling. A dozen, at least, though she hadn't counted them lately. The Stash, she called it privately, which was unknown to everyone in Natalie's life, like an alcoholic's hidden cache of forbidden liquor. She pulled out the most accessible box—when it came down to it they were all the same—and laid it on the worn navy-and-crimson Oriental rug, kneeling beside it. Already she felt better.

She opened it up. It was full to the brim with letters, as all the boxes were: letters to Natalie Daniels or Miss Natalie Daniels or Ms. Natalie Daniels, whatever the viewer deemed the most appropriate form of address for a beloved news personality. She pulled out a letter and opened it up.

> *Dear Ms. Daniels, I've been watching you so long and I just had to write! You are such an elegant newscaster and I just love . . .*

As she read, letter after letter after letter, a smile came to her lips. Though she didn't even notice.

Her hair newly washed, Kelly stood at her closet in her bra and thong, going through her wardrobe. No. No. No. The metal hangers clanged as they collided with one another, her hand slapping one into the next as she rejected outfit after outfit. No. No. She paused on a clingy black sheer top that served as her standard first-date outfit. It was transparent enough that her bra showed through, to spectacular effect. Reluctantly, no. Then, two hangers down, yes. Perfect for what she had to do that day at work.

Out it came: a long-sleeved U-necked black lace-up top with what could safely be described as extreme décolleté. Leather, no less. She could pair it with a simple black skirt: nobody would notice her south of the border, anyway. The top made her look like a beer-slinging

Heidi ready at any moment to drop her steins but so be it. Men loved that shit. With a jacket, she could get away with it on air.

But no need to wear the jacket when she was chatting with Scoppio. Kelly chuckled and dropped the top on her unmade bed. With Natalie practically self-destructing on air, the timing for this conversation could not be more perfect.

A thought occurred to her. Kelly ran to the heavy oak armoire in the living room that had served in college and the few years since as an entertainment center. Decrepit TV and VCR on top; videotapes, mostly work-related, in the cabinet below. She knelt down to rummage for the tape she needed: KPSG PALM SPRINGS CHANNEL 8 / / KELLY DEVLIN.

Her résumé reel from her first job in TV news, complete with its precious footage of her substitute anchoring. She pulled it out and slapped it against her hand. She'd gotten to fill-in anchor only once.

But Scoppio didn't know that.

The phone rang.

She dropped the tape and crawled across the carpet to answer. "Yup?" She leaned back on her ankles, absently running her hand down the back of her thong. The crawling had gotten it badly wedged.

"Yeah, it's Grant from the *Insider*."

Immediately she rose on her haunches. "Good morning, Grant. How are you?"

"It's afternoon."

She forced herself to laugh lightly. "I'm working the three to eleven today and it's easy on that shift to lose track of the time. What can I do for you?"

"I want to know how to get the aircheck back to you."

She thought quickly. The *Insider*, as she'd known they would, had used a frame from the prior night's aircheck—which she, of course, had provided—to generate the photo of Natalie that had appeared in that morning's edition. Pilfering airchecks was a major no-no. So far she was safe: nobody had seen her take it. She certainly didn't want anybody to catch her putting it back. *Or* to see her at the *Insider*'s editorial offices picking it up.

But all in all, it was better to have it back at the station.

"How about mailing it back to me at my home address?" she suggested. "In an unmarked envelope?"

The guy laughed. "I can do that. Good thinking." He laughed again. "Keep that up and you'll go far." After Kelly gave him her address information, and made him recite it back, he hung up.

She rose to amble over to her bedroom. *Keep that up and you'll go far.* She eyed the leather top lying tantalizingly on the bed. *No shit, Sherlock.*

Berta Powers was a formidable woman, Natalie decided for the umpteenth time. Natalie sat on a damask sofa in Berta's sleek ivory-colored office, watching her attorney tear into some poor bastard over the phone. She looked like she was having a fine time doing it, too. Everything about Berta seemed wired for action. Her bright red suit. Her Manhattan-style, mile-a-minute patter. Even her dark hair, frizzy but contained in a professional bun. *If I have to get divorced,* Natalie thought, *I want this woman on my team.*

As Tony would say.

"Sorry about that." Berta hung up and crossed her expansive office to rejoin Natalie in the east forty, where the upholstered seating was tastefully arranged beneath a huge de Kooning. "Cream?"

Natalie nodded and Berta expertly poured a dollop into her porcelain cup. She then pressed the RECORD button on the dictaphone that perched between them like a nosy relation. "You were telling me about discovering that the prenup was gone from the safe-deposit box," Berta prompted.

"Yes, last week." Natalie returned her cup to its saucer. "The bank clerk confirmed that Miles had been inside the box."

"But the clerk didn't actually see him remove anything?"

"No."

"It was your only copy?"

"Yes."

"You're sure the prenup was in the box prior to that day?"

Natalie frowned. "*Fairly* sure. I went into it from time to time, to put something in or take something out. I vaguely recall seeing it on occasion."

Berta bit her lip and scribbled in a spiral-bound notebook. Natalie felt a rush of humiliation, as though a more competent person would have taken notes after every foray into her safe-deposit box.

Berta looked up. "I presume Miles had a key to the box?"

"No. He was a signatory but I had both keys."

"Then how would he have been able to get in?"

Natalie hesitated. "I believe he took one of my keys the night before he went to the bank."

Berta frowned. "Took it? From where?"

"He knew that I had it taped to the underside of a desk drawer. In my study at home. Now it's gone."

"At home." Berta arched her brows. "And how would he have gotten into your home? I thought you two were living separately."

Natalie felt a flush rise on her cheeks. "He got in . . . on a pretext."

"Ah." Berta nodded slowly. "I think I get the picture."

Natalie felt her face grow hotter. *I think we both do.* "I'm still amazed there's no copy of the prenup in the file you inherited from Henry," she said hurriedly, anxious to move on. "He was my attorney for years and I would swear he kept a copy of every document he drafted."

"I'm sure he did. The only way I can explain it is that the paralegal who went through Henry's files after he died threw it out. Or misfiled it. You'd be amazed how often that happens. And now we're looking for a needle in a haystack."

"Aren't these things a matter of public record? Filed in a court somewhere?"

Berta shook her head. "No. They're like wills."

It boggled the mind. People's lives depending on slips

of paper so easily lost. "And I suppose Miles's former attorney has no incentive to come forward with *his* copy?"

"None, even if he still has one. So far he hasn't returned my phone calls. I'll subpoena him if I have to."

"And Miles's *new* attorney?"

Berta threw up her hands. "For all we know, Miles is telling *him* there's no prenup. That's certainly what Johnny would want to believe. That makes it a much more compelling case. More money. A better story, so more publicity. Two of John Bangs Jr.'s greatest motivators."

Berta pronounced the name with the derision it deserved, in Natalie's opinion. She'd never liked "Johnny," as he called himself, from the moment he'd started making headlines as the divorce attorney to the stars. He'd quickly become as famous as his clients, routinely appearing in the tabloids alongside his plaintiff or defendant du jour. Johnny Bangs with his mane of silver hair, deeply tanned face, and bespoke suits and shoes.

The women stared at each other, the pristine ivory office silent save for the soft whir of the dictaphone.

"Without a prenup," Natalie murmured, "Miles could claim half the assets remaining from the marriage?"

Berta nodded. "According to the community-property laws in the state of California."

"And the fact that I'm the one who created almost all those assets is irrelevant?"

"When it comes down to it, who earned what is not relevant. But remember, the only thing that's unusual in *your* case, and even *that's* becoming more common, is that the high earner was the wife, not the husband."

"Great." Natalie smiled ruefully. "I'm a pioneer." A dozen years of marriage and Miles's income was spotty at best, though to all appearances he'd made a fortune before she met him. How could he score such a huge early success in the sitcom world and then fare so badly?

Berta was brisk. "Natalie, I'll need you to compile financial records from all twelve years of the marriage. We'll review them together and then provide photocopies to Miles and Johnny. They'll have to go through the same exercise, of course."

Natalie grimaced. "I'm embarrassed to admit it but Miles handled all our finances. I literally have no idea what's there."

"Well, now's the time to find out."

Natalie nodded, suddenly unable to speak. She felt her throat constrict as if strong-fingered hands were clutching it, choking off the air. *What if Miles gets away with this outrageous claim? I'd lose the house. I'd lose a huge chunk of my investments, and my retirement savings.*

Right when I could lose my job.

Berta must have picked up on something, because she leaned forward to rub Natalie's hand. "We'll fight them. Don't worry. I'll have a paralegal go through what's left of Henry's files, again. We may still find the prenup."

Natalie nodded, mute.

"Look." Berta clicked off the dictaphone. "It's not an ideal situation, but don't despair. We're just getting started."

Natalie raised the porcelain cup with a shaky hand. *You're right, Berta. A lying, cheating, thieving husband suing for half your property is not an ideal situation.*

Tony stared at the spread on pages six and seven of the catalogue he'd picked up at John Morse Lexus/Cadillac, careful to keep it flat on his desk so no one in the newsroom could see what he was reading. It didn't exactly qualify as news-related.

He licked his lips. The Cadillac DeVille DTS. Big, silver, three hundred horsepower, the kind of car Old Man Bergamini cruised around in on Sunday mornings in Queens to take the family to 9:15 Mass at Most Holy Redeemer. All six Bergaminis fit inside, and looked damned comfortable, too, even Two-Ton Tina in the backseat.

A helluva contrast to the Scoppio clan, the five of them crammed inside the '53 Chevy his parents had owned for a decade, the interior stinked up by the acetone his father used to scrub off the shoe polish that stained his fingers his entire life. All those years Cosimo

Scoppio owned that goddamn shoe repair shop and never once did his hands lose the stain of that polish.

Tony looked down at his own thick fingers clutching the catalogue. He could picture his own Sunday scene: Anna-Maria in the DeVille, her silver-blond hair dolled up, wearing something she'd picked up from Neiman or Saks, and not from the sale rack, either. Other men in his position might want a Beemer or a Mercedes but he knew what he liked. Anna-Maria would look good in a Caddy. 'Course they couldn't get the kids to go with them to Mass, that had ended years ago, but he and Anna-Maria could park in a primo spot, then stroll up the aisle to a front pew, tossing a couple twenties in the collection basket when the time came. Not even use the church envelopes, just so everybody could see how much they gave.

And it *could* happen. *If* he got the newscast to number one in the ratings. *If* he got the news department out of the red. And *if* that pecker Pemberley stuck to the incentive deal he'd promised when Tony had signed.

"May I bother you for a moment?"

Damn. Kelly. He shoved the catalogue underneath some folders but knew he hadn't been fast enough. He saw her big brown eyes flicker down, then up again. Damn. Was she laughing at him?

And what the hell was she wearing?

"I know this is a difficult time, Tony, what with all the problems with Natalie. I feel just terrible for her." Kelly settled herself in the chair in front of his desk and raised her eyes to his. He struggled not to let his own eyes drop, where, goddamn, there was a helluva view. "And for you," she added.

He squinted at her. This chick was a sly one. "Why for me?" he asked.

"Well, here you are, Tony, trying to repair the damage to this newsroom from years of poor management, and your main female anchor is having emotional problems that are affecting her work on air. I know you're being sensitive to her needs, but you have a newsroom to run. It puts a great deal of pressure on you."

He settled back and crossed his hands over his

paunch, peering at Kelly over his half glasses. What the hell did she want? And why was she dressed like a streetwalker?

"After all, I owe a great deal to Natalie," she added.

Yeah, he'd heard something about that. Natalie was some kind of mentor to Kelly when Kelly was in college, even got her an internship at KXLA. The things women did—it was nuts sometimes.

He glanced at Kelly and noticed her staring at him. Then—was he seeing things?—he could swear she batted her eyes.

Tony squirmed. It made him uncomfortable—that's all he knew. *Very* uncomfortable.

"I have to admit I have an ulterior motive," she went on. Giggle, giggle. Bat, bat. No, he hadn't imagined it. She looked away, which gave him a chance to scan the scenery. Hot damn. He felt himself stir, which hadn't happened for a long time. Christ, he'd had the *other* problem lately.

"I'm thinking Natalie will want to take a few days off, what with everything that's been going on."

He practically guffawed, but Kelly didn't seem to notice. He'd have to blast Princess out of the anchor chair. She probably had it soldered to her butt.

"Personally, as a woman, I think it would do her a world of good to get some well-deserved R and R." Kelly raised her eyes to his and instantly Tony snapped to attention. "If that happens, Tony, would you let me fill in for her?"

That was it. Interesting. Howard had come babbling to him with something about Kelly filling in.

"You may not be aware," she went on, "that I did a great deal of fill-in anchoring when I worked in Palm Springs." She held up a tape. "May I?"

Why the hell not? He nodded and she made her way across his office, her hips bumping and grinding like nobody's business. Shit, if he did let her fill in, maybe she and Ken could do the news standing up. He thought it looked stupid on Channel 14 but they didn't have this kind of raw material to work with.

Kelly rolled the tape, and he had to admit, she wasn't bad. Too much makeup but that rarely hurt the numbers.

They watched in silence and he saw her glance at him a time or two, like she hoped he didn't notice. He kept his face noncommittal.

"So what do you think?" She was up close then—how the hell had she made it across his office so fast?—leaning toward him, her voice husky. He kept his eyes glued to her face, which required big-time effort. Her boobs were practically falling out onto his desk.

"How about filling in Friday night?" he heard himself ask.

She smiled. "Perfect." Then she leaned over more and he got a good whiff of her. Baby powder and musky perfume. "Tony, you won't regret giving me this opportunity."

He watched her sashay out. True. He saw no regrets on the horizon. But he did want to make one change to her plan. Not Kelly and Ken. Kelly and *Natalie*. Now *that* he'd like to see.

Geoff stood in the contemporary two-storied space that served as his living room, studying with uncharacteristic nervousness the sleek green Italian marble clock on the pristine white wall. Its ticking reverberated in the modern hollowness. When he saw that the clock's slim gold hands indicated 9:54 P.M., his heart rate picked up yet again.

It was ten o'clock and he hadn't asked her yet. He'd meant to do it at dinner but hadn't. Somehow the right moment never came.

He reached into his jacket pocket and touched the little black velvet box. Still there.

He doffed his jacket and tossed it on the sofa. Well, he decided, this would keep. He could hear Janet upstairs running a bath and knew she'd be happily occupied for some time. No doubt, he told himself, an opportunity would present itself later in the weekend.

He strode across the hardwood to the spindly metal-and-glass sideboard, the only other item in the room apart from the sofa and two writhing metallic sculptures. His designer had thrown up her hands and dismissed the decor as "spartan" but Geoff didn't care. Long before the designer's fussy arrival, he had decided that naturally beautiful spaces didn't require much decoration. He sloshed two fingers of scotch in a tumbler and threw it back.

He refreshed his glass and walked into the adjacent home theater, the only room that made any concession to plushness. It was thickly carpeted and equipped with an enormous screen and four rows of crimson velvet seats, three on each side, the same as would be found in any cinema, only wildly more comfortable. He played with a few knobs at the rear controls and switched from video to television, surfing for Channel 12. It was 9:58. He might as well catch *The KXLA Primetime News* while Janet was soaking.

The show opened. An unfamiliar female voice pierced the theater's silence. Geoff frowned and settled himself in a seat, watching the screen fill with video of a gargantuan fire.

"Tonight, allegations that yesterday's deadly refinery fire in Torrance may have stemmed from human error."

Who was *that*? The screen wiped from the fire video to a warship at sea. To his relief he heard Natalie's husky, commanding voice.

"The Pentagon sends another battalion to the Adriatic Sea, as U.S. troops already in that region remain on high alert."

Then the other woman again, in a lighter tone, over video of a Hollywood party. "And actress Hope Dalmont wraps her final scene on the final film of her career, just weeks before taking on the biggest role of her life—bride to the world's most eligible bachelor, Prince Albert of Monaco."

KXLA's pulsating news theme filled the theater. Geoff put aside his scotch and leaned forward, hands clasped between his knees, impatient to see Natalie and this mystery coanchor.

Fade up from black to a wide shot of the two anchors on set. He focused his gaze first on Natalie.

A vision in a turquoise suit, she looked in control, confident. He realized that he'd begun to worry about her on-air performance. Those flubs she'd made in the last few weeks were the first chinks he'd ever seen in her professional armor. It was jarring, like a star quarterback suddenly throwing interceptions.

The director cut to a single shot of the other anchor.

"Good evening," she said, "I'm Kelly Devlin, substituting tonight for Ken Oro. It is now official—"

Geoff's eyes narrowed. This was not good. This Kelly woman was even more striking at the anchor desk than she was reporting from the field, in a back-of-the-motorcycle, groupie kind of way. Big dark eyes, full lips, heavy makeup. And young. "The death toll from yesterday's refinery fire in Torrance is up to three," she read. "And local authorities now admit—"

"Who's that?" Janet padded into the theater, barefoot and in a thick white fleecy robe. She sat next to Geoff and nuzzled his neck. She had a sweet smell from the bath and her blond hair was heaped prettily on her head. "I thought that woman was a reporter."

"She is." He patted Janet's knee, his eyes riveted on the screen.

"Is she a client?"

He shook his head.

"Why is she anchoring and not reporting?"

"Janet!" He threw up his hands. "I'm trying to watch!"

"Fine. I'll go make tea."

Now he felt bad. He grabbed her hand to halt her as she rose. "I'm sorry, sweetie, but I'd just like to see this."

"No problem," she conceded and tiptoed out.

Relieved, he returned his attention to the screen, where a male reporter was finishing the refinery fire live shot. Next appeared Natalie, reading the lead-in to the Pentagon piece. He smiled and hiked the volume. He loved that voice. Great for TV.

"Another seven thousand troops, some from Camp Pendleton just north of San Diego, will head—"

Janet came padding back in and returned to the seat next to him. She was silent for a time. Then she asked quietly, "Geoff, do you remember that my mom's fund-raiser for the Huntington Museum is tomorrow night? Black tie." She paused. "Geoff?"

The director was back to a two-shot. He should talk to Scoppio about tweaking the lighting, if he could ever get him on the phone. It was a tad harsh on Natalie's side of the anchor desk.

"Geoff?"

Although, had Natalie gone to soft focus? Not a bad idea, truth be told. If it was good enough for Dan Rather, it was . . .

The screen went black. He reeled around, startled. Janet was standing at the rear of the theater.

"That's it." She locked his gaze. "No more news."

At first he felt a snap of irritation. But then as she moved closer, he began to reconsider. One step away she untied her sash and her robe fell open, offering a tantalizing glimpse of smooth white skin. She bent to kiss his mouth.

"Let's go upstairs," she whispered.

He reached up to push the robe off Janet's shoulders. God, she smelled sweet. "Here," he muttered, licking her throat.

"Upstairs."

Momentarily he halted, frustrated, but then in one fleet motion rose to his feet and swung her into his arms Rhett Butler style, striding out of the theater and up the staircase. She giggled until he'd kicked the master suite door shut behind them.

Fifty minutes later, Geoff extricated himself from a dozing Janet and returned downstairs. He switched the television back on just in time to hear Natalie doing a voice-over to video of Monegasques scurrying to ready the palace for the upcoming royal wedding.

"—next month, when an expected one billion viewers worldwide will witness the nuptials live on television."

He listened to the smile in Natalie's voice as the video switched to B-roll of the groom-to-be at some miscellaneous banquet, slapping backs and shaking hands. Geoff hated this celebrity shit on newscasts and knew Natalie did, too, but she was doing a good job of appearing deeply interested.

"The usually very visible Prince Albert is spending his last weeks as the world's most eligible bachelor in seclusion," she went on, "while the actress Hope Dalmont wraps up her affairs here in Los Angeles. The incredible interest in the pair has heightened with every day that both bride and groom decline requests for interviews."

Natalie made a half turn toward Kelly, inviting the anchor chitchat that invariably wrapped the newscast.

"I sure hope Hope Dalmont doesn't end up the same way Grace Kelly did," Kelly said, "dead in a car wreck."

Geoff reeled back in his seat. He watched shock flash across Natalie's face.

"That was certainly tragic," she said swiftly. "Hope Dalmont has said how much she'll miss her own mother on her wedding day. Apparently she died when Hope was just a child. It's very sad that neither mother lived to see her child marry."

Mercifully Kelly had no pithy rejoinder to that so both anchors turned back to camera on a two-shot as Natalie delivered the good-byes.

Geoff's mind raced. This Kelly Devlin woman had to be one of the loosest cannons he'd ever seen on live air. But she was edgy in a way that lots of news directors liked. Geoff watched the credits scroll past, unnerved and unseeing. Was Tony Scoppio one of them?

Natalie seethed as she watched Kelly unceremoniously dump her script in the trash bin behind the anchor desk. "What was that?"

"What?" Kelly looked genuinely taken aback.

"That Grace Kelly remark?" Natalie yanked her earpiece cord from the console beneath the anchor desk. "What were you thinking?"

"I only said what everybody *watching* was thinking." Kelly spoke mildly. "What's wrong with that?"

Natalie shook her head, disgusted both with Kelly and

herself. How could she ever in a million years have thought this woman was worth mentoring? How could she ever have expended so much time and energy teaching her the ropes, even opening her home to her?

Natalie grabbed up her script, legal pad, and earpiece and hurried down the few carpeted steps from the set to the concrete studio floor. It amazed her that years ago they'd actually been close. At the time, Kelly's desire to learn, and hers to teach, had been well matched.

Natalie had felt a strong compulsion to mentor another woman just starting out. Basically it sprang from her desire to pay back, somehow, for how much Evie had helped *her*. When *she* was a student at U.C.L.A. and KXLA reporter Evie Parker had taught one of her classes. For the next ten years, the veteran reporter had taught Natalie the TV-news ropes, even helping her get her first on-air job in Sacramento, and later a shot at KXLA.

Natalie had met Kelly much the same way, when Natalie had delivered a speech at Cal State Northridge, where Kelly was enrolled. Kelly had raced up to her after her talk and finagled an appointment. Before long Natalie was helping Kelly get an internship at KXLA, then even letting her move in temporarily with her and Miles while Kelly was between apartments.

But after a few months of shepherding Kelly through the ins and outs of KXLA, Natalie had had enough. She'd started to feel like Kelly was sucking her dry. And she wanted no more of having another woman in the house with her and Miles. A couple needed privacy.

So she pulled some strings to line up a TV reporter job for Kelly in Palm Springs, a tiny entry-level market. She hoped that would be the last she'd see of her. It was just her luck that a few years later Kelly sweet-talked her way back into KXLA, this time in a reporter slot. Talk about a fast-moving career: from the market ranked one hundred sixty to the market ranked two, in just two years.

Natalie had just made it past the massive studio doors when Kelly raced up beside her. "Natalie, I've been thinking about it and I apologize if that Grace Kelly comment bothered you. You've been at this so long, I really value your opinion."

Natalie stayed mum and kept walking. *You've been at this so long*. Had she taken a page from Scoppio's book? How snide was that?

They reached the newsroom's security door and Kelly launched ahead of her to punch the code into the keypad. "I'm glad I've got you alone," she murmured over her shoulder. "I've been wanting to talk to you."

Natalie couldn't avoid it. Kelly buttonholed her inside the newsroom, forcing Natalie back against the wall next to Tony's darkened office. Across the nearly empty after-hours newsroom a knot of producers sat chatting with Howard, and on the Assignment Desk the lone graveyard shifter was taking up his post.

Kelly leaned in close, as though she and Natalie were the most intimate of confidantes. Her face twisted in an expression of deep concern. "Natalie, I just want you to know that you can talk to me. You know, if you need someone to talk to."

"What?"

"I'm sorry. This is so awkward for me. I have such deep respect for you." Kelly leaned in even closer. Natalie got a whiff of breath mint and musky perfume. "You've been so helpful to me, I was just thinking that with you going through—what should I call it?" Kelly's big dark eyes gazed up at the newsroom ceiling, as though she expected to find the right word strung there among the fluorescent lights. "Your . . . *troubles*? I thought I might be able to help you out somehow." She paused. "You know, be a friend."

There was something so very false about this woman. "I'm fine," Natalie responded curtly. She tried to get around Kelly but the younger woman made a quick move and blocked her path.

"Really, Natalie?" Kelly's features contorted into a mask of even greater concern. "Are you *really* all right? I mean, anybody would understand if you weren't."

"What does *that* mean?"

Kelly's eyes opened wide, all innocence. "I'm sorry. I don't mean to be too personal. I just meant . . . with Miles leaving."

Natalie could feel the heat rise on her face. "This conversation is over." This time she succeeded in escaping Kelly, by shouldering roughly past her. Natalie stalked across the newsroom to the computer she'd been using before the newscast and jabbed a few keys to log off. By the time she looked up, Kelly was gone.

Natalie remained at the terminal, deeply disturbed.

What was it about that woman? She was everything Natalie hated about most TV news: slick and false and self-promoting.

But it was also true that Kelly was moving up. In leaps and bounds. Into the territory Natalie considered her own, the anchor desk. Natalie realized, with stunning clarity, that Kelly was the competition. It was a major miscalculation still to think of her as an intern, so inexperienced she didn't know a voice-over from a sound-on-tape.

Kelly Devlin knew exactly what she was doing.

"Where are you going with that?"

Kelly heard Howard's voice echo across the open space between the studio and the loading-dock exit doors. It was 11:20 P.M. and no one else was around. She spun on her heels to see him striding toward her. *Shit.*

She hoisted her satchel strap higher on her shoulder and turned again toward the exit. Maybe he hadn't actually *seen* her stuff the dub inside her bag. She kept her voice casual when he caught up. "What're you doing here so late?"

"Never mind." He grabbed her by the elbow and pointed accusingly at her satchel. "What did you just put in there?"

"What?" She opened her arms and glanced down at her body, as if she didn't even know what "in there" referred to.

"In your bag." He tried to grab the satchel strap off her shoulder but she wrestled away from him.

"Hey!" She moved a few steps back. "What's your problem?"

"I saw you walk out of Archives and shove a tape in your bag." He glared at her. "You *know* nothing from Archives can leave the lot."

"Oh, so you're the Archives police now?"

He jabbed a thumb at his button-down chest. "*I* am the managing editor of this station!"

"Ooh!" She licked her finger and made a sizzling sound as she touched his arm. "You're hot shit!"

But that was a mistake, because Howard used that opening to grab Kelly's satchel off her shoulder and throw it to the ground, where he went at it like a shark on a seal carcass. He pulled out the dub with a triumphant expression on his Ivy League face.

"Aha!" He turned it sideways to read Kelly's girlish script on the label and his face sank from victory to defeat. "What the fuck?"

She tried to yank the dub out of his hand but he held it too far away. "Don't ask," she warned.

"What are you doing with a dub of the car-accident video?"

He was such a moron. She couldn't believe she'd fucked him for so long. Then again it had made for some good assignments.

He bent back down to rummage in her bag again and this time she kicked him. But still he came up with the FedEx packaging. And read *that* label, too. He looked like he'd been struck dumb. "You're sending the tape to *Hard Line*?"

This time Kelly was able to snatch the dub from his hand. "I *said* don't ask."

"Kelly!" He shook his head, with this amazed look on his face. It seemed like he could barely string two words together. "You narrowly avoided a lawsuit, for chrissake! What's wrong with you?"

That pissed her off. There was nothing wrong with *her*. There was something wrong with *him*, and with everybody else who didn't grab opportunities however and whenever they showed up. She jabbed a finger in his direction. "You don't say one word to anybody. You got me, loverboy? Not one word." She wrested the FedEx envelope from him. It had taken her all week to get this dub. She'd had to call *Hard Line* twice to explain.

But Howard was shaking his big, fat, stubborn head. "I can't let you do this, Kelly. This could *easily* risk a lawsuit for the station. I cannot be party to this kind of—"

"Yes, you can, and you *will*," she hissed. She'd had enough of Howard Bjorkman. He'd been as useful as he was going to be. "Unless you want me calling Tony at home over the weekend to tell him how you forced me to sleep with you to get assignments!"

His eyes widened, as if he'd just seen that he was about to be run over by a Mack truck. When he could finally talk, he sounded a lot less sure of himself. "Nobody's gonna buy it, Kelly."

"Oh, no?" She stood up real close to him, so close she could smell his fear. "You don't think I'm a good enough actress to pull it off?" She hoisted her satchel strap higher on her shoulder. "I've got three words for you, big boy. Remember the Manns." Then she turned on her heel and stalked out of KXLA's loading dock, leaving Howard Bjorkman staring after her, stunned into silence.

JULY

CHAPTER SEVEN

Monday, July 8, 2:36 P.M.

"But, Ruth, don't you see that it's a fabulous idea?" Natalie was insistent. "I've come up with the perfect angle to land an interview with Hope Dalmont."

Natalie paced in front of Ruth's desk, imagining the journalistic stir she'd create by nailing an interview with the actress about to wed Monaco's Prince Albert. "I'll grant you, though, that getting her is a long shot."

"That's the understatement of the year." Ruth ambled around to the front of her gray metal desk and leaned back against it, straightening the bright yellow sweater she'd paired with black stirrup pants. "Hope is today's Grace Kelly. And she hasn't given a single interview. If she's shunning Barbara and Diane and Maria and Katie, no offense, but what makes you think she'll talk to *you*?"

"Partly because this is L.A., Hope's hometown and not exactly small potatoes, and partly because I've come up with a great angle. How much the orphaned bride-to-be misses her long-dead mother as she prepares for her wedding day. Who better to understand that than another woman who's gone through the same thing?"

Ruth shook her head. "You're grasping at straws. I know you want to do something dramatic to get back on track, but this—"

Natalie stopped listening. Over the last week she'd exhaustively analyzed the Hope Dalmont idea and convinced herself she had to give it a go, as idiotic as it might seem on the surface. Landing Hope Dalmont would be a journalistic coup of mammoth proportions, like Barbara Walters landing Monica Lewinsky. Nobody would remember the flubbed remote. Or the eight point three on the Richter scale mistake. Natalie Daniels would be back on top. Even if Tony failed to renew her, another station would snap her up.

She squared off against Ruth. "Just imagine how the ratings would skyrocket if I land this interview!"

"True, but—"

"Tony would have to sit up and take notice." *He'd scramble to renew me,* she added silently, *three months before my contract's up.*

"The problem is I don't see any way to pull it off."

Their conversation was interrupted by an insistent beeping. Instantly both women checked the identical pagers on their waistbands. "Me," Ruth muttered, then pushed a button and squinted down at the display. She began to circle back around her desk. "You know, Natalie, for weeks I've been talking to Hope's P.R. people and trying all the usual tricks to bypass them and get right to her. Flowers, personal notes—that sort of thing. But no go." Ruth picked up her phone. "I just think it's a nonstarter. Hold on a sec. I have to take care of this."

Natalie absently eyed the monitor bolted into an upper corner of Ruth's office, on which talk-show guests were throwing their chairs. It was a good thing the monitor was bolted to the wall because there was no unoccupied flat surface. Like Ruth's home, her office was chockablock with doodads and thingamabobs, all under the heading PERSONAL MEMENTO.

Natalie resumed her pacing, another thought wriggling into her brain. *This is something Kelly Devlin would* never *be able to pull off. Isn't it about time to remind her who's the star here?*

Natalie smiled and headed for the second phone in Ruth's office, deciding on impulse to call Geoff. Even if Ruth wasn't keen on the idea, Geoff would be. He loved it when she came up with kick-ass story ideas. Showed "gumption," he told her.

Shows Scoppio was dead wrong when he told me I've "gone soft" from being in the anchor chair.

She punched in Geoff's direct number and instantly he picked up.

"Hi, it's Natalie."

"Hey!" She could hear the creak of his ergo chair. "What's shaking?"

"I have an idea you're going to love."

"Shoot."

"What do you think," she paused for dramatic effect, "about my interviewing Hope Dalmont?"

"How do you propose to do that?"

Briefly she outlined her idea.

"I don't like it."

"What?"

"I don't like it. First, it won't work. Second, you don't do that celebrity-fawning horseshit."

"It's not . . . Geoff, she's the most sought after interview out there! If I—"

"*If* you land her, which is highly unlikely to begin with, you get to ask her such probing journalistic questions as who designed her wedding gown and how will she redecorate the palace. Why not go back to investigative pieces? *That's* where you shine."

"I'm not talking about not doing investigative pieces." She was frustrated. "Just landing Hope *first.*"

"Don't bother. Let the Kelly Devlins of the world do that stuff."

That ticked her off.

"Play to your strength, Natalie," he went on. "Hard-news reporting."

She remained silent.

"You're not going to listen, are you?" he asked.

"No."

"Fine, just don't waste a lot of time chasing her. Gotta take this next call, Nats." He hung up.

She replaced the receiver, deflated. So neither Ruth nor Geoff was behind her.

But she didn't want to give up on the idea. She wanted to do something big, something to resuscitate her reputation. To wipe that snide grin off Kelly's face. Not to mention off Tony's.

She sat down and logged on to the nearest computer. She'd take part of Geoff's advice. She wouldn't spend eons pursuing Hope but she had one idea she wanted to try.

Ruth hung up her phone, curiosity on her face. "What're you doing?"

Natalie was momentarily silent, pecking at the keyboard and squinting at the screen. She was trolling through one of the numerous logs maintained by the Assignment Desk, which listed addresses for recent live shots. "Here it is. 848 Stradella Road."

Ruth narrowed her eyes. "That's the address of Hope Dalmont's estate. What're you up to?"

Natalie scribbled the address on Ruth's KXLA memo pad, beneath the station logo of a satellite dish next to a palm tree. Only after she tore off the sheet did she meet Ruth's suspicious eyes. "Giving it one good shot."

Kelly pushed the rest of her chili dog into her mouth and sank back against the cracked blue Naugahyde of ENG Truck 2's passenger seat. She wiped her hands on the useless rectangle of paper napkin Fatburger had provided. What a revolting meal. The kind she ate only when hunger pangs drove her over the edge.

It was 1:40 A.M. on a Monday night—no, Tuesday morning—and she hadn't eaten since lunch, thanks to this hostage crisis at an elementary school. It just wouldn't end! And *she* had to wait and see how it "played out" so she could feed the morning shows, whose producers were apparently on tenterhooks for her live reports. Whose producers apparently didn't give a damn that she'd already been there for twelve fucking hours.

And she was supposed to be grateful! This was a hot story, a lead story, a high-stakes story, the kind of story reporters would kill to cover.

Right. Because some third-grade summer schoolers got holed up by a gun-toting deadbeat dad? Like that didn't happen all the time.

Kelly kicked open the truck's door. *Thanks a lot, Howard Bjorkman.* He probably thought he was doing her a favor by assigning her this story. Or more likely he was so terrified she'd bust him for "sexual harassment" that he was shitting in his pants from dawn till dusk and prayed this would convince her to go easy on him.

She hopped out of the truck, ignoring the mound the chili dog had made in her stomach, and headed toward the run-down beige brick pile that looked like every public school in America, except for the cop floodlights that tonight were lighting up the facade like Disneyland's Magic Castle. She felt like she'd been staring at it her entire life. Two nondescript stories, its windows pock-marked by brightly colored construction paper cut into all shapes and sizes, the masking tape that stuck them to the windows looking like wadded-up bubble gum. The school was rimmed in front and on both sides by browned-out lawn, which gave way after a yard or two to wire fence, then to sidewalk and parking lot. Every inch of asphalt had been taken over since lunchtime by a motley crew of cop cars and satellite trucks, the latter kept fifty yards away by yellow crime tape.

Kelly sidled up to Harry, one of the older, wiser photogs lined up at the tape. "Anything new?"

Harry shrugged. Like all the photogs he was held hostage by his camera. Kelly and the other reporters could, and did, hang out in the trucks, but the shooters had to stay on guard in case something went down. Which could happen at any time. There were no second takes and a photog who missed the action wasn't a photog for long.

Harry fiddled with the bulky camera battery, checking the power. "The cop P.R. guy says they'll hold a newscon around four a.m. I guess the negotiator will come on camera then, too."

That would be seven a.m. on the East Coast. Perfect for the national correspondent bigwigs to go live for the network morning shows, all of which were drooling over this kiddie hostage crisis. She and the other small-fry local reporters would use sound bites for their early-morning newscasts, most of which started at five.

"So nothing's happened since four p.m." She bit her lip and visualized the sad state of the video they had for the morning. Not a single new frame.

"But that shooting stuff this afternoon was pretty powerful," Harry reminded her, running his thick tongue over his lips.

Kelly watched spittle gather at the sides of Harry's mouth. The man was disgusting. And how could he get so excited over this shit?

"I love the audio of the gunshots, and the screaming." Harry shook his gray head from side to side, apparently recalling those moments of high drama. "Man, that rookie's in trouble."

On that, Kelly could agree. The shooting had erupted after some rookie numbskull just out of cop school got spooked and started firing off his gun when a car in the neighborhood backfired. The gunman must've thought it was a raid or something because then *he* started shooting. He was screaming like a wild man, the kids were screaming, the teachers were screaming. Kelly thought it was fantastic audio. She'd made heavy use of it during the live shots and at ten.

But since then, it'd been boring as hell.

"I hope we're not still here at four a.m." But even as she said it she knew that at the rate things were going, they'd be there long past four a.m.

Harry just shrugged again. She could feel the disapproval emanating from his fat, down-jacketed self, his amazement that she wasn't as psyched by this hot news story as he was. Apparently he didn't realize that he was a pathetic turd who lacked something so basic as a life.

She abandoned Harry to pace behind the line of photogs. She recognized most of them but had never spoken with any. It was pointless networking with techies: they couldn't do a damn thing for you, not unless they worked for your station.

She started to feel cold again. July in southern California and it was freezing at night. The photogs and most reporters kept backup clothes in their vehicles but she never bothered. She carried makeup and a mirror; that was all she really needed. By rights she should be anchoring anyway, not still reporting after two goddamn years.

Even the cops looked bored. Why didn't they get off their butts and storm the building? Or get their negotiator to dream up some brilliant idea? Kelly snorted softly. They were probably just too comfortable, lolling around half in and half out of their cop cars, drinking coffee out of Styrofoam cups.

To try to warm up, she half jogged along the sidewalk on the school's north side, also cordoned off by crime tape. A few black-and-whites were parked on that side of the building but no cops were in evidence. She kicked restlessly at a loose piece of asphalt, which ricocheted off a tree and landed near something shiny.

She bent down. A high-beam flashlight. How weird, out here by the schoolyard. A cop must've dropped it. She picked it up and flipped the switch. It worked. She played with it, sending a beam of light in arcing circles down the street.

Then it hit her.

Why not? Maybe she could make something happen, speed this thing up. Get home before *dawn.*

She looked around. Nobody. She shrugged. It was worth a shot.

She switched on the flashlight, then raked the beam across the darkened windows of the second floor. Where was the gunman, anyway? Probably asleep while everybody else was outside freezing to death. She finished with the second floor and went to work on the first.

Nothing.

Shit. This was never gonna end.

She turned to head back to the truck but decided to give it one last go. On went the flashlight. This time she sent the beam in wild raging circles across both floors, up and down, left and right, round and round . . .

Wake up, you idiot! she screamed silently. *Talk to the stupid negotiator so we can all go home!*

Then she heard a pop. Then a series of pops.

Holy shit! Shooting.

Kelly stood in place, mesmerized by the gunfire. Was it the gunman or the cops? Hard to know. Boy, she hadn't *really* expected anything to happen. But it was like four p.m. all over again. Only this time the screaming sounded even worse, if that was possible. She could see reporters scrambling out of the trucks, and cops running around like crazy.

A knot of them tore past her, one cop screaming at her to get back where it was safe, by the other reporters. Real quick she hid the flashlight under her jacket as the cops raced past, then ran to the ENG truck, pulled open the passenger door, and dumped it inside. Then she slammed the door shut and leaned back against it, panting.

She had to get to Harry, she realized. But first she should check her makeup. So she could get in a standup before the shooting stopped.

Natalie drove with reverent slowness along the curved length of Stradella Road, twined like a precious necklace through the wooded labyrinthine enclave of Bel Air, L.A.'s toniest neighborhood. Ten-foot hedges lined the narrow road, trees forming a leafy canopy. All Natalie could glimpse of the most exquisite properties money can buy were sun-dappled Spanish tile rooftops.

About thirty yards past Hope Dalmont's estate, she executed a U-turn and rolled to a halt. Her vantage point offered a clear view of the tall iron gate. She turned off the ignition and the Mercedes lapsed into silence, the guttural rumbling of its engine replaced by birdsong and the distant roar of a leaf blower.

Natalie settled into the soft leather bucket seat, Geoff's advice reverberating in her brain: Don't waste a lot of time chasing Hope. *I'm not wasting time,* she told herself. *This is only the fourth day I'm waiting outside her estate. If I don't get her today I'll give up.*

She'd tried to imagine what Hope Dalmont would do during her final weeks in L.A., before marrying into Monaco's royal family in what would be one of the most watched weddings of all time. What would a woman do?

Natalie pondered what *she* would do, and concocted an agenda:

Wake up late and eat a lazy breakfast.

Chat on the phone with her fiancé.

Work out.

Have assorted personal-care services: massage, manicure, pedicure, blow-dry.

Eat lunch with girlfriends.

Chat on the phone with her fiancé.

Nap.

Read, then eat a quiet dinner, and maybe watch a girl movie she'd never convince even a besotted new husband to see.

That involved at least one foray into the great wide world and Natalie was ready for it. She didn't allow herself to dwell overlong on the depressing truth that *no* forays by Hope had yet occurred, at least none that she had witnessed.

That morning, though, a veritable parade of visitors entered the estate. Three rapid-fire deliveries (flowers, dry-cleaning, and groceries) and two gardening trucks.

All these vehicles came and went. At 12:43 P.M., after Natalie had been watching for more than an hour, a lone blue Mercedes sedan emerged through the gate and turned south toward Beverly Hills.

Natalie bolted forward in the bucket seat. Was that Hope behind the wheel of the blue Mercedes? In black sunglasses and a silk scarf tied around her head in the very style Grace Kelly had made famous?

Natalie turned the key in the ignition and began to tail the vehicle at what she hoped was a discreet distance. Adrenaline began to pulse in her veins.

By God, this may actually work . . .

The twin Mercedes maneuvered sedately down the hill, and at one point Natalie was cheered by escaped strands of golden blond hair flapping from the open driver's side window of the blue Mercedes. The hair was well kept and Hope's color, though both were standard in Bel Air. Natalie followed the sedan as it exited Bel Air and turned right on Sunset Boulevard, heading west for a few blocks before it turned left down a main thoroughfare.

Minutes later, the Mercedes pulled onto the sweep of asphalt driveway that fronted the grand, white-columned facade of the Millennium Club, a neoclassical oddity on tacky Sepulveda Boulevard in West Los Angeles. Natalie knew the place well. It was without question the most exclusive gym and spa in L.A., where stars old and young could exercise without fear of mingling with the great unwashed. Natalie herself had paid a small fortune to join when the club opened, then let her membership lapse when she and Miles had moved to the Hollywood Hills.

She sat in her car, pondering what to do next. And she had to decide quickly. Because the woman stepping out of the blue Mercedes and handing her keys to the valet was undeniably Hope Dalmont. Natalie could never mistake that lithe body, just shy of six feet tall; the exquisite classical profile; the graceful stance and radiant smile—all were instantly recognizable.

Gym bag in hand, Hope tripped through the club's main door, flanked on both sides by squat palm trees in terra-cotta pots, and disappeared inside.

So what do I do now? Natalie clutched her steering wheel. *I can't lose her. This is my only chance. But how do I get in there? I'm not a member anymore, and with Hope there the place is probably crawling with security . . .*

She took a deep breath. *Go in like you own the place. No guts, no glory.* She forced herself to roll the Mercedes forward, then stepped out and handed the valet her key. "Good afternoon," she said cheerily.

The boy, uniformed in a white soldierlike getup with gold epaulets, gave her a bashful smile. "Good afternoon, Miss Daniels. You have your invitation with you?"

"Of course," she lied, and smiled again. Invitation? For what? And why were the valets outfitted like toy soldiers in the Nutcracker Ballet?

She turned and strode smartly up the few steps to the entrance. Once inside, she continued briskly past reception, eyes straight ahead, heading for where she remembered the women's dressing room to be. The heels of her pumps clicked noisily on the Portuguese tile. Why was the place so quiet? None of the usual music; not a sign of the rail-thin patrons who even in aerobic excess managed to look well off. Today the Millennium Club was like a mausoleum. She was nearly to the stairs when she felt a touch on her elbow.

"Ma'am?"

She spun as though irritated, which in a way she was. "Yes?" she inquired in her most imperious tone.

But she could tell at a glance that the ponytailed brunette staring back at her wasn't the least deterred. The girl was done up in a kind of Clinique salesgirl lab coat and clearly recognized her, but apparently had too much experience with Hollywood stars to be cowed by a mere local anchor.

"Miss Daniels, I'm afraid I have to ask for your invitation."

"Oh! I'm not sure I remembered to bring it with me." Natalie bent her head to rummage in her small black purse, thinking frantically. Then she looked up, trying to plaster regret on her features. "Oh, dear, I seem to have forgotten it."

Now the brunette had regret written all over *her*. "Oh, dear," she echoed. "Miss Dalmont made it clear that all her friends were to bring their invitations."

"I'm sure Hope won't mind," Natalie declared brightly, turning again to face the stairs. *That explains it,* she thought: the invitations, the toy-soldier uniforms on the valets, the unreal quiet. Hope had hired out the Millennium Club for a private party.

"I'm sorry." The brunette laid her hand on Natalie's arm again, and this time the touch wasn't so light. "Please come with me. I'll check you in."

But Natalie refused to budge. She threw an irritated glance at her watch. "Is this going to take long? This delay is highly inconvenient." She fixed the ponytailed minx with a laser glare.

The girl didn't even blink. "It won't take a minute."

The vixen must make heavy use of the equipment, Natalie judged, *because for her size she is surprisingly strong.* She tugged Natalie back toward reception, a white marble curve of a desk behind which several lab-coated females conducted mysterious business via telephone and computer. The brunette set herself up at a portal and pecked at a few keys. Natalie did her best to look affronted.

Then the brunette got a phone call. A must-take phone call. "Mr. Schwarzenegger!" she cooed into the receiver, angling her body away from Natalie. "How are you?"

Here's my chance. Natalie edged away from the desk. The brunette was riffling through a file folder and making small talk over the phone. *Damn the torpedoes, I'm going in!* She began to move nonchalantly across the tile. All the lab coats were still enmeshed in their work. She hit the stairs and started running. Down one flight, then another three. Right turn after the last stair. Partway down the hall she spied the heavy oak door to the women's dressing room. She pushed it open and slid inside, leaning back against the highly buffed wood to catch her breath.

Nothing. She waited, panting. Still nothing. But where was everybody? Where were Hope's guests? Where were . . .

She felt the door push against her back. *Damn! Could it be the brunette?* Instantly Natalie tore across the mosaic floor and pulled open the door directly in front of her. The sauna. Frantically she closed herself inside, just as a gaggle of women pitched into the dressing room.

Natalie stood a few feet back from the sauna door's narrow rectangular glass panel, desperately hoping no one could see her, squinting so she herself could see through the foggy glass. *Oh, my God.* Her breath caught in her throat. Hope Dalmont. Hope Dalmont rapidly getting naked. The same Hope Dalmont upon whom the world's eyes would feast in less than one week, though they would see far less than Natalie was seeing right now. Hope strode around the dressing room tearing off her top, her bra, laughing at a joke, and bending down to shed her sweatpants . . . *Oh, my God.* Natalie jerked backward, mutely praying that no one would enter, starting to sweat in the hundred-twenty-degree heat.

Mesmerized, she peered through the glass, hearing the muted happy chatter. Women, about a dozen of them, all young, all beautiful, and all in various stages of undress, milling about the dressing room like modern Hollywood versions of Degas's dancers, talking and striking poses as they pulled on workout clothes or draped their unbelievably fit bodies in fluffy white towels. Hope pulled on a Speedo and gathered her blond hair under a bathing cap, then grabbed goggles and a towel and scampered out the door, throwing a laughing comment over her shoulder as she disappeared.

Gradually the dressing room emptied. Mercifully saunas weren't at the top of the party agenda. Natalie sank onto a bench, now sweating in earnest beneath her pink suit.

After a few minutes she gathered the courage to move. Everybody had to be gone by now. She rose from the bench and peeked through the glass. Not a soul. She reached out a tentative hand and pushed open the door, feeling a delicious wave of cool air waft over her body. She stood for a moment, her head thrown back, her eyes closed, relishing the chilly blast.

But then she heard the unmistakable groan of the dressing room door being pushed open. Hastily she stepped back into the sauna's baking heat, pulling the door shut behind her, staring at the outer door, opening, opening . . .

In walked the brunette from reception, accompanied by a female behemoth in a cop uniform who looked like she could single-handedly arm-wrestle the entire L.A.P.D. The brunette began stalking the dressing room like a trained beagle at baggage claim sniffing for contraband. Her eyes darted left to right, her ponytail slapped the sides of her head. The behemoth followed a few steps behind.

Natalie fell back against the sauna bench, her hand

clutched to her chest as though that way she could slow the pounding of her heart. By now sweat was running in rivulets down her panty-hosed legs. She wedged her body into the sauna's darkest corner, praying they couldn't see her. But through the foggy glass she could vaguely make out their shapes as the two women repeatedly crossed the rectangle of glass.

Finally the behemoth threw up her hands and stood at the outer door, clearly ready to leave. The brunette looked anything but ready. Natalie held her breath. She watched the brunette stand by the sinks, her lips pursed, her eyes raking the ceiling as if she expected Natalie to be poised there, motionless, like a spider on a wall.

Because it was quite clear Natalie was the one they were looking for. She was a demented journalist stalker as far as they were concerned, a maniacal party-crasher who, no surprise, had not made the list of Hope Dalmont's nearest and dearest female friends.

Then all of a sudden they left. As swiftly as they had come. They pulled open the door and walked out. But not before the brunette threw one last reluctant glance behind her.

Natalie sank back onto the sauna's hard wood bench. Minutes passed. What now?

Get out of that damn sauna and take off your clothes. They were shockingly wet. She could never step outside in her current state.

She ventured out of the sauna into the chill air and stripped rapidly, all efficiency now, hanging up her jacket, skirt, blouse, bra, and hose so they'd have some hope of drying. She snagged a towel and only then dared look in the mirror. *Oh, God.* Her eyes were black hollows, rimmed by melted liner and mascara, and her makeup base was streaked by violent gashes of sweat.

She washed her face, and as she toweled her cleansed skin, stared at her reflection.

I'm going to stay and wait. I've come this far.

Tony sat behind a big rectangular pane of one-way glass in a dull beige suite of offices in Burbank, observing a group of ordinary news-watching Americans who'd been brought together that July lunchtime for his benefit.

Focus group, shmocus group. He shifted his bulk on the orange plastic-and-metal chair they'd set up for him, which looked like it had been swiped from the NBC commissary down the street. Geez, was he hungry. Why did he do this shit? Why, when he had a golden gut? He understood what viewers liked and what they didn't.

Still, sometimes at these things he gathered the occasional pearl of wisdom. It was like watching résumé reels that came in over the transom. Every once in a while you stumbled on something surprising.

Through the one-way glass, Tony could see that all eyes in the office were fixed on the television in the corner. On it was playing a dub of Friday night's *The KXLA Primetime News*, on which he'd teamed Natalie with Kelly. An anorexic-looking fiftyish broad in a bright blue suit was leading the focus group. A "marketing analyst," she'd told him—whatever the hell that was. She looked like Ruth's skinny sister. She fast-forwarded through a package, then played the tape at normal speed while Kelly read a lead-in. All the assembled watched, bug-eyed. Then the broad hit PAUSE, freezing Kelly on-screen in what even Tony had to admit was an unflattering openmouthed pose.

"Immediate impressions, immediate impressions," she yelled.

People piped up, even the old ones. "Seems sassy." "Looks like maybe she understands the news." "Reminds me of that actress who posed naked in *Playboy*." "Too much makeup." "Too young to be anchoring." "Makeup just right." "Very sparkly."

What'd I tell you. Tony slurped lukewarm coffee from a Styrofoam cup. *They love Kelly.*

The broad again punched FAST FORWARD, this time halting on Natalie reading a story. The crowd got quiet again. When she hit PAUSE, they knew exactly what to do.

"Classy." "Seems really smart." "Kinda cold." "Very

elegant and seems knowledgeable." "I like her voice." "Too aloof." "Reads like she really knows the news."

That settled it. Tony tossed the Styrofoam cup. He wasn't the only one. Everybody thought Natalie was an ice princess. That was her problem, pure and simple. Maybe that had worked in another era, like ancient times, but not anymore.

He stood up. He'd heard all he needed to hear.

"Are they getting rid of the older one for the younger one?" He was almost at the door when that gem popped out of some old lady. He paused.

"Now why would you think that?" asked the marketing broad.

"Because they do that all the time and I don't like it. It's like what they did to Jane Pauley and Joan Lunden. I don't like it."

The crowd got boisterous, all piping up with opinions.

Tony shuffled out, thinking. If he got rid of Princess, he risked a backlash. He knew that. Unless, of course, she left on her own. He chuckled. Stranger things had happened.

Natalie sat on a wooden bench in the Millennium Club dressing room, looking at her watch, the only thing she was sporting apart from earrings and a towel. *Two more minutes and I'll get dressed, even if my clothes are still damp.*

She waited. The room was silent save for a low hum generated by who knew what equipment. After what seemed like an eternity the two minutes were up. She rose, just as the dressing room's outer door creaked open and Hope reappeared in the doorway. Alone.

Natalie wasn't sure whether Hope's return was good or bad. But one thing was clear. *It's now or never, naked or not.* She forced a smile at the tall, lean beauty in the navy Speedo dripping water onto the mosaic. She held out her hand. "I'm Natalie Daniels."

Hope frowned and ignored the hand, her arm still propping open the dressing room door. Her eyes darted around the room. "How did you get in here?"

"I walked past reception. No, please don't go." Natalie took a step toward Hope, who had backed away slightly.

"I don't know you. And why are you in a towel? This is too weird. I rented out this entire club for a private party." Again Hope made a move to retreat. "This is unacceptable."

"No, please. *Please.* Hear me out. It'll only take a minute, I promise." Natalie held her breath.

Hope stilled, eyeing her narrowly. Then, with an annoyed look on her face, she shook her head and walked inside, the door slamming noisily shut behind her. She held up a finger, "*One* minute." Then she cocked her wet blond head. "You look familiar."

"You may recognize me from Channel 12. *The KXLA Primetime News.* Natalie Daniels," she repeated.

"Ah, yes." Hope smiled a brief smile of recognition. Then again a shadow dropped across her face. "Oh, no. You're here to—"

"No." Natalie clutched her towel. "Well, yes, but hear me out. Here, sit down." Natalie waved her arm, inviting Hope to sit next to her on the bench. As though she had a right to. She felt driven by an odd mix of idiocy and courage. Here she was, naked but for a towel, pitching an interview to a dripping wet soon-to-be-princess in a Speedo, who just happened to be the most sought-after interview of the year. The whole thing was lunatic but somehow seemed to have taken on a crazy life of its own.

"Please," Natalie repeated, and then the gods smiled, because Hope nodded almost imperceptibly and sank next to her on the bench. Hope turned to face her, her knees carefully together, her hands resting on her wet thighs, her clear blue young eyes, their long lashes beaded with moisture, gazing quizzically at Natalie.

Natalie took a deep breath. "You and I have something in common. I too lost my mother when I was a child. I was seven. She died of cervical cancer."

Hope shook her head. "How is that relevant now?"

"I believe it creates a bond between us. I—"

Hope spoke impatiently. "I don't mean to be rude but I hardly think that creates a *bond* between us." She stretched out the word, as though Natalie were insane to think such a thing.

" 'Bond' may be too strong a word." Natalie paused. "It does mean that I have a certain understanding of what you must be feeling in these last days before your wedding."

Hope made a dismissive noise. "I doubt it."

"I remember how *I* felt when I got married," Natalie went on hastily. "Nobody understood how much I missed my mother. And how could they? No one understands unless they've gone through it themselves."

Hope looked down at her lap. She was quiet for a time. "It is funny how much I'm thinking about her these days," she admitted.

An opening. "I don't think it's funny at all," Natalie said. "I think it's perfectly natural."

She waited, watching Hope drift with her own thoughts. "Hope, I know you've rejected all interview requests but I would very much like to profile you from this angle. How a woman feels as she takes one of life's biggest steps without her mother's guiding hand."

"No." Instantly Hope shook her head. "Too personal."

"It's *powerful.*" Natalie leaned forward. "Your situation, of course, is unique. In fact, it's tremendously poignant." That was stretching it, but nothing worked better than flattery. "You're marrying under the glare of publicity. And for you more than most brides, the marriage truly marks the beginning of a new life."

"Be that as it may—" Hope began to rise from the bench.

"I know you're involved in Big Sisters." Natalie threw out what she hoped would be her trump card. Months before she'd spied the name DALMONT, HOPE above her own on a list of local celebrity sponsors. "So am I."

"Really?" Hope halted halfway off the bench. "What got *you* involved?"

"The same thing as you, probably. A real concern for

girls who went through what I did. I've been a Big Sister to three girls now."

"I've done it for two." Slowly Hope sat again on the bench.

"You know," Natalie said, "we could use an interview to generate support for the organization."

Hope was silent and Natalie waited for the idea to take root. When Hope did speak again it was in a murmur, almost as if she were speaking to herself. "My mother died when I was eight." She met Natalie's eyes. "Did your father remarry?"

"Six months later. And he never had much time for me then."

"The whole second family thing." Hope shook her head. "New wife, new kids. My dad sort of lost interest until I became an actress. A *successful* actress, that is."

"My father's interest never revived, even after I started doing well in news. I could never really get his attention. My stepmom had something to do with that, too."

Natalie felt Hope's eyes and looked up to find understanding, and sympathy, there. Then amusement. Both women laughed.

"Stepmommy dearest," Hope said.

"Exactly."

Hope made a restless gesture and again stood up. She pulled her goggles off her neck, sending a strong whiff of chlorine into Natalie's nostrils. "So you want to interview me."

Natalie threw up her hands. "I do." Her admission hung in the air, a refreshingly straightforward counterpoint to the day's lunacy.

"I've said no to everybody. I decided months ago that I wanted to have some control over how much my life became tabloid fodder."

"But here's a chance to use publicity to further your own ends."

Hope gave Natalie a wry look. "Not to mention *yours*."

Natalie grinned. "It's win-win."

Hope smiled as well and began to pace the mosaic, there in her Speedo, lovely, gracious, so young, and even in this odd situation, pondering this fly-by-night request, a powerful self-contained presence. She halted after a bit, suddenly frowning. "How did you even know I was going to be here today?"

"I followed you."

Hope's eyes narrowed. "You *what*? From my home?"

"Every reporter in town knows where you live." Natalie paused. "I waited in my car until you came out."

"Then you followed me here and sneaked in, past reception?"

"Yes."

Hope retreated a few steps, vigorously shaking her head. "I can't accept that. That's going way too far."

Oh, no, Natalie thought, *that was a mistake.* But she had no chance to regroup, because just then, as she sat on the bench in plain sight, the outer dressing room door slammed open and in burst the ponytailed brunette and the behemoth cop, followed by a stampeding herd of more female behemoth cops.

"Her!" The brunette halted triumphantly in front of Natalie, who was frozen into horrified immobility on the bench. The brunette's young face was twisted in perverse glee. She raised an accusing finger to Natalie's face. "This is her!"

Swiftly the behemoths encircled her. *This cannot be happening.* "You are under arrest for trespassing," one of them said, and snapped a handcuff on her right wrist. *This cannot be happening.* "You have the right to remain silent . . ." The cop continued to read Natalie her Miranda rights as she forced her roughly to her feet.

Desperately, Natalie looked over at Hope, who was standing by the sinks. She was shocked at what she saw on Hope's face. Anger. Vindication.

She's not going to help me. It's all over . . .

It was when the behemoths were forcing Natalie toward the door that the horror rocketed toward fever pitch. She couldn't hold on to the towel, not with the cops manhandling her, and all at once it fell away. *Oh, my God, no . . .* She was stunned by a paroxysm of humiliation so huge it was beyond imagining. The brunette started cackling and one of the cops said something like "We can't take her in like that." There was some discussion before another one thought of looking for a robe.

Which took a hellacious eternity to find, because the brunette refused to help. And all the while Natalie stood nude in the dressing room, unable to cover herself, handcuffed to one of the amazon cops, able to do nothing more than wallow in the whole crazy horror that she herself had created.

CHAPTER EIGHT

Thursday, July 11, 3:16 P.M.

Kelly sat in the darkness of Edit Bay 3, staring with disgust at the boring-as-hell video from that goddamn funeral. A kid died in the school shootout and *she* had to cover the service. "You covered the shooting," Ruth told her. "This is the natural progression of the reporter's involvement." To top it off, Ruth said she couldn't do a stand-up. "The focus isn't on you," she said.

Kelly snorted. Maybe it should be.

She swiveled away from the monitor to face the computer screen head-on. Once she got done writing her script for *The KXLA Primetime News,* and a shorter version for the morning newscast, that would be the end of it. She'd never have to think about that goddamn shooting again. No one had seen her with that flashlight. The next night she'd driven to the Santa Monica Pier and tossed it into the Pacific. And even if somebody *had* seen her use it, no way did she have anything to do with what went down. She'd thought about it since and that was what she'd decided. The gunman was crazy and shit just happened.

She ran her eyes down the script. A minute forty of the dullest crap she'd ever written in her life. But if Ruth was gonna make her cover funerals, then Ruth was gonna have to air a funeral piece that would make every last viewer die of boredom. It would serve the hog right.

Kelly punched a few keys to print the script upstairs

in the copy room next to Ruth's office, then gathered up her tapes and dragged herself up there. What a pain in the ass. Now she had to get script approval from Ruth. Even Tony said she couldn't bypass her, as she had for the car-accident story. The old battle-ax must have gotten to him somehow.

Kelly was in the hallway just outside Ruth's office when she heard Ruth's voice, all loud and upset. "*What?* What do you mean you got arrested?"

Kelly stopped short. Who was Ruth talking to? Who the fuck would *she* know who'd get arrested? Kelly inched forward to peek inside the office, where Ruth was on the phone.

"*Hope Dalmont* had you arrested?"

Kelly snapped backward. *Ruth* knew somebody that *Hope Dalmont* had arrested?

"Natalie, slow down! *What in God's name did you do?*"

Natalie? Despite the wall and the ten feet that separated them, Kelly could tell that Ruth was appalled. She, on the other hand, was thrilled. And not entirely surprised. On some primal level she'd half expected Natalie to screw up again. She was wound tighter than a drum. But what in the world could she have done that would've gotten her arrested—by Hope Dalmont, no less? This was big. Kelly's every instinct went into overdrive. In fact, this was enormous.

Kelly glanced furtively both ways down the hall and behind her down the stairs, her heart thumping. Not a soul around. Down below she could hear the afternoon tape editors schmoozing with the receptionist. But there was nobody but her and Ruth up here on the second floor. Silently she waited, shifting the betatapes to her other arm.

"Where are you now?"

Kelly cocked her ear and heard the scratch of pen on paper.

"Hollywood Division?"

Kelly arched her brows. Wow. That was where the real perverts got booked.

"And when are you getting out?" Silence. "Of *course* I'm not going to tell anybody! But how do you expect to keep something like this a secret?"

Shit! Somebody at the end of the hall. Kelly pirouetted to race down the stairs, bypassing the chattering tape editors on her way to the newsroom. Swiftly she organized the jumble of her thoughts into a plan. She snorted softly. What a day this was turning out to be. It would more than make up for having to cover that idiotic funeral.

Her cubicle was all the way at the back of the newsroom, by the beehive of the Assignment Desk. Like everybody else's, her desk was piled high with tapes, newspapers, and magazines, every inch of the cubicle wall's light gray padding covered with tacked-on newspaper articles and jotted reminders. She dumped the funeral tapes in the only open space and stared at her phone. Eight of the ten newsroom lines were lit up in bright unblinking red. She glanced around. It was three in the afternoon and the newsroom was full. Most of the morning reporters were back from their shoots, logging video and writing scripts. It was dangerous to make a phone call here. Somebody might overhear. She smirked. *That* had been known to happen.

She snapped her fingers. Yes! That was the place to do it. She trolled through the Cs in her Rolodex, scrawled a telephone number on a memo pad, then flipped back the cards so nobody could see anything interesting if they bothered to look.

The ladies' room by the executive wing was empty as usual. And the phone had a dial tone, which wasn't always the case. Kelly perched on the beat-up pink couch and rehearsed her pitch. Then she punched nine for an outside line, plus the number she'd jotted down.

"City News Service," a bored female voice answered.

"Yes." Kelly cleared her throat. "I'm calling to tip you off to a story every station in town will want to run. Get ready to put this on your urgent wire."

Tony pushed open the double doors that separated KXLA's executive suites from the production wing.

Once back on the production side, he had the same thought he always did: it was like going from a rich country to a poor country. From carpet to concrete. From walls hung with oil paintings to walls with cracking paint. From fancy-shmancy cappuccinos in ceramic mugs to percolated coffee in Styrofoam cups.

That was fine with him. Every day he thanked God he wasn't one of the suits. He'd get bored in ten minutes from the shit they had to deal with.

He turned left at the end of the hall by the hair and makeup departments and lumbered past the studio, heading for the newsroom security door. He hated budget meetings, and this one had been particularly bad. Not only weren't the suits going to give him another ENG truck—they might cancel the lease on one of the three he had. But whose ass was on the line if three monster stories hit at the same time and he had only two satellite trucks for live shots? Like that never happened in L.A. Christ, he could have riots, earthquakes, and wildfires at the same time, with a celeb murder or two thrown in for good measure.

He got back to his office and poked around in the bottom right-hand drawer of his desk for his afternoon snack. Every few weeks Anna-Maria bought him one of those home-economy size bags of chocolate bars, not that so-called bite-size shit but the normal-size bars grown men could eat. He was working on a bag of Three Musketeers now, which was high on his favorites list, right up there with Snickers and the ones with the coconut—he could never remember the name. He tore off the wrapping and took a chomp. "Maxine!" he bellowed out his door. "Coffee!" He was just about to take another bite when he glanced up at his row of monitors.

Holy shit.

He rose and edged closer to the second monitor from the left, almost not believing his eyes. It was Channel 8 doing a live shot, he couldn't immediately tell where. But clear as day, right in the middle of all the action, was Natalie Daniels. She was being led down the outside stairs at . . . *Hollywood Division?* And she was wearing—he couldn't believe it—one of those bright orange jail jumpsuits. Propped up by that fancy agent of hers, she looked like absolute shit, especially with all the flashbulbs going off in her face. A monster crowd of reporters and cameramen bumped into her so much she almost fell down, except that the agent held her by the elbow. Jesus fucking Christ.

Mechanically Tony crossed himself, as he always did after a really big swear, the Three Musketeers bar clutched in his right hand hitting his forehead, stomach, left and right shoulders in turn. He raced forward and punched the up volume button to hear veteran street reporter Phil Davies from over at Channel 8 do his live shot.

"Sources say Dalmont may file stalking charges, though details on that are still pending," Davies reported. "No official comment from her camp, but the actress is said to be holed up at her Bel Air estate. We'll have more details on this incredible breaking story at five when—"

"You saw it?" Howard stood panting at his doorway.

Tony nodded. "We had a crew there?"

"Yeah, an urgent wire came over City News Service while you were in the budget meeting. I was sure it was a prank, so I didn't call you out of there. But I did send a crew and a reporter."

"What the hell was Daniels doing going after Hope Dalmont?"

"I have no idea."

Tony was stunned. Princess was a Psycho Anchor. Stalker by day, anchor by night. In all his years of TV news he'd never had *this* problem before.

He trudged back to his desk, pondering. Jesus, she must have been really close to the edge. All he'd done was tell her she was on the bubble and off she went stalking celebs?

So now what was he gonna do?

First order of business. He plopped in his chair and polished off his Three Musketeers. On one hand, he thought, Princess getting arrested would be good for the numbers. Because, by God, this was something people would want to see. Psycho Anchor, news at ten. But what if she was really looney tunes? By this point he had to wonder.

"Get Elaine from Legal," he ordered Howard. "I want her in here ASAP. And tell Kelly she's gonna fill in for Natalie tonight." He looked up. Howard looked dazed. "What's *your* problem?"

Howard shifted from one foot to another, like he was agitated or something. "Are you sure you want Kelly filling in for Natalie?"

"You got a problem with that?"

"No, no," Howard stammered, but he still had a weird expression, like he couldn't believe what was happening. Tony watched him back out. Sometimes he wondered what his managing editor had for balls.

He pulled out the bottom drawer of the wide metal file cabinet behind him where he stored all the talent contracts. DANIELS, NATALIE. He pulled out the thick manila folder and slapped it open on his desk, putting on his bifocals at the same time.

"Tony, there is an explanation for—"

"Save it, Ruth." He looked up to see her filling his doorway like a huge bee in some black-and-yellow sweater getup, her face red as if she'd just run down the stairs. "I don't wanna hear it. Elaine, get in here."

He motioned in Elaine Nance, the station's senior attorney. Tony thought she looked like a tree hugger who'd accidentally gone to law school instead of Earth First. She dressed in goddamn green corduroy every day of the week. She edged her skinny ass past Ruth's fat one and slid into the chair in front of Tony's desk, her granny glasses sliding down her nose.

He tossed Natalie's contract folder in Elaine's direction, ignoring Ruth, then leaned back and crossed his hands over his belly. "Okay. Tell me what we have to do to suspend her."

Natalie tried to calm down by staring out the closed passenger window of Geoff's navy blue XJS as he drove west at a virtual crawl along sweltering Hollywood Boulevard. They'd left the horde of reporters and camera crews behind at Hollywood Division, but late on a July afternoon the gritty, potholed street was jammed with both tourists and locals. Everything from the cinemas to the sex stores was doing blockbuster business.

The car was silent save for the hum of the air-conditioner, which Geoff had cranked to the max. She glanced down at her bright orange polyester jailhouse jumpsuit, hot and stiff and uncomfortable even under the blast of artificially generated cold air. She wanted nothing more than to get home, lock the doors, peel the damn thing off, and crawl into bed. She glanced sideways at Geoff and felt a surge of gratitude. He'd made no recriminations. He'd simply shown up, bailed her out, and whisked her through the mob to his car. "Thank you for doing all this, Geoff," she said quietly.

"Don't worry about it, Natalie."

He was composed, businesslike. Impossible to read. *What an embarrassment I must be to him.* She realized that she cared a great deal about his opinion of her and until recently had never doubted that it was high. She sighed, then ventured, "You're awfully quiet."

He switched lanes to speed past an especially slow car, then shrugged. "I don't know what to say."

"Somebody else would say 'I told you so.' "

He shook his head. "I just never thought the celebrity stuff suited you. Play to your strength—that's what I said."

She laughed ruefully. "At the moment it's hard to know what my strength is."

He was silent. Mercifully they left Hollywood's traffic behind as he made the right turn onto Outpost Drive, a steep curving residential canyon that led up to Mulholland Drive. And home. He gunned the accelerator and the Jag shot up the slope. "I don't know if I've ever told you this, Natalie," he said finally. "You're the best damn anchor I've ever seen. I'm not kidding. Bar none."

She stared at him, too stunned and grateful to speak. Tears pricked her eyes but she held them back, not wanting to cry in front of him. His being her agent required that she maintain a certain facade. She tried to manage a light tone. "Even after today?"

"Today hasn't changed anything." He negotiated a switchback, the Jag's tires squealing. "Now you're the best damn anchor I've ever seen who's been arrested. You're in a category all your own."

He gave her a sideways grin then and she let out a hiccupy laugh because she was almost crying. He edged the car too close to the right and a protruding branch slapped the Jag's windshield.

She reached into her purse for a tissue. "There's something I never told you." It felt like a confessional moment. "The day of the quake, when Tony told me he wasn't planning to renew me, he said that maybe my judgment isn't what it used to be. That I'd been behind the anchor desk so long I'd gotten soft."

Geoff shook his head. "Don't start doubting yourself, Natalie. This was a misstep but everybody makes those. What separates the winners is how they recover."

She gazed out the window. The Jag had arrived at the hill's steep crest and Geoff turned left onto an open and dusty stretch of Mulholland that had killer views of the L.A. basin. Natalie let her head drop back and stared up at the black ragtop. "The thing is, I don't know how to recover. I've made a laughingstock of myself. Viewers who didn't see me blow up at the remote will see this. I've cut off my own head and handed it to Tony on a plate."

"Don't be so sure. This will make you more of a ratings draw than ever and Scoppio is smart enough to recognize that."

She was not convinced. She could too easily imagine Scoppio sitting at his desk, wolfing down a chocolate bar, and snickering at her comeuppance. She shut her eyes and they drove the remaining half mile in silence.

Geoff rolled the car to a halt outside her house and turned off the ignition. The narrow canyon road was quiet.

Natalie fidgeted with the balled-up tissue in her hand,

shredding it into bits that piled like tiny snowflakes on her orange polyestered thigh. She was reluctant to get out of the car and go inside. *An empty house. Again.* She raised her head and stared unseeing through the windshield. "I'm just so petrified that I'm going to lose this job, Geoff." Tears gathered behind her eyes. "I feel like everything I've built up over all these years is slipping away and I can't stop it. Everything I do to *try* to stop it only makes it worse."

Finally it was just too much. The tears broke over the dam of her resolve, spilling over her cheeks in a great unchecked rush. It was too humiliating, but there it was: every last shred of dignity she had was now officially gone. No doubt Geoff would want to cut bait soon and then she'd really be marooned. But instead she felt him reach out to massage her shaking shoulder.

"You just have to keep pushing, Nats," he whispered. A few houses down, an SUV pulled into a driveway. Out spilled its cargo, a harried mom and two little leaguers, loud and boisterous and without a care in the world. "Besides," Geoff went on, "you Yanks love underdogs. That'll work to your advantage."

"But the one thing I could always fall back on is my reputation. Now that's shot. By *me*!" She jabbed at her chest, her cheeks wet. "*I'm* the one who killed it! I mean, I'm forty goddamned years old. I can't compete on the basis of looks anymore, if I ever could. And if you don't have looks in this business, and you don't have reputation, what the hell do you have? Nothing! Not a damn thing."

Geoff kept his hand on her shoulder. "Nats," he said finally, "you are a beautiful woman. You are also one of the few people in this lunatic business who competes on the basis of experience and skill. Any news director who doesn't see that has got a screw loose."

She shook her head helplessly. That was sweet but what did it mean at the end of the day? Probably he just didn't know what to say. Maybe a woman's tears undid Geoff Marner just like they undid every other man.

A car whizzed past, rap music blaring. After it passed, silence again descended. The closed Jag began to heat up from the relentless July sun but still Geoff sat there patiently and still she was reluctant to get out. "I'm just so frightened." She dabbed at her face with the mangled tissue. "I've only got three months till my contract runs out and I can't—I *can't*—lose this job." *If I do I might end up like Evie, living by myself and scrabbling away at some fourth-rate newspaper for a pittance.* "It's all I've got."

"That's not true." He shook his head vigorously. "You are not defined by one hour of nightly airtime."

"Like hell I'm not!" She shrieked the words.

As if he didn't know what else to do, Geoff suddenly reached across the gearshift and bundled her into his arms. She let herself crumple onto the broad expanse of his chest, let her wet face drop onto his starchy pin-striped collar. He felt so solid and smelled so good, of soap and aftershave and maleness. She pulled back and stared at him. He gazed back, wonderful, hazel-eyed, pillar-of-strength Geoff, who even at this moment had a smile in his eyes. Crazy, manic Geoff, but Geoff whom she could always, always count on.

She was surprised to watch those smiling eyes grow somber, then fall to her lips. Completely without warning, to her utter surprise, he bent his head and kissed her.

Geoff. She felt as though real life had ceased, and been replaced by some bizarre yet entrancing reality. His lips were slow and undemanding, totally unlike Miles, totally unlike what she might have expected of Geoff had she ever had any wild imaginings of kissing him. It was like being nestled in soft sand, enveloping and delicious. She didn't want to move. She didn't want him to move. His skin, slightly rough from late-afternoon stubble, gently grazed her cheek as then he bent his head to kiss her throat.

Delicious sensations overcame her, so sweet as almost to be painful. *Oh, my God,* she heard herself murmur. She was so surprised. *Geoff?* Her hands rose to pull him closer. It so rarely felt right, but with this man it did. Somewhere deep in her mind's recesses she realized she hadn't kissed any man but Miles for a dozen years. But even that fleeting bit of rationality, that might in a more lucid moment have drawn her back to the real world, fell by the wayside as Geoff's kisses grew more urgent. "Inside," she heard herself whisper, her eyes closed, her head thrown back, her throat fully exposed to Geoff's caresses.

His head reared up. He looked startled. "Inside?"

"The house."

Understanding dawned and he moved quickly, as did she, getting out of the Jag, grabbing her purse, foraging for keys. Once inside, she turned off the security alarm and again, wordlessly, they reached for each other.

They stood clasped in the foyer, kissing. She felt the long, hard length of him pressed against her. He was so different from Miles, tall and lean where Miles was pudgy and almost formless. Geoff's tongue darted tantalizingly across her lips, then softly into her mouth.

Somewhere in the recesses of her brain a worry niggled. *What are you doing? This is Geoff! Your agent!* But the pull was so powerful. And Geoff she could trust, she could talk to. Why had she never thought of him like this before?

He pulled back and grasped her by the shoulders. "Upstairs?"

"Here." The word came instantly and without thought. No time for upstairs. No need. She led him by the hand into the living room and he followed without complaint. Somehow her customary caution had abandoned her. Maybe she was without caution that day. Or had lost it somewhere in the Millennium Club.

She was almost giddy with need of him. At the sofa she turned and they faced each other. He stood a few feet away, motionless, as though if he moved at all this craziness that had taken possession of them both might suddenly wear off.

She kicked off her shoes and her hand reached for the jumpsuit's zipper. Slowly she pulled it down, watching Geoff's eyes trail down her body with the movement. It was silly, of course, doing a striptease in a jailhouse jumpsuit, but there it was. She didn't care. It didn't matter.

The zipper ended below her navel. After a moment's hesitation she pulled the rough orange fabric off her shoulders, then bent from the waist to push it down her legs. She rose and stepped out of it, kicking it aside. She was naked, her clothes in a plastic jailhouse bag in Geoff's car.

He came toward her and ran his hands down her body. She reached for the buttons on his starchy pin-striped shirt, complaining, "So many," plucking cuff links off his wrists and tossing them carelessly aside so that they skipped along the tiled floor. She pushed his shirt off as he bent to step out of his trousers. Warm skin, strong muscles, thick light brown hair . . . She caught her breath as again he raised himself to his full height and pulled her against him, his body hard and lean and, now, demanding. Without another thought, without letting him go, she backed against the sofa's plump white cushions and pulled him atop her.

"God," he muttered, then bent his head to take a breast into his mouth.

I can't believe I'm doing this, Natalie thought vaguely, but hadn't the least desire to stop. She arched her back, looking sightlessly at the rough-hewn beams that criss-crossed the ceiling, rubbing her body against his. She felt delirious. It was the easiest, the most natural thing in the world to then take him inside her, as though he had been before and would be again. *Geoff.*

The wave that swept them both was sweet and yet relentless. When finally they each gave in, afternoon light pouring through the paned windows, Natalie couldn't find within herself the least regret, the least guilt, the least worry. It was Geoff, and that made it right.

They must have fallen asleep, she realized later, because the light was much softer when somewhere, vaguely, she became conscious of the phone ringing, the answering machine picking up. And a male voice speaking. "Yeah, this is Scoppio. You're not gonna anchor tonight. You're suspended. I'm gonna put it in writing—"

Her eyes opened. The room around her snapped into focus. Reality hit like a thunderclap. *What?* She scrambled from beneath Geoff and seized the jumpsuit, holding it in front of her. She whirled to face Geoff.

He lay still, rubbing his eyes and looking bewildered. "What's wrong?"

"Tony called. I heard him on the answering machine."

Geoff rolled his eyes and held out his arms, beckoning her. "Come back here, Nats. We'll deal with him later."

"No." How could she possibly wait? "I really need to hear Tony's message now. I think he said he's suspending me."

Geoff seemed to consider that. Then a moment later he abruptly rose from the sofa with an irritated expression on his face. "Right. The anchor desk comes first. I'll get out of your hair." He grabbed his trousers, abandoned on the floor.

"It's not that. It's . . . I don't know. I'm sorry," she repeated lamely, though by now he didn't seem to be listening to her and she no longer knew what she wanted to say.

Geoff reattached his belt. "We should listen to the message."

Back to business, apparently. She was oddly disappointed. But wasn't it she who'd insisted on listening to the message?

"Where's the machine?" he asked.

"In the kitchen."

Dutifully they both tromped in that direction, though Natalie felt like a fool walking around nude with a jailhouse jumpsuit clutched in front of her.

Geoff found the machine on the granite counter and punched the blinking MAILBOX 1 button. "5:55 P.M.," recited an automated voice, followed by Tony's clipped tones. "Yeah, this is Scoppio. You're not gonna anchor tonight. You're suspended. I'm gonna put it in writing but take this as notification that you're off the air without pay for a week."

"Can he *do* that?" Her voice sounded as if it came from someone else, shrill and unnerved.

Geoff was frowning. "Contractually, I'm sure he can. You've got a moral turpitude clause, like everybody else." Somehow the phrase "moral turpitude" hung oddly in the silent kitchen. He picked up the phone. "What's Scoppio's direct line?"

"555-4837."

He punched in the numbers, facing away from her. "Maxine, it's Geoff Marner. Will you put Tony on the line for me?" Silence. "Do me a favor then and make sure he doesn't leave. I'm coming by." Silence. "Thanks, Maxine." He hung up and without meeting Natalie's eyes strode out of the kitchen. "Right. I'm off then."

She padded after him helplessly. It was as though a wall had gone up between them, right after they'd been closer than they'd ever been before. *And I'm off the air. Suspended.* Panic rose in her throat. In eighteen years of television news that had never happened. Never come close to happening. "What should I do?"

"Nothing." He met her eyes briefly before letting himself out the front door. "I'd say we've both done enough already."

"I'll say it again. Reinstate Natalie." Geoff stood in front of Tony's desk, his demeanor belligerent, forcing himself to keep his mind on business even though he felt like an alien man had taken over his body. An alien man who seemed to think he could bonk a client and then blame her for his own folly.

That had been one hell of an afternoon with Natalie and even hours later he didn't know what to make of it. So he pushed it into a corner of his brain, a rarely probed corner, a corner where he could box it up and paper it over and pretend it didn't exist. And deal with business instead, one thing he could understand.

"Forget it," Scoppio was saying for the umpteenth time. "She's off the air for a week, without pay, and that's the end of it."

"That's completely unjustifiable. You should be promoting her rather than suspending her. Her going after

Hope Dalmont is the kind of aggressive reporting that hikes the numbers."

"Yeah, right." Tony sat behind his desk, his reading glasses pushed far down his nose, rubbing his reddened eyes. "And my aunt Carmina doesn't have a mustache. Listen, Marner, 'aggressive reporting,' like you wanna call it, doesn't end up in stalking charges."

"No charges have been filed."

"Not yet, but that doesn't mean a damn thing." Tony spread his hands wide, as though he were a mere slave to events. "I'm not gonna just pretend this didn't happen. She should be glad I'm only suspending her."

Geoff sat down and leaned forward. "Look, we can both agree that Natalie edged over the line." Tony scoffed at that. "But it was in a good-faith effort to get *you* what *you* want—a hot story and bigger numbers. What sense does it make to punish her for that?"

Tony shrugged, momentarily silenced. Geoff had tangled with Tony plenty in the past, back when Tony was a news director in Dallas. He'd concluded then that Tony Scoppio had banished the human element from his calculations. He was all pragmatism: all he wanted was to get the highest ratings for the least money. If that meant sidelining veteran talent, so be it.

Geoff tried another tack. "The smart play is to have Natalie on the air *more* than usual so you can sit back and watch the ratings skyrocket from all this free publicity."

"Nice try but no cigar. She'll be on the air in a week and not before."

"And who will fill in for her during that time?"

"Kelly Devlin."

"Kelly Devlin." Geoff shook his head as though he were dealing with someone particularly thickheaded. "Don't kid yourself, Tony. You can't trade in a racehorse for a donkey's ass and hope nobody'll notice. The difference in experience, in perspective, not to mention in sheer talent, is enormous."

"Yeah, well, you and your hoity-toity friends might notice a huge difference but I don't think most people who watch the news will. And that's who *I* care about." Tony jabbed a thumb at his chest. "*Most* people who watch the news."

That pissed Geoff off. He wasn't some effete intellectual who watched PBS and nothing but. And Natalie was popular with the public, for whom *he* had a higher regard than Scoppio apparently did.

"You'd better hope we don't have another earthquake this week, Scoppio." He rose from the chair, beginning to despise this man. "Because if we do, you'll have to rely on Kelly Devlin for wall-to-wall coverage. You think she can ad-lib? You think she can go live without PrompTer? In thirty seconds you'll be wishing you had Natalie back."

"You know what?" Tony raised his chin. "Kelly'll be rough the first time out. I know that. But she's smart. She'll learn. You think Natalie was perfect fifteen years ago? I don't think so."

"That's the bottom line here, isn't it?" Geoff felt anger bubble up within him, like a pot ready to boil. And like his lust hours earlier, he was having trouble bottling it up.

"What is?"

"That's why you've been gunning for Natalie ever since you got here." Even he could hear that his voice had turned quietly lethal. The two men eyed each other warily across Tony's desk. "Her age. That's it, isn't that right, Scoppio?"

Tony said nothing. Both men knew they had moved onto dangerous terrain.

"That's why you're not promoting the newscast," Geoff went on, "so you can use the lower numbers as an excuse to trade her in for somebody younger. Somebody cheaper."

Tony shrugged. "I make no excuses for investing in somebody for the future."

"Tony, Natalie is a *star*." Geoff laid his hands on Tony's desk and leaned forward aggressively. "She stands head and shoulders above Kelly. You can't replace her with a pretty little no-name and get the same punch."

Tony shrugged. "Not immediately. But give anybody enough airtime and you'll make 'em a star."

"And meanwhile you see the difference on the bottom line."

"Hey, let's not pretend this is a charity operation. I gotta worry about the bottom line."

"Especially since how it reads determines whether or not you take home a bonus."

Scoppio snorted. "You got a lot of nerve talking to me about money, Marner! You get fifteen percent off Natalie Daniels. What's that this year? A hundred ten, a hundred fifteen thousand smackers? No wonder you want her to keep her job."

That pissed him off: this newsroom pasha presuming to judge what motivated Geoff Marner. He jabbed at the air in Tony's direction. "Natalie Daniels means a hell of a lot more to me than a commission!"

The admission hung in the air, as telling a blunder as lipstick on a man's collar. Geoff cursed himself. Scoppio only smiled.

"Then you got a bigger problem than me, Marner." Tony casually clasped his hands over his paunch. "I'm ending this conversation. I got a newsroom to run."

Geoff clenched his jaw. He was almost shaking from anger. That was two times he'd lost control that day. That was totally unacceptable. He towered over Tony's desk and delivered his final salvo. "It's not over, Scoppio. Not by a long shot."

CHAPTER NINE

Tuesday, July 16, 4:49 P.M.

Natalie parked the Mercedes in her reserved space on the KXLA lot, thinking how much she lived her life by ritual. It was day three of her suspension. Day three that she was off the air. Still, on each of those days, she'd forced herself to go through the same ritualistic exercise of going to work, despite the stupefying reality that she had nothing to do there. She'd been purged from *The KXLA Primetime News* as thoroughly as if the letters of her name had been deleted from the alphabet.

She pulled the key from the ignition and set the hand brake. To her at least this ritual did have a point. Everyone expected her to stay home and out of sight. That was what all suspended people did: retreat into their humiliation. But Natalie would neither skulk nor hide. *Out of sight, out of mind. So I refuse to go out of sight.*

She grabbed her purse and briefcase and headed for the loading dock entrance to the gray fortresslike news building. Nor was her suspension the only vigil she was maintaining. The other was the wait for Geoff's call. They'd spoken only once, by phone, since the day of her arrest. It had been a brief, unsatisfying conversation in which neither of them had neared the topic of their lovemaking. Now it almost felt as if *that* had never occurred.

Almost. She couldn't truly forget it, not the tactile sense of it. The feel of him was buried deep in her pores and could not so easily be excised. The possibility that he could simply cut her out, like a surgeon eliminating a malignancy, was too hurtful to fathom.

Glumly she walked through the loading dock and into the station, greeting the few coworkers who weren't too embarrassed to look at her, then made a pit stop in the basement mailroom to pick up her snail mail. This was the one thing buoying her up. Not only had her viewer mail ballooned since her suspension, but four to one, viewers thought she should promptly be reinstated to the anchor desk. Natalie carried the load to her yellow cubbyhole of an office and carefully set it on her desk. "I'm still here," she declared sternly to the empty room, punctuating her pronouncement with a slap on her desk blotter. The rap sent a shiver of pain up her arm and made her pens rattle in their copper holder. "I am."

She cleared a space on her desk next to the letters, shaking out the *Los Angeles Times* to give it a good read. This was yet another of her suspension rituals: reading the *Times* in the evening at the station rather than in the morning over coffee. It gave her something to do during those hellacious hours between five and eleven p.m., when normally she would be reviewing scripts, taping teases, anchoring a newscast.

She pored over the front section, Metro, Calendar, and Business, even reading the articles about obscure foreign countries and unknown corporations. Then she moved on to Sports, going through it item by item, learning more than she cared to know about wrestling and Nascar. The only section she allowed herself to toss was the classifieds, and the only thing she saved, as a kind of newsprint dessert, was the *Hollywood Insider*. That day an item in *Tidbits* leaped off the page.

LAMBERT NETS LUCRATIVE PAYDAY

Sources at Heartbeat Studios tell The Insider *that the creator of the season's most anticipated new sitcom,* Forget Maui, *will pocket a whopping three million dollars for his efforts. Miles Lambert will take home the princely sum for executive producing one full season of the comedy, which NBC already has slated into a coveted Thursday prime-time slot.*

Natalie's hand flew to her throat. *Three million dollars? She* was the one footing the bill the entire time they were married—*twelve years!*—and then a few months after he walks out on her he lands a three-million-dollar gig?

She reared up from her chair and began pacing her small office, four steps in one direction, four steps back. It was unbelievable. It was infuriating. What did it mean?

She raced back to her phone. Berta picked up on the first ring and Natalie relayed the gist of the item.

"Good news," Berta declared instantly.

"How so?"

"Miles never filed for legal separation and neither did you. So the three million qualifies as marital property."

She was puzzled. "What do you mean? He moved out. We—"

"No. *Legal* separation is a specific process, Natalie." She paused. "Since Miles is claiming there's no prenuptial agreement, this sitcom money is fair game."

"You mean we can go after it?"

"Absolutely." Berta spoke wryly. "As his wife, in this community-property state, you can lay claim to half."

One point five million dollars. It would render divorcing Miles even less painful than it already was.

Berta ended their conversation with a reminder to Natalie to assemble the financial documents from all twelve years of the marriage, for the discovery process soon to begin. Natalie got off the phone and resumed her pacing, finally halting in the center of her office to glare at a crack in the yellow paint.

Geoff. What a polar opposite he was to Miles. Honorable where Miles was slimy. Hardworking. Understanding. Kind. It amazed her how blind she'd been about him. How could she have missed it?

Because you were married to Miles, an inner voice reminded her. She shook her head. What a mistake. And how much time wasted.

Slowly she returned to her desk. *But Geoff is your agent.* That made getting involved with him risky. What if it didn't work out? She'd probably have to go elsewhere for representation. And good agents were nearly as hard to find as good men.

But Geoff was so exceptional. She laid her head on her desk and shut her eyes. Maybe that explained why he hadn't called. He probably had a zillion other options. And no doubt she was geriatric compared to most of them.

Not to mention that she'd insulted his pride. She understood that now. She'd insulted him by zeroing in on Tony's voice mail and using Geoff only to parse what Tony meant. He would be justified in thinking her wildly self-absorbed.

She reached for the phone, then drew back her hand. No, better not to call. Better not to crowd him. When he wanted to talk, he would call. *Just wait.*

Exactly what she hated doing. But the right play. For now.

Forget it. I'm not waiting anymore. Geoff ignored the illuminated seat belt sign and freed himself from the woven strap across his lap. He reached beneath the seat in front of him for his briefcase, wanting both to work and to get some sleep before the United Airlines 767 landed at dawn at Kennedy Airport.

He had a great deal of travel over the next few weeks. He'd barely get back to L.A. from this round of meetings before he had to fly to Boston, then continue on to London. But perhaps it was good to be out of L.A. for a time. Get some distance. Some perspective.

He winced, remembering that mortifying conversation the prior week with Scoppio. *Natalie Daniels means a hell of a lot more to me than just a commission!* And that smug grin on Scoppio's face. *Then you got a bigger problem than me, Marner.*

He got hold of the well-worn leather briefcase just as

the guy one row ahead cranked his seat into the recline position, conking Geoff on the skull. He stayed doubled over, head between his knees, and a throb began to reverberate in his cranium. Damned uncomfortable business, flying, even first class, even with every imaginable perk the airline could squeeze onto this high-tech tin can hurtling through space.

He dislodged his briefcase and pulled out his laptop, booting it up. He didn't bother with the overhead light: he liked working by the computer screen's dim glow. Everyone around him in the darkened cabin was quiet, either reading or asleep. He felt alone, as he usually did even among people, but it was a pleasant, productive alone, an alone he knew how to handle.

He punched a few keys, trolling the e-mails not yet read, the tapping of the keys a staccato accompaniment to the soft rustlings around him. Forty-two e-mails. Geoff scanned the list. Most were run-of-the-mill work-related but one caught his eye: jroswell@hotmail.com. He stared at it, then punched a key to bring the missive full screen:

Honey, remember how we talked about doing a long Labor Day weekend with Liddy's family in Tahoe? Turns out we need to confirm the cabin within 24 hours or lose it. Are you game?
xoxoxo Janet

Geoff stared at the screen, the 767 bobbing in a sudden bout with turbulence. Great. A long weekend in a small cabin with Janet's less-than-exciting oldest sister and her boor of a husband, not to mention their drooling two-year-old, whom he'd met once and swiftly decided didn't merit a subsequent viewing.

He shook his head. Not a pleasing prospect. Yet no woman came without some downside, Janet no exception. He'd concluded long ago that, when it came to such a serious business as marriage, it was a matter of choosing the best total package.

He sat silently in the half dark, idly staring out his

small rectangle of tempered glass, his computer screen going black from neglect. Janet pleased him in nearly every way. On the key dimensions of looks, temperament, and athleticism, she was clearly a keeper. And her family . . . The Roswells had a solidity, a permanence, he hadn't run across since he'd left Sydney. They were a long-time San Marino clan, Establishment by southern California standards. They owned a lovely home on a gracious tree-lined street near the venerable Huntington Museum; they were on the A List for the best blue hair parties; they made him feel anchored and secure in a way he never did in the Hollywood whirl. And he liked—he *admired*—John Roswell, Janet's father—a cardiologist, one of the best in town, a smart, solid man who clearly loved all three of his daughters but had a special twinkle when it came to his youngest.

Yet—

Truth be told, Janet wasn't always the most scintillating companion. She was prone to chattering on about how houses were decorated or people were dressed. Of course, all of that mattered a great deal to a San Marino Junior Leaguer. And, no surprise, she talked nonstop about children. He *truly* shouldn't fault her for that, she was after all a teacher. But the ins and outs of first-grade education didn't exactly grab him.

Sometimes, odd as it seemed, he had the feeling that he slid neatly into an open slot in Janet's life, labeled, for the moment at least, BOYFRIEND. Geoff Marner, lucky him, had what it took: he was a Dewey, Climer senior partner; he made a lot of money; he dressed and spoke well; and being Aussie, he did it all with a dash of exotic flair. Sometimes it felt as though another guy who fit the same bill might just as well slide into his place if need be, that it wasn't really about *him* at all.

Geoff accepted a scotch from the Asian stewardess servicing first class and squinted into the cabin's dimness. Never once with Natalie had he felt replaceable. Somehow she made him feel truly singular. He remembered how Natalie looked after they first kissed—like he was the only man in the world.

He forced his logic to kick in, the same logic that had

earned him a First at the University of Sydney and a spot on the Law Review at the U.C.L.A. School of Law. Methodically he ran through Natalie's negatives, starting with her age. In and of itself he didn't mind her being three years older, but her being forty pretty much put the kibosh on kids. And he liked keeping that option open. And of course she was "in the throes of divorce," as people were wont to say. Still battling Miles legally. A wounded bird. Vulnerable.

Not to mention that she was a client! Briefly he shut his eyes. That thought was almost painful. It wasn't *verboten*, an agent/client romance, but it was certainly frowned upon. Bonking clients was definitely not included in the professional code of ethics. And he hadn't worked his ass off at Dewey, Climer to commit career suicide.

He had to admit one other thing bothered him, parochial though it was—Natalie was so damn wrapped up in her career. He remembered how she had completely closed off to him when she got the call that Scoppio was suspending her. One minute they were making love; the next all she could think about was her beloved airtime. He'd been shunted aside with a swiftness that stunned him.

Geoff rolled the tumbler between his palms, becoming perplexed, as he often did, when he thought about Natalie. So many downsides and yet the pull toward her was shatteringly powerful. There was something so vital about her, so unpredictable. That afternoon, once the veil had lifted and he saw her not as an anchor, not as a client, but as a woman, he didn't think he'd ever felt quite the same rush before. It was like catching a truly wild wave and wanting to ride it so bad you didn't give a damn whether or not it killed you.

Forcefully Geoff shook his head. He knew he had that side in him, that maverick side that hankered after all the wrong waves, and for years he'd fought it. Dangerous, that side. Foolhardy. What more proof did he need? He'd let himself ride the wave only to take advantage of one woman—a *client!*—and cheat on another.

Geoff had long prided himself on being smart when

it came to serious matters. He wanted to do things right. He wanted to succeed. And the *smart* thing, when it came to choosing between these two women, was to select the one who would make his life easier, better, calmer. The one who would help him control his wild side.

Janet. He nodded to himself. Janet. From the moment he'd met her, he'd seen what a rare find she was. In a land of starlets and wannabes, Janet was both down-to-earth and beautiful. And though she wasn't brainy, exactly, she was smart. And sensible. And anchored.

Janet.

Janet Roswell. Janet Roswell Marner. Janet Marner.

It worked, he told himself. It sounded right. It was smart.

Right then and there, thirty-five thousand feet above the earth, Geoff made up his mind. He slapped the armrest to punctuate his resolve. When he got back to L.A. after the London trip, he would ask Janet to marry him. He should have done it long ago. But he would do it now.

He couldn't believe it.

Tony leaned both elbows on his desk and peered at the overnight ratings, slurping his morning coffee without raising his eyes from the neat columns of numbers. Maybe the ratings were wrong. But Nielsen was never wrong. Or even if it *was*, nobody could do a damn thing about it because Nielsen was the only game in town. Nobody else did TV ratings. It was Nielsen, beginning and end of story.

He closed his eyes and opened them again. The same numbers reappeared in the column labeled KXLA, smack dab in the ten to eleven p.m. slot. So. *The KXLA Primetime News* got a 5.1 rating the prior night, the third night in a row it had come in over 5.0. The third night that Kelly had anchored in Natalie's place. And they were only three-tenths of a point behind KYYR, the bane of Tony's existence, the only other well-run independent TV operation in La La Land, the one station between him and his hundred-grand bonus.

And the higher ratings weren't because of the lead-in. Tony leaned back to think, resting his crossed hands on his belly. KYYR had creamed the competition from nine to ten with a reality show called *Behind Bars.* Incarcerated females, secret-camera video, the kind of thing that came out every ratings period, in this case the July sweep. It was hot, far grabbier than the bullshit teen drama he'd been forced to air. A bunch of Valley girls moaning and groaning and getting beaten up by their low-life boyfriends. At least they were running around in those cutoff midriff tops, but still . . . Tony had had to force himself to watch and he'd switched to KYYR at every commercial break.

He picked up the overnights to analyze the numbers quarter hour by quarter hour. Viewers had *changed channels* at ten to watch his newscast. Viewers had *abandoned* KYYR to watch him. Viewers had *stuck with* him for the entire hour.

Not him, exactly. Kelly. Well, not *only* Kelly. Ken, too. But who was he kidding? It was really Kelly.

Viewers saw what *he* saw: she was young, she was hot, she was new. Higher scores in all those key dimensions than Natalie Daniels got, that was damn straight.

But were viewers hoping to see Psycho Anchor? That whole Hope Dalmont saga sure had gotten a lot of publicity. Maybe viewers initially tuned in to see if Psycho Anchor would be on, he concluded, but they figured out fast she wouldn't. Still, they stayed. What did *that* tell him? They saw *something* they liked. Ken, who he'd had the smarts to bring in. And Kelly, who he'd had the smarts to have fill in.

His intercom buzzed and Maxine's nasally voice whined out into the silence. "You have a Suzanne Anderson and a Martin Van Davies here from Peterson and Drake, the public relations firm."

"Who?" Shit. Some P.R. flaks who wanted to foist some asinine story . . .

"They represent Hope Dalmont."

Even Maxine, who'd seen and heard everything twenty times over, sounded impressed. Tony frowned. What were *they* doing here? Then it hit him. Of course.

The courtesy call to tell him, the boss of Psycho Anchor, that Hope Dalmont was going to charge his crackpot employee with stalking, or trespassing, or whatever the hell other felonies she'd committed.

Fine. But he wanted backup. "All right, send 'em in, Maxine, but get Elaine over here pronto."

Tony set up a third chair and scuttled back behind his desk just as the P.R. types showed up at his door. He took one look and his jaw nearly hit the ground. The redhead was a major babe-alicious and the guy looked like Cary Grant in the good old days. He thought the two of them should give up P.R. to go forth and multiply.

"Mr. Scoppio," Cary said, holding out his hand, "we are here on behalf of Hope Dalmont."

Tony shook his hand. Cary had a damn strong grip. The redhead's wasn't bad, either. Where the hell was Elaine? He felt cowed by these people. His entire wardrobe probably cost as much as Cary's shoes.

"We apologize for not having scheduled an appointment," Cary went on, "but hope that in light of what we have to say you'll forgive our intrusion."

"How is Miss Dalmont doing?" Tony asked, stalling.

The redhead arched her brows, like she couldn't believe he was civilized enough to ask. "Very well, thank you." She had the huskiest voice he'd heard this side of *The Exorcist*. "She's flying to Monaco today, as you know, with the rest of the bridal party."

Tony nodded. Why the hell should *he* know? Unlike Psycho Anchor, he wasn't tracking Hope Dalmont's movements. But that's what these P.R. people were like, always convinced their story was the biggest dot on everybody's radar screen.

"Tony?"

Elaine. He waved her in. He was glad to see her, but damn, did she look like a tree-hugger today. She'd pulled out all the stops and mixed green *and* brown corduroy. He saw the P.R. pair look at each other.

"Elaine Nance, from our Legal Department," Tony said. Elaine arranged herself next to the redhead, who moved her chair away a few inches like she was afraid her hair would frizz if she got too close. "You were saying?" he prompted. Now he wanted to get this show on the road.

Cary cleared his throat. "Miss Dalmont has spent a great deal of time thinking about the unfortunate events of last week and has made an important decision."

He paused. *Jesus,* Tony thought, *does the guy want a drumroll?*

"Miss Dalmont felt a certain . . . *kinship* with Miss Daniels," Cary went on. "I gather both of them suffered similar personal losses when they were children. And while Miss Dalmont believes Miss Daniels was, perhaps, *overassertive* in pursuing an interview, nonetheless she has selected her to tape an exclusive interview this Friday in Monaco, on the eve of the nuptials."

Tony sat up straighter in his chair. He could not have heard what he just heard. "Say what?"

The redhead piped up. "That is correct, Mr. Scoppio," she said. "Miss Dalmont has come to believe that Miss Daniels will bring a unique perspective to an interview." She shook her head, as if she thought Dalmont was as fruity as Psycho Anchor.

"Now let me see if I've got this straight." *There's no way I do,* Tony thought, *unless hell froze over this morning and the newsroom failed to report it.* "You're telling me that Hope Dalmont wants Psych . . . uh, Natalie Daniels, to tape an interview? In Monaco?"

"On Friday, yes."

"And did somebody use the word 'exclusive?' "

"Yes." The redhead nodded.

Tony struggled to process that. So Psycho Anchor, who got herself arrested, now got herself *an exclusive interview*? Beating out *every goddamn reporter in the U.S. of A.?* Tony closed his mouth, which he realized was hanging open. He looked at Elaine. She looked as if a big limb from one of her favorite trees had fallen right on top of her head.

Then the redhead spoke up again. "Though I should point out that we will require KXLA to provide dubs of the interview to all news organizations that request them."

"Whoa." He threw up his hands. "What's up with that?"

Cary took over. "Miss Dalmont was taken with Miss Daniels's proposal precisely because it would generate publicity for the Big Sisters organization, which Miss Dalmont has supported for some time. Of course, the more widely the interview is aired, the more support Big Sisters will receive." He paused. "Naturally, every time any news organization airs excerpts of the interview, it will be required to give KXLA an on-air credit."

Naturally. It hit Tony like a ton of bricks.

He sagged in his chair. He could see it now. So if those shitheads at KYYR, for example, wanted to air excerpts, fine—so long as they aired a graphic saying the video was courtesy of KXLA. Same thing with KKBR in Dallas and WNNC in New York and KJDO in Podunk, Nebraska. And Jesus Christ, same thing with the networks, too. CBS, NBC, CNN, Fox . . .

Because every newsroom in America would want to air excerpts.

KXLA would get national credit.

He would get national credit, in every general manager's office from Maine to California.

He started to flush. This was good. This was very good. Maybe *too* good. He narrowed his eyes at the redhead. "So what about the stalking charges?"

She hesitated. It was clear she didn't like this part one bit. "Miss Dalmont has decided that filing charges is unwarranted."

Hot damn. The whole thing was going away, just like that. He pulled out his handkerchief and mopped his forehead. Psycho Anchor hadn't only dodged a bullet: she'd been resurrected and was levitating straight to heaven.

That was just fine. 'Cause he was going with her.

Cary reached into his briefcase and pulled out some documents. He yammered for a while about press credentials and hotel suites. Then the redhead got up and laid a business card on Tony's desk. "Please get us the names of the producer and crew who will accompany Miss Daniels so we can process those credentials and flight arrangements. We'll have a limousine meet the group at Nice Airport. Good day, Mr. Scoppio." She sailed out, followed by Cary, after another bone-crushing handshake.

Tony dropped back into his chair. He and Elaine stared at each other.

Tony spoke first, but only after he'd reached into his bottom right-hand drawer and pulled out his last two Three Musketeers bars. Even skinny-ass Elaine polished hers off PDQ. "Okay," he said, feeling fortified, "so what do we do to get Daniels *un*suspended?"

"What do you mean, I should be thanking you?" Natalie narrowed her eyes at Tony, holding court per usual from behind his desk. She'd been in her office going through her suspension ritual, day four, when Maxine called and asked her to come by Tony's office. She still didn't understand why, though Tony looked even cockier than his usual annoying self.

"You should be thanking me," he repeated, "because if I hadn't lit a fire under your butt you never would've gone all out to get an interview with Hope Dalmont."

Amazing. The gall of this man could fill Dodger Stadium. She put her hands on her hips. "How perverse is that? Now *you* want to get credit for me getting charged with a felony?"

"My sources tell me you won't get charged." His eyes glittered.

Her heart rate sped up. "What sources are those?"

"Let's just say they're impeccable." All of a sudden he grinned. "Here." He tossed her what looked like a travel-agency ticket packet.

She opened it up. It *was* a travel-agency ticket packet. "Airline tickets to *Nice, France*? Departing tomorrow? And a suite at Monaco's Hotel de Paris? Where did this come from? Why—" Realization dawned. "Oh, my God." Her hand flew to her throat.

"You got it," Tony said. "I don't know what you slipped in her Evian bottle but Hope Dalmont is convinced you're the one and only gal in the U.S. of A. who can interview her. Something about Big Sisters. I don't know. I don't get this women's stuff. But go ahead, Daniels." He spread his arms wide, still grinning. "Go ahead and start thanking me."

She stared at him, one idea after another crashing around in her brain like pinballs in a machine gone haywire. She was so happy, so stunned, she couldn't even manage to be mad at him.

She'd done it. Somehow, some way, she'd gotten through to Hope. Somehow in that lunatic episode, she'd convinced Hope Dalmont that Natalie Daniels was the one TV journalist who could tell her story.

It was unfathomable. She felt tears prick behind her eyes and rapidly looked down so Tony couldn't see. Apparently those old instincts about how to go after a story were still there. Apparently she hadn't gone soft after all. She looked up at Tony again. "So I guess going after Hope turned out to be a damn good idea. My judgment must not be so bad after all."

He waved his hand dismissively. "Doesn't matter whose idea it was. All that matters is that this interview will air fucking everywhere and that KXLA will get credit every time."

He explained the entire arrangement then and it rapidly became clear how much responsibility would be riding on her shoulders. True, a Hope Dalmont interview might be "celebrity-fawning horseshit" as Geoff had put it, but it was also the hottest interview of the year.

Her heart began to pound. This interview was likely to air on most of the television stations in the country. It was more exposure than she'd ever had in eighteen years of television news and she'd damn well better do a good job on it. "I want Ruth to produce for me," she announced.

"I've already decided that," Tony said. "And I'll tell you what I'm gonna tell her. I want three reports a day.

One for each of the morning shows and one for the prime-time news. And live shots—"

"Slow down. I don't want to have to file so many reports that the quality suffers. Two a day, morning and evening. That'll be hellacious enough. Given the time difference, I'll have to file for the morning shows mid-afternoon Monaco time and for prime time in the early morning. As it is, Ruth and I will be working constantly."

He fought her for a while but eventually he agreed, then eyed her narrowly. "So, Daniels, you up to it?"

"I'm more than up to it, Tony," she bristled.

"Good." The challenge in his eyes was unmistakable. "Because I'd say you have a lot riding on this trip."

She stood up. "I'd say we both do." She walked out, her pulse racing. Why did he always get her so lathered up? It irritated her. It also irritated her that there was a grain of truth in his pronouncement that *he* was the one who'd fired her up to go after Hope in the first place. In a way he had, by telling her he didn't plan to renew her contract. Management by fear. It had worked.

But now you'll have to renew me, Tony, she told herself. *Maybe you'll even have to hike my salary to keep me.*

She made tracks getting back to her office. She had a huge amount to do. Get her passport out of that damn safe-deposit box. Get her hair highlighted. Pack the perfect on-air wardrobe. And troll the Web for every last shred of information she could gather on Hope Dalmont.

She reached her office and stopped dead, a thought smashing into her brain. This was an excuse to call Geoff. In fact, she reasoned, she was *obliged* to call him. This was huge career news and he was her agent. He needed to hear it. She ran for the phone, only to remember that he was in New York until that night.

Fine, she told herself. *I'll stop by Dewey, Climer tomorrow on my way to the airport.* No matter that it was well out of the way.

* * *

Kelly poured a packet of Equal into her iced tea and gazed over her Jackie O sunglasses at the well-dressed hordes populating the outdoor food court at the Century City Mall. Dressed in casual California chic, their wealth was evident in everything from their soft leather accessories to their just-out-of-the-gym physiques to their flawlessly highlighted hair.

Kelly swizzled her straw, studying the crowd carefully. This was where she belonged. Or where she *wanted* to belong. Among the privileged locals from the sun-kissed acres of Beverly Hills, Holmby Hills, and Bel Air. She wanted to understand what they did, what they bought, what they said. She'd wanted to understand that ever since she'd been a kid back in Fresno. After all, a beautiful woman like her deserved to be one of them, and usually got to be after marrying some rich asshole. But she'd do it all on her own, so no one could ever take it away from her. And TV news was her ticket. Not some rich jerk she'd have to fuck six ways to Sunday.

Kelly speared an asparagus from her salad. She was tired from all the shopping. What with filling in for Natalie, she needed new anchor outfits in the worst way. She glanced down at the three shopping bags arrayed around her sandaled feet, stuffed to the gills. She'd worry about the bills later: her credit cards were so maxed out anyway, another few thou hardly mattered. Although, she realized, all this buying was keeping her from putting together a down payment. And if she really wanted to be like these people, she should live among them. How to achieve that, she had no idea.

Dispiritedly, Kelly polished off her salad, swabbing up the last bits of dressing with the one slice of unbuttered French bread she allowed herself, and reached into her purse for a cigarette. Thank God for nicotine. Without it, she'd be two hundred pounds. Her eating regimen left no leeway for extra calories: she prided herself on being rail-thin, regardless of the near-starvation required. Not to mention the workouts: five weekly, at least an hour per. She'd started dieting at fourteen and smoking at fifteen, deciding the greatest single threat to her future wasn't cancer, but fat.

The beeper attached to the waistband of her white capri pants buzzed. Shit. Was it Howard wanting something? She glanced at the readout. 212-555-8697.

Her eyes widened. *Hard Line*! She recognized the number from when they called before.

Instantly she stubbed out her cigarette and pulled out her cell phone. What did they want? They must've gotten the dub by now. Wasn't it good enough?

"This is Kelly Devlin responding to your page," she said as soon as the receptionist answered.

"Yeah," the woman rasped. She sounded bored as hell. "We're getting ready to air the killer natural disasters special and wanted to confirm that you have a signed release from the Mann family allowing the video to be aired."

"A signed release," Kelly repeated.

"Right. Hold on."

The receptionist put her on hold. Kelly's mind whirled. Of course she didn't have a signed release! It was just her luck that *Hard Line* would want one, to cover their butt in case anybody got mad at what aired. But no way could she could get the Manns to sign anything! She might as well try to drive her new Beemer to the moon.

She smashed her fist down hard on the table, making everything on it jump. This was her big chance! If *Hard Line* liked her, who knew what could happen? They might offer her a national anchor job!

The receptionist came back on the line. "Still there?"

"Yes." She bit her lip. "I have a release," she lied.

"Fax it to us. You know the number?"

Kelly cringed. "Yes."

"We'll let you know when the special airs."

"Please do that," Kelly tried to get out, but the woman had already hung up.

Kelly slapped her cell phone shut. Her hands were shaking. *Fuck!* Now why did that have to happen?

She dropped the cell phone back into her satchel and pulled out another cigarette, thinking fast.

I'll just ignore it, she decided. She flicked her lighter and lit the cigarette, closing her eyes behind her sunglasses and letting the nicotine work its relaxing magic. You had to take risks to play in the big leagues. You *had* to. It was just that simple.

"That's fantastic, Natalie. Really, I'm thrilled for you," Geoff repeated. From across his office Natalie watched him at his desk as his eyes dropped from hers and he began to shuffle some papers. He hadn't emerged from behind his desk the entire quarter hour she'd been there. And though he'd offered numerous variations on the congratulations theme for her Hope Dalmont coup, he seemed oddly lacking in . . . *warmth.*

She flushed. Or was it heat?

Maybe another tack. "So how are you?" She made her voice light and friendly. "How was the trip to New York?"

"Quick. Fine." Still he didn't meet her eyes. "I'll be doing a lot of traveling over the next few weeks, actually. I'm flying to London later today—" He stopped.

Today? Her brain cranked into overdrive. "So you'll be in London while I'm in Monaco?" *We won't be that far apart. Maybe we could . . .*

"Seems so." He punched a few computer keys, then stared at the screen, his chin in his hand.

Natalie felt a surge of disappointment, quickly replaced by annoyance. That was certainly a nonstarter. And it bordered on rudeness, didn't it, that he was going about his business as if she weren't even there? "Maybe I should get out of your hair," she offered coolly, though she didn't move a muscle. "I don't want to be late for my flight and you seem preoccupied."

"I'm swamped, frankly." But at that he did raise his eyes to hers.

She flinched. Not a flicker of the old Geoff there. Just the aloof gaze of an agent toward a rather pesky client.

"Really," he said, the distance in his hazel eyes belying his words, "I couldn't be more pleased about your news. I'll be anxious to hear how it goes in Monaco."

She nodded, tremendously hurt. She bent to retrieve her briefcase but couldn't quite make herself go. *You have to say something now or you're never going to stop wondering.* Without giving herself time to think she pivoted on her heels and faced him.

His eyes rose from his paperwork, with apparent reluctance.

"You've been very standoffish since"—she paused—"since the day of my arrest."

A look of guilt flashed across his face, unmistakable. He cleared his throat. "I'm very sorry about that, Natalie."

Her breath caught. *No.* "Sorry about what, exactly? That we've barely spoken since? Or that—"

"Sorry that it happened."

"That the arrest happened?" She tried to sound joking.

He threw down his pen, then pinched the bridge of his nose, sagging in his chair.

She watched him, frozen. *No.*

"Natalie, that was reprehensible behavior on my part. You're my client. We've known each other for a long time, and I took advantage of you in a vulnerable moment." He shook his head. "I hope you can forgive me."

"There's nothing to forgive," she began, but he was speaking again, as if he were delivering a rehearsed speech.

"I put an extremely high value on our business relationship, not to mention on our friendship, and I would hate for one idiotic mistake to jeopardize that."

Idiotic mistake. That cut deeply. She wished desperately that she'd left when she'd had the chance, that she hadn't had to hear any of this. *Don't ask a question unless you're sure you want to know the answer.* She took one last stab, though her pride was screeching at her to stop. "I'm not sorry," she said firmly. "I don't consider it a mistake." But the words bouncing off

Geoff's office walls sounded increasingly pointless. *It's over. Before it even started.*

He looked shaken and said nothing for a few moments. Then he said quietly, "I'm afraid I do."

No. She forced her voice to be strong. "Geoff, that afternoon was not my imagination. There was something—"

He cut her off. "That doesn't mean it was right." A pained expression crossed his face. "I'm seeing someone."

"What?"

"I'm seeing someone."

Her heart battered against her ribs. It was Miles all over again, in their bedroom, packing a suitcase. That terrible, horrible Sunday afternoon. *"I've met someone."*

No. Not Geoff, too.

Geoff spoke again. "I've betrayed her trust as well. I've been a cad all around and I'm terribly sorry. Please forgive me."

"You keep saying that!" Anger was taking over. It felt good, actually, better than the pain shooting through her. "Who is she? Does she know what happened?"

He shook his head.

"Do I know her?"

"I don't believe so."

"How old is she?"

He threw up his hands. "Natalie, that's hardly relevant!" He sounded exasperated. "The only thing that matters now is that you and I get past this. The sooner the better."

She was infuriated. "The better for whom?"

That shut him up, but only temporarily. "Both of us. Our relationship is beneficial to both of us."

"I'll just bet it is." She knew full well how beneficial her commission checks were to Dewey, Climer. In her heart of hearts, buried deep, she also knew what a fine agent Geoff had been to her, time and again, and that not for a heartbeat did he view her as a commission check. Still. She grabbed her briefcase and strode for the door. "Fine. See you on television." She banged his door shut behind her, tears pricking her eyelids. In the adjoining office two sets of curious male eyes rose from a mound of paperwork to regard her. She stomped past, averting her face.

When the humiliation came, seconds later, it was with a vengeance. *Again! Always too old, always not right.*

Even with Geoff.

CHAPTER TEN

Friday, July 19, 7:11 A.M.

"That's right. Natalie Daniels has wrapped the Hope Dalmont interview," Tony informed CNN's senior foreign-news producer, one of the half dozen national news types who'd succeeded in getting him on the phone so far that morning. Tony wasn't bothering with the locals: Howard could deal with them. "The first dubs should be available in two hours."

Tony chatted a while longer, then hung up and consulted his watch. He didn't really need to because he knew the timing by heart. If it was 7:15 A.M. in L.A., it was 4:15 P.M. in Monaco. Princess and Hope Dalmont should be just finishing their girly-girl chat. Fine. All he had to do was sit back and let the congrats roll in.

His intercom buzzed. "Mr. Pemberley on line three," Maxine rasped.

Tony first frowned, then chuckled. Ah, yes. The chairman of Sunshine Broadcasting, KXLA's esteemed parent company, no doubt calling to offer his kudos.

He picked up the receiver, prepared to be jovial. It was a real effort for him to do this corporate slap-on-the-back shit. "Rhett," he bellowed, "how are you?"

"Never better," Pemberley replied. Tony detected a trace of Southern twang in Pemberley's speech, which not even decades in the executive suite could erase. "And how is the most enviable news director in Sunshine's illustrious corporate crown?"

Tony forced himself to laugh. Ha ha ha. He could just see Pemberley holding court in the corner office of Sunshine's Phoenix headquarters, the mental wheels turning underneath that mane of silver hair, the tailored dress shirt crisp and blindingly white.

"I'd have to say everything here is going well," Tony said.

Pemberley laughed. "Modesty does not suit you, my friend. But I daresay you're pleased. These developments in Monaco certainly have you inching closer to 'the grand prize,' shall we say?"

Tony bristled. *Inching?* He was goddamn leapfrogging. But he kept his voice matter-of-fact. "The ratings are up. We're beating KYYR now. We're the number one newscast at ten." He pulled the overnight Nielsens closer. Who knew how long it would last? But right now it was true. With Natalie reporting from Monaco and Kelly at the anchor desk, *The KXLA Primetime News* was over a 5.0 rating every night and beating KYYR routinely.

"I'm sure you're dreaming of numbers every night." Pemberley laughed again and Tony's jaw tightened. "More power to you. I admire a man who wants to win."

"I don't want to win, Pemberley. I do win." Instantly Tony regretted the remark. But Pemberley ticked him off. Who was *he* to be so snide about Tony's incentive deal? He'd agreed to it.

"Scoppio, you're a hard-ass but I like you."

Oh, peachy.

"But don't forget the second half of the equation," Pemberley went on. "Not just coming in first at ten but getting the news department out of the red."

Tony forced himself to respond with some "confident he'd do exactly that" bullshit, then hung up.

He rose and paced his office. He hardly needed Rhett Pemberley to remind him of the terms of his deal. He knew them as well as his own name. But there was only one surefire way to get out of the red and that was to cut the talent payroll. Of which Natalie Daniels's salary was by far the biggest chunk.

He lumbered back to his desk and stared down at the Nielsens. They were over a 5.0 rating every night but who had gotten them there? Kelly. She was on the anchor desk.

Still, he had to admit, now that Princess was doing such a bang-up job reporting, and getting him such good publicity, he was less anxious to get rid of her. But she cost him a goddamn fortune.

He rubbed his forehead. What to do.

Then it hit him.

Of course.

Tony laughed and slapped the side of his head. Sometimes he was so goddamn clever he surprised even himself.

Natalie shut the bedroom door of her suite in Monaco's Hotel de Paris and leaned her exhausted body back against it. In the main room behind her, she could hear Ruth puttering about, channel-surfing to find CNN and calling room service to order in dinner.

Natalie kicked off her pumps. They landed with soft thuds on the plush white carpet. Pure white, like the fur on a Persian cat. That was true luxury everywhere else in the world, but in the Hotel de Paris's penthouse suite, white with gold accents was *de rigueur*.

She perched on the canopied bed, turned down for the night with a single peach rose centered on the pillows, and rubbed her sore feet. They throbbed from twelve plus hours pinched into the pointy-toed pumps she'd bought for Hope Dalmont's interview. She grimaced. After all these years in TV news she should have known enough to wear either low-heel runaround shoes or seriously broken-in high heels. There was no in-between when it came to female reporter footgear.

But the interview had gone well and that was all that mattered. Afterward, when they were saying their goodbyes, Hope had even given her her private phone number and asked her to keep in touch. It was amazing. She was the only reporter to interview Hope. The only reporter lodged in a Hotel de Paris suite, six magnificent rooms restocked daily with flowers and chocolates and champagne. The only reporter whose bills were sent directly to the Palais Princier. She was a journalistic luminary of the highest order. *Take that, Tony Scoppio!*

She smiled with satisfaction, then hoisted herself to her feet to shed her ivory suit and hose. They'd finished their shooting for the day so she could relax at last. In the main room beyond, half of which she and Ruth had converted into a makeshift edit bay, Ruth was talking back to the TV, castigating CNN for some journalistic transgression real or imagined. Natalie donned the hotel's thick white fleece robe and threw open the double doors to her narrow balcony, walking out to lean over the railing. Late afternoon was softening into twilight. Far below, the port was awash with the lights of countless enormous yachts, people lingering on deck as though reluctant to bid adieu to the day's magic. She could vaguely make out their laughter. The breeze was thick with humidity and scented by the verbena that grew in profusion on her balcony. Her gaze drifted above the harbor, where the Palais Princier glimmered like a pastel fortress from the peak of ancient Monaco-Ville.

Natalie hugged her waist, the robe's sash thick around her middle. *Odd. When have I been in such a beautiful place? Scored such a professional triumph?* Yet still she felt vaguely unsatisfied.

For a second, there on the balcony, she worried that she had done her life all wrong. Maybe she'd been misguided to be so career-obsessed, so dominated by desire to get into TV news, succeed in TV news, hold on to her TV-news job? But you *had* to be obsessed to play that game, didn't you? Wasn't it so competitive that even minuscule lapses in fervor were enough to knock you out of the race?

And she *loved* the game, always had. How could she not play it? And really, what else did she have going on?

She shook her head, banishing the image of the tall, hazel-eyed man that all at once rose in her mind. How pointless, harboring romantic fantasies about a man who'd made it abundantly clear that he wasn't interested. And even worse, how naive to think that a man could satisfy every desire. She had too much common sense to believe that fairy-tale mush. No, much better to focus on work—work that she loved, work that was always there.

Natalie forced herself back inside and shut the doors to close out the heavy moisture-laden air. *Relax,* she ordered herself. *You'll rally. You always do.* And at the moment she *had* to, because she and Ruth had three hours of videotape to log, one script to write, and a two-minute package to edit. To be fed by satellite to Los Angeles by four a.m. Monaco time for air not only on *The KXLA Primetime News* but on most other television stations in the country. She was staring at an all-nighter.

She sighed. She was exhausted already. But in career terms this might well be the most important night of her life. Resolutely, she tightened the robe's sash and opened her bedroom door to rejoin Ruth at their makeshift edit bay.

"Goddammit, would you lie still? I'm trying to get some sleep here!" Kelly shivered and tugged the duvet higher around her naked shoulders. Staying overnight in Malibu reminded her of the downside of beach living: it was too damn cold at night, even in July. She was smart to want to buy in Bel Air.

Well, if she played her cards right, she'd be able to.

"Sorry, baby." Miles sighed heavily and Kelly rolled her eyes. She'd been back with him only one night and already she was sick of his angst. "But now that we're in production, I can't get *Forget Maui* out of my mind."

These Hollywood types! "Fine. But don't keep *me* awake."

"You sure?" he muttered huskily, and started nibbling on her shoulder, lingering wet kisses meant to arouse her.

She twisted away, cutting off his access to her bare skin. "Not again!" Finally she rolled out of the king-size bed and grabbed Miles's abandoned dress shirt from a heap of clothes on the floor, pulling it on. "I'm getting some air. No, you stay here." She left him wearing a stupid, disappointed expression and padded across the whitewashed pine floor.

She was drawn across the big, high-ceilinged living room toward the huge window that faced the ocean. All that lay between her and the Pacific Ocean was fifty yards of clean white sand. The moon was big and everything was nice and quiet.

She laid her cheek against the cool glass. This was the kind of spread rich people had. This was the kind of spread *she* should have. After all, she couldn't be a real news celebrity and live in a smarmy apartment, could she?

But there was that gnarly problem of a down payment. And on a major house, like one in Bel Air, it was humungous. Miles might be a pain in the ass, but how was she going to get a down payment without him? Plus, she'd been so pissed off when Natalie had suddenly risen from the dead and gone off in glory to Monaco. So she'd called Miles, out of the blue. Why not? She'd read all about him in the trades: how all of a sudden he was a big muckety-muck with a new sitcom about to go on the air. It struck her: why not kill two birds with one stone? Get a down payment. *And* get back at Natalie. Fucking Natalie's husband was getting back at her for sure, even if Natalie didn't know about it.

And of course Miles had accepted her dinner invitation. He was the kind of guy who took what he could get. She'd figured that out long ago.

Kelly remembered when she'd first met Miles. He'd been good for laughs back then. They'd conducted their affair behind Natalie's back, while she'd interned at KXLA and lived in Natalie and Miles's house. Natalie had been so completely clueless, it was hilarious. But Kelly had gotten sick of it fast. Miles was old and seemed like kind of a loser.

But not anymore. Not judging from his house, anyway.

Kelly sighed. She should go back to bed. It was fucking four o'clock in the morning. Slowly she made her way back to the bedroom, where Miles seemed to be asleep. But no such luck. As soon as she crawled into bed, he rolled over and kissed her shoulder. She could barely keep herself from cringing.

"Go to sleep," he murmured. "Isn't it great we're back together?"

Kelly rolled her eyes and snuggled deeper into the pillow. Miles was as delusional as his future ex-wife.

Geoff stood in his room in London's Claridge's Hotel, sipping tepid afternoon tea and staring at the fax that his secretary had forwarded from Los Angeles. He set his jaw. What a bastard Scoppio was. What a sniveling wally. Cowering behind bureaucratic procedure, delivering the blow in black-and-white type, while Natalie was in Monaco no less, all to protect himself from the awkwardness of a face-to-face confrontation.

Too messy, that. Coward.

Geoff skimmed the document a third time. Given its life-changing contents, it was surprisingly brief. He wanted to tear it to smithereens but instead tossed it on the bedside table and began to pace the small area of beige carpet between the window and the four-poster bed, his mind ricocheting among the options before him.

His meetings would be over the next morning and his flight immediately followed. His IN box at Dewey, Climer was piled high with must-dos, most of them urgent.

Still . . . Natalie was in Monaco for another twenty-four hours. She was an important client and this was shattering news. She should hear it sooner rather than later and she should hear it from him.

He grimaced. Perhaps with ingenious phrasing he could soften the blow. Not that she was positively inclined toward him or anything he had to say at the moment. Still . . . He halted at the window. If she found out in Monaco, she could get her thoughts in order before she returned to L.A. And if she wouldn't open up to him, she had Ruth with her to commiserate.

He moved aside the filmy white drapery and peered

out the rain-streaked window, where London, gray and damp in weak afternoon light, bustled three floors below. His heart ached for her. It was so unfair, so idiotic of Scoppio. He would come to rue the decision, Geoff was sure. And the ironic, painful twist was that Scoppio had acted on the heels of Natalie's triumph with Hope Dalmont. What a cruel, crazy business.

His hand dropped uselessly to his side. What would he have done a few weeks ago? Would he have flown to Monaco? It seemed his relationship with Natalie broke down into Before and After. Would he have waited until they'd both gotten back to Los Angeles? He didn't want to act differently than he would have Before.

Tentatively he reached for the bedside phone.

It was twenty-four hours later when Natalie and Ruth heard the knock on the door of their Hotel de Paris suite. Both were exhausted from working round the clock; both were dressed in the hotel's fleecy white robes and sitting at a small round linen-draped table with the dirty plates from their room-service lunch arrayed around them.

"Do you want to get it or should I?" Ruth asked.

The knock was repeated, louder this time.

"I'll get it." Natalie rose, her body aching. "It's probably room service wanting to clean up."

"I'll tell you, room service here is faster than a Catholic girl on prom night." Ruth pushed back a strand of errant hair that had escaped from her nest of pink rollers. Her black-rimmed half glasses drooped down her nose, her eyes tired and makeup cakey behind the thick lenses.

Natalie forced herself toward the door. She knew she didn't look one whit better than Ruth did. In fact she looked worse, given the juniper-berry sauce from her *Côtes de Porc Marinées* she'd spilled down the front of her robe. She gave her sash a quick tightening tug and pulled open the door. "My God!" The last person in the world she'd expected to see in Monaco. Or wanted to, for that matter.

"I have a way of surprising you, don't I, Natalie?" Geoff smiled. His hazel eyes ran down the robe to her bare feet, then swiftly back up to her face. "And of catching you when you're not properly dressed."

She stared at him, not sure whether to be pleased or worried by his sudden appearance. *What's he doing here?* Her heart leaped. *To apologize? To start over?* "I'm sorry. I'm forgetting myself." She stepped back and waved him inside. "Please come in. I'm so surprised to see you." She felt awkward. "Ruth and I are just finishing lunch."

He brushed past her, his brows arched in surprise. "You're eating room service on your last day in Monaco?"

"We still have editing to do this afternoon. Plus we're both zonked from filing a million reports."

He nodded. Then his eyes cut sharply away.

Something clanged in her consciousness, like a note strangely out of tune. Slowly she shut the door. No, he hadn't come to start over, some instinct told her. The distance between them was still there, almost tangible, like a NO TRESPASSING sign slung around his neck.

Ruth rose from the table, a linen napkin clutched in one hand and bafflement on her face. Natalie swiftly made introductions.

Geoff stooped to set his briefcase on the pure white carpet, then turned to face Natalie.

She analyzed his face and began to feel truly frightened. He didn't look like himself. He looked like an exhausted, pained version of the Geoff Marner she knew. "What have you come all the way from Los Angeles to tell me? What is it?"

"I was in London, actually." He took her elbow and tried to lead her to the couch.

She refused to budge. *Why does he look so uncomfortable? What did he come to tell me?* Instinctively her hand rose to her throat. Ruth moved behind her, rubbing her hand soothingly down Natalie's back.

"Please," Geoff said. "Sit down."

This time, with Ruth's help, he did get her to sit. She

perched stiffly on the sofa's silken cushions, Ruth beside her. "What is it?" She felt a catch in her throat. "Scoppio did something?"

He met her gaze. The pain she'd glimpsed in his eyes before now took solid shape. "Yes."

She took a deep breath. "Did he fire me?" Her voice shook. "Is that it? He fired me?"

"No, he didn't fire you." Geoff sighed and looked down at his clasped hands. "He demoted you."

"*Demoted* her?" Ruth repeated. "What the hell are you talking about?"

"Natalie, he's making you a reporter." He glanced at Ruth. "Believe it or not, he's moving Kelly Devlin to the anchor desk in Natalie's place."

"Kelly Devlin!" Ruth hollered. "How in hell could he replace Natalie with that birdbrained pinup?" Ruth leaped to her feet and began storming back and forth across the pristine white carpet.

Natalie remained still on the couch. She was surprised how little she felt. Sad, mostly. Drained. Her brain struggled to life, dully at first, then in fits and starts. "Is this just another step in trying to get rid of me? He thinks I'll be so disgusted I'll quit?"

Geoff paused. "Possibly. Though I'm sure he wants to keep you, but in a radically reduced role." He looked at her. "And when your contract comes up he'll want you at a radically reduced salary."

Of course. While he acceded to a radically higher salary for the woman who replaced her. "When did you hear about this?"

"My secretary forwarded the fax to me. He sent it Friday. I got him on the phone this morning but couldn't budge him."

Scoppio had issued the directive *Friday*. The day she'd interviewed Hope. Natalie shut her eyes. How ironic was that. He'd demoted her on the very day she believed her career was shifting into its highest gear. She threw up her hands. "But can he do this? Doesn't my contract specify that I anchor the prime-time news?"

Geoff shook his head. "Your contract leaves him

enough wriggle room to use you in other capacities. 'From time to time,' it says, you can be required to do a range of other things, including report."

"But why now? The ratings are up!"

"Natalie." He rose and stood at the balcony doors, facing the pastel hulk of the Palais Princier. "He says that it was while you were *reporting* that the newscast got over a five."

Ruth guffawed loudly. Natalie processed that final twist in silence. Then a thought occurred to her. "I could refuse to do it."

"You could." Geoff returned to the sofa. "Though in that case KXLA wouldn't have to pay you, because you'd be violating the terms of your contract."

"But they *do* have to pay me at my current salary even though I'm reporting and not anchoring?"

"For the duration of this contract, yes."

Natalie tried to take it in. *He has to pay me my full salary through October fourth. But if I refuse to report, he doesn't have to pay me. And gets me gone entirely.* For the first time, she realized how fragile was the foundation on which her life was built. How one brick, suddenly removed, could topple the entire edifice.

And her television career was more than one brick. It was her entire life. She had nothing else.

She looked at Geoff and again saw the invisible barrier between them. She was alone. She had no one but herself to depend on. "That's it, then," she murmured. "It's over." The words hung in the air.

Geoff stared at her for a moment. "No, it's not over." His features set. "First, there's no reason to believe this switch is permanent. Scoppio's experimenting, I guarantee you. Second, I'll fly to Phoenix to meet with Rhett Pemberley. I may be able to talk some sense into *him*. And there's the obvious other option." He paused. "We get you another offer, in or out of L.A. Thanks to all this"—he waved his arm expansively—"you're a hotter property than ever. I'm confident that at this point we can line you up elsewhere." He paused. "It's not over. We'll fight it."

She nodded, unable to take heart from his bravado. The reality that she'd lost the job she'd loved for fourteen years bobbed stubbornly on the surface of her brain, like trash dumped on ocean water. *That's it, then. Everything I've struggled for. Gone.*

"We'll fight it, Natalie," she heard Geoff repeat. But by then she'd risen and walked away and closeted herself inside her room. Alone, as ever.

CHAPTER ELEVEN

Wednesday, July 24, 11:08 A.M.

Tony leaned back in his chair, cradling the phone in his hand, flushed with the pleasure of one of his favorite pastimes. Contract negotiations. It was like a miniwar, every time. Made him feel like fucking Caesar, one of the all-time best wops. He liked every single step: masterminding his battle plan, seeking out his opponent's weakness, then using it to drive the poor schmuck into submission. May the biggest prick win. And that meant him, every time.

He forced himself to focus on the monologue his current windbag of an adversary was delivering. "—unreasonable to come in below the compensation your morning anchor is now receiving."

Rico Jimenez paused and Tony knew it was for dramatic effect. Tony could just picture him in his Manhattan office, sitting in his thousand-dollar Italian suit eyeing his fingernails, which Tony heard he actually had manicured. The guy was like a spic George Hamilton. Funny how anchors and their agents were like dogs and their masters: after a while they started to look the same. And no question this guy was a lot like Kelly: fast-talking, good-looking, and on his way up.

"Look, Rico," Tony said, "I gave you a number and both you and I know your client should be happy with it. Shit, a hundred twenty-five grand a year is nothing to sneeze at."

"But she's making seventy-five now as a *reporter*. She should be making a *lot* more if she's going to be anchoring prime time!"

"She should be *grateful* she's going to be anchoring prime time." Tony paused. This was *his* turn for dramatic effect. "Not greedy."

Jimenez, sighed, as if he was dealing with a skinflint. Tony snorted softly. Who else was gonna slide this guy's untested twenty-four-year-old client into an anchor slot? In L.A. no less, where anchor jobs were as hard to come by as ice storms? And sure the ratings were popping now, but that was no guarantee they'd pop forever.

But Tony had already planned for that. The negotiation and all the paperwork would take a good month. He'd see how Kelly did during that time. How the *ratings* did. Until he signed the contract, he could always back out. And if Kelly did good, then he'd lock her in at a salary he could live with.

Tony cleared his throat. He was in the driver's seat on this one. He knew it. Jimenez knew it. The only question was whether Kelly would know it. "That's the deal. One twenty-five the first year, one thirty-five the second, one fifty the third."

"One fifty, one seventy-five, two hundred."

Tony consulted the legal pad on which he'd jotted down what he'd known in advance would be the final figures. "One thirty, one forty-five, one sixty. That's it."

He leaned back, grinning. And when Princess's contract came up in a few months he could cut her salary big-time, since she'd be reporting and not anchoring. *Or* get rid of her entirely. Either way he'd bring down his talent payroll so much that good old Rhett Pemberley would have to cut his bonus check. He'd have Anna-Maria in a Caddy by the time they drove down to San Diego for vacation.

Jimenez sighed again, as if he was badly wounded that this was the best Tony could do. "Well, I'll run these past her. But, Tony, you're getting her for a song. Kelly has real star—"

"Save it." He was getting irritated now. A song? How

many songs cost a hundred thirty grand a year? "Plus I want you to tell her she's gotta be more careful with what she says and does. She's an anchor now."

"I understand."

"And even though she's an anchor, I'm not going to have her sitting around on her duff." Tony wasn't going to repeat *that* mistake. "She's going to have to go out and report once she gets settled at the anchor desk."

"Sure, sure." Jimenez was quiet for a while. When he started up again he sounded wheedly.

Tony relaxed. Fine. They were into the flattery phase.

"Tony," came the guy's insinuating voice, "I have a suggestion to sweeten the pot for Kelly."

Right. That pot needed sweetening like his Nonna Lucia's cannoli. "What is it?"

"We've talked in the past about Kelly hosting an hour-long prime-time special. Now's the perfect time. It'll launch her formally into the anchor job, bring in some nice publicity." He paused and Tony cocked his ear. Jimenez wanted something more. No, *Kelly* wanted something more and Jimenez was her mouthpiece. "We could offer it to Sunshine's sister stations."

So *that* was it. Kelly wanted prime-time exposure in the six other cities where Sunshine Broadcasting owned stations. So the minx had national ambitions.

Tony quashed his mild annoyance. Well, airtime was the name of the game—they all knew that. And it wasn't really such a bad idea. Especially since it wouldn't cost him anything.

"Maybe we could do something playing off that school gunman shootout," Jimenez suggested. "You know, how dangerous it is for kids these days, something like that."

Tony arched his brows, jotting "Kids in Danger" on his legal pad. Not a bad idea from old Rico. He could imagine the opening now, Kelly in that leather jacket of hers doing a stand-up by a wall loaded with graffiti.

"I'll think about it," he told him.

Languorously Kelly raised her left arm in the air, lilac-scented bath bubbles slithering down her skin like sea foam retreating on smooth white sand. This was another good thing about anchoring prime time: she could take baths in Miles's Jacuzzi during the day. She cocked her head to better admire her arm's slimness and ponder her agent's plea.

"No, Rico," she declared finally into her cell phone. "For the last time, no! That's a lowball offer from Tony and you must think I have shit for brains to take it."

"Kelly, it's seventy-five percent more than you're making now."

"That's because I'm making diddly now." She settled deeper into the hot water, her wet skin squeaking against the porcelain, observing how her breasts still jutted straight out even though she was lying almost flat. That was the beauty of implants for you.

"I tell you, we're not gonna get more than this!" Rico bellowed.

Now he was p.o.'ed. Kelly rolled her eyes. *She* was the one who should be p.o.'ed. She had an agent who didn't know jackshit about negotiating.

"I'm telling you, Kelly," Rico went on, "don't fuck this up by getting greedy! Sure, I'd like more, too, but that'll come when you've got a track record. Do you know how amazing it is that you're even *getting* this offer?"

Amazing to *him*, maybe. Not to her. She snorted and stared out the massive window of Miles's Japanese-style bathroom. The bottom of the window was level with the top of the Jacuzzi tub, and on the other side of the window, level with the black-bottomed lap pool. Beyond that was sand, then ocean. She let rip another snort. All these men—Miles, Scoppio, now Rico—they shoveled so much shit.

"Listen, Rico," she snarled, "don't give me a line about a track record. Scoppio's trading in somebody with a hundred years of track record for *me*, so don't try to tell me it matters. I ain't buyin'."

He shut up for a while. "One more thing," he said finally.

She slapped her open hand down on the water. "What now?"

"Scoppio says, and it's true, you gotta be more careful

about what you say on air. It *matters*, Kelly. You're playing at a higher level now. You—"

She cut him off. "I know, I know, I know! Just make Scoppio pay!" She pulled the cell phone away from her ear and stared at it a second before putting it back. "And that's final!" She slapped the cell phone shut with a satisfying smack.

It was *pathetic*. She tossed the phone on the slate floor, where it skittered a few feet, then slid to a stop by the ficus. What did Natalie make, like seven hundred fifty grand a year? And they wanted her to take *one thirty*?

Forget it. She rose abruptly and stepped out of the tub, wrapping a thick black towel around her body and reaching for the cigarettes she'd left by the sink. She'd just bide her time and watch the ratings rise. And when they did, Tony would jump all over himself to sweeten the deal. *She* knew that, even if the agent she paid fifteen percent of her gross was too goddamn stupid to.

Across town, Natalie shifted uncomfortably on News Van 10's cracked blue Naugahyde passenger seat, blazing hot from the late-afternoon sun. For two hours she'd waited for the mayor to get his behind back to City Hall so she could grab a sound bite for her package about his Safe Streets campaign. Now her sweaty legs stuck to the Naugahyde and she had a serious need to pee and her script was going nowhere fast. And she had only one person to thank for sticking her back in the hellhole of reporting.

Not true, she reminded herself. *I have* myself *to thank, because I could quit. If I were a quitter. If I were willing to let Scoppio win.*

"I saw the mayor's limo." Her cameraman Julio appeared at her window. "I'm pretty sure he was inside."

"I'll bet he was. Let's make another run by his office." She grabbed her cell phone to check in with the Desk. Julio took a swig from what by now had to be a lukewarm Diet Coke.

A female intern answered. "Assignment Desk."

"Natalie Daniels. Any new Safe Streets stuff on the wires?"

"A few new quotes. A pissed-off Watts resident, a cop from the gang unit—"

Nothing earth-shattering. She cut the intern off. "Fine. The mayor's back, so we'll go nab him."

"You heard about the aftershock?"

"What aftershock?"

"A three point five. Not that big but people called in. So Tony bumped you to the second block."

Natalie clutched the cell phone. *Again*?

"And you've got a minute forty-five," the intern reported blithely.

"A minute forty-five? Last I heard I had two fifteen!"

"You haven't had two fifteen since the three-thirty." The midafternoon rundown meeting for *The KXLA Primetime News*. "Wait, I gotta put you on hold."

Natalie clenched her jaw. She used to get an hour of airtime a night and now she was down to one minute forty-five seconds. And even *that* was a battle. The last three days were reminding her just how frustrating TV reporting could be: your story got bumped, or cut, and you ran around town often not knowing till the eleventh hour what piece you would actually file.

Or if you would make air at all.

The intern came back, sounding seriously uncomfortable. "Uh, bad news. Your story's been cut again."

Silence. Natalie had a very bad feeling. "If it's been cut again," she said slowly, "that probably means it's become a v/o."

The intern hesitated. "It *has* become a v/o."

A voice-over, video over which the anchor would read. Over which *Kelly* would read.

This has Tony Scoppio written all over it. Natalie hung up on the intern and turned to Julio. He was still standing outside the van. "We're going back," she told him.

His eyes flew open. "What?"

"We're going back. Pronto." *As Tony would say*, she added silently. *We're having it out. He's not dodging me today, too.*

For a fat man Scoppio was surprisingly nimble. Not once since she'd been back from Monaco and off the anchor desk had she been able to catch him alone. But by God, this afternoon she would.

Julio sped the van back to the station without her saying another word. She hopped out before he could park and raced inside through the loading dock.

Not in his office.

Not at the Assignment Desk.

Not in the lunchroom, or editing, or Satellite Operations.

Where the hell was he?

Then inspiration struck.

Tony Scoppio was just wiping his hands on a towel when she burst into the men's room.

I wish I had a camera to record the look on his face, she thought with satisfaction. *For once* he's *on the receiving end of a shock.*

She let the door slam shut behind her. "You having a good time watching me run ragged through the streets of Los Angeles?"

He smiled. He looked so damn arrogant. "Beats professional bowling."

"All week you've been sending me on wild-goose chases."

"Hey, reporters get reassigned all the time." His voice was casual. "It's the crush of events. You've just been off the streets so long you've forgotten."

Maybe you've gotten a little soft from all those years behind the anchor desk.

"You're trying to tell me this is just happenstance?" She advanced a step and set her hands on her hips, her stance aggressive. "I don't see any other reporter getting chopped every night of the week."

"That's because you're not aware of anybody but yourself." He tossed his towel and turned away from her to face the mirror, smoothing back what hair he still had. "Look at it this way, Daniels. It'll do you good. Remind you how people work in the real world."

Then Howard walked inside the men's room. His eyes behind his tortoiseshell frames went wide when he saw her.

"Out, Bjorkman," she ordered. He backed through

the door and she slammed it shut behind him, whirling again to face Tony. "What is this 'real world' crap? What I asked you is what other reporter hasn't made air this week? You tell me!"

His jaw set. She took grim pleasure in finally making him mad. "I don't have to tell you a damn thing." He pushed past her.

"You are just reveling in your power over me, aren't you?" She spoke to his back, so angry herself she could barely speak. "Even after all the publicity I got for this station in Monaco. Even—"

"Give me a break." He drew out each word. "You don't give a good goddamn about the so-called 'publicity you got this station.' " He turned and raised his hands to write big quotation marks in the air, his voice mocking. "You're just pissed off that now you've got to do some real work."

She was flabbergasted. "You don't think anchoring's real work? Who's kidding who here? Performing live five nights a week—"

"If that's real work then sign me up."

"I just don't get you." She shook her head. "I honestly don't get what you have against me."

"You wanna know what it is, Daniels? You really wanna know?" He advanced toward her and she retreated with the force of what she saw in his eyes. Contempt. Sheer contempt. "You don't want to get down in the muck. You don't want to get your hands dirty. You want to waltz in here at six in your high heels and your silk suit and work in fucking ease for five hours. Pulling down seven hundred fifty thou a year."

She shook her head. "That is simply not true. I am one of the few anchors who *does* report. I—"

"When you *choose* to. When some story gets you all hot and bothered you get off your pampered butt for an afternoon. I got news for you. That's not how it works. Not in my shop." He turned his back to her and pulled open the door. "Divas, every last one of you," he muttered as he walked out, "whether you're in L.A. or Lone Pine."

* * *

Geoff stood just off the eighteenth green of the Adobe Course at the Arizona Biltmore Hotel, watching Rhett Pemberley prepare to pitch up from about seventy-five yards out. Pemberley took a single practice swing, then hit an easy wedge, though the ball flew over the flag and rolled to a stop a testy twenty feet past the pin.

Clearly annoyed at himself, Pemberley smacked the wedge into the fairway. Then a moment later he bent to repair both the new mark and the divot. *He's basically a good guy,* Geoff thought. *A tad cocksure, but that usually comes with success and wealth.* Both of which Pemberley had in spades as chairman of Sunshine Broadcasting, which owned ten television and radio properties in seven states.

Geoff mopped his forehead with an already damp handkerchief, though he couldn't do much about the sweat trickling down his back beneath his polo shirt and sports jacket. Noon and it was a hundred ten degrees in the shade. That was why in Scottsdale in late July only stalwart locals like Pemberley who'd snagged early morning tee times could be found on the links. Geoff was already looking forward to his shuttle flight back to L.A., though his stomach clenched when he thought of the upcoming weekend. Of course he would see Janet. And of course he would "pop the question" this time.

He mopped his brow again, and this time not from the heat.

Pemberley closed his round with a tap-in second putt, then said his good-byes to his playing partners, clearly a regular foursome.

"Nice par," Geoff told Pemberley as the older man ambled up.

They shook hands. Geoff assessed Pemberley, who as ever looked the picture of affluent good health. Mid-fifties, tanned and fit, his hair white but thick, he looked like a poster boy for "The Good Life," corporate American style.

"Not a bad round." Geoff caught a glimpse of the scorecard: five over. "Care for an early lunch at the hotel?" Pemberley suggested. "Should be tolerably cool on the patio."

"Sounds great."

Pemberley stowed his clubs and the men made their way toward the Biltmore, a set of striking, low-slung buildings designed by a Frank Lloyd Wright disciple. They settled at a well-shaded patio table, waiters scurrying to procure drinks and menus for Mr. Pemberley and His Guest.

"Come here often?" Geoff grinned as two water boys almost collided in their haste.

Pemberley smiled easily. "You could say so. I like the courses, especially Adobe."

"That's saying a lot, given the options. TPC Scottsdale, of course, and isn't Troon North just up the road?"

Pemberley nodded. "Troon is outstanding." He patted his washboard-flat abdomen. "And they let you walk the course so you can actually get some exercise."

"You like the Weiskopf design?" Geoff asked. He didn't golf but could talk the talk, and he wanted Pemberley warmed up. He kept up the links chatter long enough for their steak sandwiches to show up.

"Geoff, I know you're not here on a social call," Pemberley observed as the waiters scuttled off.

"Correct. I'm here to talk about Natalie Daniels."

Pemberley narrowed his eyes. "Shouldn't you be talking to Tony Scoppio about Natalie Daniels?"

"I already have. Which is why I'm here talking to you. Are you aware that he's replaced Natalie at the anchor desk with Kelly Devlin?"

"I am."

Geoff had expected that. Scoppio was too shrewd an operator to make that bold a move without alerting his higher-ups. Especially higher-ups whose pens were hovering over mammoth bonus checks.

Pemberley went on. "And though I'll tell you I'm surprised, I don't interfere in my stations except in exceptional circumstances."

Geoff leaned forward, elbows on the small table that separated them. "That's what I consider this to be, Rhett. This decision takes the cake for ill-advised."

Pemberley shrugged. "Who's to know? I'm not there on the ground."

Geoff launched into his analysis, how Scoppio was gunning for Natalie for age and money reasons, followed by a litany of Natalie's achievements. Pemberley listened but offered little. Geoff persisted though he feared much of the information was neither new nor, to Pemberley's mind, relevant.

The sandwich plates were cleared away. Both men ordered new beers.

"Geoff," Pemberley said finally, "I know you're supporting your client. I admire that, but I can't help you. Scoppio may not cut a dashing figure but he's brought every news department he's ever headed to number one. I see no reason to question his judgment."

Geoff let the cold beer run down his throat. He knew Pemberley fancied himself a small-scale Jack Welch, the famed longtime chairman of General Electric whose hands-off policy made Rhett Pemberley look like a micromanager. Welch gave his division heads the same directive every year, and the same warning: raise profits fifteen percent or lose your job. How they did it was their business. And Geoff couldn't deny that Scoppio produced along the only two dimensions that really counted in TV news: ratings and profitability.

"You run the risk of losing Natalie," Geoff pointed out as he and Pemberley left the shaded restaurant patio for the blast furnace of the parking lot. Heat radiated from the asphalt in blistering waves. Geoff broke into a sweat that within seconds reattached his polo shirt to his skin.

"*Scoppio* runs the risk of losing Natalie," Pemberley retorted. "And apparently that's fine with him."

"Your entire organization is hurt if you lose a talent of Natalie's caliber," Geoff insisted. "You know how much every Sunshine station relies on her reports when a huge story breaks. Remember it was *Natalie* who covered the JFK Jr. plane crash and filed reports for all your stations. *Natalie* who covered the election fiasco and 9/11. Not to mention nailing the exclusive on Hope Dalmont."

Pemberley seemed to weigh that. "Granted," he admitted finally. When they'd arrived at his gleaming white

Mercedes 450 SL, the older man let fly something Geoff hadn't in the least anticipated. "I just heard today that WITW is looking for a new prime-time female."

WITW, Sunshine's station in New York City. Geoff narrowed his eyes against the sun's glare, ignoring the tightness that suddenly gripped his stomach.

"Tell you what," Pemberley went on, halting at the driver's side door, "I'll give Dean Drosher a call." WITW's news director. "I'll recommend that he look at Natalie. Who knows? She might be perfect for him. And Sunshine could keep her in the family, so to speak."

The men shook hands. "I'd very much appreciate whatever you can do," Geoff told Pemberley, then waited while the Mercedes sped off. Head down, he returned slowly to his own car, the sort of nondescript maroon Ford that seemed destined from the assembly line to live life as a rental.

WITW. New York. Thoughtfully Geoff extracted the Ford's key from his trouser pocket and inserted it into the lock. This was certainly unexpected. He'd wanted Pemberley to intercede with *Scoppio*. Geoff settled himself in the saunalike front seat, rolling down the windows and blasting the air conditioner. Minutes ticked by while he waited both for the Ford's interior to move from broiling to bearable and to get used to the idea of Natalie living in New York.

He would be in Los Angeles and Natalie would be in New York.

Geoff dropped the car into reverse and backed slowly out of the parking space, finding himself surprisingly downhearted. He castigated himself for the reaction. This was good news, he told himself. If this job came through, Natalie would actually move up in the TV-news world, to the only media market larger than Los Angeles. He pointed the Ford toward the freeway, making tracks for the airport. Only one thing was clear to him at that moment, though. He was planning to propose to Janet, and Natalie might move to New York. Life was certainly changing, and it wasn't at all clear that it was for the better.

* * *

Kneeling on the floor of her study, surrounded on all sides by untidy piles of paperwork, Natalie paused in her labors just long enough to listen to the grandfather clock chime eleven. After the final note, the lone sound in the big Mediterranean-style house was the breeze riffling the study's lacy white curtains. The brass lamp on the rosewood desk provided the only illumination.

What a sorry way to spend a Friday night. She sighed, closing her tired eyes to massage the lids. Maybe she needed more light. The documents spread all over the worn crimson-and-navy Oriental carpet contained a great deal of fine print. Mortgage-payment coupons. Tax returns. Bank statements. Year-end financial reports from investment houses. Credit card bills. Pension paperwork from AFTRA, the union for television and radio artists. 1099s, W-2s, from all the years of her marriage.

It was like tax season in hell, where documents from twelve years were required in one shot. On a week's notice.

The discovery phase of the divorce had begun, Berta had told her. Natalie winced. Discovery was a euphemism for being forced to lay bare the nuts and bolts of her financial life so Miles's attorney could peruse the whole and cut out his half for his client. All she was discovering was that twelve years of marriage had been reduced to statements to be pored over in the half-light, the joy and passion sucked out like lemonade through a straw, leaving her nothing but the bitter aftertaste.

She moved from the chair to the carpet, kneeling on the thin woven wool to stare down at the numbers. Had they spent *so much* money? Why was there so little left?

She sat back on her haunches. During their marriage she'd left the money stuff to Miles, doing little more than arranging automatic deposit of her KXLA checks into their joint account and signing their joint tax returns. It was easier and, she'd thought, wiser. Miles seemed to know exactly what he was doing. When they'd married she was twenty-eight and he was forty-three. She'd been a KXLA anchor for two years, and though her salary was impressive, it hadn't yet reached the stratospheric heights it would later attain. And though Miles made only a piddling income, from occasionally selling a pilot script that never went anywhere, he certainly seemed to have amassed a fortune from his first sitcom, the one he'd created with his former writing partner Jerry Cohen, the one that won so many awards and stayed on the air for so many years before moving into highly lucrative syndication. When she met Miles, he owned a beautiful house and a fancy car and jet-setted her around. Surely such a man knew how to manage money?

But now, staring at these shockingly small numbers, she had to wonder. Maybe all Miles knew about money was how to spend it.

Why did I stay with him? The question perplexed her now. She knew that she'd loved Miles. Perhaps more to the point, she knew that she'd loved her life with him. And while doubts about her husband occasionally niggled to the surface, she'd ignored them. Because, she now recognized, she hadn't wanted to roil the happy placidity of her life.

Perhaps, too, she'd felt a trifle guilty, as her career and salary skyrocketed and Miles labored on scripts that failed to take off. She winced. He'd never seemed resentful until the day he'd walked out.

Her knees hurt. Natalie hobbled to her feet. God, she was forty years old and felt like an old woman. She arched backward to try to work out the kink in her spine, her mind racing ahead to ponder the imponderable. *What if Miles succeeds in claiming there's no prenup? He'd make off with half what's left. I'd have almost no cushion*, Natalie realized dazedly. *At age forty.*

Berta had told her not to give up on finding a copy of the prenup. She'd subpoenaed Miles's former attorney. He never returned her phone calls but might hop to when he received a legal summons.

Natalie shook her head dubiously. *The guy was a slime then and he's a slime now.* Why hadn't she seen that? You could tell a lot about a man from the company he kept and Natalie had liked only one of Miles's associates. Jerry Cohen, whom Miles had dumped.

She surveyed the heaps of documents. There was so much she didn't understand. So much she didn't want to think about. Being banished to reporterdom. The divorce. Geoff's standoffishness. Her future stretched before her in unrelieved murkiness. *Enough*, she told herself. *Tomorrow's Saturday. I'll deal with it then.*

She felt a rush of relief, then tiptoed among the paperwork piles to turn off the desk lamp and climb the pitch-black stairs to her bedroom. There, soft light glowed in warm welcome from two bedside lamps. Pillows and plump duvet beckoned enticingly. Nothing more was required than giving in to her overwhelming fatigue.

Which she did. Gladly.

CHAPTER TWELVE

Monday, July 29, 9:45 A.M.

"I'm dead serious, Natalie," Geoff said. He observed her from behind his Dewey, Climer desk as she finally, *finally*, cracked a smile. "WITW wants to audition you for the prime-time anchor job. Tomorrow."

"Tomorrow?" The smile faded. "Why so fast?"

"We have to strike while the iron's hot. You won't be ready?"

"Of course I'll be ready. I'll have to call in sick and fly a red-eye but I'll be ready."

He nodded and raised a warning finger. "I'm not making any guarantees. You've got to wow them. And I mean *wow* them."

"I can do that," she replied and set to pacing his office.

Geoff watched her, drawing a relieved breath. For the first time in a long time he'd made her happy. He'd broken through a bit of the awkwardness. And it was clearly because they were talking business. Making this audition possible was no more than any good agent would do but he felt especially gratified. He'd done wrong by her lately. This time he'd done right.

She halted in front of him. "So Rhett Pemberley made the initial call and you followed up?"

Geoff nodded. "Dean Drosher and I spoke, yes."

"And he's as much of a hotshot news director as ever?"

"More than ever. In the May sweep WITW won the noon, six, and eleven."

"So why now?" Natalie narrowed her eyes. "Why is Drosher looking to change anchors if they won the book?"

It was a truism that on-air changes typically occurred in two circumstances: when new management came in and when ratings were in the dumper. Often the two went hand in hand: new management was brought in *because* ratings were in the dumper.

But Geoff knew neither was true in WITW's case. He spoke carefully. "Natalie, it's my belief that the same thing's happening at WITW that's happening at KXLA. The management wants the demographics to skew younger. And Sally O'Day is pushing sixty. She's also pulling down a million and a half a year."

Sally O'Day was a New York institution: she'd been on WITW's anchor desk for decades, thanks to God knew how many lifts and peels and rejuvenations. The woman did a good imitation of forty-five, at least with soft focus and kind lighting. But she was sixty all the same, and management knew it, and viewers knew it, and advertisers knew it.

Natalie grimaced. "Great. So I'm to Sally O'Day what Kelly Devlin is to me. Younger and cheaper."

"That's about it."

She shook her head. "I hate to profit from another older woman getting forced out of her job."

"This is business." He leaned forward, his elbows on his desk. "Do you want to rail against the system or do you want another anchor job?"

"I want both."

"Can't have both."

She sighed. "That's why I don't want to file an age-discrimination suit against KXLA. I guess if I were a nobler woman I would. But what I really want is another anchor job."

"Which you'd never get if you *did* file."

With a pensive look on her face she resumed pacing. "You think the timing would work out with WITW? If

Drosher wanted me he'd be willing to wait till early October, when my KXLA contract runs out? That's still two months away."

"Scoppio might let you go early. That way he'd get out of paying you." He eyed Natalie, still pacing. What was it about her that he liked? She was unstoppable—maybe that was it. Unsentimental when it came to business. He rose and perched on the edge of his desk. "So how's it going with old Tony these days?"

"Oh, since our latest knockdown-dragout, which by the way took place in KXLA's men's room, we're getting along famously." Her voice had an edge. "I steer clear of him—that's why."

Geoff watched as Natalie threw back her head and shut her eyes. For a moment another image flashed into his brain. Natalie above him on her sofa. Naked. Her head thrown back, her eyes closed . . .

He obeyed a compulsion to abandon his desk and approach her. Her eyes grew wary but she didn't draw back. "You're a fabulous anchor, Natalie. And you'll land on your feet."

She stared at him. "At WITW in New York?"

"Why not?" He was close to her now. He could smell her faintly musky perfume, see how smooth her skin was. She was wearing less makeup these days, now that she was in the field and not in the studio. A more natural look. Very becoming.

She said nothing. Their eyes met. "Thanks for paving the way for the audition, Geoff," she said softly.

"Just doing my job." He said it automatically, without thinking, and something in her face hardened.

"Right." She turned away.

Damn. He forced himself back behind the fortress of his desk and made his voice businesslike. "We both know what an opportunity WITW would be for you. I'd be delighted to have you land there."

"I'm sure you would." She returned to his desk and bent to retrieve her briefcase when she stopped and frowned.

He followed her gaze and grimaced. Janet's photo. A

glossy eight-by-ten by a hotshot photographer. He'd given her the shoot as a birthday present.

"The woman you're seeing?" Natalie inquired coolly.

He nodded. Why did the look on her face make him feel guilty?

She grabbed her briefcase. "I'll let you know how it goes in New York." Then she was gone.

The office felt oddly vacant after she left. He slapped his desk, the sound echoing in the silence. *I'm doing the right thing*, he told himself. *WITW would be great for her.*

He slapped his desk a second time, not thinking about WITW at all. *I'm doing the right thing.*

Tony slouched over his Jack Daniel's at Chadney's, the Burbank watering hole favored since time immemorial by NBCers anxious to drown the day's sorrows. He squinted in the semidark at the muumuued, red-lipsticked Bobbi Dominguez, BD, the local NBC news director who this Monday evening personified the type. At that very moment she was pouring back a Long Island Iced Tea. Shit, Tony thought, those things had like seven kinds of liquor in them and they were taller than glasses of Kool-Aid. Either BD had a wooden leg or she could drink the Russian army under the table.

Just another reason to admire her, he thought. He swizzled the ice in his glass. And he liked a woman with hair on her chest, at least in a work context.

He stuffed a handful of popcorn in his mouth. He and BD had a big basket of it between them on the little wooden table. It tasted like those foam things you put in packing boxes, only with tons of salt. He loved it.

"All right, Tony, enough already," BD complained, sucking down the rest of her drink. He watched in amazement as she raised a finger to order another. "So once and for all, what's the scoop with Kelly anchoring and Natalie reporting?"

He pretended to look reluctant to say. That had been his MO all week, in an attempt to get BD really anxious to get "the scoop." Apparently it was working. "BD, I'd rather not get into it," he said. He stifled a grin by swigging the last of his scotch. He was proud of himself. He was a real master.

"Spit it out, Scoppio."

He sighed heavily and occupied himself with ordering another Jack Daniel's so it'd look like he was carefully choosing his words. BD would never guess he'd been crafting this line all week. He sighed again. "All right, BD, but only because it's you. And I have to insist that you keep this to yourself. It's, shall we say, *personal.*"

BD nearly choked on an ice cube. She nodded vigorously. Tony knew BD lived for "personal." She loved "personal" so much she spent half her life looking for it and the other half spreading it around.

That was why he judged her perfect for this little assignment. If there was a queen bee in the TV-news hive, BD was it. She knew everything and got it all right. He sniggered to himself. At least, she *used* to get it all right.

Tony tried to look pained. He leaned across the table confidingly. BD followed suit, her huge muumuued boobs knocking into the popcorn basket. "Let's just say," he whispered, "that Natalie is suffering from"—he paused dramatically—"*nervous exhaustion.* And that she's better off"—he squinted, as though he were trying to come up with exactly the right phrase—"in a less *stressful* position."

BD's black eyes flew open until they looked as big as eight balls. "Are you telling me *Natalie Daniels had a nervous breakdown*?"

He winced. "The doctors say we shouldn't use that phrase."

"The doctors?"

He tried to look mournful. "It's against their advice that I have her on the air at all. But"—he shook his head—"I just can't bring myself not to."

"Does Dean Drosher know about this?" BD blurted. Then her mouth slammed shut.

Tony frowned. "What?"

"No." BD shook her head from side to side like a dog who just got out of a bath. "I shouldn't have said anything."

"Come on, BD. I laid myself open to *you.*"

"I really shouldn't."

"Come *on*, BD."

She rolled her eyes, then leaned forward and whispered, "Well, you know Drosher wants to get rid of Sally O'Day."

Tony put a look on his face that said, *Yes, I know that,* even though this was the first he was hearing of it.

"Well," BD went on, "I hear he's going to audition Natalie."

Tony almost knocked over his drink. "What?"

BD nodded sagely.

Tony was shocked. *Dean Drosher*, that prick news director who had everybody thinking he walked on water? He was thinking of hiring *Princess*? And Princess had called in sick that very day, the two-timing minx. She was probably on a plane right now.

He frowned. This was bad. He did not want her to have another option. This had to stop.

Well, he was staring at just the woman to stop it.

He took some time to craft a plausible line. "I certainly would hate to lose her," he told BD, "but I could only wish Natalie the best if she gets an opportunity in New York. I just hope Dean Drosher doesn't get wind of her . . . difficulties."

Seconds passed while he slugged his scotch and watched BD process that last. He could almost see the wheels turning underneath her mop of dyed black hair. "You will keep all this to yourself," he reiterated at one point, by way of a test.

She nodded obediently but her gaze skittered away.

Bingo. By tomorrow every news director in L.A., not to mention New York, would think Natalie Daniels was one live shot away from a straitjacket.

He grinned furtively. *That* should limit the incoming offers.

Natalie leaned into the mirror in the makeup room at New York station WITW, scanning her heavy studio makeup for flaws. As in every makeup room everywhere the mirror dominated the space, running the length of the room waist-high to ceiling, its perimeter dotted with bulbs. And here, as everywhere, the light the bulbs cast was unforgiving, as it must be to approximate harsh studio conditions. Natalie narrowed her eyes. She did look tired, there was no way around it. Who wouldn't be, after a red-eye? And was that a new line around her mouth? Sure looked like one.

"Miss Daniels." A female intern grasping a clipboard poked her head inside the small room. "You're wanted on set."

"I'll be right there."

The girl retreated and again Natalie stared at her reflection. Her heart was pounding. *How can I be so nervous? I've done this a million times.*

She'd anchored a million times, for sure. But she'd auditioned only once, and that was fourteen years ago, for the prime-time anchor job at KXLA.

Which you got, remember? You're good at this. Relax.

But it was damn hard to relax when she felt like her entire life rested on a single performance. She'd always considered herself a clutch player, but the last months had depleted her confidence. She shook her head vigorously and stared down at her hands, compulsively clutching the narrow shelf that ran beneath the mirror. *This must be what it feels like to be a skater who's one triple axel away from Olympic gold. Or an actor one audition away from a Broadway role.*

If she nailed this audition and got this job, her problems would be solved. At least her professional ones. She'd be resuscitated in an even bigger job than the one she'd lost. She'd be back on the anchor desk. She'd have to move, sure, but what was there to keep her in L.A.?

A vision of Geoff rose in her mind. She banished it. He had no qualms about sending her off; she should have none about going.

Plus she had a strong sense of time running out. Her contract expired in exactly sixty-six days. How many other major-market anchor jobs were likely to open up during that time? And even if they did, how many other news directors would want to audition Natalie Daniels?

I have to get this. I simply have to get this. It could easily be my last chance.

She closed her eyes and counted backward from twenty-one. Lucky twenty-one. It was a relaxation exercise, a trick she played on herself, telling herself that when she opened her eyes she'd be calm and ready.

Three. Two. One. Natalie took a deep breath. *Here goes nothing.* She forced herself out of the makeup room and down the blue-carpeted hall to the studio.

A blond man who had anchor written all over him walked toward her and claimed her hand in a hearty grip. "Pleasure to meet you, Natalie," he boomed. He looked like a star quarterback who'd given up the gridiron for TV. "Jim Fuller. I anchor the morning show," he informed her, "and I'll join you on the audition, if you don't mind." He grinned. Klieg lighting reflected off his brilliant white teeth.

"I'd be delighted," Natalie said, though a warning bell sounded in her brain. Why wasn't the male who anchored prime time, the one she'd be working with, auditioning with her? Wouldn't the management want to see how the two of them looked as a team? Maybe they thought it was too early in the day to bring him in, she told herself. After all, it was only one p.m. He probably didn't come in most days till three for the five o'clock news.

Jim guided her to the set, a monster anchor desk that looked like mission control.

"When does the shuttle launch?" she joked and Jim guffawed. She couldn't tell whether his joviality was false or congenial.

"Which side do you like?" he asked when he recovered.

That's considerate, she thought. Most anchors did have a preference. "The left, if you don't mind."

He waved an arm expansively. "Left it is."

They switched positions and Natalie set herself up. *Fix the height of the chair, plug in the earpiece, dress the mike.* "Might I have a glass of lukewarm water?" she asked. Her mouth felt full of cotton. An intern scurried.

A voice boomed over the studio intercom. "Natalie, this is Dean Drosher."

The news director, whom she was surprised she hadn't met yet. To her, the single most important man in the building. She smiled warmly into the lens on Camera One, knowing he was in the control booth and watching.

"We'll chat afterward," he went on. "This is the drill. You and Jim will do the first and last segments of the morning show. Ignore sports and weather. You've got the script and a rundown?"

She nodded. Everything was arranged in front of her on the anchor desk.

"We'll give you a few minutes to read everything over," Drosher said. "By the way, you don't happen to have a different jacket?"

She tried not to frown. Of course not. Who walked around with more than one jacket? She'd worn red, her best red suit, because news directors loved red on women anchors. And because it warmed up her pale skin. She shook her head no.

Silence.

"Okay," he said eventually. "That'll have to do. By the way, after the last section, we want to do an ad-lib thing where Jim will ask you a few questions so you can talk about yourself. We'll roll tape in, oh, three minutes."

Then she heard the intercom system switch off. He was gone.

Great. Three minutes to read a totally unfamiliar script. And what did Drosher have against red? He was the only news director in the Western Hemisphere who didn't like red.

The reason became clear when the crew illuminated the anchor desk's backdrop. In big red letters—letters that clashed wildly with the color of her jacket—were the station call letters: WITW.

Wonderful. She'd be a huge jarring note in the whole tableau.

"Two minutes," the floor manager announced. The intern returned with a Styrofoam cup of water, which

Natalie eyed warily, recalling that horrendous night of the quake when spilled water had rendered the wires unreadable.

Hastily she bent her head to skim the script, mouthing the phrases. It was lifted from the morning newscast and written in straight NewsSpeak, but still she found it awkward. Normally she edited her script to fit her own speech patterns. No chance to do that here. At least there were no weird place names.

"One minute."

She glanced up and got another shock. The TelePrompTer. At KXLA it was black letters on a white background. Here it was the reverse, white letters on a black background. Yet another unfamiliarity, along with the mission-control anchor desk and the uncomfortable chair and the odd angles at which the crew set the monitors.

Jim wasn't even bothering to review his script, but then again he already had the job. He was fully occupied checking his face in a small handheld mirror. Whoever thought men were less vain than women had never met a male anchor.

"Rolling tape," the floor manager announced.

Her heart took another lurch. She knew what that meant. The audition would be taped; then the tape would be viewed by all the relevant layers of station management as they made their hiring decision.

The intercom system buzzed on. "Ready?" Drosher asked.

Her mind screamed no but her head nodded yes. She mustered her most confident smile. No, she wasn't ready. She hadn't read the whole script and her heart was in her throat and her palms were so moist she was leaving a wet spot on her skirt. But she knew that in this crazy game, when you were called upon to jump, you jumped.

So yes. She was ready.

Kelly stood with her real-estate agent in the foyer of a Bel Air house that was for sale. She tapped her toe on the floor. "What's this?"

"Limestone slab," the agent cooed, bending down to pet it like it was a dog or something.

Kelly arched her brows. "Wasn't there limestone someplace else, too? Lots of limestone in this place."

"In the kitchen, yes," the woman said. She was skinny and mid-forties and looked as if she wanted the commission badly. She was exactly the kind of woman Kelly lived her life not to become. "Also limestone slab on the floor, and limestone counters."

Yeah, yeah, yeah. Kelly mounted the stairs. Enough with the limestone.

The agent yammered to her back. "This is a custom staircase. And we have three bedrooms on the upper level, and two full baths, one of them en suite."

At the top of the stairs the woman darted ahead of her to lead the way. Kelly rolled her eyes. The fake French shit was driving her nuts. And she couldn't stand the way the agent kept trying to guide her around, as if she'd get lost otherwise. The place wasn't *that* big.

The woman corralled her into the master bedroom. "Coved ceilings, as you can see, and sea-grass floor coverings." She pointed up and down like a model from *The Price Is Right*, then ran across the room to throw open what Kelly had learned were French doors. Figured. "And because this is a hillside property, from this level we can walk out to the garden."

The woman traipsed out and Kelly followed. "Oh, it has a pool," Kelly said. She liked pools. Rich people had pools. And not those blue plastic ones, either, like her family had in Fresno. That embarrassing kind that you took out of a box every summer and set up in the backyard and that trashed the lawn by Labor Day.

"This pool has an exercise jet," the agent went on. "And of course, a Jacuzzi."

Of course. Everything was "of course." "Of course" a Sub-Zero. "Of course" a Thermador range. "Of course" a convection oven. Like Kelly knew what any of that was.

"So what do they want for this place?" Kelly asked.

"Seven fifty." The woman leaned in closer. Kelly got

a whiff of stale coffee and plain old bad breath. "But I expect the sellers to exhibit some flexibility."

"What, they're hard up for cash?"

The agent looked shocked. "I wouldn't say that. But they've already purchased a new home and are anxious to close a deal on this property."

"Right." Hard up for cash. Kelly made a loop around the pool, then went back inside and down to the first floor. She walked out the front door to look at the house again from the street.

She just wasn't sure it was fancy enough. English Country, the agent told her, but all she knew was that it said "doing pretty well" and not "raging." After all, she was a prime-time anchor now. Her house should make a statement.

But maybe it was the best statement she could make. As it was, it was kind of a stretch. The rule of thumb somebody told her was that she should spend no more than three times her annual income buying a house. Even though Scoppio seemed stuck on a hundred thirty grand a year, she was pretty sure Rico could get him up to a quarter million. Then *pas de problem.*

"What would be the down payment on this?" she asked the agent, who'd scurried outside to stand next to her on the curb.

The woman's eyes lit up. *Pathetic,* Kelly thought. *She really needs the bucks.*

"Assuming you were able to get it for, say, seven twenty-five"—the woman pulled a calculator out of her purse and punched some buttons—"the standard twenty percent down would be one forty-five. And you should expect an additional ten thousand in closing costs."

Kelly processed that. So all that stood between her and a Bel Air address was a hundred fifty-five grand.

Which she had no doubt she could pry out of Miles. He was just the kind of guy who liked to show how big and important he was by throwing cash around.

"Give me a day or two," she told the agent. "I might make an offer."

* * *

So far, so good. Natalie moved aside script pages L04 and L05 and listened to Jim read page L06, the final story of the final section. They were almost done with the audition's newscast portion and she hadn't made a single flub. Her ability to read PrompTer without stumbling had once again gotten her through.

Jim paused and made a half turn in her direction, signaling the start of the chitchat. She smiled, anticipating a specific question to which she could craft a clever response.

"So, Natalie," he said, "tell me about yourself."

She stared at him. *Thanks, idiot.* But then she smiled instead. "Well, Jim," she began, "I was born and raised in Los Angeles but have always taken whatever chance I had to come here to New York." She inclined her head slightly to include the camera in the conversation, as though it were another person in the room. "I remember years ago when I first visited the Metropolitan Museum—" She went on briefly, relating a funny anecdote from the trip, which she'd taken during spring break her junior year in college.

Jim chuckled and Natalie laughed, giving him a chance to ask another question.

He never did.

Instead the intercom system buzzed on. "Thanks, Natalie." It was Dean Drosher. "An intern will escort you to my office."

That's it? That was nothing by way of an interview, nothing. She'd deliberately kept her first response short because she'd expected several questions, a real conversation. In fact, she had a few questions lined up to ask Jim.

Who had already stood up. "Thanks, Natalie." He shook her hand and walked off.

That's it? She tried to ignore the warning bells that were by now sounding a cacophony in her brain. *Am I just here as a courtesy? Are they not really considering me for this job?*

Because it didn't seem like they were. She unplugged her earpiece from the console and carefully removed the mike, trying to contain the sinking feeling in her gut. Things just didn't add up. Having her audition with the morning guy. Giving her almost no time to prep the script. Truncating her interview segment. Not even bothering to have her meet the news director beforehand.

"Right this way, Miss Daniels." The same intern who'd summoned Natalie from the makeup room now stood by the anchor desk to lead her away.

Natalie smoothed her skirt and jacket and followed the girl through a maze of hallways. *Don't worry about it,* she told herself. *The audition went fine. Focus now on charming the hell out of Dean Drosher.*

Because she'd learned long ago that getting hired for on-air jobs was like getting asked out on dates. Similar dynamics were at play. It was usually a male who did the deciding. The judgments were subjective, when it came right down to it, made on a gut level. If he liked you, you were in. If he didn't like you, you had to cut your losses and move on.

They arrived at the news director's office. Natalie held out her hand and flashed Dean Drosher her most brilliant smile, the one that had worked wonders on the two news directors in her past who'd hired her for anchor jobs, in Sacramento and Los Angeles.

And that had worked such magic on Miles. He'd proposed in two months. Of course she'd been younger then. By a lot.

She assessed her smile's effect on Dean Drosher.

Nothing.

Then the real shocker. He glanced at his watch, furtively, as if he didn't want her to notice.

He's already bored and we haven't even started? The date equivalent was requesting the check right after the appetizer.

"Sit down, Natalie." He motioned her toward a brown Naugahyde couch that hunched beneath the lone window. His office looked like every other news director's office. Stacks of videotapes and periodicals. Numerous awards, of the plaque and statuette variety. Mementoes from cities past, where he'd earned his journalistic stripes. Rochester and Pittsburgh, in Dean Drosher's case.

The man himself looked preppy and intense. He was small and wiry, with a receding hairline and round tortoiseshell glasses. Natalie knew him to be in his early thirties, a TV-news wunderkind. She knew Tony Scoppio resented the hell out of him.

And he's almost a decade younger than me. What a switch. The other two news directors for whom she'd auditioned in the past had been old enough to be her father.

"I enjoyed your work from Monaco," he said. "Very impressive."

"Thank you. I—"

"I'm surprised KXLA is willing to let you go."

He was giving her a funny look but she'd anticipated the question. "Dean, there's only one way I can explain it. It basically stems from a personality conflict with Tony Scoppio. This is the first time—"

He cut her off again. "I don't want to hear about you and Scoppio. Tell me about the stories on your reel."

For a beat, she was silent. *I didn't think I'd ever find a news director who's more abrupt than Scoppio.* But then she began to talk about the stories and she and Drosher had a real give and take. There was no question he was engaged. And the packages on her reel were good—she knew it. The story about the Korean shopkeeper who'd lost everything in the L.A. riots, for which she'd won both an Emmy and a Golden Mike. The piece from Kobe, in the aftermath of the quake, in which a local boy walked her down a street on which every single house had been destroyed and every single family had lost a loved one. And of course, a segment from the Hope Dalmont interview, hastily edited on to the reel before Geoff had FedExed it to Dean Drosher.

When she stopped speaking, she noticed Drosher was eyeing her carefully. Steadily she returned his stare, keeping a light in her eyes and a smile on her lips. But she was stunned when totally out of left field he asked her a question she'd never before in her life heard from a news director.

"Is there any reason you might not be psychologically equipped to handle the day-to-day stress of an anchor position?"

Before she could respond his intercom buzzed. "The two o'clock's here," a female voice said.

His hand snapped out. "Thanks for coming out, Natalie."

What in the world kind of question was that? And who in hell is "the two o'clock"? They'd barely talked for fifteen minutes and their conversation had ended on the oddest of odd notes. Nor had he said word one about the actual job, though both of them knew exactly what it entailed. Prime-time anchor jobs were prime-time anchor jobs, the same everywhere.

He rose and stood by his door. This time he looked at his watch with no attempt to hide the gesture. He might as well have said, "Shoo," he was so clearly anxious for her to leave.

Slowly she rose as well, reluctant to leave. But he was standing by his door, looking damned impatient. "Thank you, Dean," she said and again shook his hand. She held on to it. "Please know there is nothing that would limit my ability to perform this role. If there is any other tape I might show you or references—"

"We don't need to see anything more." He pulled his hand away and nodded, not meeting her eyes. The same intern appeared to spirit her away.

It was over. She'd been dismissed. She emerged into the bright Manhattan sunshine, the July afternoon glorious and hot. On the wide sidewalk pedestrians jostled past: businesspeople, matrons, joggers with dogs on leash—all apparently with somewhere to go and something to do.

In a daze she forced herself to move purposefully in the direction of the Met. She'd walk there, even if it took forever, even if she sweated like a pig, even if her feet killed by the time she arrived.

Who cared, anyway? She had nothing better to do.

Geoff watched Janet. She was laughing, her head thrown back, her long blond hair whipped by the wind as the forty-four-foot *Island Lady* cut through the waves on its way from Long Beach to Catalina Island. He'd hired the oceangoing sloop and a man to sail it so that he could be on the water with Janet but not have to focus on the boating. Geoff loved the sea. He'd made most of his big-life decisions on the water, like the Sunday morning when he was twenty-one and surfing off Bell's Beach and finally decided that, yes, he would leave Sydney for Los Angeles. So this was the right place to be this afternoon.

He'd left work much earlier than usual and asked Janet to meet him at his house. Now, hours later, he gazed at her, in her white shorts and white sleeveless tee. She looked exquisite, he thought, as if she should live on the water. *And she's such a classic, she'll always be beautiful. And warm and giving and good with children and dogs.*

He glanced away from the woman he was planning to make his wife and stared into the distance, the salty sea air making his eyes water. Ahead of him Catalina Island rose hulking from the sea, verdant and green. It was a spectacular day. A regatta was sailing out of the harbor, colorful spinnakers slapping gaily in the wind. His heart was pounding, which amazed him. Janet was so perfect and still he was nervous.

Perhaps it shouldn't surprise him. Men must always be nervous before they propose, he reasoned. Nervous because she might say no. Nervous because she might say yes. And he, especially, should be nervous, because he had never been anxious to climb aboard the commitment bandwagon. Already he'd put it off for longer than most men. And once he married, that would be it. Done. No turning back.

He really should do it now. He wiped his palms on his shorts. They'd already been out on the water for three hours and he hadn't done it yet. They were almost to Catalina. He hadn't done it yet.

He checked his pocket again, just to be sure. Yes, the little black velvet box was there. Waiting. He took a deep breath.

All right.

Ready.

Carefully he moved into the center of the boat and got down on one knee on the floorboards in front of Janet. She looked down at him, laughing still, and riffled his hair. Then, almost imperceptibly, her face changed. He couldn't put a finger on quite how. A slight tilt of the head, maybe, a stillness in her demeanor. What must be in my face? he wondered. He had no idea. But she sees something there. *Of course she does. She knows me so well.*

Their gazes locked. "Janet." He stopped. His heart was pounding. It must be from happiness, he thought. This must be how all men feel. "Janet," he repeated, "will you be my wife?"

Her face was still for a moment more, and then it contorted into an expression of such unbounded joy he was instantly relieved. *It must be right. Look how happy she is.* She catapulted into his body and threw her arms around his neck and he felt her tears against his skin. "Oh, yes, Geoff, yes, yes," she was saying, and then a strong wave hit and they toppled backward onto the deck, the man who was sailing the boat letting out a big uproarious whoop. It was a glorious moment, what with her happy tears, and then his, he was surprised to see, the sort of moment you believe you will remember all your life, just like people tell you it will be.

Natalie sat at a tiny table in the lobby bar of the New York Hilton, a mammoth tower on the Avenue of the Americas that played temporary home to thousands of guests a night. They broke down into two categories, she decided, assessing her fellow travelers from behind a glass of chardonnay. Businesspeople who ranked too low on the corporate totem pole to pull off a stay at a ritzier hotel. And tourists using discount awards to be able to afford a Midtown room. *Which category am I in?* she wondered. A businessperson whose sponsor, in this case WITW, wanted to spend the least possible money and still get a passable hotel room?

She glanced down at the paperback she was keeping open, though it was serving more as a prop than as reading material. It kept some of those traveling businessmen at bay, though not all. A few bold souls made lame pickup attempts, unfazed by her wall of uninterest. Not to mention by their own wedding rings. Or by the telltale untanned skin on their ring fingers where their wedding rings normally were located and would no doubt be reinstated by their return home.

She sighed. It was very difficult, as a soon-to-be divorcée and even more recent rejectee, to sit in a hotel bar fending off married men not to be damned cynical about love and marriage.

And not to feel conspicuous. By now, a little after seven p.m., the pancake makeup she'd applied for the audition had gotten seriously cakey. And her red suit, which had fallen far from its previous perch as her favorite outfit, felt garish and overdone.

She downed her chardonnay and raised a finger to request the check. She knew that a better woman would use this rare evening in Manhattan to dine in a fabulous restaurant, perhaps go to the theater. In fact, she'd booked the night for just that purpose, figuring why not call in sick to KXLA the extra day. But in the end she would do nothing more elaborate than repair to her room for a shower, room service, and a movie on the in-house system. She was too exhausted and disillusioned to attempt a grander plan.

She signed the bill, grabbed her purse and paperback, and stood up. A man across the bar, staring away from her toward the lobby, caught her eye. Tall, commanding, thick mane of silver-gray hair. Vaguely familiar. She squinted. It was Ben Stilwell, one of the most prominent TV-news agents in the business. A powerhouse. Natalie would have signed with him if Dewey, Climer hadn't won her over. She smiled. What a happy coincidence. She hadn't seen Ben in years. She'd go say hello.

She halted a few feet away when a drop-dead blonde got to him first. Truly drop-dead, not to mention gorgeously turned out in a stunning teal suit. Natalie stopped and stared. Around her, heads swiveled, businessmen on the prowl newly attentive, though this creature was clearly out of their league. But the blonde—twenty-five if she was a day—was oblivious to everyone but Ben Stilwell. And to judge from the look on her face, absolutely delighted with what he had to say.

Natalie sidled closer. Though she was at Ben's back, she could make out his words. "—bowled them over. Absolutely bowled them over. Drosher wouldn't give me a number but I assure you, Tina, we'll have an offer in writing by the end of the week."

The blonde's eyes filled with tears. She just held on to Ben's arms, helplessly. Natalie watched her, unable to move. She was still trying to process the words. And grasp that they had been spoken to someone other than her.

Time moved in slow motion. She stared at the blonde. How happy she was. How thrilled. How young. She could barely hold it in, Natalie could tell. She was so happy she was shaking. *What a triumph for her,* Natalie thought, mesmerized. *What a day she's having, a day she'll always remember. It's how I felt when I got hired at KXLA.*

But that had been years before. That wouldn't happen again. Not here. Not now. Maybe not ever. *Maybe you've been at this too long.*

Someone jostled Natalie's elbow, snapping her to attention. She maneuvered past the duo, of course not saying hello. It was a private moment, a moment of benediction, though not for her. She walked across the lobby, crowded with travelers and bellboys, and made the mistake of entering an elevator crammed with Japanese tourists in search of a tempura bar and a Midwestern family who couldn't remember which floor they were on.

Finally she alighted on eighteen and made the right turn down the hall, halting outside number 1842. Her key card worked. She was home, such as it was. She was blessedly alone.

She sat on the bed and kicked off her pumps. The room smelled of Lysol and cigarette smoke. It was silent save for the muted roar of traffic eighteen floors below and a game show playing on the TV next door. The only indication that it was her room at all were the cosmetics on the nightstand.

The cosmetics she'd used that morning when she still believed she had a chance at an anchor job in New York. When she still believed she had a chance at an anchor job at all. Now that illusion was shot. She was two months away from her contract expiring and as far from an anchor job as if she had never stood in front of a broadcast camera in her life.

AUGUST

CHAPTER THIRTEEN

Saturday, August 3, 9:24 P.M.

Kelly was damn irritated and who wouldn't be? Here she was on a Saturday night, in this chichi Santa Monica restaurant that Miles had taken over for his sitcom's launch party, and he wasn't paying a damn bit of attention to her! Who did he think she was, his *wife*? Sure, there were all these starlets around, but she wasn't going to put out more than a slap in the face later unless he shaped up but quick.

Or unless he gave her what she wanted. And wrote the check tonight.

One of the waiters cruised by with a tray and she snatched an oyster in cucumber sauce. Chinois on Main, the restaurant was called, one of those Eurasian places, but here the food was actually good. The place was small and all done up in pastels, with exotic Chinese shit on the walls. The studio must have paid a pretty penny to take it entirely over on a Saturday night. But Miles probably whined to high heaven until they gave in. That would be classic Miles. Living large, on somebody else's dime.

One of the starlets sidled up wearing a slinky white dress that was even shorter than Kelly's sequined blue one. Suzy, her name was, the blond bimbo star of *Forget Maui.* Kelly barely knew her but already hated her.

Suzy cocked her head at Miles, who was standing with some groupies across the restaurant. "So you're seeing Miles now?"

Kelly just smiled. She knew it gave her status big-time to be dating the executive producer. He was *the* big dog.

"Miles and I saw each other for a while," Suzy said. "So what do you do?"

Like she didn't know. "I anchor *The KXLA Prime-time News,*" Kelly informed her.

"Oh." Suzy looked bored, then sauntered off.

Bitch. Like the only thing that counted was acting! And those implants of hers were huge. They were really fake-looking.

A motion across the restaurant caught Kelly's eye. Great. Miles was taking over the center of the room, as if he was going to make a speech. And he was looking all slick and proud of himself.

Jeez, it was just a sitcom going on the air! These people acted as if they were sending a man to Mars.

Miles stood there awhile and eventually people quieted down. Were they sucking up or what? It amazed her. Then they started applauding and he took a few bows. Kelly rolled her eyes and snagged a glass of champagne.

"People," he said, holding out his hands as if he were a preacher, "we're here tonight to celebrate the launch of *Forget Maui.*"

Everyone started applauding again, wildly this time. Some of the guys whooped, including a cute young one with curly black hair and a go-to-hell ass. Someone had told Kelly he was one of the writers. She waited till he looked at her; then she winked at him. His big dark eyes shot open as if he was shocked, but then he smiled back.

Oh, yeah, he smiled back. Kelly forced her gaze back to Miles, but she could feel the young guy watching. She arched her back so that her spaghetti strap dropped from her shoulder; then she left it down. She could almost feel the guy's heat from across the restaurant.

Miles was talking again. "We're finally getting our due. Heartbeat Studios, and NBC, recognize what a gem they have in *Forget Maui*—"

Loads of people cheered at that. Jesus Christ.

"—and I'm here to tell you they're right! I guarantee

you"—Miles opened his arms wide—"we'll be gathered here again celebrating our Emmy for best comedy series!"

Everybody cheered again. At least the booze was flowing at this shindig. Kelly threw back some more champagne. She'd given herself a night off her diet regimen just to get through.

She tried to get next to the cute guy, but now that she didn't want Miles's attention, she had it. He was like a fly on paper the rest of the goddamn night.

Finally, after what seemed like an eternity, it was over. They sped to Malibu in Miles's Porsche, him talking the whole way about how great he was.

But if he's so proud of himself, Kelly realized, *this is the perfect time to go for it.*

He parked the Porsche in the driveway, but before he could get out, Kelly laid her hand on his thigh. "Baby," she purred.

He looked at her, then grinned. "You're hot, aren't you?" He put his finger on her lower lip, then stared at her mouth. "I could really feel it tonight."

What an idiot, she thought. *He thinks I'm hot for* him, *not the writer who's half his age.*

But of course she couldn't tell him that. She sucked on his finger until she had him totally mesmerized. "Oh, I'm hot, Miles," she whispered. "But I need something from you."

His voice was husky. "What do you need?"

"I need some cash to buy that house I told you about." She paused. "A hundred fifty grand for the down payment." She could get the other five thousand from maxing out her credit cards. And then Kelly Devlin, L.A. Anchorwoman, would have a Bel Air address.

"Whoa." He pulled back, his eyes wide with shock. "That's a big number."

"You don't have it?"

"Of course I have it. I'm just saying, that's a big number."

She let her gaze drop to his lap. "Everything about you is big, Miles."

He laughed. "You're right about that, sweetcakes." Then he stared out the front window and got all serious again.

She waited. He'd cave. No way he'd bypass a chance to show what a big man he was.

"I suppose I could do a loan," he said eventually. "What the hell?" He laughed. "I'll draft something for you to sign."

"Great." Whatever. So long as she got the bucks. Eventually Scoppio would cave, too, and hike her offer and then she'd have no problem paying Miles back.

She smiled at Miles. Now she did owe him a treat. Maybe she could close her eyes and pretend he was the young guy with the drop-dead ass. She met his eyes. "Let's go fuck on the beach," she suggested.

For that, Miles needed no convincing.

Not what you like to see first thing Monday morning.

Tony stood in front of his desk, briefcase still in hand, staring down at the ratings from Friday night that Maxine had put in his IN box. *The KXLA Primetime News*, 4.6. *The KYYR News at 10*, 5.0.

Harrumph.

Three nights in a row that he'd fallen back below a 5 rating. Three nights that KYYR had kicked his butt. But how in hell could that happen with a hot number like Kelly Devlin at the anchor desk?

He shrugged out of his sport coat and tossed it on the plaid couch on the far side of his office, its sagging cushions half hidden by stacks of yellowing *Los Angeles Times*. Then he unpacked his briefcase, varying his morning routine by immediately tearing into the new bag of chocolate bars Anna-Maria had given him.

"Maxine!" he bellowed out his door. "Coffee!" He paused, considering. "And get Bjorkman in here!"

Maxine had just deposited his coffee on his desk when Howard showed up, stinking to high heaven of that cologne shit he doused himself with every morning. " 'Morning, Tony." Howard threw himself on a chair. "How'd your son's wrestling match go over the weekend?"

"Don't ask." Tony rolled his eyes. It was one of God's cruel jokes that all the Scoppio men were built as wide as they were short, and the only athletic field on which they could hope to compete was the wrestling mat. But even that was failing his kid now. It'd been no fun sitting with Anna-Maria in that high school gym watching their son get pinned so often and so hard. "Snickers?" He held up the bag.

Bjorkman looked startled. "No, thanks."

Tony shrugged. Fine. More for him. He tore off the wrapping and took a chomp, then threw the overnights in Howard's direction. "What gives with the ratings?"

Bjorkman studied the numbers. He might be a putz but he was good at this, Tony knew. He remembered every story in every segment, which was useful for analyzing the ratings by quarter hour.

Finally Howard looked up. "Well, we held our own for the first half hour, then plummeted at ten-thirty."

"I got that, Bjorkman. What piece finished right before we dropped?"

"Natalie's spot on DMV corruption. I thought it was good," Howard added.

Tony was silent. He'd thought it was good, too. Since he'd lit a fire under her pampered behind, Princess was shaping up to be a good reporter. All of a sudden she was doing research on the Web. Staking people out. And she did that shit where she asked the bad guy the tough question and prearranged it so the cameraman would shoot that part real close-up so you could see the guy sweat. It made Tony look good, too, 'cause it made his newscast look like *60 Minutes*.

But he didn't like it that viewers switched away right after she got off the air.

He had an explanation, though. "This is the summer doldrums," he told Bjorkman. Ratings always dropped in July and August. People watched less TV because of repeats and because they were outside enjoying the weather.

Howard nodded, then laughed. "But why are we in the summer doldrums more than KYYR? It's the same season across the street."

That wasn't funny. Then, just to add to the nonhilarity, Ruth popped her head in. She was dolled up in a bright pink suit with enough gold buttons to start another rush. She cocked her head at the Nielsen overnights. "Having a pity party and didn't invite me?" She came in and plopped next to Howard, pointing at Tony's Snickers bag. "Didn't Mommy teach you to share?"

Grudgingly he tossed her a bar.

"We were just discussing the ratings," Howard offered. Tony could've throttled him. He knew what Ruthie would think about *those.*

"I hope neither of you is surprised. This is what you get when you put a twit on the anchor desk." She focused her beady blue eyes on Tony. "You can't fool viewers forever. They're too smart."

He just stared at her. Ruth Sperry was damn annoying. But he couldn't fire her because she was one of the few people he had who knew what she was doing.

"Speaking of twits," she went on, "has Kelly signed her contract yet?"

Bjorkman's eyes flew open. "You made Kelly a *formal offer* for the anchor job?"

Damn both of them. And damn Kelly, too, for trying to bully him into coughing up bigger bucks. She *was* a twit if she thought she'd get them, especially now with the ratings dropping like shit down a sinkhole.

"Outta here, both of you," he ordered.

"Oh, did I hit a sore spot, Tony?" Ruth laughed. "Don't you want her to sign before Rhett Pemberley visits in a few weeks? So you can formally introduce him to your new prime-time anchor?"

By now he could've punched Ruth, except that she was a woman. Instead he stood up. "Out." He herded both of them out of his office, then hollered at Maxine to call Willa from Promotions, pronto. He needed billboards—that was what he needed. *Now* he'd launch the ad campaign, with Kelly front and center, so it'd be in place before that pecker Pemberley rode into town on his white horse.

Across the newsroom a bunch of staffers were standing at the notice board reading the overnights, which every morning Maxine posted for everybody to see. Tony walked right into the group and tore down the sheet. He'd keep the ratings to himself for a while.

"Of course, all of this is an exercise in futility," Berta Powers declared. Natalie sat in Dewey, Climer's sun-filled penthouse conference room and watched her attorney produce a confident smile. That afternoon, in honor of the so-called discovery meeting with Miles and his attorney, Berta's dark frizzy hair was contained in a bun and she wore her signature red: red suit, red pumps, red lipstick. She wore red for legal battles like Tiger Woods wore red for tournament Sundays. "It will all become moot"—Berta kept smiling—"when the prenup surfaces."

Either she's the best actress in the world, Natalie thought, *or she truly expects the thing will pop up again, like Lazarus from the dead. By this point its reappearance* would *be miraculous.*

"Counsel, I advise you not to hold your breath." Miles's attorney, Johnny Bangs, smiled, too, the sort of smile a boa constrictor might sport if it had a human face. "You might as well wait for the *Titanic* to resurface."

Berta chuckled. Natalie glanced around the sleek glass-topped table. Except for her, everyone was smiling, even Miles, even the male accountant whose name she couldn't remember. All of them sporting big, fake, we're-going-to-win smiles, while she had all she could do not to stand up and throw a punch at Miles's lying, thieving, cheating face. It was painful even to be in the same room with him.

Berta noisily slapped a folder on the conference table. "The next order of business is the payment from Heartbeat Studios to Mr. Lambert for executive producing *Forget Maui.* In the amount of three million dollars."

"Not relevant." Johnny Bangs smiled again.

"Of course it's relevant. You know as well as I do that since Ms. Daniels and Mr. Lambert are not legally separated, his earnings are marital property."

"It is not relevant because my client will not receive

the three million dollars during the marriage," Johnny Bangs replied smoothly.

Berta flashed the *Hollywood Insider* that contained the item on Miles's *Forget Maui* deal. "It is a matter of public record that Heartbeat will pay your client three million dollars for executive producing the program this upcoming season."

Johnny Bangs grinned lazily. "You believe everything you read in the trades, Ms. Powers?"

"Your point?"

"My *point* is that Mr. Lambert has an unorthodox deal with the studio. He is so confident that *Forget Maui* will succeed, and be renewed next season, that he has deferred compensation until this time next year. At which time he will receive the fee *plus* a renewal bonus."

So he makes even more than the three million, when the divorce will be final and the takings entirely his. Natalie glanced at Berta and was disconcerted to see that her attorney looked stunned. Miles, on the other hand, just looked smug.

"I never heard of such an arrangement," Berta said.

Bangs shrugged. "As I said, it's unorthodox. It's also a tribute to my client's justifiable confidence in his script writing."

Berta tapped a fingernail on the glass table. "I expect written documentation of that studio deal, Johnny. And be aware that this payment-delay tactic of yours will not magically erase the three million dollars from the marital property. Your client never obtained a legal separation, hence any money he earns, or is contracted for, while legally married, still counts."

Bangs scoffed. "That's highly disputable."

"I would dearly love to argue the point before a judge." Berta's voice then took on the quietly threatening quality mastered by the most fearsome nuns and schoolmarms. "And unless you are forthcoming on this, I will subpoena Heartbeat Studios for all paperwork relating to its so-called unorthodox deal with your client."

"Be my guest." Johnny Bangs just smiled again, that same loathsome smile. But Natalie noted with satisfaction that Miles had paled a shade or two beneath his salon-induced tan. *That's how it feels, bucko,* she communicated to him silently across the table. *That's how it feels to have somebody lay claim to half your income. Having fun?*

"Moving on to maintenance for my client," Johnny Bangs said.

Berta snorted. "You must be kidding. It's not enough that Ms. Daniels supported Mr. Lambert for twelve years while he waited in vain for his muse? Who very conveniently showed up shortly before he walked out on his wife?"

"Save it for the judge, Berta." Miles's attorney slapped open a file of his own, extracting a sheet of paper and handing it to Berta. "This is what we require for monthly expenses."

Berta barely glanced at the neat columns of numbers. "This is outrageous."

"It reflects my client's reasonable expenses."

"Only if your client were the Sultan of Brunei. Forget it. We won't give you a dime without a judge's order." She slapped the page dismissively. "And what is this seven thousand dollars for window replacement on Mr. Lambert's house?"

"Ask your client." Natalie refused to recoil when Johnny Bangs turned his predatory gaze on her, though she felt as though she'd encountered a barracuda. "I'm sure she can fill you in."

Natalie met his eyes but held her tongue. Berta had warned her that Johnny Bangs would bait her and instructed her to keep her cool.

"Forget that, too," Berta said.

Johnny Bangs shook his head as if with regret. "We'll get it sooner or later, Berta. Don't make me take it to the wall. Last item." He turned to the accountant. "Do we have a final figure for the value of the marital property?"

The man nodded. "We do," he declared in a portentous tone. Then he produced two slips of paper on each of which was typed a single figure, handing one to

Johnny Bangs and one to Berta Powers. Natalie noted that Berta did not look at hers, but at the team opposite.

Natalie focused her gaze on her husband's face. She knew him well enough to know that he was stunned at what he was seeing. Not only did he pale another few shades, but when he spoke, he stuttered.

"This is *it*?" he said. "*This* can't be right!"

She felt a shiver of satisfaction. *That's what's left after you spent my money on whatever the hell you wanted all those years. That's what's left, Miles.*

Perverse as it was, she couldn't help but take some pleasure in her assets being as reduced as they were, simply because it produced that stupefied expression on her husband's face.

How can you be so surprised? she questioned him mutely, watching as he struggled to compose himself. You *were the one managing the money. Were you so lousy at it that you had no idea how little would be left? Apparently so.*

Johnny Bangs held up a warning finger as Miles opened his mouth to speak again. "Not now," Natalie heard him mutter. Then he looked at Berta, plastering that same detestable smile on his face. "I will of course need to run the numbers myself." Bangs rose from his chair. "We're done here," he announced and ushered Miles out.

Her husband hadn't met her eyes once during the entire meeting, Natalie realized. He was a coward. That should have been obvious to her long ago, but now it came as a realization.

She looked at Berta. "How did it go?"

Her attorney smiled. "Pretty well. We got them squirming."

Natalie went through her usual ritual when she got to the station for her three-to-eleven p.m. shift. She stopped off in the basement mailroom to pick up her latest load of correspondence, then systematically dumped the viewer letters in an overflowing box underneath her desk. So far they were going unanswered because she hadn't yet composed a form letter response. What to say? *Thank you for your concern. Let me be a lesson to you: either be like Tinkerbell and don't grow old, or choose a profession in which you're as valued when you're forty as you are when you're twenty-one.*

One missive stood out: an invitation-size parchment envelope with her address engraved in an elegant font. On the reverse was the return address: *Dewey, Climer, Fipton and Marner.* She studied it. No doubt an invitation to the firm's annual yacht-club picnic, though this stationery was ritzier than usual. She tore it open.

Dewey, Climer, Fipton and Marner
invite you to please join us on
Thursday, August 15
at 6 o'clock in the evening
for a champagne reception
to celebrate the engagement of
Geoff Marner and Janet Roswell
Regrets Only

Natalie stared dumbly at the stiff ivory-colored parchment. *The engagement of Geoff Marner?* It didn't seem possible. She slumped back in her chair, feeling as if she'd been steamrolled on the railroad tracks by the noon express.

Geoff had asked another woman to marry him? So soon after making love with her? Apparently he'd dismissed that interlude as of no importance. He'd moved on, so much so as to get engaged.

Now her back was up. What a coward he was. He hadn't even had the balls to tell her.

Yet he had no obligation to, she realized swiftly. *Do you honestly think he went through his Palm Pilot and methodically called every client? Or every woman he ever slept with? Get real, Natalie.*

She dropped the invitation on her desk blotter yet the words continued to stare up at her defiantly. She couldn't help it: she felt shoved aside. Passed over. She bent forward and hugged herself around the waist. What was it about this Janet woman? Natalie had never met her, though she'd seen that damn photo. Which was enough to tell her that Janet Roswell was beautiful. And young.

Which was apparently what it took to become Geoff Marner's fiancée.

Natalie grabbed the invitation and tore it into smithereens, which took some doing because the parchment was so thick. But she felt no better when she was done. She stared down at the shredded remains, remembering every damn bit of what it said, the date and time, even the champagne reception. And knowing full well that morbid curiosity would not allow her to stay away.

CHAPTER FOURTEEN

Friday, August 9, 7:32 P.M.

Hands on hips, Geoff stared out the floor-to-ceiling windows of his penthouse office. The Century City tower that housed Dewey, Climer and its identical twin were notable landmarks on L.A.'s west side: two glass skyscrapers in opposing triangular shapes jutting into the blue, blue California sky. His view faced north, and at seven-thirty on an August evening the setting sun turned the windows of the twin tower a flaming shade of gold. The sight dazzled, but on this occasion failed to move him.

He rubbed his forehead, where a headache had begun a low-grade throb. Natalie, Natalie, Natalie. What in the world was he going to do with her? Where was he going to place her? Her contract expired in seven weeks and there was no offer in sight.

In truth he wasn't surprised that she'd been rejected by WITW. It'd been a long shot, even with Rhett Pemberley's help. It was a long shot getting *any* anchor job, let alone a prime-time slot in the nation's number one media market. And the woman Dean Drosher did hire, Tina Boone? Well . . . Geoff would sign her as a client in a heartbeat. She had real star potential.

Geoff returned to his desk and punched a few computer keys to pull up notes from that day's conversations with L.A. news directors. At Channel 8 the news director had said his only opening was in the morning and

Natalie was too expensive. In that time slot, much less critical to the bottom line than prime time, the most he could pay was about a seventh of Natalie's KXLA salary. She might take it, Geoff knew, but it was dangerous. Stations liked to try out fresh faces in the morning and on weekends before promoting them to weeknight prime time. Once Channel 8 found a fresh face, and they would, they'd bounce Natalie.

It irked him that most local TV-news management considered a forty-year-old woman too old to move up. A forty-year-old man, no. But the most typical anchor pairing was an older man with a younger woman, the same bias as in Hollywood movies: fifty-year-old male stars with love interests half their age.

He scrolled through the rest of his notes. Nothing at Channel 10: they were the one shop in town whose talent was firmly entrenched. And despite numerous attempts he'd never connected with BD, Bobbi Dominguez, at the NBC-owned station. He was beginning to think she was dodging him, though he couldn't imagine why. Then there was the weird call with Channel 6. Geoff had gotten nowhere. The news director had hemmed and hawed.

What did he have against Natalie? Methodically Geoff shut down his computer files for the night. The usual? Her age? *That* the guy would be loath to spell out.

He simply had to cast his net wider, Geoff decided, though it was a struggle to introduce an "older" woman in a market where she wasn't known. News directors liked youth or familiarity. Nevertheless, he would dig in smaller markets. He'd already gone through the top twenty: nothing. So now on to twenty-one through thirty. Maybe Natalie would like San Diego. Or Portland.

Geoff consulted his watch. 7:50. He should hustle. He had an eight-fifteen reservation to dine with Janet and her mother. To discuss, he still couldn't believe it, *colors*.

Colors? Yes, Janet had told him, in all seriousness, they had to decide not only on colors for the wedding but colors for the house.

Colors? He shook his head. He had an important client in serious professional trouble but was going to spend hours discussing *colors*. An evening during which, he already knew, he'd do a great deal of nodding. And after which he'd pick up the bill.

Colors. Which of his old mates in Sydney would believe that? He rubbed his temples, where his headache was intensifying. Suddenly the lyrics from the old Broadway show tune "If They Could See Me Now" raced across his mind. "That little gang of mine," he sang under his breath, ambling to his tiny fridge for a cold beer. Aussie aspirin.

He twisted off the top and put the bottle to his mouth, letting the beer run down his throat. *I'm eating fancy chow and drinking fancy wine.* He chuckled. He could hardly be expected to give up *all* things Australian.

Natalie sat at her KXLA computer sipping morning coffee and glaring at an item on the *Hollywood Insider*'s Web site.

BOONE INKS WITW DEAL

Tina Boone, morning anchor at Syracuse station WNNC, has signed a low six-figure deal with New York powerhouse WITW to coanchor the 5, 6 and 11 P.M. newscasts. The 25-year-old Boone, only four years in the business, will replace outgoing veteran Sally O'Day, who is ending a phenomenal thirty-year tenure at the Sunshine-owned station. News Director Dean Drosher predicts that Boone will appeal to the all-important 18- to 35-year-old demographic. "We're delighted to bring Tina on board. She'll bring our news department a wonderful mix of youthful enthusiasm and hard-core broadcast experience."

"Hard-core experience." Natalie snorted. Right. Four whole years. Apparently Dean Drosher was nothing more than a young preppy version of Tony Scoppio: he certainly thought along the same convoluted lines. Did these men have a secret club or what? A treehouse somewhere where they traded information on which women were in and which out? *They* could get old and fat and fart their way to kingdom come but the women all had to meet some standard the men came up with.

Natalie rose abruptly. *It hasn't changed from when Evie hit forty-five and couldn't get another TV job after KXLA. Only this time* I'm *Evie.* She began to pace her minuscule office, every inch as familiar as her own home. Probably more so. She knew the origin of every stain on the gray industrial carpet; she could name the mishap that had caused every blemish on the yellow walls. Her hand reached out to touch a jagged hairline crack, a memento of the Northridge quake. She'd anchored nonstop for nineteen hours that January day, winning an Emmy for her efforts.

But these days she was as likely to split the atom as get another anchor job. And Scoppio had made her feel guilty for even wanting one. *You don't want to get down in the muck. You don't want to get your hands dirty. You want to waltz in here at six. . . .*

True. Every word. Natalie returned to her desk and punched a few computer keys. That was what was so goddamn irritating!

And now she had only half an hour to do some research before heading out with Julio for a full day of shooting. She'd mapped out an aggressive program because anything less felt like shirking. No way would she do that with Tony's accusations ringing in her brain.

Her package that night was on environmental problems at a Superfund site outside Los Angeles. She did a quick Web search and was instantly rewarded with forty hits. Information at her fingertips. *That* was easier than eighteen years ago. She began printing pages to read in the van while Julio drove to the first location, then conducted a quick search of the L.A. station Web sites. She'd heard another local station had done a Superfund piece the prior night but didn't know which one.

Nothing. Nothing. Nothing. Only ten minutes left. Nothing.

Damn. Couldn't find it.

Julio poked his head in her office doorway, broadcast camera dangling from his right hand. "Ready?"

"Yup." Too late now. She stuffed a spiral-bound reporter's notebook and an Aquafina bottle into her briefcase, then hoisted its strap onto her shoulder, where it dug into her skin. The other night she'd been surprised to see a welt there. "Let's go. I just have to stop by the printer to pick up something on our way out."

It took just one pissed-off instant for Kelly to drop her usual care and punch her index finger way too hard into the PAUSE button on the betatape machine, wreaking havoc on the chocolate-brown nail polish that bitch of a manicurist had painted on less than twenty-four hours before. Damn! She jammed her body back into the hard steel spine of Edit Bay 4's chair and nibbled angrily at the nail's jagged edge. Another sixteen dollars down the drain, unless she could force herself back to that crappy minimall and listen to that woman whine about her nonexistent love life while she grudged out a repair.

Kelly swiveled around to face the computer screen head-on. She had a ton of work to do, thanks to that relic Ruth Sperry. Talk about good news and bad news! Rico had convinced Scoppio to let her host a one-hour prime-time special called *Kids in Danger*, which would air on all seven—count 'em, *seven!*—TV stations Sunshine Broadcasting owned, including the one in New York. So she'd get a ton of exposure and on a hot topic, too: kids and guns. The special would make heavy use of the school hostage incident, and she already knew how fabulous she looked in *those* stand-ups.

But the bad news was that Scoppio had assigned Ruth to executive produce, so for the next month Kelly was big-time under the old battle-ax's thumb.

All of a sudden the door opened and hallway light poured in. "How're you doing?" Ruth asked.

"Just dandy," Kelly snarled.

Ruth narrowed her eyes. "You're almost done logging the dubs we got from CNN?"

"Hardly! There's nine hours' worth."

Ruth just smiled. Kelly wanted to smack her. *She's loving this,* Kelly thought. *She asks for a ton of video from CNN, because of its sharing arrangement with KXLA, even though she knows it takes an eternity to log one hour of video, let alone* nine.

"Have you come across CNN's video of the school shootout yet?" Ruth asked.

"Not yet."

"Log it carefully when you do. I only scanned it briefly but it looked like pretty powerful stuff."

"Right." Ruth wouldn't know powerful if it rammed her bowlegged.

"And be sure to return all the tapes to me when you're done." Ruth started to back out, but that didn't stop her from still blabbing. "I've made extra dubs but I don't want to lose a frame. We've got an hour of prime time to fill."

Blah, blah, blah. Finally Ruth left, and Kelly scanned the CNN dubs till she found the one with the shootout. She stuck it on the bottom of the pile. She'd log it last, just to serve Ruth right.

She was irritated now, irritated and, she had to admit, kind of worried. No one had seen her with that flashlight, no one! But still, part of her wished the whole thing had just gone away. Now, as much as she wanted to host this special, it still meant that she'd have to relive the damn thing day in and day out. Somehow it just gave her the willies.

Fuck Ruth Sperry for upsetting her, Kelly thought, though she knew that in a million years Ruth'd never find a man to do *that* job.

Natalie stood in Dewey, Climer's elegant, wood-paneled reception area, nursing a glass of champagne and wishing desperately that she hadn't come to Geoff and Janet's engagement party. She knew only a few people and had zero desire to mingle. Ruth, whom she'd strong-armed into coming along, stood a few feet away, dressed with typical flamboyance in a turquoise pantsuit with a yellow-and-lime-green scarf tied jauntily around her neck. Natalie could overhear her telling one of the senior partners a ribald story about midnight and a six-pack. All six patrician feet of the man looked completely entranced.

Natalie sipped her champagne. She should be careful how much she drank. She had to do a live shot later that night and already could feel a flush rising on her cheeks. Around her on the Oriental carpets a few dozen people stood in clusters, their voices low, their bearing elegant, and, apart from Ruth, their clothing muted. Geoff's fellow attorneys, most of them, with a few on-air clients sprinkled in. No sign yet of the guests of honor. Natalie caught the eye of a fellow female reporter and raised her glass in greeting. The woman grinned and reciprocated, then instantly went back to chatting with the fortyish man next to her. She was on the hunt, clearly.

More power to her. Natalie fidgeted with the slippery stem of her crystal champagne flute. *She's willing to be in the fray.*

"Don't worry. No one will ever suspect," Ruth murmured, sidling up alongside her.

Natalie started. "Suspect what?" She tried to make her voice casual.

"That you couldn't get a date. Bringing your fifty-year-old female executive producer with you is a fabulous cover."

Natalie sipped her champagne, relieved. "Thanks for coming with me, Ruth."

"My pleasure." Ruth snatched a tandoori kabob from a passing tray. "Nice spread. So have you met this Janet gal?"

Natalie shook her head. "No."

"What do you know about her?"

Natalie could feel Ruth's eyes on her face. "Oh, not much." She shrugged, trying to appear nonchalant. "That she's a teacher. First grade, I believe. Her dad's a cardiologist. She grew up in San Marino and lives in Pasadena now, I think."

Ruth narrowed her eyes. "Don't tell me. Her dad's in the Jonathan Club and her mom's big-time on the charity circuit."

"How did you know that?" Natalie was amazed. "It was at some Jonathan Club function that Geoff met her, actually."

"I'll bet she does the Junior League thing, too." Ruth fell silent, finishing her kabob. She wiped her lips with a cocktail napkin, smearing it with bright pink lipstick. "I'm surprised you haven't met her. Does Geoff talk about her much?"

"Not really." That was a big part of the shock. Geoff had dated Janet on and off for a few years—Natalie had known that, but she'd had no indication that Geoff was really serious about the woman.

"Well, I'd say it's a perfect example of the Duck Mating Theory." Ruth winked at the senior partner, who was gaily raising his champagne flute to her from across the reception area.

"The *what*?"

"The Duck Mating Theory," Ruth repeated matter-of-factly. "Very common in those of the male persuasion. They decide it's time to get married, for whatever reason, whether they hit a certain age or their best buddy gets married or whatever, and then boom! They get engaged to whoever they're dating at the time, whether she's no better or no worse than any of her predecessors."

"That's crazy!"

"That's men." Ruth paused to order a gin and tonic from a cruising waiter. Natalie decided instantly to go for another glass of champagne. "I thought this might happen when you told me Geoff made senior partner," Ruth went on. "And he's in his late thirties, right?"

"Thirty-seven."

Ruth nodded sagely. "Fits the profile. Oh"—she arched her brows—"there he is now."

Natalie's gaze slid to a commotion at the party's edge, where Geoff had made an entrance with a tall, slim blonde in a white suit. Natalie caught her breath. *God, no. She's even more beautiful than in that damn head shot.*

Natalie stared, mesmerized, as the couple accepted

congratulations from the group gathered around them. She could hear Geoff's boisterous laugh, see Janet's beaming face. A few men slapped Geoff's back. Natalie watched as Geoff's colleagues appraised Janet with appreciative eyes.

Natalie was crushed, as she'd known she would be. Inanely she'd held out hope that somehow the eight-by-ten had been a stroke of celluloid luck and Janet wouldn't be gorgeous. But every woman Geoff dated was stunning. It was absurd to think the woman he'd marry wouldn't be a knockout.

He's like a news director, she thought, deflated. *The younger and prettier, the better.*

"I'd say I called it," Ruth observed in a low murmur, "though I'd put her at about thirty. Older than I would have expected. I give Geoff credit for that. Still"—Ruth narrowed her eyes appraisingly—"she looks like a Breck girl. One of those sweet types men typically go for. Not ornery like us."

"Speak for yourself!"

Ruth shrugged. "Okay, you're only ornery at work. I'm ornery constantly. I have yet to find the man who appreciates that. Shall we go say hello?"

Ruth propelled Natalie by the elbow across the Oriental carpets. The path opened before them and before Natalie could prepare herself she was face-to-face with the Happy Couple. The tall, dazzling, all-of-life-before-them Happy Couple. For a moment she was flummoxed. Then she gathered herself and forced out her free hand to Janet, who was looking at her with big blue expectant eyes.

"It's a real pleasure to meet you," Natalie heard herself say. She hesitated. She couldn't very well say, *I've heard so much about you.* "I'm so delighted for you," she managed, though that was hardly true. *Why in the world is this happening?* was more like it. "I'm Natalie Daniels, one of Geoff's clients," she added.

"One of Geoff's *favorite* clients!" Janet grasped her hand. "I'm thrilled to finally meet you. Geoff has told me so much about you."

Did he tell you we made love? Natalie quashed the thought as she watched Janet look up at Geoff teasingly, giving him a happy possessive look, a look that spoke of private conversations, conversations in bed, conversations in which they talked of everything and nothing, talked casually of Natalie Daniels, Geoff's client. Geoff's client, Natalie Daniels. Someone not nearly so important in Geoff's universe as his fiancée, Janet . . .

I don't even remember her last name.

Natalie tried to meet Geoff's eyes but he was looking above her head across the reception area, laughing at something or someone. Then he was moving on. Already someone else had stolen his attention.

She stood paralyzed next to Ruth as the bustle moved beyond them. "I'm ready to leave now," she declared abruptly. She threw back her champagne and set the empty flute on the mahogany reception desk.

"What?" Ruth's eyes flew open. "They just got here!" Then she gazed at Natalie a moment more. "Fine. Let's blow this pop stand."

Natalie moved swiftly toward the door and beyond to the bank of elevators. As she waited impatiently, rummaging in her small black purse for her valet ticket, she could hear behind her Geoff's distinctive laughter and Janet's accompanying giggle.

He won't miss me. He won't even notice I'm gone.

Finally an elevator arrived. Natalie entered, Ruth a bulwark beside her. By the time the doors closed to spirit them away, Natalie could see through the glass walls of Dewey, Climer's reception area that senior partner Geoff Marner had his arm around his beaming bride-to-be. And was bending his head to place the gentlest of kisses on her smiling upturned mouth.

CHAPTER FIFTEEN

Saturday, August 17, 8:18 A.M.

Geoff unloaded his surfing gear from his Jeep and stowed it in its designated corner of the garage. What a stunning day. Southern California at its glorious best, blindingly bright and invigorating, promising dry heat and endless sunshine. Not one of those summer mornings that dawns with a dreary marine layer that lingers for hours like a boorish guest. Beneath his wet suit his muscles ached pleasantly; his skin still stung from sea air and salt. Ahead of him stretched nothing but free time.

He punched a button to lower the garage door and leaped the few concrete steps to the interior door. Once inside he heard the blender running, no doubt Janet concocting one of her post-run a.m. protein drinks.

"I'm in here!" she called.

He joined her in the kitchen, nuzzling up behind her. She was aglow in a shaft of sunlight, wearing a thin white tee and very short running shorts, smelling slightly of sweat. He raised his hands to cup her small breasts, naked under the cotton, and immediately felt himself grow hard. "Um"—he rubbed against her—"upstairs."

She giggled. "I can't believe you want to. I'm so gross." Then she turned to kiss him on the nose. "But maybe I'll indulge you if you promise me something."

"Anything."

"That we register today."

He rested his forearms on her shoulders and kissed

her forehead, where her blond hair was downy and white like a baby's. "Register?" God, was she soft. "Register for what?"

"Wedding gifts."

He wasn't computing, nor trying to. "Why would we register for wedding gifts?"

"You have to ask?" She pulled away, still smiling but looking genuinely puzzled, which jolted him out of his reverie.

"It's easier for everybody if we register." She swiveled to face the blender, giving him her back and jabbing the PULVERIZE button. "We won't get what we don't want. And people will know what to buy. Nobody's flailing around."

He strode to the coffeepot and pulled open a drawer for a filter. "But we've already got two households' worth of stuff. I was even thinking we should tell people not to do gifts."

"Not do gifts?" She looked astounded now. "Who doesn't do gifts? As it is I've been planning to get rid of most of my stuff and surely you have as well?"

She asked it like it was a question but it certainly didn't sound like one. Carefully Geoff measured coffee beans into the grinder. Maybe that was because there was only one right answer?

She put her hands on her hips. "You must understand that I want to stamp our house with my own style?"

Another nonquestion question, and one he found fairly irritating. "I hadn't thought about it," he snapped, his surfing high rapidly getting obliterated. He started the grinder and raised his voice over the din. "Anyway, we can't register till we've set a date."

"That's *another* thing." Immediately she waltzed over to the kitchen wall calendar.

He stared at her in astonishment. "What's the rush? We just got engaged."

She lifted a page, then another, staring at October. Then she dropped the pages and turned to face him, hands on hips. "What do you think, spring or fall?"

"Next fall?"

"This fall."

"Then spring," he countered instantly.

"Then May." She cracked a sudden smile, as though glimpsing some distant happy scene. "I've always dreamed of a spring wedding."

Geoff flipped the grinder and slapped its base to loosen the ground coffee. "I must say, I don't get how you could 'always dream' of something like this. We just got engaged."

"It has nothing to do with you, silly!" She was restored to sweetness and light now, her voice teasing. She returned to the blender to pour its foamy peach-colored contents into a tall glass. "A woman dreams of her wedding day from the time she's a little girl. You're the least important part."

"How reassuring." This entire conversation had annoyed him in a way he couldn't quite identify. Since when had Janet been obsessed with trivialities? Insisting on registering for wedding gifts because it was "the done thing"? Maybe it was the weirdness that took over a woman once she got engaged. More than one buddy had warned him of it, but Geoff hadn't believed he'd witness the phenomenon in Janet.

She was halfway out of the kitchen when she called back over her shoulder, "So let's get out of here by nine-thirty."

"You *still* want to register today?"

"Of course!" She turned at the kitchen door and faced him down. "Besides, the sooner we get that done, the sooner we can plan the trip to Sydney."

He halted, his finger poised at the coffeepot's ON/OFF switch. "We're going to Sydney?"

"Unless you want to fly your entire family out here." She made it sound painfully obvious. "We should meet, don't you think?"

He stopped himself from telling her that his family had no clue he was engaged. Or had even so much as heard the name Janet Roswell.

Janet turned to race upstairs, not bothering to wait for his answer. *Well, why should she?* he thought. *She knows she's won.*

Geoff stood alone in his kitchen and pressed the coffeepot's ON switch. It bloomed the same bright red as a stop sign.

"You're not going to believe the latest," Natalie heard Berta Powers predict over the phone bright and early Tuesday morning. Natalie clutched at the receiver and shot up in bed, instinctively fortifying herself against bad news. Her free hand pulled the duvet tighter around her body, her negligee doing little to ward off the chill created both by the early-morning air wafting through the open window and the irritation in her attorney's voice. "What won't I believe?"

"Do you remember that I subpoenaed Heartbeat Studios for all the paperwork relating to Miles's sitcom deal? So we could get the nitty-gritty on the three-million-dollar payment?"

"Right."

"Well, I got the boxes from the studio late yesterday. A dozen of them."

"*A dozen boxes?* How could there be that much paperwork? His sitcom isn't even on the air yet!"

"Natalie, they sent such a pile of crap. Including documents from twenty years ago when his *first* sitcom was on."

Heartbeat Studios had also produced that sitcom, Natalie knew, the one Miles had done with Jerry Cohen.

"They sent duplicates of all kinds of stuff," Berta went on. "It'll take forever to sort through and probably get us nowhere."

Natalie fell back against her pillows. "Why would the studio do that?"

"Because its loyalty is to Miles. And they have no reason to make it easy for us."

"So what do we do now?"

Berta sighed. "I read them the riot act and subpoena them again. But there's no guarantee they'll be more forthcoming next time."

Natalie stared at the ceiling, pine beams crossing the white expanse like rough-hewn stripes. "And you still haven't gotten anything useful from subpoenaing Miles's former attorney?"

"No. He still insists he has no recollection of a prenuptial agreement between you and Miles."

This was so goddamn frustrating! "How can that *be*? Can't lawyers be disbarred for flat-out lying about this sort of thing?"

"Natalie, you'd be amazed how often lawyers risk their licenses. And it's always possible that Miles paid the guy off to shut him up. I've seen it before. And if Miles did it in cash, then of course there's no paper trail."

Natalie was silent. There sure as hell was no paper trail. Her prenup might as well have been written in sand at low tide.

"I'll subpoena the studio again and keep you posted."

"Thanks, Berta." Natalie replaced the receiver. *There has to be a way to get hold of documentation on Miles's sitcom deal. But how?*

Some odd compulsion propelled her out of bed, into old gray sweat clothes, and into her car. Given her late work hours, she was rarely awake that hour of the morning. But this was a wonderful day to be rousted so early, chilly and clear.

She pointed the Mercedes west on Mulholland Drive, following its narrow winding curves in what had to be the least direct route to the coast. It wasn't until she was clear of the hills and heading north on Pacific Coast Highway that she admitted to herself where she was going.

A few miles farther, she spied Miles's beachfront house. She rolled the Mercedes onto PCH's graveled right shoulder and stared across the busy street at the property. It looked quiet. Two cars, Miles's red Porshe and a black 323i, sat in the driveway. Natalie shook her head, disgusted. Suzy's Beemer, no doubt.

What do I think I'm doing here, anyway? Planning to break in? Find the sitcom documentation and abscond with it?

As she was pondering just what she did intend to do, a woman dressed in a light blue sweat suit, with the hood up and sunglasses on, emerged from the house and approached the Beemer. Natalie shook her head in disgust. Suzy. So much for Miles and her being broken up. The woman opened the trunk and tossed in a duffel bag, then shook the hood down from her head and plumped her brunette hair.

Oh, my God. Natalie's hand rose to her throat. *Not Suzy.*

The woman unlocked the driver's-side door and got into the Beemer. The car's engine sprang to life.

It's Kelly Devlin. Undeniably Kelly Devlin.

Natalie sank into the soft leather bucket seat, trying to catch her suddenly short breath. *Kelly is sleeping with Miles. Kelly is sleeping with Miles.* The truth slammed across her brain like a pinball in a machine. Why else would Kelly be leaving Miles's house with a duffel bag so early in the morning?

When had this started? Anger shot through her. *When Kelly was living in my house? When I got her an internship at KXLA? Was Miles cheating on me even then? And Kelly? Sleeping with my husband all the while she was playing the eager student, grateful to lap up any tidbit about TV news that I might drop?*

The woman who now has my job at KXLA.

Natalie remained in the bucket seat, her body shaking. She had known for eons that she couldn't trust Kelly, but she had never imagined a betrayal of this magnitude. And Miles? Had he *ever* told her the truth about *anything*?

You won't get away with it, Miles, she vowed silently, staring across PCH at her scumbag of a husband's multimillion-dollar beachfront love nest. *Somehow I'll find a way to stop you.*

"I'm off-limits!" Tony bellowed out his office door to Maxine. Then he set down on his desk the three doughnuts he'd plucked from the box standing open in the newsroom.

He grabbed a Reese's Pieces doughnut and started sorting through the dozen phone messages that had already come in that morning. One was from Rico Jimenez, Kelly's agent. Greedy prick. Tony had a thing or two to say to *him*. He paused to lick some peanut butter off his fingers, instantly feeling better. He could use a few of these later in the week, when Rhett Pemberley would show up in town and Tony would have to face the dreaded tee time at the Riviera Country Club. He knew he was going to embarrass himself, despite the golf lessons he'd taken. The only question was how badly.

Tony moved on to an Almond Bear Claw. These doughnuts were probably a thousand calories each. Not that he cared.

He saved the Chocolate Cheese Danish for later, then lumbered to his office door and pulled it open. "Maxine!" he yelled. "Coffee! And get Elaine in here!"

The station's senior attorney showed up a few minutes later. "I want to make Natalie Daniels an offer for another contract," Tony told her. "Her current one expires in a little over a month."

Elaine's eyebrows shot up over her granny glasses and he knew why. The way he'd demoted Princess it would shock anybody that he wanted to keep her. It sort of shocked *him*. But the fact was, she was like an insurance policy. In case Kelly exploded. In case the ratings didn't go back up, which they hadn't yet, even *with* the billboard campaign. In case a huge story broke and he needed good reporters. He'd been around long enough to know *you just never knew*. In TV news, as in birth control, it was better to be safe than sorry.

"The thing is," he went on, "I don't want to pay her the same kind of money." He paused. He didn't add what he was really thinking. *If I do, I'll never get the news department in the black. And I'll never get my bonus check.*

They stared at each other and that same old amazing thing happened again between him and Elaine. Sometimes, as pro-ACLU, antigun, marshland-protecting as Elaine was, he felt like he understood her. And she, him.

Elaine got that he liked keeping options open. Elaine got that he wanted to get his hands on that goddamn bonus check before he and Anna-Maria died of old age. And Elaine got that all of the above meant keeping Natalie Daniels on an inexpensive string.

In fact, he realized suddenly, it probably pissed Elaine off too that the anchors made so much money. She might not mind helping take Princess down a peg or two.

"How low do you want to go?" she asked him.

"As low as I can," he admitted, "and still keep her."

Elaine nodded, then smiled. "We can do that."

Kelly, lying on her stomach on a Millennium Club massage table, lifted her head from the padded rest to reread the loan document that Miles had drafted. It was typed on his personal stationery, with his Malibu address printed in fancy gold letters on top. What amazed her was that the thing was only two paragraphs long.

> *I, Kelly Devlin, hereby promise to repay Miles Lambert a loan in the amount of one hundred fifty thousand dollars. I will repay this loan in two installments of seventy-five thousand dollars each, the first to be paid one year from the date of this agreement, as noted above, and the second to be made two years from the above date.*

Then there was a bunch of legal shit that Miles had told her his attorney said to put in. Below that was Miles's signature and space for her own. He'd attached carbon paper and a single copy to the original. The thing was really primitive, considering that a hundred fifty thousand smackers was changing hands.

In fact, had *already* changed hands. Miles had given her the check. And it had cleared. When the escrow closed, she'd have to sign a buttload of documents and cough up the whole wad of cash, along with the five thousand she'd advanced on her credit cards.

"Roll over, Kelly," Sven murmured. "I'm done with your back and I want to finish your quadriceps."

Why in the world did anybody ever hire a woman to give them a massage? Kelly didn't bother to keep the towel tight as she rolled onto her back, but Sven, as usual, kept his green eyes trained on the wall, using the break to readjust his ponytail. She didn't think she could get him to look even if she did a full-out striptease. He was gay, but still.

She sat halfway up, balancing herself on one elbow, and held out the document. "Will you stuff this in my satchel?"

He backed off, a horrified look on his face. "My hands, they are oily."

She shrugged. Who cared? It would still be legal even if it had almond balm on it.

Sven finally took the papers, holding them by the corner with his pinkie stretched out.

"Ever buy a house, Sven?" She lay back down. God, his hands were magic. She knew he lived with some retired actor in a mansion in Pacific Palisades, basically waiting for the guy to croak and leave Sven all his money. But with the massages the old fart probably got, no wonder he refused to kick.

"No." He grinned at her. "Too much responsibility."

"Yeah, that's what everybody says." But she needed a house. It was part of keeping up appearances. You got successful, you needed to look successful, you bought a house.

Her cell phone rang.

"Shit," she murmured, her eyes still closed. "Sven, get my phone for me."

She heard him rummaging around in her satchel; then he came back with it. "Yeah?" she answered.

"It's Rico."

Great. "What do *you* want?"

Kelly listened to him let out this big sigh, as if she was putting him through TV-news hell or something. "I just got off the phone with Tony Scoppio and I'm gonna say it one more time. *Sign . . . the . . . effing . . . contract!* He's *not* gonna go any higher—*he's not*—and I'm getting seriously worried that this whole deal will blow up in your face!"

"Your face, too, Rico," she snarled.

"Both our faces, I agree," he said real fast. Then he got all whiny, as if *that* would convince her. "Kelly, this is your first big contract. You'll earn more in the future, I *promise* you, but—"

"Forget it." She couldn't settle for a hundred thirty grand a year! It was too humiliating for an L.A. prime-time anchor to make so little. Plus she just couldn't survive on it. Her mortage payments alone would be four thousand a month, *plus* she had to pay back Miles, *plus* she needed new furniture for the house, *plus* a better wardrobe, *plus* the Millennium Club dues . . .

"Listen, Rico," she growled into the phone, "you didn't have to do diddly to get me this job. I got it all on my own. All *you* have to do is sit on your ass and get me the money I deserve. So either get me the quarter million a year or I'll get a new agent. You got that? Good-bye."

She slapped the cell phone shut, then reared up and threw it in the direction of the satchel. It hit the wall above the bag, then plopped in. Nice shot. Again Sven was looking someplace else, as if he hadn't seen or heard a thing. That was what made him so goddamn good. "I'm booking you for another half hour," she told him.

He nodded silently. She thought for a moment that she'd scared him.

Fine. So long as he kept his hands moving.

I don't feel like doing this. I don't feel like doing this. I don't feel like doing this. Natalie grabbed her briefcase in one hand and Julio's tripod in the other and trudged across Pasadena's Colorado Boulevard toward the converted redbrick warehouse that housed the subject of tonight's package. A Web business called MetroSeek. It was going gangbusters, which couldn't be said of many Web businesses these days, and making its youthful founders rich beyond their wildest imaginings. She was already in a pissy mood and interviewing twenty-something multimillionaires would hardly help.

"Let me get the tripod," Julio offered from behind her as they approached the entry door.

"I've got it." She hated when female reporters never carried anything. And that was what she was now. A female reporter. Forty years old and back doing what she'd been doing years ago.

For a lot more money, an inner voice reminded her. *But still powerless,* her pissy inner voice shot back.

"What's this company do?" Julio asked.

Awkwardly she wrested open the heavy glass door, the tripod banging painfully against her shin. "They're an on-line guide to entertainment, restaurants, city tours—that kind of thing," she panted. "City by city, so you plug in L.A. and all kinds of info pops out."

"Can you buy stuff through them?"

"Tickets, yes. And you can make reservations. They have other services on their site, too, apparently. Even a little local news."

Julio made an appreciative grunt but Natalie couldn't summon even that degree of interest. Business stories were hell to do on TV, the main reason they were done so rarely. Boring pictures, at best. Lots of talking heads. Difficult and time-consuming and dull, dull, dull.

Which was no doubt why Tony had assigned it to *her.*

They made their way deep into the bowels of the warehouse, heading in the direction of the loudest noise, and eventually arrived at MetroSeek's beehive of an office, crammed to bursting with desks and computers and phones and people. Slowly Natalie lowered the tripod to the ground, Julio at her side. "This isn't what I expected."

"None too corporate, is it?"

"It's like a newsroom." It was the same open, semidecrepit space, with a similar buzz, except that it was even noisier and more crowded. Everyone was young and casually dressed and moving at high speed. There were no cubicles or separations of any kind; desks were cheek by jowl, everywhere; there was a lot of shouting across the high-ceilinged, fluorescent-lit room. "I like it." Natalie turned to Julio, her interest piqued. "We can do a lot with this."

"I agree."

"You must be the TV people." A young blond man in Dockers khakis and a light green polo shirt approached and held out his hand to Natalie, grinning. "I'm Brad Fenton."

Involuntarily Natalie's eyes widened. "The CEO?" He looked mid-twenties, max.

"Founder and. Come with me." He wrested the tripod out of Natalie's hand and ushered her and Julio across the mayhem, stopping at a central module that could easily pass for an Assignment Desk. "Sound bites or B-roll first?" he asked Natalie.

She arched her brows. "You certainly know the lingo."

"There's a little TV news in my past." He grinned. "Before I wised up to where the real action is. Coffee? Water?"

Both Natalie and Julio accepted the former and Brad Fenton loped off. Julio laughed. "He's not old enough to have a past."

"You're telling me."

"I say we get the interview first." Julio began to attach the broadcast camera to the tripod.

"Sure." *Before he wised up to where the real action is?*

Brad Fenton returned with two Styrofoam cups full of coffee and Natalie eyed him as he handed her hers. "I was telling Julio you even do a little local news on your Web site."

"Too little." He raked his hand through his close-cropped hair. "We don't have the bandwidth to do more."

"Come again?"

"The resources, even the time to figure out how to do it right. We're all going flat-out doing just what we absolutely have to." He arranged himself in the chair Julio set up. "It's hard to believe but great opportunities fall by the wayside that way."

She sat in the chair opposite and began to dress her mike for the interview. "You mean you think there are great opportunities on the Web in local news?"

"Absolutely."

"Even these days when it's harder than ever to make money?"

"I repeat, absolutely."

Natalie noticed Julio giving her a funny look. She ignored him and focused on Brad Fenton. "Maybe when we're done with the interview I can get you to tell me more."

CHAPTER SIXTEEN

Friday, August 23, 7:26 P.M.

One more tape and she'd finally be done.

Kelly popped the last of the nine CNN cassettes for the *Kids in Danger* special in the betatape machine. She was alone in the darkened editing booth, her butt sore from sitting so many hours logging tapes, her fingers stiff from typing so many time codes and video notations.

And this particular cassette, CNN's footage from the school shootout, she wanted to log least of all. Every time she thought about having to cover that frigging story, waiting for hours while that lunatic gun-toting dad held a bunch of kiddies hostage only to go off and shoot one dead, she got the willies.

But no one had seen her with that flashlight, not when she'd been shining it at the windows or afterward when she'd thrown it off Santa Monica Pier. And even if someone had, no one could prove that she'd had anything to do with what went down.

A wide shot of the school suddenly filled the monitor. It looked just as she remembered it: a run-down, two-story, brick-and-concrete structure, its windows as dark as the night sky. The CNN cameraman had an angle different from the one Harry had had, because from his vantage point she could also make out the school's north side, where lots of cop cars were parked at crazy angles.

Where she had stood with the flashlight.

Kelly shivered but forced herself to keep working. She reset the time code to zero, then rolled the tape at slo-mo. Her eyes bounced among the monitor, the computer screen, and the digital time-code display, while her fingers typed the log notes. It required mucho concentration, and she hated it, but she had no choice: did she want to host *Kids in Danger* or not? Tony must be pissed at her or something, because he'd told her that either she did what Ruth said or he'd can the special.

Who said men didn't get PMS?

But maybe he was just irked that *The KXLA Prime-time News* ratings hadn't stayed up. Hey, summer doldrums! Everybody knew about those. Or maybe the real problem was that buffoon Ken Oro. If Scoppio got her a stud as coanchor, *then* he could watch the ratings fly.

She was forty-two minutes into the CNN shootout tape when she glimpsed herself on screen. Or *thought* she did, but couldn't believe it.

She reracked the tape, then set it to super slo-mo and watched again, focusing on the extreme left, the north side of the school.

Damn!

Kelly jabbed STOP and reared backward, her heart pounding. *It was unbelievable!* But nobody must have noticed her, not even the CNN cameraman who shot the damn thing, because if anybody had, the shit would have hit the fan big-time.

Holding her breath, she pressed PLAY and watched a third time. There was no question about it. If somebody looked *really*, *really* hard, they could see her, shrouded in darkness, her black skirt and dark aviator jacket tough to make out but her white tee-shirt kind of obvious, standing on the school's north side and shining the flashlight up at the windows.

Then, instantly, the shooting started.

Fuck! She pressed STOP again and held her cold hands against her face, rocking back and forth, trying to think. Nobody could see this. Nobody could *ever* see this.

And nobody ever would. She halted her rocking, reality crashing into her brain. Because *she* had the tape.

And she'd simply degauss it. Then the footage would be gone—*poof!*—as if it had never existed.

She didn't have time to think about how CNN had other

copies. All that mattered was getting rid of *this* one, now, before Ruth or anybody else at KXLA saw it.

Kelly let out a breath. That was it. She'd erase the tape. That was what she had to do.

She rose from the chair, struggling to stop her legs from shaking. Boy, had she dodged a bullet. If Ruth had logged this tape and seen her, Kelly would have ended up back in Fresno making minimum wage at Dairy Queen. Or even worse, pounding out license plates in the Big House. She pulled open the editing booth door and stood blinking in the bright hallway light. *Well,* she told herself, *this just goes to show that Kelly Devlin has what it takes to get to the top. She sees what has to be done; she does it.*

She made her way down the hall past the other editing bays, crowded with editors and reporters cutting pieces for *The KXLA Primetime News*. She got to Archives and sidled inside, pulling the heavy metal door shut behind her. Her heart was racing like during kickboxing. But she had a right to be there, she told herself. She couldn't take anything *out* of Archives, although she sure as hell had more than once, but she had a right to be *inside*.

Now for the degaussing machine. It was in the back, she knew, behind the seven or eight tall, metal, rolling stacks on which were stored KXLA's archival footage.

Her heels clicked on the concrete floor as she made her way to the rear of the silent, high-ceilinged room. It was cold and spooky, what with all those dusty tapes, and she couldn't see behind all the stacks, so it felt as if somebody was watching. And the stacks kind of *groaned*. No wonder people didn't go into Archives more than they had to.

The degausser, a steel machine the size of a fax, sat on a grimy TV table in the back. It was turned off unless it was in use, which wasn't often. She flipped the ON switch and the machine began to hum.

The tape went in. She pressed START, waiting for the machine to neutralize the tape's magnetic field, basically erasing it.

Nothing. None of the usual clicky noises.

Damn!

Calm down, she ordered herself. *Try it again.*

She pressed the button.

Again, nothing. Total silence.

Okay. She took a deep breath. *It's not working. But there's more than one way to dispose of a tape.*

She ejected the cassette and pried off its plastic side, revealing the tape underneath. Her fingers tore at it, pulling it off its dual spools. Within seconds she had several yards of the sticky tape in a wadded mess in her hands.

Now what? A garbage can stood beneath the degausser's TV table. Should she just toss it? But what if somebody saw it and got curious and . . .

No. There was only one way to be sure it was trashed. By doing what she had done with the flashlight.

Throwing if off Santa Monica Pier.

She glanced at her watch: 8:15 P.M. She couldn't get all the way from the KXLA lot in Hollywood to the pier and back before the newscast, and even if she *did* go now, there'd be a ton of people on the pier and they'd see her.

So she'd do it after the newscast, when there'd only be winos there. And it didn't matter if any of them saw her. None of them counted.

Tony entered KXLA through the loading dock, deathly quiet after hours, lumbering past Archives toward his office. His muscles ached with every step. He felt like absolute shit. But who wouldn't after five hours chasing a little white ball around a golf course? Humiliating himself in front of Rhett Pemberley by coming off the eighteenth green with what would have been a respectable *bowling* score?

At least now he was clean and fed. He'd gone home to shower and grab dinner, bypassing an open bottle of pinot grigio. Because tonight he had to be on top of things. Because tonight Rhett Pemberley, whom Tony was starting to think of as the Station Owner from Hell, had decided he wanted to watch *The KXLA Primetime News* live from the control booth.

Great.

Tony had to admit it made him nervous and he had to admit why: Kelly Devlin. It was a month now that she'd been anchoring and goddamn if she didn't mispronounce something or stumble over something or let fly some asinine remark every single night. Like the time she declared that Vienna was the capital of Australia. Or that Bishop Desmond Tutu was next in line to be pope. They were ignorant mistakes. And careless.

Tony punched the four-digit code into the keypad and pulled open the newsroom security door when the buzzer sounded. Maybe he'd be lucky and there'd be no breaking stories. No surprises. First time in his career he'd ever wanted that. He marched inside his office and switched on the overhead fluorescent lights. Too bad Princess wasn't babe-alicious anymore. *Cheap* and babe-alicious. This having to trade off looks against experience was a major pain in the ass.

He picked up his phone and punched in Ruth's newsroom extension. He didn't feel like dealing with her face-to-face.

"Sperry," she answered.

"Scoppio. Wanted to give you a heads-up that Pemberley's gonna watch from the booth tonight."

"No shit." Then she chuckled. "So you want me to call in Natalie to anchor instead?"

He hated how this broad could read his mind. "Yeah, right," he guffawed, hoping he sounded as if he thought that was an idiotic idea. Then he made his voice all casual. "So anything big happening?"

"Nope. It's as quiet as a pool hall in downtown Salt Lake City."

Tony let out a breath. "Too bad," he lied. "I would've liked to put on a big show for the brass."

"Yeah, right," Ruth said, mimicking his tone exactly. Man, she got on his nerves. "I'll try to get little Miss Fancy Pants on the set more than thirty seconds before airtime," she said, then hung up.

Tony winced, replacing the receiver. He'd forgotten

about that. Kelly had actually missed the newscast open once and Ken had had to start alone. Lost track of the time, she'd told him.

Should he warn Kelly that Pemberley would be watching from the booth? He sat back and pondered. He didn't know if that would make her perform better or worse. Would it make her inspired or nervous? Careful or cocksure?

He stared blankly at the monitors across his office. No, he decided finally, he wouldn't warn her. Better leave well enough alone. At least, he *hoped* it was better. He realized, sitting there in his news director's office, that he could no more predict what Kelly Devlin would do than he could walk on water.

Just back from work, briefcase still in hand, Natalie bent down to retrieve the stiff FedEx envelope propped in the shadows outside her front door. She held it up to the sconce to read the sender's name, then froze as the smudged typewritten letters took clear shape. *T. Scoppio.*

Her heart thumping, she unlocked the door and let herself in the dark two-story foyer, the security system beeping insistently. One hand reached out to punch in the alarm code; the other dropped the FedEx envelope on the side table as if it were wired to detonate.

The distinctive red, white, and blue FedEx packaging taunted her.

It's got to be a dismissal. She stared at it warily. *What else would Scoppio send? Anchors don't get reupped by overnight mail.* She forced herself to pick it up, then pulled the wiry tab that sliced the package open. Out dropped a manila envelope, labeled with her name and address and two red stamps: PERSONAL. CONFIDENTIAL.

Briefly she closed her eyes. *It's got to be a dismissal.* Her hand trembling, she pried open the manila envelope, then scanned the letter within. Apart from the requisite legalese, it was surprisingly brief.

This is to inform you that the management of KXLA-TV (hereinafter to be referred to as "Sta-

tion") will extend an offer of employment to Natalie Daniels (hereinafter to be referred to as "Performer") for a one-year period commencing on . . .

What? KXLA was making her an offer? Stunned, her eyes raced down the first page.

Station offers Performer annual compensation in the amount of one hundred fifty thousand dollars . . .

What? For a *fifth* what she was making now?

. . . to serve as general-assignment reporter for all KXLA-TV news programs . . .

A reporter. No anchor job. That was gone, for good it seemed.

She sagged against the side table. The news was so unexpected she didn't know what to make of it. A television offer, definitely good. At the station she'd loved for fourteen years, wonderful. For a much less prominent job making much less money? Lousy.

And also for only one year. Every other offer she'd ever gotten from KXLA had been for three. Scoppio would know that. Her gaze fell back on the document, homing in on his name. This one man, rendering judgment on her professional worthiness like a pasha grown tired of one of the concubines in his harem.

No, she realized, *that's not right. It's not just one news director: it's all of them. No one else is clamoring to hire me. If anyone were, Scoppio couldn't butcher my salary and hope to keep me.*

It was amazing. Eighteen years of experience and still she served at the whim of whoever happened to be news director at any given moment. It was exactly the same as when she'd gotten started.

This exact thing probably happened to Evie. The first step in a TV reporter's decline was getting only one bad offer. The next step was getting no offer at all.

She drooped toward the kitchen, flicking light switches

as she went. Some things were undeniably true. An L.A. TV reporter job was highly desirable. A hundred fifty thousand dollars a year was no joke. But still, both were a comedown for her.

She leaned against the granite kitchen counter. And still to be under Scoppio's thumb? Forced to run around reporting whatever stories he deemed newsworthy? Of course he would know that she hadn't gotten another offer, because she certainly would have left if she had. He would be so condescending. And she so powerless.

She threw back her head and closed her eyes. Could she even keep up as a reporter? It was so much tougher than anchoring, so much tougher than when she was twenty-two years old.

Tony's contemptuous tone rose in her memory. *You don't want to get down in the muck. You don't want to get your hands dirty.*

She opened her eyes. *He's right. So what does that say about me?*

Her gaze fell upon the phone, then the big white-faced kitchen clock: 9:37. *I should tell Geoff about this.* But at this hour on a Friday night he was unlikely to be in his office.

Of course he won't be in his office, you fool. He'll be out to dinner, or at home. Or away. With Janet, whatever he's doing.

She remained leaning against the counter, so spent that trudging upstairs and washing off her makeup seemed unbelievably daunting. Around her the big Mediterranean-style house was silent, as it ever was these days, save for the relentless ticking of the kitchen clock. *Time. I have so little time.* Her contract expired in exactly six weeks and the only option she had was to keep slaving away for Tony Scoppio.

Slowly, methodically, she did what she had done so many times before, when she was low, when she wanted to feel better, when she needed reassurance that her life meant something to someone, somewhere. She walked to the study and pulled open the double closet doors. Then she knelt and overturned the nearest box to dump its contents on the worn Oriental carpet. Out poured letters, in all shapes and sizes, many tattered and yellow from age and handling. But to Natalie that rendered them no less precious.

"Rhett, you want coffee or anything?" Tony watched the master of his universe claim a prime seat in the control booth, just behind the director. Coincidentally, the same seat that Tony picked when he watched the show from the booth.

"Thank you, no. I'm just fine." Rhett smiled his Pepsodent smile and crossed his ankle over his knee in a maneuver that Tony's fat legs couldn't manage in a hundred years. It irritated him that even at ten at night Rhett Pemberley looked as fresh as a daisy. He even smelled good. He had his thick white hair all slicked back; a striped shirt that looked like it didn't even know how to wrinkle; tan slacks with a perfect crease; and a navy blue jacket in some expensive-looking material. The guy looked as if he could go straight from the control booth to a yacht party.

Tony was forced to set up a metal folding chair in the back of the booth, because what with Ruth, the director, the technical director, the graphics operator, the chyron operator, and Pemberley, they had a full house. He stared at the bank of monitors that dominated the front wall, the three in the center corresponding to the studio cameras. A huge red digital clock read out the time: 09:58:28. One minute to air and no Kelly Devlin on set.

Jesus Christ. Maybe he'd been wrong not to warn her.

At 09:59:34 she raced on set. Tony cast a sidelong glance at Pemberley, who was frowning. At least Kelly looked good. She was wearing white, which normally in TV was a no-no because of the glare, but it did look sharp against the dark backdrop they used for *The KXLA Primetime News*. Not to mention that it made a good contrast to her dark hair and eyes and, he had to admit, heavy makeup.

10:00:00. The prime-time news music started, over video of the California State Assembly. Kelly began her voice-over.

"In Sacramento, the governor squares off against legislatures, saying it's their job as elected officials to enact his vision into law."

Tony cringed. *Legislators,* not *legislatures.*

The video wiped to a wide shot of chanting protestors and Ken spoke. "In Riverside County, citizens band together to block a development that would wipe out a beloved old-town shopping area."

Then back to Kelly, over dramatic nighttime shuttle launch video. Tony held his breath. "And NASA sets a precedent as *Columbia* roars into space with a woman as commanding officer."

No more mistakes. Good.

The news music swelled, the director cut to a wide shot, and Tony glanced at Pemberley, who was staring fixedly at the monitors. And who had a frown plastered on his tanned face.

Bad.

Tony looked away. Had Kelly *read* the script in advance? Ruth told him she usually didn't but he hadn't believed her. What anchor would do a cold read if they didn't have to? He shuddered. Only a careless anchor. Or an ignorant one.

At 10:47:37 the very thing Tony most feared, happened.

Ruth slammed down the phone and turned to the director. Her voice rang out across the booth. "I told ENG Truck 2 to get the bird up. They ran into a mongo apartment fire. I want it live. No reporter, so we'll have the anchors voice it. And we might want to stay on past eleven." Then she grabbed the producer's mike to relay the latest to Ken and Kelly on the set.

Shit. Tony closed his eyes, but not before he saw Pemberley lean forward, as if now he was getting excited. Great. Perfect timing. A breaking story, with Kelly Devlin on the anchor desk.

And the man who had to sign Tony's bonus check watching from the booth.

Tony bit at what remained of his nails. So far Kelly's performance had been weak but not catastrophic. He'd counted six mistakes. But that number could easily balloon if she had to ad-lib.

It was then that the ENG truck got the bird up. One monitor suddenly filled with spectacular images of a fire, flames shooting out the windows of a beat-up brick building that looked to be about ten stories. People actually hanging out of windows screaming. Meanwhile, live on KXLA's air, the director cut to a medium shot of both anchors. Ken spoke first.

"We're going live right now to the scene of a devastating fire in Riverside County, near the 60/215 interchange, in the vicinity of Moreno Valley," he said. The director brought the live shot full screen, just at the highly dramatic moment when fire trucks roared up, sirens blaring.

"Wow, that is terrific video," Kelly said.

Tony cringed. Geoff Marner's prediction rattled across his brain. *You'd better hope we don't have another earthquake, Scoppio. Because if we do, you'll have to rely on Kelly Devlin . . . In thirty seconds you'll be wishing you had Natalie back.*

Ten, actually. But he hated when other people were right, especially tall, rich, good-looking people.

Ken kept up a running commentary about the fire, and was handling himself well, Tony thought, especially since this was the toughest live assignment of all: wall-to-wall coverage with no info. No story had hit the wires; no reporter was on the scene. Anchors were forced to wing it with nothing more to go on than the pictures and their own experience.

"Those people better get out of that building fast," Kelly said, "or they're gonna be toast."

Pemberley stood up. "What in the world kind of comment is that?"

Oh, God. Tony stayed paralyzed in the folding chair, his mind whirling. *Should I get her off the air? How?*

Ken jumped in, but not before every KXLA viewer saw him shoot his coanchor a shocked look. "Riverside County Fire Department personnel have arrived on the scene," he jabbered, "deploying fire hoses to fight this blaze. Now we are told the structure is a residential hotel."

"Oh, *that* explains it," Kelly said, and Tony shut his eyes. "These huge fires are *always* breaking out at residential hotels. It's like how tornadoes always hit trailer parks."

"What?" Pemberley roared.

That's it. "Cut to commercial!" Tony stood and yelled the order at Ruth.

She turned around real slow and stared at him. He didn't know what he saw in those pale blue eyes of hers but he knew he didn't like it.

"Cut to commercial!" he yelled again, when still she did nothing.

"We can't cut to commercial in the middle of this," Ruth declared calmly. Tony could have wrung her neck. "This is a fantastic story and we're the only crew there."

Insubordinate bitch. And goddamn if she wasn't enjoying every second of this. Tony was acutely aware of every pair of eyes in the booth, Rhett Pemberley's included, watching his every move. *"Cut to commercial,"* he repeated. His eyes didn't waver from Ruth's. *"Now."*

She shrugged and slowly turned around to pull the producer's mike to her mouth. "Ken and Kelly," she said in as casual a voice as he had ever heard, "we need you to go to commercial ASAP. Don't say we're coming back to the fire."

Tony could see on the monitors that both anchors looked stunned, Ken especially. But Tony didn't give a good goddamn what anybody thought, anybody except the one person who now approached him across the booth with measured steps.

"I hope you know what you're doing," Pemberley muttered under his breath, his face inches from Tony's, "because right now I've really got to wonder."

CHAPTER SEVENTEEN

Monday, August 26, 9:20 A.M.

Natalie sat at her KXLA desk, reading for the umpteenth time the contract offer Tony had FedExed to her house on Friday. It was no more attractive now than it had been on first perusal. Over the weekend she'd left Geoff four messages on his cell phone, never getting a response. Was she going to wait till her agent surfaced from God knew where to confront Tony?

It took her a minute flat to get to his office, a second more to get as deflated as a pizza box run over by a Mack truck. He wasn't there.

She walked in anyway, shaking her head in disgust at the newspapers, videotapes, magazines, manila folders, boxes, crumbs, and wrappers in which the man habitually wallowed. Two half-empty Styrofoam cups of coffee enjoyed pride of place next to his IN box, both with dribble marks that ended in staining brown puddles on his desk blotter. During Scoppio's tenure, KXLA's news director's office was less a bastion of journalistic enterprise than a pigpen.

She glanced in his IN box and her interest piqued. Right on top, plain as day, the Nielsen overnights. She hadn't seen those in ages. For some reason Maxine had stopped posting them on the newsroom notice board. Not even Ruth knew what *The KXLA Primetime News* ratings had been lately.

Natalie glanced out Tony's newsroom windows to

make sure nobody was looking before she swiped the single typewritten sheet and expertly scanned its neat columns. *The KXLA Primetime News*: 4.6. She smiled. And KYYR's *News at 10?* 5.0. So. With Kelly at the helm, the newscast was back below a 5.0 rating. She laughed out loud.

"Enjoying yourself, Daniels?"

"I'm having a grand old time," she told Tony in her sweetest voice. Without missing a beat she laid the overnights back in his IN box. "It's such a joy knowing you can no longer blame *me* for the ratings."

He guffawed noisily but she could tell she'd hit home.

"I got your contract offer," she went on. Her tone hardened. "I cannot believe you seriously expect me to accept it."

"You're free to go elsewhere." He plodded behind his desk and sat down, his chair squealing in protest of his weight.

"I certainly *will* if the best you can do is an eighty-percent pay cut."

He shrugged, his beady brown eyes glittering.

So smug, so self-assured. *So confident I won't get a better deal.*

"Ever heard of market forces?" he inquired casually.

"Your point is?"

"This offer reflects what I judge to be your current price in the marketplace." He leaned forward and set his elbows on his desk blotter, dangerously close to the coffee puddles. Unfortunately not close enough. "I'm willing to pay that. But no more."

"In that case you'd better start screening those tapes." She cocked her head at a teetering stack of résumé reels rising halfway to the ceiling. "You're going to need some new talent. Who can report and anchor and ad-lib on demand. In other words, prepare to lose me."

"Right." He laughed. "To WITW New York?"

Momentarily she was stunned into silence. How had he found out about *that*? Or maybe she'd been naive to think he wouldn't. TV news was a very, very small world. And talent auditioning in another newsroom, particularly one that shared the same corporate parent, ran the distinct risk of being recognized. And ratted on. "I would think you'd be delighted if I went elsewhere," she managed. "Given how poor my judgment is and how soft I've gotten."

"Well, Daniels, all I can say is that my diet and exercise regimen has put you back in fighting trim." He lolled back in his chair and linked his hands behind his head. Huge sweat stains marred the armpits of his yellow button-down shirt. "Now I think you're worth keeping."

"As a reporter. Even though the ratings are hardly on the rise with Kelly on the anchor desk."

"Give it time. They will be."

She shook her head. He was so damn cocky. And the galling reality was, she couldn't fight him. Not unless she was willing to go elsewhere. "Consider this fair warning. Unless you improve this offer, be prepared for me to walk."

He laughed. "I learned long ago to be prepared for every eventuality, Daniels. However unlikely." He leaned forward to consult his calendar. "Even you getting another offer. That fancy agent of yours still has, what, five or so weeks to line something else up."

"What makes you so sure he won't?"

He just shrugged, saying nothing, though his eyes shone with an odd triumphant light. Then his intercom buzzed. "Your wife on line one," Maxine rasped. Tony looked up at her. "Gotta take this."

Natalie nodded and walked out, her blood boiling as ever after an encounter with Tony Scoppio, though this one had been particularly bizarre. What made him so supremely confident she wouldn't get another offer? Was it crystal clear to everyone but her that she was no longer marketable as anchor talent? She entered her office to find her phone ringing. "Natalie Daniels," she answered.

"It's Berta. Bad news."

Natalie sank into her desk chair, propping up her forehead with her hand. "Just what I need. What now?"

"Johnny Bangs is trying to get a discovery closure date."

She shook her head. "What in the world is that?"

"A date to end the discovery process, such that all relevant information must be available to both parties by that time."

Natalie frowned, her mind working. "Meaning if we don't get our hands on Miles's sitcom contract by then—"

"The fee is out of the picture. We can't go for it as part of the marital property. Exactly."

"What date does Bangs want for this discovery closure?"

"September sixth. A week from Friday. He and I go into court to slug it out tomorrow."

"Any chance it won't happen?"

"Not much. I'll put up a fight, but I can't tell you it looks good." Natalie heard Berta flip through some papers. "Tomorrow's also the deadline for the second subpoena on Heartbeat Studios. Let's see what they send us *this* time."

"This is unbelievable."

"But not over. I'll keep you posted." Berta hung up.

Natalie was pensive as she replaced the receiver. As quickly as she set it down, she picked it up again, first calling Burbank Directory Assistance, then a series of numbers at Heartbeat Studios.

"Production offices," a young man answered.

"For *Forget Maui?*"

The guy grunted a bored affirmative.

"Great. What night is the show taped, please?"

"Thursday, 6:30 P.M."

"And how long does the taping last?"

"Two to five hours. You wanna be in the audience?" The guy was starting to sound impatient. "I can put you in touch with the company that handles that."

"So there'll be a taping this Thursday, the twenty-ninth?"

"No, the next one's September fifth."

Her heart dropped. "What? Not till then?"

"Can't wait, huh?" The guy laughed.

"Thank you." Natalie hung up.

September fifth. Miles would *have* to be out of his

house for the taping of his own show. That gave her one chance to carry out her plan. And one chance only.

Tony was proud of himself for putting on such a confident show while Princess was in his office. He should win a Best Actor Oscar. Because the reality was far from encouraging.

He had Kelly making cockamamie remarks on air. His ratings were in the dumper. The news department budget was still in the red. And thanks to all of the above, Rhett Pemberley had Tony's bonus check wedged in his pocket tighter than a C-note in a hooker's fist.

Pemberley was really pissing him off. Questioning his judgment left, right, and center. He was supposed to be such a hands-off manager. What was so goddamn hands-off about flying into town and watching the newscast from the control booth? Not a damn thing.

Tony cringed, remembering what had popped out of Kelly's mouth on Friday's newscast. *Those people better get out of that building fast or they're gonna be toast! These huge fires are always breaking out at residential hotels. It's like how tornadoes always hit trailer parks.*

What was it? Did she just say whatever came into her head at any given moment? He understood that ad-lib situations gave talent almost no cushion between brain and mouth but still, they had to show *some* judgment. That was why they got paid the big bucks.

He leaned forward and buzzed Maxine. "Get that coach guy on the phone," he ordered her. "That one from Jersey you hire to come out to the station. Feinstein, Feingold, Feinman—you know who I mean." Maxine would sniff the guy out. The old broad could've been a P.I. if she hadn't drowned in the secretarial pool first.

He slapped his desk. It'd be worth ten grand or so to get Kelly up to snuff. Despite all her mistakes, he wasn't ready to give up on her yet. Everybody would think he was a fool if he changed course midstream. And besides, maybe in Hollywood stars were born and not made, but not in TV news.

* * *

"Bring the loan document with you when you come over," Miles instructed Kelly over the phone.

She stood at the bar that separated her minuscule kitchen from the rest of her apartment and rolled her eyes in disgust.

"You *have* signed it, right?"

"Doesn't your sitcom go on the air in like a few weeks?" Kelly shrieked into the receiver. "Don't you have better things to worry about than whether or not I signed your goddamn loan document?"

He got all apologetic then, as if he was afraid that otherwise he might not get laid later. "Baby, it's a lotta money, that's all."

"I thought to Big Sitcom Producer Miles Lambert it wasn't!"

"Well, not as much as to most people, but still."

Arrogant turd. "Fine, I'll bring it with me," she snarled, then punctuated her point by slamming down the phone. *Jesus.*

But not even Miles was making her as mad these days as Scoppio. Coaching! He'd told her she needed coaching! All because of some realistic observations she'd made Friday night on the air.

Kelly stalked to the fridge and grabbed herself a Gatorade, surveying the damage wreaked that afternoon by the movers from Starving Students, who were so expensive no way they could be starving. But she wouldn't pack herself. It wasn't what anchorwomen did. They hired people and didn't care how much it cost.

Though, Kelly had to admit, *she* kind of cared. Because she was still living on her diddly-squat salary of seventy-five grand a year and wouldn't get a dime more until she inked Scoppio's contract. Which she wouldn't do until he hiked the offer.

Kelly tossed the empty Gatorade bottle and made her way among the boxes to her bedroom, deciding suddenly not to give Miles his stupid document. He was pissing her off.

She'd just stuffed it in a drawer when she noticed a

blinking red light on her answering machine. It was probably her real-estate agent. Since escrow on the Bel Air house was almost closed, she was messaging Kelly constantly with every phase of the operation, like they were infiltrating Cuba. She pressed the mailbox button and a woman with a heavy Brooklyn accent started speaking.

"Kelly, this is Hard Line. *We still haven't gotten the release from the Mann family to air your spot. That's slated to go right after Labor Day so please fax the release to 212-555- . . ."*

Kelly pressed STOP and stared at the machine, a chill of both excitement and anxiety rippling along her spine. Her first national appearance! And just after she moved into Bel Air. Things were going right big-time.

But she didn't have the release and would never have it. What if *Hard Line* wouldn't run her piece unless they got it? She couldn't let that happen.

Kelly grabbed a slip of paper and jotted down *Hard Line*'s fax number. Tomorrow from KXLA she'd fax them a letter saying she'd put the release in snail mail. That should pacify them. Hell, maybe they'd even forget about it.

She deleted the message and slung the strap of her overnight bag over her shoulder. It wouldn't be long before she got used to playing on the edge. Then she'd *really* be in the big time.

Natalie pulled a steaming hot Lean Cuisine from her microwave and tossed it on the trivet she'd set on the granite kitchen counter. Off came the plastic wrap to reveal the puny serving of Chicken Piccata Stouffer's apparently considered an adult portion. No wonder it packed a grand total of two hundred eighty calories: it was an hors d'oeuvre posing as an entrée.

She poured a glass of chardonnay and carried both to the study, setting them beside the computer. Eyes glued to the screen, she sipped her wine and began to search the Web in earnest.

Very interesting. It was exactly as Brad Fenton from

MetroSeek had described. There wasn't a single site on the Web that provided substantial local news coverage from a variety of sources. Absently she stabbed a piece of chicken with her fork. Maybe that was because it was a lousy business idea. Or maybe it was because the right person to start the business hadn't come along yet.

Am I the right person? Part of her couldn't believe she was even asking that question. What did she know but television news? Nothing. What other field had she ever worked in? None. And her insight into the Web was pitiful, though it was greater than two weeks ago, thanks to all the surfing she'd done and questions she'd asked.

But, her internal devil's advocate demanded, *what did Evie know about writing for a newspaper before she started?* To which Natalie had an instant answer: *Nothing, but it didn't much matter. Reporting for a newspaper isn't fundamentally different from reporting for television. But running a Web business has nothing to do with anchoring the news.*

Her doorbell rang. She threw down her fork. Who could it be at nine forty-five on a Tuesday night? She stepped to the door and pulled open the tiny window grate at eye level. Then her heart skittered to a place it hadn't traveled in some time. "Geoff."

He laughed lightly. "I've done it again, haven't I? Shown up when I'm least expected."

"You do have a way of surprising me. Hold on a second." She shut the grate and tore off her headband, plumping her matted-down hair while examining her cotton pajamas for food stains. *I look like hell. And I haven't seen him since that damn engagement party.* A pang shot through her. *Remember that? He's engaged. This is business.* She gathered herself and pulled open the door. "Sorry I'm not dressed."

"I'm the one who should apologize, showing up this late without warning." He swept past her into the foyer, bringing with him a waft of cool night air. "But I'm just back from New York and got your messages."

"Yes, of course. I didn't realize you were out of

town." She closed the door behind him. *Why did he come all the way over? He could've called.* "I wanted to tell you about the contract offer I got from Tony."

"I've seen it." He stood across from her in the foyer, carrying a briefcase and wearing both a trench coat and a trace of five o'clock shadow. "What do you think?"

"Please sit down." She motioned him into the living room and bustled about turning on lamps. "Well, I hate the idea of having to keep working for Tony and getting paid less for it. And of course with zero hope of getting back on the anchor desk. But I suppose since I don't have any other option I have to take it seriously."

He linked his hands and studied them. "I think we should regard Scoppio's offer as a fallback. We're only now getting into the hot time, the last month before your contract expires. On October fourth, right?"

She nodded.

"Well, now the real opportunities will pop up." He reached inside his briefcase and extracted a sheet of paper. "Till now I've focused on the top twenty markets but it's time to cast the net wider. I've taken the liberty of drafting a list of smaller markets you might consider." He held it out to her.

She took it. *Have we ever been this formal with one another? "I've taken the liberty—"* She cleared her throat, quickly scanning the neat column. "St. Louis. San Antonio. New Orleans. I probably could get excited about Baltimore."

He nodded. "I'll start making phone calls. And RTNDA is coming up in a few weeks. That's always a plum hunting ground."

The annual confab of radio and TV news directors. A must-show for agents, especially those hawking hard-to-place clients.

All at once Natalie felt exhausted. Talk about an uphill battle. Starting over, in a new city, where she knew no one and no one knew her. *But it's worth it, right? For an anchor job?* It had to be. Her ruminations were interrupted by the undeniable sound of a stomach growling. Not her own. She chuckled. "Hungry?"

Geoff looked abashed. "There was some foul-up with the ovens on the plane, so I ended up not eating."

"Let me get you something." She rose. "Are you willing to try Lean Cuisine? It's all I've got in the house."

"At this point even female diet food sounds appetizing." He shed his trench coat and followed her to the kitchen, where she selected two meals and popped both in the microwave.

She held up a bottle of wine. "Chardonnay?"

"Please."

She poured two glasses and Geoff perched atop a stool at the kitchen bar, accepting one.

"May I tell you my crazy idea?" The moment the words slipped out she regretted them. Geoff would think that her launching a Web business was idiotic. Not to mention that he had a vested interest in her continuing on-air. And that *she* had a vested interest in his aggressively seeking an anchor post for her, which he might not do if he judged her not fully committed.

"Shoot." His hazel eyes fixed on her expectantly.

But there seemed no way out of it now. "Well, a few weeks ago I did a story about a Web business called MetroSeek."

"I've used the site."

"Really? Well, the CEO got me thinking about a potential local-news Web site. One he thought was promising." She stopped. So far Geoff's expression remained unchanged, which emboldened her. "Specifically," she went on, "a local-news portal for the L.A. market. So people here in town could watch local TV news on their computer. In a box in the corner of their computer screen."

The microwave pinged. Geoff rose and helped Natalie serve the double dose of Lean Cuisines, then returned to the stool. "This isn't being done yet?"

"Individual stations are doing it on their own sites but there's no one portal that accesses material from various sources. So there's an opportunity for someone to be first. And even if competing sites pop up, well, CBS and NBC and ABC and Fox manage to coexist."

"And people could pull up whatever they want from whatever station they want?"

"*Whenever* they want, too. People could watch local news when it was convenient for *them*, not have to wait till the news came on. And watch just the stories they want."

He chewed for a while. "You'd need cooperation from local stations, obviously. For rundowns and video."

"Right." She nodded. "And I'm thinking radio and newspapers, too, to round out the site."

"I gather you think this might be an opportunity for you?" He pushed away one Lean Cuisine and started in on the next, not looking at her.

She felt suddenly on thin ice. "This is very early stages," she hedged. "All I'm doing now is tossing around the idea. Very preliminarily. Of course my heart lies in anchoring the news."

He nodded and was silent for a while. "Natalie, I don't want to rain on your parade, but do you know how many Web businesses have gone belly up?"

"Everybody does."

"So—"

"Look, I'm not saying I'm just going to abandon TV news to pursue this." She couldn't help it—she was sounding defensive. "It's just that I think I should look into it further. And by the way, it's not like I have a ton of options in TV news."

"I agree. You should look into it further."

"What?"

"I said I agree."

Now she was confused. "But—"

He raised his head from his meal to regard her. "Do you seriously expect me to argue that all you should consider is a new anchor job? Maybe just so I can keep collecting commissions?"

She was embarrassed. "Something like that."

"Come on, Nats. I want you to be happy. And if that means you ride off into the Internet, so be it. I just want you to know what you're getting into." He paused, swirling the chardonnay in his glass, staring at it, not her. He spoke softly. "The good thing about it, of course, is that you'd stay in L.A." He raised his eyes to meet hers.

The air seemed to still as they stared at each other.

"And when your startup goes public," he went on, holding her gaze, "and your personal net worth is valued at hundreds of millions of dollars, you'll *still* be in L.A. And every once in a while you'll take your old agent out to the best, most expensive restaurants." Then he grinned, breaking the spell, his mischievous smile making him look like a teenager.

It was impossible to resist. She laughed out loud. "Geoff Marner, you have a way of making me feel better."

He tipped an imaginary cap. "Aim to please, ma'am." He returned his attention to his meal, mopping up the last remnants of Lean Cuisine. "I take it this doesn't mean, though, that I'm to stop ferreting about for anchor jobs."

"By no means. This is all highly speculative."

He grinned. "You already sound like a businesswoman." He threw back the last of his chardonnay. "I have another thought. A buddy of mine from law school is a venture capitalist. I'm sure he'd be happy to talk to you, though I'm not so sure you'd like what he has to say."

"I'd love to talk to him. Thank you, Geoff." Amazing. He was actually helping her. Even though it wasn't in his best interests.

"My pleasure." He rose to carry his plates to the counter, and the two of them danced around each other loading the dishwasher. It was the most comfortable Natalie had felt with him for weeks.

At one point she broke the silence. "You look zonked."

"I'm exhausted." He rinsed his cutlery in the sink. "And home is forty minutes away."

She nodded. Her heart began to thump.

"I dread what awaits me there, too." He loaded the last of his dishes, shaking his head. "A gargantuan pile of newspapers and mail and dying plants crying out for water."

"Stay here." Her offer surprised even her. "You're too jet-lagged to drive that far and the guest bed has clean sheets."

He seemed to ponder the offer, which pleased her. "Are you sure it's all right? I mean, not too inconvenient?"

"It's not remotely inconvenient."

He shrugged, not meeting her eyes. "Well then, maybe I'll take you up on your offer. Thank you."

"The guest room's upstairs, the third door on the left." She turned her back to him to wipe down the sink, flummoxed by her inordinate pleasure that he would stay over. "Everything you need should be up there," she called over her shoulder.

"I'll go get my stuff from the car," he called back. Then she heard him let himself out the front door and return a minute later, rolling a suitcase. He disappeared upstairs.

She busied herself in the kitchen, unnecessarily swabbing down counters, feeling oddly excited. Above her, she could hear him in the guest bathroom, then the guest bedroom. Then all was quiet.

Methodically she toured the first floor, shutting lights. It was somehow exciting just to have him in the house. It was also a bit of a coup, she decided: so much for his fiancée, Janet. Apparently *she* wasn't the woman Geoff most wanted to see when he got back to L.A.

Natalie mounted the stairs. She was still surprised he'd come over at all. Maybe it was an extension of the olive branch. They'd been awkward with each other for so long. Maybe Geoff wanted things back the way they were and was going out of his way to make that happen.

Well, she'd go out of her way, too. Returning to some semblance of normalcy would be an enormous relief.

Natalie climbed the last stair and arrived at the landing outside the master suite. The unlit hall beyond was silent and cloaked in shadow. She hesitated, then continued noiselessly down the hall toward the guest bedroom. The door was shut. No light shone beneath.

She waited for a moment, then grasped the doorknob and twisted it. The door pushed open without resistance. Slowly her eyes adjusted to the dimness, and her ears to the rhythmic breathing of the man in the four-poster bed.

It was some time that Natalie stood there, listening, her eyes half closed, before she forced herself to retreat to her own room.

Geoff returned home at dawn to find a white Miata, wet with dew, parked in his driveway. He slid the Jag next to it, frowning. Janet must have come to his house the prior night. While he was at Natalie's.

Had staying over been a mistake? He wasn't sure. He just knew that he'd wanted to. He knew that it was a great relief talking about something other than canapés for the reception or whether to wallpaper the bathroom. And he'd justified it on the basis that he and Natalie needed to get back on an even keel. Nor was there anything wrong with being good friends with a client, he told himself. In fact, it was desirable.

Geoff pulled his key from the ignition, staring at Janet's convertible. How would she even have known he was coming back? Or—a thought crossed his mind that filled him with dismay. Maybe she'd been there the whole time? Maybe she'd moved in while he was away?

Dread propelled him out of the Jag and into the house, briefcase and rolling suitcase in tow. He found her in bed, asleep. Quietly he deposited his things and conducted an inspection. Minutes later he was in the kitchen, calmer, brewing a pot of coffee. Nothing had changed. She hadn't moved in. The house was still his.

"You're home." Janet's just-woken voice was soft, as was her touch as she snuggled up behind him, clasping him about the middle, smelling sweet. "Did you get back so late you slept in the guest room?" She nuzzled his back. "Didn't want to wake me?"

He forced an uncomfortable chuckle. "Sort of." He

turned to face her. "Let me give you a proper kiss." She tasted of sleep. Her long straight blond hair was loosely contained in a ponytail, falling down the back of her standard sleepwear, a pastel cotton nightdress. He made his voice casual. "So how did you know I was coming back? I'm a day early."

"I had a feeling," she murmured into his chest, "so I called your secretary." She pulled back, still clasping him, and regarded him through half-lidded eyes. "I'm surprised you didn't call to let me know."

"Oh, it happened so fast." He turned his back to her, gazing out the window beyond the coffeepot. The *Los Angeles Times* delivery boy, conducting his rounds from a bicycle, was doing his usual hit-and-miss job. Geoff's issue landed somewhere on the lawn, where the dew would render it a sodden mess within minutes. "I'm going to rescue the newspaper," he told Janet.

She padded after him all the while that he retrieved the *Times*, poured coffee, and set himself up in the breakfast room. "What time *did* you get back last night?" she asked. Was it his imagination or now did her voice have an edge?

He raised his eyes from the front page. "All right, let's get it over with. I got into L.A.X. a bit before nine and went round to a client who's going through a bad patch. I ended up spending the night in her guest room."

She waited a beat. "*Her* guest room. What client?"

"Natalie Daniels."

"I knew it!" Janet's voice ratcheted higher. "I *knew* there was something going on! I had a feeling at the engagement party."

"There's nothing 'going on,' " he heard himself insist. "She simply offered me a glass of wine, we talked about her situation—which, may I remind you, is dire—and it rapidly became clear that I wasn't fit to drive home. I was jet-lagged, remember. I'd barely eaten. It was two in the morning New York time."

Janet was shaking her head. "You make it sound so sensible but somehow I find it hard to believe."

"You're doubting me?" He shook his head. "I find that very disappointing."

"So do I, because this isn't the way it's supposed to be. I'm not supposed to be questioning my fiancé's commitment." She raised her lovely eyes to his, blue and accusing. "I want you to dump her. Let her find another agent."

That angered him. "No. Absolutely not. I told you, she's in serious professional trouble. And, Janet, you do not have a say over who is my client and who isn't. Natalie Daniels needs a new job and she needs me. Period."

"*I* need you. And I'm about to become your wife. That should take precedence over everything else." She paused, the sudden silence deafening. "So do you want to marry me or not?"

"I proposed, didn't I?"

Then Janet came forth with a declaration that shook him to the core. "I want to get married now. Not wait till May."

He tried not to stutter. "Now? I mean, *now*? We settled on May. Why change it?"

But she was at the kitchen calendar, holding up pages. That was at least better than an instant elopement, which was what Geoff now most feared. "October fifth. That feels like a good day."

"Janet, this is nuts." He abandoned the newspaper to walk closer to her, careful to soften his voice. "There's no reason to put ourselves through this. May is a fine month to marry. It'll give you time to plan everything exactly the way you want it."

She was still looking at the calendar. "No, the fourth. A Friday, because it'll be hard to book everything on a Saturday at this late date. My mom will help me. We'll get it done."

"Janet." He forced her to look at him. "Don't do this. This doesn't make sense."

"It makes sense to me." She met his eyes. "And if you loved me, it would make sense to you, too."

What to say to that? She'd boxed him in. And October fourth was better than eloping here and now. He shook his head, outdone. Perhaps Janet should give up teaching first grade and become a trial attorney. She could certainly win an argument.

SEPTEMBER

☆

CHAPTER EIGHTEEN

Thursday, September 5, 6:32 P.M.

Natalie had decided in advance that it was wiser to park up the street. Safer. It just didn't feel like a good idea for her to park for all the world to see in Miles's driveway. What if he came home unexpectedly? That was unlikely, which was why she'd chosen this particular evening for her mission, but still it was possible that *Forget Maui*'s taping would finish early and Miles would return home before she was done with her business. She *might* be able to get away undetected if that happened, but not if her car was smack-dab in the middle of his driveway.

Natalie carefully parked the Mercedes about a quarter mile north on Pacific Coast Highway, near a signal and a crosswalk. A pedestrian needed both to get across PCH's four hazardous lanes without meeting her Maker. Traffic whizzed by at phenomenally high speeds, despite the road's sharp curves and stunning beachfront vistas. Apparently neither Angeleno nor tourist could be bothered to slow down for either safety's or beauty's sake.

She pulled the key from the ignition but remained in the car, reviewing her game plan. She'd gone over it countless times and only a few unavoidable flaws remained. One was that Kelly might show up. Natalie was betting that that wouldn't happen with Miles not home. The other risk was Suzy, who for all Natalie knew Miles might still be seeing. She snorted softly. Her husband wasn't exactly faithful. But Suzy was *Forget Maui*'s star, so she had to be at the taping even more than Miles did.

Natalie clutched the steering wheel. Her plan *had* to work: Miles's attorney Johnny Bangs had gotten a judge to agree that September sixth, the very next day, marked discovery closure. She refused to let the day dawn without having her hands on documentation of Miles's sitcom fee. Which his damn studio, despite two subpoenas, still hadn't provided.

She exited the car and for a moment just stood still, cars whizzing past. It was a hot, dry evening. In her break-in getup of sweatshirt and leggings, she was unpleasantly warm even here at the coast.

Natalie finally got across PCH and made her way south toward Miles's house, the ocean to her right, her sneakered feet crunching on gravel. This stretch of PCH had no sidewalks, which didn't exactly make for a pleasant stroll. Traffic careened past at killer speeds, a lowlife hooted obscenities out his window, gravel dust blew up into her face. But soon she arrived.

The one-story beige clapboard beachfront home looked as gorgeous as ever, what with all the windows replaced and the remodeling apparently completed. Natalie walked around to the main door, on the south side. It was repainted a Colonial gray, and at its left, just as she remembered from her window-breaking foray, was a tall ficus in a terra-cotta pot.

She bent and felt carefully around the pot's base, soon hitting pay dirt. She smiled, closing her fingers around a key. That was the handy thing about being married to a man for a dozen years. You knew his habits.

And yes, there was an alarm system—she could tell from the Westec decal pasted on a small window next to the door. But chances were excellent that the code was *101147*. Miles's birthday. That had been his code in the house he'd owned when she met him. And he'd insisted they use that code on Nichols Canyon, saying it was the only one he could be expected to remember. How like Miles, she realized now.

If by some trick of fate that *wasn't* his code, she'd just

bolt. She could run the quarter mile back to her car with no difficulty. She didn't work out for nothing. By the time the cops showed up to check out the intrusion, she'd be back in the Mercedes heading for the Hollywood Hills.

She took a deep breath and advanced the key toward the lock.

"Hey, wait a minute!" A man, a gruff-voiced man. But not Miles. At least that.

She froze, her heart pounding, the key just in the lock.

"Who are you?" the man demanded.

She arranged her features in what she hoped was an imperious mien and spun around to face the man who now stood just behind her. Tall. Beefy. Workman's clothes. Scowling. "Who are *you*?" she demanded, and the man's big dark eyes flew open. With, she realized instantly, recognition.

"Oh, ma'am. I'm sorry, ma'am." He stepped back and doffed his baseball cap, holding it in front of his plaid-shirted chest. "Natalie Daniels—I mean, Ms. Daniels," he stuttered. "I'm Dale, ma'am, pleased to make your acquaintance, ma'am. I didn't realize you and Mr.—"

"Mr. Lambert and I are married, yes." Absolutely true, at least until that happy day when California's legal system worked its magic. "My husband didn't tell me you'd be here this late." She tried to sound annoyed.

He made a waving motion with a big callused hand. "It took longer than usual to finish up, ma'am. You know how it goes."

"Yes, I suppose."

Still he stood there. *What in hell do I do now? I don't want to open the door with him here! What if the alarm goes off and it turns out I don't know the code?*

"Actually, I need to get back inside, ma'am," he said, and her heart dropped. "I forgot my needlenose pliers and I'm gonna need 'em tomorrow at another job."

He could see plain as day that she'd already put the key in the lock, so she couldn't exactly have *him* open the door, now could she?

"I see." She turned her back to him to face the door,

then tried to work up a casual tone. "By the way, did you reset the alarm before you locked up?"

"Yes, ma'am," he replied proudly.

God, no. She closed her eyes. *Please make the code be 101147.* She twisted the key, then pushed the door open. The alarm system began its insistent beep, beginning the inexorable twenty-second countdown to a full-out siren and the imminent arrival of the authorities. It was at that moment that she realized she hadn't the slightest idea where the code pad might be.

Kelly perched on one of the dozens of moving boxes piled high in the living room of her Bel Air house, staring at her new flat-panel television. The *Hard Line* anchorwoman was reading a tag to a piece on killer tornadoes.

I could do better than her, Kelly thought. She had to be mid-thirties, minimum. And she didn't look exactly *bad* but she'd look a helluva lot better if she had on more makeup.

Kelly was nervous—she had to admit it. How wild was it that her first national appearance was the very same night she moved into her new house? Was that some kind of sign or what?

The anchorwoman finished the tag and segued into a tease of Kelly's accident spot. That got Kelly's heart really pumping.

"When we come back, a Los Angeles man loses his life when a killer earthquake forces his car headlong into a reinforced light pole. Metal meets metal with deadly results. When Killer Disasters *continues . . . here on* Hard Line."

Kelly stared at the screen, irritated. Why didn't that bitch use her name in the tease? She could just as easily have said, *As Kelly Devlin reports, a Los Angeles man . . .*

Well, she told herself, what *really* mattered was that her spot was making national air. And *Hard Line* would *have* to use her name when they tossed to her package.

She guessed they must have just forgotten about the release from the Manns, because of course they never got it. Because of course she never *sent* it.

Impatiently Kelly played with the chain at her neck, desperate for the commercial break to be over. Finally it was. The anchor reappeared, her face serious. Fake serious, Kelly could tell.

> *"When Los Angeles fell victim to a huge earthquake in June, one man on his way home from a fun-filled weekend in Las Vegas drove straight into a nightmare."*

Then the screen filled with quake video, the shaky kind where the camera captures the tremors and people scream and stuff falls off shelves. Kelly watched, her chain in her mouth, confused. Why hadn't the anchor said Kelly's name? Then, to her amazement, she heard the anchor begin to voice over her piece.

> *"Darryl Mann was returning to his Santa Monica apartment from Las Vegas when—"*

That Hard Line *woman is voicing my piece?* Kelly listened, disbelieving. It took her a while to grasp that, yes, she really was.

Then she got so mad she stopped listening. The video from her spot, only slightly recut, flew past. But she barely saw it. Because she was so mad she couldn't see straight. They'd cut her out of it? They'd used her video but cut *her* completely out of it? *This sucks! This totally sucks!*

Then it was over. *That was it?*

The bitch anchorwoman came back on screen, not a care in the world. Kelly would've jumped through the screen to kill her if she could've managed it.

Everything she went through? All that trouble? Getting the dub? Running the risk of the Manns seeing it and going ballistic? That was all to impress *Hard Line*! Get a shot at a national job! Not for some *Hard Line* anchor to voice the video! Kelly was stunned at the unfairness of it all. It was as if they thought she was a producer or something, providing video for somebody else to voice!

She grabbed the remote and stabbed the POWER button until the TV finally went black. She sat in her silent new house, shaking with anger. *Fuck* Hard Line *and everybody on it.*

It all sucked and there was only one thing she could think of to make herself feel better. She stood up from the packing box, starting to search for her duffel bag. She couldn't believe how much crap she had to take. People really dished it out in TV news—that much was for damn straight.

Natalie advanced slowly into Miles's Malibu house, Dale the workman clomping in behind her. She could feel his eyes on her back as her own gaze darted left, then right in desperate search of the alarm code pad.

Where in the world would it be? It sure as hell wasn't obvious. At least not to her, at least not now with the alarm beeping insistently and Dale as close on her heels as a puppy. In front of her in the pristine high-ceilinged foyer was a white wall with nothing on it. To the left was Miles's huge living room, with massive windows offering a Pacific view. To the right were steps down to a sleek, modern kitchen. She veered right, her gut telling her that was more promising. Of course Dale followed.

Her mind raced. She probably had only ten seconds left before the siren began to wail. *Is there any way I can ask Dale where it is, without him getting suspicious? Play the ditz? Oh, silly me, we haven't lived here long and I forget where the code pad is!*

Then she found it, totally by chance, when her frenzied eyes lit upon a phone alcove in the kitchen. At that point her next problem reared its ugly head. *Make the code be 101147!*

Holding her breath, she punched in the numbers.

The gods must have been smiling, because the alarm's high-pitched beeping gave way to a few final peeps, then blessed silence. Briefly she remained motionless, leaning her forehead against the wall.

"Got what I needed," Dale said. She jumped. "Hey, sorry I startled you."

"My fault." She had her hand at her throat.

"I'll be off then." He turned to go.

"Um, excuse me? Dale?" Natalie turned her smile on full force.

He turned to face her, one foot on the kitchen stairs leading up to the foyer, dark eyes expectant.

"I have a favor to ask you."

"Shoot."

"I'd appreciate it if you wouldn't tell anybody you saw me here at the house today."

His eyebrows shot up.

"Security reasons," she added hastily. "Because—"

"Because you're on TV!" Dale laughed, obviously pleased to have added two and two correctly. "You don't want folks to know where you live." His face grew solemn. "Can't be too careful these days. Our little secret, Ms. Daniels." He nodded sagely.

"Thank you." She walked forward to shake his hand. "Thank you very much."

Dale let himself out, and Natalie found herself alone in Miles's Malibu beach house.

She conducted a brief tour. Kitchen, dining room, living room, study, three bedrooms, two-and-a-half baths, deck with Jacuzzi, pool. Whitewashed pine floors and lots of big windows so nearly every room had killer ocean views. She stood in the living room, hands on hips, surveying the Pacific as the sun made its last stand for the day. Typical multimillion-dollar Malibu beach house. Typical Miles for wanting it, no doubt less for his own enjoyment than to flaunt his new success. And either the housekeeper had come that day or her husband was getting fastidious in his old age. Nothing was out of place, not that there was much to *be* out of place. The furniture was minimal and designer-procured, clearly: metal and glass and marble to go with the property's sleek contemporary lines. Not at all the tile and stucco and beams and dark gleaming hardwood of the house on Nichols Canyon. She grimaced. *We picked it out together but maybe he secretly hated it. Or now is on to a new phase. Which includes Kelly and Suzy and who knows who else.* A jolt of bitterness rippled through her. What a lowlife her husband was. What a comeuppance he deserved.

Then she'd better get cracking to give it to him.

Natalie made her way to the study, whose built-in bookshelves were crammed with more scripts than books, and whose white space-age desk held pride of place in the center of the room. She knelt by a file cabinet beside the desk and pulled open a drawer.

It didn't take long to find a set of thick files labeled *Forget Maui* with Roman numerals I through VI. She pulled out all six and hauled them to the desk.

Number I had interesting stuff, but not what she was looking for. She moved on to II. Ditto. She was getting a kink in her neck. She rubbed it and glanced at her watch: 8:17. On to III.

III was . . . *very* interesting. One document in particular, with Heartbeat Studios letterhead, that looked like a contract. Carefully she pulled it out and ran her eyes down the first neatly typewritten page. Then the second.

Phrases leaped out at her: . . . *one-million-dollar signing bonus in one lump-sum payment . . . executive producing* Forget Maui *for a total twenty-two episodes . . . two-million-dollar fee to be paid over fifty-two-week period . . .*

No mention anywhere of the "unorthodox" deal Johnny Bangs had described, that Miles had deferred compensation until the studio renewed the sitcom for a second season, so that Miles could receive a balloon bonus payment.

She frowned, flipped open file IV and caught her breath. Check stubs. Lots of them. And all from Heartbeat Studios, made out to Miles Lambert.

She caught her breath. One for a million dollars, dated March fifteenth! *The signing bonus.* Quickly, she checked the date Heartbeat Studios had signed the contract. It jibed. March sixth.

And there were so many more, all for roughly thirty-eight thousand dollars. One a week, she realized flipping through them, starting June third. *It's probably the two million divided over fifty-two weeks,* she calculated. *Just like the contract says.*

She reared up, heart pounding. Miles and Johnny Bangs had been lying. There was no unorthodox arrangement with the studio. Miles hadn't deferred compensation. He was getting paid right along, like all executive producers did. And he'd already cashed checks worth over a million-and-a-half dollars, which probably explained how he'd made the down payment on the very house in which she was standing.

And I'd be entitled to half that if there were no prenup, since he earned it while we're still legally married.

But Miles couldn't lie anymore. She'd found him out. This would give her and Berta the ammo they needed to end his thievish claim for half the marital property.

And get this divorce over with once and for all . . .

Her eyes fell on the digital desk clock. 8:28. She had to copy these documents. But there was no home copier to be found.

Fine, she decided swiftly. *The hell with Miles.* She'd take the originals.

Leaving the studio contract and check stubs on the desk, she grabbed the files to return them to the file cabinet. One particularly hefty document slipped loose and landed facedown on the whitewashed pine floor. Judging from the look of it, it was probably a script. Natalie put the files back in the cabinet, then bent and flipped the document over. It *was* a script.

A very marked-up script, she soon realized. She knelt by the file cabinet with it heavy in her hands. Even the title page was marked up. The original title, *Jamaica Beach*, was crossed out, and above it was scrawled *Forget Maui.* Beneath the typewritten words *"Written by,"* the name *"Jerry Cohen"* was crossed out and *"Miles Lambert"* was written in. All the writing was Miles's distinctive chicken scratch.

How odd. Natalie stared at the title page, her brow furrowed, then flipped to the middle. It, too, was marked up. Some lines were crossed out, with new lines written in, though not many. It was that way throughout.

The script slid out of her hands and onto the floor. She raised her head and stared sightlessly across the study at the built-in bookshelves, loaded with scripts. *Oh, my God.* Her mind began to whirl. *Is it possible?*

Miles had dumped Jerry Cohen as a writing partner eight years before. Jerry went on to even greater sitcom success, then took a sabbatical to write a screenplay. He'd moved to Tuscany, she thought she'd heard, though she hadn't spoken to him since he and Miles broke up. For all she knew he was still in Italy.

But his script for *Jamaica Beach* was here. In Miles's study. Retitled *Forget Maui.* And under another script-writer's name. Miles Lambert.

It could only add up to one thing.

Miles hadn't written *Forget Maui* in a creative burst, a sudden outpouring of long dormant but prodigious tal-ent. He had plagiarized it. He had sat in that study on Nichols Canyon and decided to steal the words and ideas of his former writing partner.

A memory rose in her mind. Miles, when they'd been married three or four years. By then he'd started bad-mouthing Jerry. He was sick of carrying him, Miles had told her. The guy was a parasite, he said. Untalented. The battle raged for weeks, then a month, then a few months. One night she'd come home from anchoring the news to find Miles in his study, typing furiously on his computer keyboard. His dark eyes were feverish with excitement.

"You must have found your muse today," she'd observed.

"Read this." He'd moved aside to let her see the com-puter screen.

She'd read the first lines eagerly, a few more less so. It was a diatribe against Jerry. Vitriolic, hateful. Almost incoherent. She remembered staring at it, shocked that her husband could generate such bile.

"I'm dumping him." Miles's jaw set. "I may sue. He's stolen more than one idea from me."

She'd been stunned. "Jerry hasn't stolen anything from you."

Miles had scoffed at that. "I can make it sound like he did."

There in Miles's study in Malibu, Natalie knelt immobilized on the hardwood floor. Then she heard a sound.

The front door opening. Slamming shut. Heels sounding on the hardwood. Too quick and light to be Miles's walk.

Instantly Natalie scurried behind the desk, her heart racing. It was a woman. Suzy? Kelly? It was somebody who had a key and was very much at home. The woman walked into the kitchen and opened the fridge, then slammed it shut. Ditto with a cupboard door. Whoever it was did a lot of slamming. Then she heard a cork being pulled.

More steps. Natalie crouched lower behind the desk and held her breath. The woman walked past. Seconds ticked by. Maybe she could sneak out. She *had* to sneak out. Then she heard a wonderful sound. The bath running.

She waited a minute more, then rose cautiously and advanced to the door. She could see across the living room to the master suite, where the woman was making noise. Drawers and closet doors opening and slamming shut. A strong scent of lilac filled the air. Bath salts, Natalie concluded. Suzy or Kelly, it didn't matter a damn. She just had to take what she'd found and get out.

She raced back to the desk and stuffed the studio contract and check stubs into her purse, then stared at the plagiarized script, lying on the floor.

No way I'm going to leave this. The gloves are off now, Miles.

With the script cradled in her left arm like a football, Natalie tiptoed out of the study and into the living room. The woman was in the tub, she concluded. The Jacuzzi jets were whirring and water was sloshing.

Carefully, Natalie made her way to the foyer, her sneakered feet noiseless on the whitewashed pine floor. When she got outside and silently pulled the door shut behind her, she returned the key to its hiding place beneath the potted ficus. Then, in the darkness that had fallen, she bent low and scampered across the width of the house, then rose and sprinted north on PCH toward her car.

As she ran, a grin spread across her face.

Her TV-news career was in a shambles. Her love life was nonexistent. But the universe was tilting in her direction where one Miles Lambert was concerned.

CHAPTER NINETEEN

Monday, September 9, 10:36 A.M.

Tony punched his intercom button. “Maxine, get Ruth in here.” Then he pushed a button on his remote to rewind the hour-long special *Kids in Danger*, hosted by Kelly Devlin and produced by Ruth Sperry, that he'd just screened for the first time.

What a disappointment. The thing never made it out of first gear. Sure, it conked you on the head with info, but who the hell cared? Plus, he had to admit, Kelly came off as a lightweight, even mouthing all those statistics Ruth had fed her.

Ruth showed up in his doorway, looking like a huge lemon in a bright yellow suit. “What's up?” she asked him, sitting down in front of his desk. Never one for preamble, old Ruth.

“You need to jazz up *Kids in Danger*. Big-time.” He pressed EJECT on the remote and the tape popped out, like a period on his sentence.

She narrowed her beady blue eyes at him. “What do you mean, jazz it up? What's wrong with it?”

“It's not sexy enough. Not enough effects, not enough quick cuts, not enough music. Jazz it up.”

“But we're doing a serious special . . . ah, forgive me.” She slapped her forehead. “I forgot. Kelly Devlin's the anchor. It can't be a serious special.”

“Save it, Ruth. Just jazz the thing up.”

“Let me get this straight.” Tony watched her prepare

to beat this dead horse into the ground. "You want me to make a special about how today's young people are at risk from unpredictable violent outbursts 'sexy' and 'jazzy' "—she drew big imaginary quotation marks in the air—"with more effects than, say, an action movie."

He didn't like the way she said it, but basically, yeah. "Basically, yeah."

"Like a music video?" she went on.

He shrugged. "That's what sells."

She looked disgusted. "And heaven knows we've got to sell, since the ratings are still in the dumper."

"The ratings are fine," he lied, but didn't know why he bothered. Broads like Ruth Sperry were like the nuns in his elementary school: they could see right through you.

"Fine. I'll review the CNN dubs and see what else we can use. But only up to a point." She stood up. "I'm not going to have my moniker attached to a special I'm not proud of."

He watched her walk out of his office. He hated when Ruth got all self-righteous. This was TV news, not Sunday school. Everybody was just doing what they had to to survive.

Geoff stretched his arms across the back rest of the park bench, happily waiting for Natalie and the bag lunch she'd promised. She'd told him she wanted to report back on her get-together with his venture capitalist buddy and in his estimation this was a fine place to do it.

He'd always liked Roxbury Park. It was a spot of green in the southern part of Beverly Hills, where the surrounding multimillion-dollar houses would have passed for plain old middle-class in a more rational part of the country. To the west, toward the beach, rose the graceful white towers of Century City, one of them housing Dewey, Climer, Fipton and Marner. To the east lay a series of residential blocks, complete with neat squares of lawn daily watered by hired help so they wouldn't brown in southern California's relentless sun.

On this hot, bright September afternoon, the sky was

clear, the air dry. He'd long since shed his suit jacket. Not far away a group of boys played soccer, madly chasing the ball, falling on the ground, screeching, yelling at one another to pass or run or kick. None of it was to much effect but none of them seemed to care much. When was the last time he'd done anything just for fun? Geoff wondered. Eventually he'd reduced even surfing to a competition, though his only rival was himself.

His gaze traveled east and he spied Natalie walking toward him. She was in beautifully cut white trousers and a turquoise blouse, hair loose, ever-present black bag dangling from her shoulder. He grinned. He liked her out of her anchor armor, the power suits and French-twisted hair and heavy studio makeup. She drew near and their eyes met. She'd known immediately where to find him, of course, because every time they met at Roxbury Park it was at the same bench. Creatures of habit, both of them.

"Sorry I'm late." She smiled and the sun made a halo of her blond hair.

He found himself smiling, too. "No problem. I've been soaking up the rays."

"Amazing any are getting through the smog. I got you the usual." She pulled sandwiches wrapped in waxed paper out of a paper bag. "Plus two *enormous* pickles and a Coke." She sat next to him, plunked her bag on the ground, and proceeded to unwrap what he knew would be a California Veggie. "Have you been able to reach Tony?"

"No. I've left three messages with Maxine, who's quite the guard dog. She's better than a Doberman. Clearly he's dodging me."

"Bad sign or good sign?"

"Good sign. I bet he's rethinking his offer."

She frowned. "You mean to pull it?"

"No, to raise it."

"Good! At least that." She smiled; then the smile faded. "Though the idea of still working for him a year from now kills me. Any nibbles from other news directors?"

"Hmm." He'd prefer to dodge that question. "Let's say we're making progress."

Natalie nodded and he knew he hadn't fooled her. They were silent for a time, both eating, before Geoff asked about her meeting with the venture capitalist.

"Helpful, though I can't say it left me very optimistic." She sighed, and he heard her weariness. "He said it's just so hard to get funding for a new company these days. Even the established ones are having trouble."

Geoff nodded, secretly pleased. Just what he'd hoped for: Natalie getting a dose of hard reality about the Web idea but from someone other than him. He didn't like it, never had, but had disillusioned her on so many other fronts that he hardly wanted to add this one to the list.

Her voice perked up. "But he *did* say this site could find an audience and that would go a long way toward making it a viable business. And how the audience could be anyone wired who wants to watch local news when it's convenient for them, not necessarily when it's on. Businesspeople, for example. We'd have numerous features they'd find attractive. Frequent updating. Seasoned reporters providing analysis and commentary."

He smiled. "I note you use the word 'seasoned.' "

She rolled her eyes. "What a concept. Experience actually being valued."

They were interrupted by the soccer ball rolling up to Geoff's feet. He kicked it back to a boy who turned and scuttled back to his friends. Geoff returned his gaze to Natalie. "What else?"

"How important the management team is. How in many ways that matters more than the idea." Her face lit up. "Of course I immediately thought of Ruth."

"Really? As a cofounder?"

"There's no one I'd rather work with. And her experience and contacts complement mine."

"Do you think she'd do it?"

"That's the problem. I'd have to blast her out of that station. She hates what's happening under Tony, but still, it's the devil she knows. And she's older than I am, even less willing to take risks."

"How willing are you?"

She looked into the distance. He watched thoughts play out on the planes of her face. As for himself, he found it hard to picture a Natalie Daniels who wasn't on the air. It seemed as fundamental to her as breathing.

"If I have to, I will," she said eventually. "I can't imagine not being an anchor anymore but I have to admit I like the idea of running my own shop. Not being at the beck and call of Tony Scoppio or some other news director. Maybe what Ruth said way back when is right: we all get beached eventually. Maybe it's better to swim to shore on my own power than wait till I'm tossed off the boat. And if I do it now, I can leverage my experience and contacts and name recognition."

A proactive strategy, he thought. *Smart. And admirable.* But then again he was always finding admirable qualities in Natalie. How unstoppable she was. How getting shunted aside in the business she loved hadn't knocked her out of the game but geared her up to fight. Even losing that lout of a husband hadn't left her bitter, just sad. He could tell that from the moments when she got quiet, and distant, as if her mind were lost in a different time. *Maybe that's another reason she wants to launch a business,* he realized. *To drown herself in work. To have at least one arena in which she feels in control.* He knew the strategy.

Her voice became even more somber. "Geoff, I really appreciate your willingness to discuss this with me. But I know it's a conflict of interest for you to help a client into an area where she'll stop generating commissions for Dewey, Climer. I don't want—"

"Let *me* worry about my conflicts of interest."

She eyed him dubiously. "Are you sure? You—for that matter *everyone* at Dewey, Climer—have been very good to me. I—"

"I'm sure, Natalie." He found himself reaching out to pat her knee reassuringly. He was surprised how few qualms he felt, because indeed she raised a good point. But he wanted to help her, regardless of any ill effect on Dewey, Climer. Plus, in truth, he could always find another high-earning client. He couldn't find another Natalie.

"Well, then I have a favor to ask you."

"Shoot."

"Will you help me draft a business plan? That's the next step and I'm out of my depth."

"Sure. I'd be delighted," he heard himself say. Now how had that popped out? He didn't even like this Web business idea. Then his cell phone rang. "Damn. Hold on a second." He snapped it open. "Marner."

"Hi!"

"Janet." Damn. He watched as Natalie politely angled her body away from him. "I'm right in the middle of—"

"This is important." Her voice was excited. "My mom and I are down to two locations for the reception and I'd like you to come see them both so we can make a final decision."

"Fine. We'll do it tonight. I—"

"We have to do it *today,* not tonight." She had moved into a scrupulously patient tone, which irritated him. "We don't have much time."

"I can't do this during business hours." He kept his voice patient. "I'll tell you what. You and your mom go ahead and choose. I'm sure I'll be happy with whatever you decide."

Something in the quality of Janet's silence brought him abruptly to the realization he had said the wrong thing. But didn't women decide all this anyway? All they really wanted was his stamp of approval.

"I'll tell you what," he repeated, backpedaling fast. "How about I rearrange a few things and meet you at four?"

That seemed to mollify her. Geoff got the address, then after a quick good-bye slapped his cell phone shut.

Natalie angled herself back into a forward position on the bench.

"Sorry about that." Somehow he felt embarrassed about Natalie having overheard that call. "It's just that Janet and I have to pick a place for the reception because the wedding's so soon." Then he remembered, from the sudden stricken look on her face that she swiftly wiped off, that Natalie didn't even know he and Janet had set a date. Let alone that it was three weeks away.

"When is it?" she asked.

"October fourth. A Friday because we can't book what we need on a Saturday at this late date."

An expression of shock passed across her face. "That really is soon. October fourth," she repeated, and again she looked pained. "That's the day my contract expires."

"I hadn't thought of that." That felt awkward though he couldn't pin down why. Why shouldn't he marry on the day Natalie's contract expired? Yet it seemed disloyal, somehow.

Natalie rose abruptly, rewrapping her sandwich as she spoke. "I should let you go. You know, with everything on your plate, I don't want to bother you with this business plan thing."

"No." He surprised himself with how firm his voice sounded. "I really want to help you with it."

She looked reluctant, but agreed and thanked him. Then, without a good-bye, she walked swiftly across Roxbury Park toward her car.

Dispiritedly, he crumpled his waxed paper into a ball and tossed it basketball style into a nearby trash bin. But he missed. His shots were off lately. Everything was.

Natalie returned from Roxbury Park to her KXLA office and found one welcome message among the nineteen on her voice mail. It was from the longtime secretary to Jerry Cohen, whom Natalie had tracked down and phoned after she'd found the plagiarized script.

"Natalie, I'll give you Jerry's address, but you should know he's undercover in Tuscany working on his screenplay. You *he'd like to hear from, I know. So get your pen. It's—"*

Natalie transcribed the unfamiliar address, in Bagni di Lucca, Italy. She could easily imagine Jerry in a glorious villa pounding away at a laptop, not waiting for his muse like Miles did, but being so productive the muse was forced to visit just to get her two cents in. She smiled, with considerable fondness. In years past she hadn't understood Miles's antipathy toward Jerry. Now she did. It was fueled by jealousy.

Was she right to disturb Jerry's sabbatical with this? Natalie stared at her desk blotter, its neat white squares marred by appointments noted and stories due. She didn't want to snitch. And Jerry had chosen to distance himself from Hollywood. Maybe he wouldn't even care.

But then again, how could he not? Those were his words and ideas that had been stolen. And she'd found out about it. If she didn't tell Jerry, she'd be an accomplice to grand theft. How could she live with that?

Yes, she would alert him, she decided. What he did with the information was his own call.

Carefully she addressed a big padded manila envelope and put a copy of the script inside, along with a *Hollywood Insider* item on *Forget Maui* and a handwritten note.

Jerry,

I believe you should see this. I think of you often and fondly.

Natalie Daniels

She would mail the missive herself, not trusting KXLA's mailroom to get the international postage right. But for a few minutes, she didn't budge. She remained at her desk, surprised how little she now felt for Miles. Disgust, revulsion, an overwhelming sense of being well rid of him. Even, oddly, a little pity. But no love at all. Not even its memory.

Kelly sat in the study of her Bel Air home, trying to decide what she really thought of the cherrywood desk that Grange Furniture had just delivered. It was French, which was probably why it cost a buttload. But she figured this was the kind of furniture she should have. English Country, the realtor had told her the house was, so French should fit in. Of course she'd had to buy the desk and chair on credit, and there'd been a sucky moment when the first MasterCard she'd handed over got rejected. She'd laughed it off but still. It was hell being poor.

She stared with disgust at her latest KXLA payroll check stub, which had come that morning from the Jimenez Agency in New York. When she'd signed with Rico, she'd agreed to the usual agent/client arrangement: her paycheck went from KXLA straight to the agency, he took his ten-percent cut, deposited the rest in her checking account, and sent her a stub. But after Rico, the feds, and California all got their take, was she getting ripped off or what? Of course, the main problem was that she was still pulling down only seventy-five K a year. So all she ended up with every two weeks was sixteen hundred bucks. How was a person supposed to live on that?

It was like how her parents had lived on some pathetic tiny amount the entire time she and her sisters were growing up in Fresno. It was embarrassing to be so poor. It was a sign you hadn't figured out how the world worked. She'd decided when she was a kid she wasn't going to go through that shit all her life. It got you old fast—she'd seen that in her mother.

Maybe Rico was right. Maybe she should just take Scoppio's offer and get more in the next deal, when she had more experience. Kelly lolled back in her new cherrywood chair and wondered. Scoppio hadn't budged from his original cheap-ass position. It was kind of impressive. She'd never met anyone who was as stubborn as her until she met Tony Scoppio. Plus, she had a feeling he wasn't as hot for her anymore. It was like dating somebody. She could always tell when a guy cooled. Now she could tell that Scoppio had.

So Scoppio offered a hundred thirty grand the first year, retroactive to the contract date. She pulled out her calculator to run the numbers. After all the deductions, that would give her a little less than three thousand every two weeks. Almost six thousand a month. With that she could swing the mortgage payments. Plus she'd get a big chunk of change from the deal being retroactive and could use that to start paying off her credit card bills, which had reached pretty scary heights.

The doorbell rang. Who the hell could it be at three in the afternoon? Bel Air didn't exactly get Jehovah's Witnesses.

Kelly ambled downstairs, still in the workout gear she'd worn to kick-boxing class, and pulled open the front door.

"Good, you're here." Miles pushed past her into the foyer, wending his way through the leaning towers of Starving Students moving boxes.

Kelly studied him, knowing instantly that something was wrong. He looked big-time agitated, but ever since *Forget Maui* had started shooting he always did. Or maybe he was high, though she hadn't seen him do much of that lately.

"You haven't unpacked the boxes yet?" he snapped at her. "What the hell are you waiting for, the moving fairies?"

"Fuck you, Miles." Lazily she bumped the front door shut with her hip. She didn't feel like fighting. "Want a Gatorade?" She headed for the kitchen.

"No, I don't want a Gatorade!"

"So why aren't you at work at three in the afternoon?" She pulled a lemon-lime Gatorade from the fridge and twisted off the top. "Or did they cancel the show already?"

"Don't you fucking say that! Don't you fucking say that!" He was screeching and pointing his finger at her, his face red as if he was gonna have a heart attack.

She stared at him, kind of amazed. "Jesus Christ, Miles, what stick got up *your* butt?"

He started pacing back and forth on her limestone slab floor, shaking his head and muttering to himself. All he needed was a brown paper bag and he would've looked like one of those crazed homeless guys who tromp up and down Rodeo Drive. What if he *did* have a heart attack, right here in her kitchen? Would that be a pain in the butt or what? It would be like her new house was cursed.

He stopped pacing. "I'm going to need you to do something for me." He didn't look at her.

Kelly stared at his profile, his hair and beard grayer than she'd remembered. She'd never been big on doing favors. "Like what?"

He shuffled his feet and looked out the window. "I'm going to need you to start paying back the loan I made you."

"*Now*?" She was shocked. "That's not the deal. My first payment's in a year."

"I can't wait a year!" he shrieked. Then he took a deep breath and made himself all calm again. "Something's happened—that's all. I helped you when you needed it and now I need you to help me."

He was in deep shit. She could smell it. He'd told her that there were some problems on the show, that the studio didn't like the new scripts. Maybe that was why he was suddenly worried about money. But she didn't want to start paying him back. She couldn't afford to.

"So why don't you just give me the signed loan document," he went on, "and get your checkbook and we'll figure out how to do this so it's easiest for everybody?"

She already knew what was easiest for *her*. Not to start paying him back.

She stared at him across her brand-new kitchen, sunshiny and bright, and had a realization. That's right. She'd never actually given him the loan document. In fact, she'd never actually signed it.

But the check had cleared. And now she had her Bel Air house.

Kelly looked away from Miles and guzzled more Gatorade, thinking. No one else knew about the loan. How much easier it would be if it just went away . . . She imagined a life in which no balloon payment loomed on the horizon, like a tornado threatening to wipe her out. That would really free her up.

Miles was pacing again. *He doesn't* really *need the*

money, she decided. *He's loaded, and has the Porsche and Malibu house to prove it.*

But *she* was just starting out. She did need the money. In fact, she deserved it. Especially from an established guy like Miles. He was like a mentor.

Plus, she was sick of him. This would make it so she wouldn't have to sleep with him again.

She pulled the bottle away from her mouth. "What loan document?"

"What do you mean, what loan document?" He looked bewildered. "The one I drew up. Come on, Kelly. Go get it. And your checkbook."

"No can do, Miles." She was very calm. "You told me that was a gift, not a loan."

Now it was his turn to stare at her. She saw something change in his eyes and for a second she got scared. But only for a second, because she knew she was in charge here.

"I told you no such thing, Kelly." He squeezed his hands open and shut, as if he were gearing up for a fistfight. But he wouldn't hit her, because he knew she'd hit him back. Probably harder.

"Sure you did." She grinned. This was almost fun.

He came a few steps closer and jabbed his finger at her, right in her face. Men liked to do that shit, to prove how big they were, but it didn't work on her. She didn't scare easy. "The game is over. That was a loan and we both know it. And I have the canceled check to prove it."

"All the canceled check proves is that you gave me a hundred fifty grand. A real generous gift. Thanks, Miles."

Then his eyes got all wild and he started screaming and jabbing his finger in her face, as if he was going out of control. He looked like a lunatic. But she didn't budge. She just waited for it to be over.

"You can't do that!" he kept screaming. "You can't just take something and lie about it and make it the opposite of what it is!"

But I just did, she thought to herself.

* * *

Geoff hated conventions, but if there was one a year he had to attend, this was it.

The Radio and Television News Directors Association annual confab drew thousands of big and small fish, to backslap, talk shop, and steal one another's talent. This year the convention site was Charlotte, North Carolina, which in mid-September boasted ninety-degree temperatures and wilting humidity. Geoff prowled the vaulted, air-conditioned convention center, ignoring producers, directors, and engineers to home in on news directors who might take an interest in one Natalie Daniels.

In an adjacent row of booths he spotted a prime target: Bobbi Dominguez, News Director KNBC Los Angeles, who in recent months had expertly dodged a good dozen of his phone calls. He ambled closer. BD, black hair big as ever and dressed in what appeared to be a hot-pink summer caftan, was working a crowd of small-market news directors with tales from the big-city trenches.

Geoff watched her dark, heavily mascaraed eyes fly open midroutine when she spotted him. But he had to hand it to her: she recovered fast and waved a bangle-laden arm.

"Now here's a player for you," she loudly informed her audience. "One of the big-time L.A. agents."

Geoff laughed. "That *still* doesn't mean BD returns my calls."

"Hey, what's ten calls in ten weeks?"

"Nothing when you can chat face-to-face. Excuse us, gentlemen?" Geoff nodded at the news directors and steered BD by her fleshy elbow toward a deserted booth across the aisle.

"Always liked a strong lead," she deadpanned.

"You're my kind of woman." Geoff manhandled BD into the booth and squared off in front of her. "Cough it up, Bobbi. You've been dodging me like the plague. What's up?"

She got a cagey look. "I know what you're selling and I'm not buying."

"That's what I don't get. You've expressed interest in Natalie many times before. Why not now?"

She shuffled in place, clearly uncomfortable.

"Come on, Bobbi. What's wrong?"

Then she scoffed, which startled him. "Nothing, unless you consider institutionalization 'something wrong.' "

He frowned, incredulous. "Institutionalization?"

"Marner, don't kid a kidder." She tried to move away.

"Bobbi." He grabbed her elbow again and forced her to face him. "What in the world are you talking about?"

She rolled her eyes. "Look, I'm a woman, too, okay? I'm not one to get all high and mighty when it comes to another member of the female persuasion having problems. But that doesn't mean I have to put her on my air. And you've got no business getting on my case for that."

He spoke very slowly. "What do you mean by 'having problems?' "

She stared at him. "You're going to make me say it? Okay." She threw up her hands. "I heard about the breakdown."

"The *breakdown*?"

"Is there a PC word for it I'm not using?"

"You think Natalie Daniels had a *breakdown*?" Pieces started to slide into place in Geoff's brain. This was incredible. Yet . . . plausible. "Why in the world would you think that?" he asked, though in some quarter of his brain he knew. Already he knew.

BD threw up her hands. "What does it matter? Everybody knows by now anyway."

Everybody knows by now anyway. Geoff felt a cold rage rush through his belly. He could see how the scenario had unfolded as clearly as if it were playing on a screen in his head. Scoppio. It was Scoppio. He'd made up the malicious lie, then fed it to BD, knowing, as did everyone in Los Angeles television, that she was more effective at spreading news gossip than all the trades combined.

That explained everything. News directors shunning him. The cold shoulder when he finally did get somebody on the phone. The absence of offers after months of beating the bushes. What news director would want to hire an anchor who'd had a nervous breakdown? Risk having her blow up on live air? Not a one. It all added up.

People jostled past them, the din in the convention center deafening. Geoff found his voice, low and cold. "The bastard."

BD frowned. "What?"

"Scoppio. He lied to you, BD. He fed you a line to quash competing offers and keep Natalie in-house for a pittance."

BD scoffed again. "Come off it, Marner. You're just trying to protect your client. Not even Scoppio would go that low."

"It's a lie," Geoff repeated. This no doubt helped explain WITW passing on Natalie as well. Scoppio hadn't limited his bile to Los Angeles; he'd spread it coast to coast. "And I for one don't have any trouble believing Scoppio is capable of this," he added.

BD's face took on an ugly scowl. "You're seriously telling me there's no truth to it? That Natalie *didn't* have a breakdown?"

"There's not one whit of truth to it."

That shut BD up. Now she looked as astounded as he felt. "I can't believe Scoppio would do that to her. Or to—" Then she clammed up and Geoff silently finished her sentence for her. *Or to me.*

"Catch you later," she muttered and angled past him out of the empty booth.

He watched her stamp up the convention center's central aisle at high speed. It might as well have been a warpath.

Tony sat in the La-Z-Boy in his family room, across from the television, screening airchecks and playing hookey. In short, killing two birds with one stone.

He hadn't gone to RTNDA, though with him out of the station that day naturally everyone would assume he had. Maxine was the only person who knew otherwise, and only because she had to forward calls. Plus, he wanted to screen *The KXLA Primetime News* airchecks in the privacy of his own home, where talent somehow looked different from the way they did on a monitor at the station. This was how viewers saw talent. Maybe if he watched Kelly here, he'd get a better idea what the hell was wrong, why his ratings were still parked below 5.0. Even *after* the coaching. Even *after* the billboard campaign.

He hoisted himself out of the La-Z-Boy to stretch his legs, looking around with disgust at the family room's fake wood paneling. It amazed him that he'd had to shell out more than half a million bucks for this house. It was in Studio City and typical for the upper-middle-class San Fernando Valley neighborhoods convenient to downtown: ranch-style tract homes that boasted little more than three nondescript bedrooms and a spot of front lawn. He knew that his, with its neat white clapboard and curved stone walk bordered by Anna-Maria's impatiens, had nothing in particular to recommend it. Nothing to indicate that one of the powerhouse news directors in Los Angeles TV lived there. But at the moment he wasn't feeling like such a powerhouse.

Anna-Maria walked in with a tray bearing a mug and a muffin. She set it down beside the La-Z-Boy. "Blueberry. Just out of the oven."

He had to smile. Well into her forties Anna-Maria was still a damn good-looking woman, a helluva lot better preserved than *he* was after twenty years of marriage. And she'd given birth to twins. Slim, blond (though now it was thanks to those monthly appointments), still did her hair up real nice, still wore pretty slacks and blouses and pink lipstick even on weekdays.

He was a lucky man.

"Tony?" His wife's face was puzzled. "Why aren't you at RTNDA?"

His smile faded. He didn't want to answer that question. He didn't want to admit that the last thing he felt like doing was hobnobbing with a bunch of TV types who'd interrogate him about his ratings and why Kelly was anchoring and how he was getting along with Rhett

Pemberley. Anna-Maria had no idea that everything wasn't just peachy at KXLA and he wanted to keep it that way.

But he was saved by the bell because the phone rang.

"I'll get it." Anna-Maria scurried off, then returned holding out the cordless. "It's Maxine."

He grabbed the phone. "Bobbi Dominguez, calling from RTNDA," Maxine informed him without preamble. He frowned. Why would BD call him from Charlotte? Maybe she had some mongo gossip.

"Scoppio," BD snarled the second he put the phone to his ear, "I'm giving you one chance and one chance only."

Talk about no preamble. "BD? Are you all right?" He tried to sound concerned. Women liked that. "What are you talking about?"

"Is it or is it not true that Natalie Daniels had a nervous breakdown?"

Uh-oh. Tony's mind started spinning. He was trying to concoct a plausible story when she snarled into the phone again.

"Time's up. You sniveling troll. If you think I'm gonna let you get away with lying to me, you've got another guess coming."

Then she hung up. Tony kept the receiver at his ear until the dial tone came on because it took him that long to believe what he'd just heard.

But he didn't much like it when he did start believing it. BD was on to him. And she wasn't the sort of broad he liked to piss off.

CHAPTER TWENTY

Wednesday, September 18, 7:19 P.M.

Kelly did what she usually did after a session with KXLA's makeup artist: she added drama. She rose from the chair, got real close to the mirror, ignored the sulking makeup girl, and brought out her own liner, shadow, and mascara for round two. Feinman the coach told her she wore too much makeup but clearly he didn't understand TV news the way she did. The true news babes wore the most makeup. It was that simple and she was amazed Feinman didn't get it. What was it everybody said: those who couldn't do, taught? Same for TV-news coaches.

7:22 P.M. She had to be on set by 7:29:55 to do a five-second live tease for *The KXLA Primetime News*. And the weird thing was she had to be as done up for those five seconds as she was for the hour-long newscast at ten.

She had a few minutes. She'd go past Intake, where an operator taped all the incoming satellite feeds and airchecks, and pick up the aircheck of the prior night's newscast. She wanted to check out her new haircut on tape. It was basically the same as the old one but cost twice as much. She'd switched to a Beverly Hills stylist because she figured that was what she needed now that she was anchoring.

Past the studio, where the klieg lights were already on, through the newsroom security door to Intake by the editing booths. Kelly snatched the aircheck off the big gray metal shelves busting with tapes, then noticed Ruth's hulking form in Edit Bay 3 viewing tape.

She turned away, then did a double take.

It couldn't be. But it was. She'd logged every single frame, so of course she recognized it.

Ruth was viewing CNN's tape of the school shootout.

Damn!

How was this possible? Kelly stood under the bright fluorescent lights in the hallway by Intake, clutching the aircheck and listening to her heart pound. She'd destroyed that tape! How in hell could that warthog be watching it? Kelly remembered it well: as soon as she discovered herself on that goddamn tape she'd personally mutilated it, then in the dead of night had tossed the mangled remains off Santa Monica Pier. Where, she didn't like to think about it, a collection of items she never wanted to see again was mounting on the ocean floor.

The station intercom system buzzed on and a male voice boomed, "Kelly Devlin, you're wanted on set. *Now*."

Damn!

Mechanically Kelly's legs began to move in the direction of the studio. When she got there she ignored the ignoramus floor manager and sat down at the anchor desk opposite Camera One. Who gave a flyer if the live tease was in less than a minute? She had a nightmare to contend with.

She had to get that tape. Kelly dressed her mike and plugged in her earpiece. Probably Ruth had made dubs of every frame of video she got from CNN; in fact Kelly vaguely remembered hearing her say that.

Fine. What Ruth Sperry could do, Kelly Devlin could undo. Kelly glared into Camera One and vowed that she would get every last dub of that goddamn tape out of her executive producer's fat hands.

Natalie claimed the chair next to Ruth in the darkness of Edit Bay 3 and wiped her damp palms on her panty-hosed legs. She couldn't deny it—she was as nervous as a high school boy gearing up to ask his dream date to the prom. But Ruth—caustic, funny, loyal Ruth—was her target, and nothing nearly like a prom was in the offing. "What are you working on?" she asked her.

"*Kids in Danger*. I tell you, I will be so happy when this piece of shit special finally airs." Ruth put the tape on slo-mo and raised her chin to squint at the monitor through her bifocal lenses. "Working with Kelly is driving me nuts. That girl has more moods than the Rockettes on Midol."

Natalie chuckled, then sobered as she watched the grim images crawl past.

Ruth gave a heavy sigh and paused the tape. "Tony wants it jazzed up, if you can believe it. So I'm reviewing the CNN material to see what else we can use." She glanced at her watch, a ladylike gold band on her left wrist, then focused her gaze on Natalie, her sharp blue eyes appraising. "So how are you?"

Natalie took a deep breath. "Funny you should ask." And then she plunged in, telling Ruth all about the Web venture. And with every detail it began to take real shape in her mind, so real that she could almost imagine setting up shop in some business park, leasing office furniture, and getting started.

When she finally shut up, Ruth just stared at her. Then, after what seemed a long time, she reached out and patted her knee and Natalie could swear that Ruth's eyes were something very close to misty. "I think it's a fantastic idea," she said quietly. "And if you really want to do this, you can make it happen. You're one of the few people I know who could."

"You don't think it's crazy?"

Ruth shrugged. "It's a leap, but the best things in life are. Wasn't it a leap when you went into TV in the first place?"

Natalie nodded. And she'd done more and gone farther in television than she'd ever dreamed she would. She rubbed her damp hands down her legs again in another futile attempt to dry them. "So, Ruth, are you ready for a leap?"

The older woman's eyes narrowed. "What are you talking about?"

She took a deep breath. "I'd like you to consider joining me. As my partner. You'd get an equity stake, a big one."

Ruth's face registered shock, a rare sight. "You want me to join you in this venture of yours?"

"Why is that so surprising? We work tremendously well together, I enjoy every minute of it, and you're the best producer I've ever known. Not to mention that this place is a hellhole since Scoppio took over. I'd be honored if you joined me. I mean"—Natalie hesitated—"if you can see your way clear to doing so. I realize you might have financial constraints. I know this is a huge life change. And it's risky. But please say you'll consider it."

Ruth looked away, as if she were imagining a private world that Natalie couldn't see. Natalie had a flash that, as long as they'd worked together, there was a great deal about Ruth Sperry that she didn't know.

"Might be good to shake me up," Ruth said slowly. "I've been sitting on my butt for a long time now. And new chances don't come up that often."

Natalie's heart began to pound. "You'll think about it?"

"You're really sure you want to take on an old biddy like me?"

"If you're an old biddy, what does that make me?"

"A young biddy." Ruth punched the EJECT button on the videotape machine and the CNN cassette popped out. "I'll think about it. And in the meantime I'll make the radio calls, see what stations we can line up to cooperate."

Natalie's eyes flew open. "You'd do that?"

"Why not? I started in radio. Those folks are my buds. They get drunk at my house on the weekend. I'll line 'em up in no time."

Natalie reached across the small expanse of KXLA's Edit Bay 3 and grasped Ruth in a hug, which seemed to embarrass her.

"So what's next?" Ruth asked gruffly.

"I sit in my office and write a business plan. Geoff agreed to help me but I'm doing the first draft. I'm going to stay late tonight to work on it."

Ruth arched her brows, suddenly a mischievous glint in her eye. "And where does all this leave Tony Scoppio?"

Natalie rose from her chair, smiling. "Out in the cold."

Kelly decided the best place to kill time after *The KXLA Primetime News* was the ladies' room by the executive wing. Nobody would be there, which was key since people would think it was weird if they saw her hanging around after the newscast. People in TV news liked their jobs but when their shifts were over they ran out of the station like it was going to detonate. Anybody still on the lot after hours was doing something bad, like making contraband dubs or stealing tapes. Exactly what Kelly was planning, in fact.

She lay down on the ratty pink couch in the anteroom, figuring she had to hang till eleven forty-five at least. By then, the station should be empty except for the intern who manned the Assignment Desk overnight and the graveyard-shift security guard. Howard Bjorkman had the intern so terrified of missing a phone call he only left the Desk for the john, and Kelly had already made sure the guard was asleep as usual in the crew room.

Damn if the couch wasn't lumpy. Kelly struggled to find a good spot, staring up morosely at the pink and silver flowered wallpaper and asbestos ceiling. Couch stuffing poked into her back and her butt. The whole place reeked of cleaning products. Minutes ticked by. She felt as if she were in a war: bored as hell but nervous at the same time, because she was about to do something scary. Break into her executive producer's locked office to make off with a tape.

Finally it was eleven forty-five. She rose from the couch and reached into her jacket pocket for the bobby pin she'd lifted from the hair studio. Thank God she'd practiced this a lot as a kid, locking her parents' bedroom door, then breaking it open again. She made her way back toward the newsroom, tiptoeing so her heels wouldn't clack on the concrete floor. Past the crew room, which, surprisingly, was empty. She paused, briefly nervous, then relaxed as she realized the guard had probably segued into phase two of his shift, sitting in Satellite Operations watching porn flicks. She didn't bother to check on the Assignment Desk intern, instead heading straight upstairs to Ruth's office.

Locked, as she expected. Out came the bobby pin. She made fast work of it. Inside she scurried, then pulled the door shut behind her. She flicked on the overhead light, blinking at the fluorescence.

For the first time, Kelly was grateful that Ruth Sperry was so organized. For behind Ruth's desk, lined up on a metal file cabinet, were tapes clearly labeled CNN/*KIDS IN DANGER*. Plain as day, even from across the office.

But which was the tape she needed? She couldn't make off with all nine of them—Ruth would know for sure something was up. Kelly ran across the office to power on the betatape VCR and monitor, both of which took an eternity to warm up. Finally they were ready. She muted the volume and popped in tape nine, which she thought was the right one.

It was nine, she could tell instantly. By now every frame of that goddamn video was seared into her brain. She ejected the cassette and powered down the equipment.

Kids in Danger was supposed to air pretty soon, so she had to hope Ruth would decide she didn't have time to call CNN for another dub. But Kelly would have to keep her eyes open. If another tape shipment came in from CNN, she'd just have to get the new dub and destroy it, too.

At that moment, the door to Ruth's office opened.

Startled, Kelly spun on her heels, the tape in her hand, realizing as she stared at Natalie Daniels standing in the doorway that the situation must look pretty damn suspicious.

"What the hell are you doing in Ruth's office at midnight?" Natalie's voice was so low and menacing that for the first time in her life, Kelly was kind of afraid of her. "Ruth always locks her door when she leaves." Natalie moved a step closer. "And what is that tape in your hand? Give me that."

"Back off," she growled. "What's your problem? This is a tape of my show. Remember? It's *my* show now!"

Natalie moved toward her and without thinking Kelly tried to run past her out the door. But Natalie was surprisingly quick—*bitch!*—and grabbed her by the elbow before she made it out.

"Give me that," Natalie snarled and tried to pull the tape away. Kelly was surprised how strong she was, but she wasn't going to let her have it. She'd never let her have it. She'd never let go . . .

"Hey!" The security guard, big and white and dumb, loomed in the doorway. For a split second Kelly's hand relaxed and Natalie jerked backward, tripping over her own feet and landing on her butt.

But with the tape in her hand.

Damn!

"What's going on here?" The security guy was wide awake now. He stepped into Ruth's office and stood between Kelly and Natalie, holding his arms wide to keep them apart.

"She broke into Ruth's office," Natalie said, getting to her feet, "and tried to steal this tape."

"I did not, you paranoid moron!" Kelly lied. She turned to the guard and made her voice reasonable. "Ruth told me I needed to screen this tape tonight and that's what I'm doing." She pointed at Natalie. "I don't know what *her* problem is."

"Fine." Natalie headed toward Ruth's desk. "Let's call Ruth at home. Just so happens I know her number."

No! Kelly lunged for Natalie and the tape, figuring that afterward she'd break for the door. But Natalie raced behind Ruth's desk and Kelly felt the security guard grab her around the waist and the tape was gone,

gone. She didn't get it and she'd never get it, and—*oh fuck!*—what was going to happen now . . . ?

Natalie looked at Kelly, her face all serious. "Looks like now I've got something on *you.* Maybe a chance to get even with you for sleeping with my husband."

Kelly's mouth dropped open. She was in deep doggie do now. She watched Natalie pick up Ruth's phone and felt as if her heart chose that exact moment to stop beating.

Natalie and Geoff kicked off their working Saturday in what Natalie judged the most sensible of ways: by not working. They took advantage of the gorgeous day by hiking up Nichols Canyon to Mulholland Drive, then continuing a half mile east along the ridge until they hit Runyan Canyon. Then down the dirt path that led to the overlook, which afforded a glorious view of the L.A. basin, all blurred and white and shimmery in September's hot haze. Hikers were everywhere, and runners, and locals with dogs off leash, everybody freer somehow, as though the weekend air had invaded their bloodstreams and buoyed their moods.

She took her eyes off the view to study Geoff's profile. Apparently he hadn't shaved that morning, because he had a bit of a shadow, and his light brown hair was tousled from the breeze. He was in khaki shorts, a white tee-shirt, and Topsiders, and he looked tall and tanned and handsome. Like a male version of *The Girl from Ipanema.* And as unattainable: two weeks from marrying another woman. Reluctantly she tore her eyes away.

He spoke still squinting out at the view. "I'm going to tell you something that's going to make you very, very angry."

She frowned. "What's that?"

Then Geoff relayed to her how Tony had concocted and spread the lie that she had suffered a nervous breakdown. By the time he finished, Natalie was apoplectic.

"That's outrageous! I should sue Scoppio's butt from here to kingdom come! That's libelous, Geoff, and it's keeping me from getting another anchor job!"

"I completely understand how outraged you are, but speaking as an attorney I believe it would be difficult to make a libel case stick."

All she could do was shake her head, even more enraged. And frustrated that once again she'd been checkmated by Tony Scoppio. "This explains the cockamamie remark that Dean Drosher made to me after my audition, asking whether I could handle the stress of an anchor job. At the time it seemed crazy but now I understand why he wanted to know!" She threw her hands up in the air. "Do you understand now? Do you understand why I cannot countenance continuing to work for that bastard?"

Geoff's voice was calm, though it failed to mollify her. "I've always understood that, Nats. And rest assured that I've begun to reverse the damage, though it's tough. People tend to believe the first story they hear, even news directors who should know better."

"Geoff, I have only two weeks left!" The reality was staggering. She had never imagined her career would come to this sorry pass. "Two weeks from today I'm unemployed unless I get another offer or re-sign with Scoppio."

"You'll get other offers, Natalie." Geoff shaded his eyes with his hand to scan the horizon, as though offers might be incoming even then and there.

But she was hard-pressed to share his confidence. By the time they returned to her house she was itching to take her life into her own hands by honing the business plan.

They repaired to her redbrick terrace for a quick lunch of grilled chicken and salad, then got down to the nitty-gritty, still sitting at the umbrella-shaded teak table where they'd eaten.

Geoff tossed aside his napkin. "The biggest hurdle you have is your lack of management experience."

"Because that makes it tougher to get funding." She toyed with the straw in her lemonade. "I believe I can manage people. There's a bit of that in being a reporter. It's a small team that puts together a story, with the reporter at the head."

"But nonetheless that's a hole in your background. Which means you have to have everything else buttoned up before you pitch to VCs."

Natalie was still trying to get used to VCs being venture capitalists and not the Viet Cong. "And I need a plan for lining up content partners from TV and radio."

"And newspapers. Most important, you need a management team. Have you broached the idea to Ruth?"

"I have." Natalie grimaced. "I hate to say it but I don't think she'll do it."

"Too much risk?"

"At her stage of life, yes. But I'm not giving up on her yet."

He nodded, thoughtful. "Have you thought of a backup?"

"What do you think of Sally O'Day?"

Geoff arched his brows. "WITW's former prime-time anchor? I know she's been beached since Drosher fired her. It's grabby, two former prime-time anchors from the two biggest media markets founding a local-news site. The downside is that your skill sets are so similar, you don't complement each other. But it might fly."

Natalie sighed. This was shaping up to be like everything else in life. Not easy. "Okay." She slapped the teak table, jarring the ice cubes in her lemonade. "What else? To be absolutely clear on what the target market is and how to hit it—"

"And how sometime in the future investors will get their money back out." He grinned. "Nothing to this game."

They got down to it in the living room, dueling laptops set up on the coffee table. At Geoff's suggestion they broke the business plan down into its component parts and divvied up the writing.

After several hours, motivated as she was, Natalie was having a tough time focusing on target markets and financial projections and value propositions. From the yard next door she could hear a man playing ball with his son, and across the narrow canyon road a radio blaring oldies entertained somebody washing a car. Happy sounds. Saturday sounds. Not business-plan sounds.

Not to mention the immense distraction of the attractive male whose lanky frame had taken over the plump white sofa. The last rays of the sun slanted through the open windows and lay bars across Geoff's bare muscular legs. By this point he'd replaced his contact lenses with glasses, round wire frames that made him look sexy as hell. Natalie watched him push them up on his forehead and pinch the bridge of his nose. She cleared her throat. "Shall we take a break?"

"You want to get this done today, right?"

"Right. But that doesn't mean we can't take a break."

"True enough." He rose from the sofa in one fluid motion.

She led him to the Sub-Zero, from which she pulled a big plastic Diet Coke bottle whose cap stubbornly refused to twist off. She handed it to him. "I hate this weak female bit but I can't get this open."

To her gratification Geoff didn't have the easiest time with it, either. Finally he gave the cap one serious wrench and not only did it twist off, but exploding Diet Coke sprayed his face, tee-shirt, and a good part of the kitchen.

Natalie leaned against the counter, laughing.

"I'm glad you're amused," he commented, but he was grinning, too.

"You've got Coke everywhere!"

"I trust you're making such brilliant observations in the business plan."

"I am," she announced, and then she was leaning one hand against his chest, still laughing, and he was laughing, and then, they were inches apart, staring into each other's eyes, the laughter dwindling. Without looking away Geoff set the Coke on the counter, then leaned forward and kissed her.

Finally. Natalie closed her eyes, wrapping her arms around him. He smelled of Diet Coke and sunshine. His unshaven face, warm from the day's heat, scratched her skin deliciously. His body within her arms was strong and muscular, his kisses as slow and tantalizing as she'd remembered.

All at once he groaned and broke away. "Damn! I'm sorry." He slapped the counter, frustration clear in his hazel eyes. "Dammit! This is exactly what I told myself I wouldn't do."

"Why not?" Her heart was pounding.

He threw up his hands. "I'm getting married in two weeks!"

"I've never understood that." All her resolutions about caution and good sense fell away. All she wanted was to feel him, his body around her and on top of her and beneath her. To continue what they had begun months before. Gently she raised her hand and laid it against his cheek. He bent his face to kiss her palm.

Then with a sudden urgency he again pulled her against him and was kissing her, deep, hungry, insistent kisses. His hands traveled beneath her cotton top, up her back, then undid her bra. She held herself still as his hands wandered to the front of her body.

"God, I shouldn't be doing this." He did, though, all the while that every fiber of her being was urging him on.

I don't want him to stop. I don't care about the goddamn wedding. I could give a hoot about Janet what's-her-name. Natalie grabbed the hem of his tee-shirt and ripped the fabric over his head, dispensing with it on the floor. She ran her hands through the fur on his muscular chest, bending to lick his nipples. She could feel his heart race and body tense as he held her head gently in his hands. She ran her tongue down his belly, then reached to undo the button on his shorts.

In one move he bested her, pulling off her top and pushing her against the Sub-Zero, forcing her back against the cold metal. He pressed his body hard into hers, insistently rubbing his erection against her pelvis. Her wrists in his hands, he forced her arms above her head and held them there, licking her mouth. Slowly he inched down from her lips, still clasping her arms. She was trapped in delicious anticipation, her breasts screaming for his mouth. With his tongue he pushed aside her bra and teased her hardened nipple, refusing to let her arms go, refusing to allow her to touch him. She writhed powerlessly against the cold metal.

He released her breast from his mouth and raised his head. "Oh, God, Nats." His voice was strangled. She stood, half naked and trembling, watching helplessly as he fought with himself, with his conscience, with his desire. And she knew, from the pained determination that came into his eyes, the exact moment at which she lost the battle.

He let her go. He retreated across the kitchen, retrieved his tee-shirt from the tile, and pulled it over his head, not looking at her. "I am such a lout. I cannot do this, Natalie. I am so sorry." He raked a hand through his hair and met her eyes.

She looked away, pulling on her own top, nearly crying from frustration. "Honestly, Geoff, I do not understand why you are marrying that woman!"

"At the moment I don't, either. Except that I don't know how to stop it."

Her heart leaped, but at that instant both of them heard Geoff's cell phone trilling from the other room. He uttered a low oath, looking not at her but at the big round-faced kitchen clock.

It was all very clear. The idyll was over.

"I'm sure it's Janet," he muttered, and her heart plummeted. "She has a helluva sense of timing. Plus I'm supposed to meet her and her mother for dinner."

Natalie watched a hangdog expression spread over his features, while she fought off the wave of disappointment that assaulted her.

"I'm sorry, Natalie." Then he walked out of the kitchen.

She stood alone, still leaning back against the Sub-Zero. She'd feel better later, she knew, when it wasn't pain that held her, but anger. For his stubborn refusal to see what was to her so obvious.

After a minute or so Geoff returned, his Topsiders back on, his laptop apparently safely stowed in his briefcase. Again awkwardness fell between them. He smiled feebly. "At least we got a lot done."

"Right."

"Have a good evening," he added, which sounded pretty lame to her. Then he was out the front door.

Can't be late! She heard the Jag's engine turn over. *Can't make Janet wait!*

For lack of anything better to do she stalked into the den and turned on the TV, where gorgeous young women with state banners across their gowned chests paraded across the screen. Miss Illinois pranced by with an irritatingly toothy smile across her glowing face.

Great. The Miss America Pageant. Where half the contestants want to be television news anchors. Natalie jabbed the remote's POWER button until the screen went black. *Probably the other half want to launch Web businesses.*

CHAPTER TWENTY-ONE

Tuesday, September 24, 11:12 A.M.

Kelly perched on her new yellow suede sofa, the only piece of furniture in her Bel Air living room, lightly blowing her still-damp Tropical Gold Sunshine nail polish. No more minimalls for her. Now the manicurist came to her house, at her convenience. Nobody who lived in Bel Air should be caught dead in a minimall.

The phone rang, for what seemed like the hundredth time that morning. Her beeper had been going off, too, but she hadn't felt like dealing with that, either. She reclined against the sofa cushions, listening to the message machine pick up in the kitchen. It was too far away to make out who was talking.

But after a few seconds she *could* make it out, because it was Rico, her agent, screaming to beat the band.

Damn.

She heaved herself to her feet and made her way awkwardly into the kitchen, her newly pedicured toes separated by little wads of cotton. Gingerly she picked up the phone so she wouldn't screw up her polish. "Yeah?"

"Why the hell aren't you answering the phone?" Rico shouted. "I've been trying to reach you for the last fucking hour!"

She snorted. "Good morning to you, too, Rico."

"I got no time for your sarcasm, Kelly. Scoppio just read me the riot act and you've got some serious explaining to do."

Kelly stiffened. Had Natalie figured out what was on

that shootout tape and told Tony? "He's upset?" she ventured.

"*Upset?* He's frigging ready to *kill* you, Kelly! Do you know that *because* of you KXLA is being sued? In *two* separate lawsuits? Because of *you*, Kelly? Do you know that?"

Kelly clutched the phone. "What do you mean, being sued?"

"You want me to spell it out? I mean that the Mann family, who I never heard of before this goddamn morning, is suing KXLA, and you personally, for giving *Hard Line* video of their kid smashed up in his car!"

Fuck! Kelly bent over the counter, thinking she was gonna hurl. This was exactly what she'd been worried about: the Manns crawling out of church and watching the spot on *Hard Line* and going ballistic. And *Hard Line* had even cut her out of the story! This was so unfair! She forgot about her manicure and banged her fist on the counter so hard it hurt. Then she had an idea. "Isn't there a limit to how often people can sue somebody? You know, double jeopardy?"

"No, Kelly," Rico snarled, and she didn't appreciate his tone. "There's no limit, particularly since the Manns *didn't* sue before because you managed to talk them out of it. Which I never heard about until today, by the way. So much for agent/client communication. And remember how you had to promise the Manns that that tape would never again see the light of day? Remember that?"

Her mind was working fast. "But they can't prove *I* gave *Hard Line* the tape. Maybe they got it some other way."

"Yeah, right, maybe that'll fly. Give that a whirl."

Kelly was shocked. Rico sounded totally disgusted.

"I gotta tell you, Kelly," he went on like he was *raving*, "you *really* fucked up this time. I swear, Scoppio is so ticked off he's two inches from firing you. *Two inches.* But if you'd listened to *me*, if you'd signed that contract when I *told* you to, he wouldn't be able to fire you so fast because he'd still have to pay you! But *noooo*, why listen to me? Why listen to your agent, Kelly?"

She ground her teeth. *Now* she got it. Rico was *so*

transparent. "You agents are all the same," she told him. "You're just worried about your goddamn commission. Fine. But I'll get you an even *bigger* commission if you can manage to get off your ass and negotiate the contract." She paused for effect. "If Scoppio fires me, I'll just go work for *Hard Line*."

He roared with laughter, which really pissed her off. "Are you nuts, Kelly? Didn't you hear me say there are two suits? *Hard Line* is suing, too! They say you lied to them about having a release from the Manns!"

"What?"

"They sure did, Kelly! So have I got your attention?"

She had no comeback to that. Now *Hard Line* would never hire her. And what if Scoppio was so ticked off he fired her from KXLA and she couldn't get another TV job?

That was just too terrifying. Kelly stood at her counter and felt as if she'd swallowed a gallon of ice-cold Gatorade, all of which got stuck in her stomach at the same time. She couldn't *survive* if she wasn't on television. She *had* to be on the air. Then something else Rico said came back to her. "Did you say the Manns aren't just suing KXLA, but me personally?"

"Yup."

She was petrified to ask the next question, but knew she had to. "How much are they suing for?"

"Thirty million. And *Hard Line*'s suing for ten million, plus legal fees."

Forty million total. Wow. Actually, that made her feel kind of important. But then she got chills. "Will I have to cough up money myself?"

"You're goddamn right you will!"

Kelly looked around her bright sunshiny Bel Air kitchen. She didn't have any money to cough up. She was behind on her mortgage already, since she'd never signed the anchor contract and was still on her piddly reporter's salary.

She could lose the house. She could lose the furniture. She could lose *everything*. And just when she'd finally arrived!

And there was stuff Rico didn't even *know* about. That whole other business of Natalie finding her in Ruth's office with the CNN shootout tape. She sure as hell wasn't going to tell Rico about that *now*. One thing really did strike her. "You know what?" she said. "I think maybe now I should sign the contract."

"Are you crazy?" he screamed, so loud that she had to pull the phone away from her ear. "Are you so *loca en la cabeza* that you think Scoppio's gonna sign a fucking anchor deal with you *now*?"

She'd had enough of Rico. She slammed down the phone and stood in her kitchen trying to decide what to do. It was a lot tougher than usual. Her head actually started to hurt and she never got headaches. By the time she went upstairs to shower, deciding to skip kick-boxing class for the first time in forever, she still hadn't figured out a damn thing.

Janet stood in Geoff's contemporary white living room, backlit by the midday sun streaming through the windows. "Can you believe our wedding is just ten days away?"

Geoff lowered *The Wall Street Journal* to regard his fiancée. "I can't believe it," he replied truthfully. He returned his gaze to the newsprint, though he had little interest in reading it. Ten days. At Janet's request he'd taken off from work that day to finalize the few remaining details, which included such monumentally important questions as which champagne flutes to use at the reception and on which linen-draped table the guest book should be laid open.

He didn't know how it had happened but somehow their initial "keep it small, keep it simple" plan had morphed into a four-hundred-person, eight-bridesmaid church ceremony, gourmet dinner, and dance extravaganza. When he'd suggested they hire out the Hollywood Bowl for midnight fireworks, Janet hadn't immediately understood he was being sarcastic.

Somehow, somewhere, he could no longer remember the exact instant, he'd realized that the woman he was planning to make his wife was obsessed with small things, superficial things, things that in the grand scheme of life didn't matter one whit. And in the days since he had felt more and more like a cog in Janet's life plan. An important cog, but a cog nonetheless.

And now the marriage was ten days away. Ten days. The tide was going out and he was being swept along. His family—clearly all of them in shock—was arriving from Sydney on the weekend; another few dozen Aussies would follow days later; the bachelor party a surfing buddy had organized was this very Saturday night.

He raised his eyes to observe his fiancée. Stunning as ever, perhaps even more so. She was radiant. She exhibited none of the confusion he felt. Or perhaps . . . He arched his brows, a jolt rippling through him. Maybe she was feeling it, too, but not saying anything? Just as he was?

He made his voice light, as though he were embarking on a joke. "So. Any cold feet, now that the wedding's so close?"

She looked amazed. "Are you kidding?"

"It would be perfectly natural, though." He found himself wanting to persist. "And I'd certainly want you to tell me." He then took a page from her book, to encourage her. "We should share everything, you know."

Her lovely eyes narrowed, grew appraising. "*You're* not having cold feet, are you, Geoff?"

"No. Of course not." The lie escaped him easily and, once told, was irretrievable.

Her face relaxed. She approached him and bent her head for a kiss. He obliged, remembering other lips.

What was wrong with him? He cursed himself. Were these simply the last gasps of his male independence, perfectly predictable and thus to be ignored? Or was he truly wanting to stop this, but was discovering that Geoff Marner was such a coward he couldn't manage it?

Suddenly he rose from the sofa. "I've got a headache. I'm going upstairs for some aspirin." He knew his abruptness startled her, but he was in too much of a muddle to deal with it. He couldn't deal with any of it—that was the problem. It was too gargantuan to take on.

Geoff practically ran to the second floor. How bizarre was this? When had circumstances ever gotten the better of him before?

He reached the second-floor landing and pressed his right hand against the wall, leaning his full weight against it. He really did have a headache. In fact, his head was spinning.

Natalie picked up her office phone on the first ring. She was being tremendously efficient. All business, all the time. "Natalie Daniels," she answered.

"It's Ruth. I'm down in editing. You know the CNN tape that Kelly tried to steal from my office?"

"How could I forget?"

"I've screened it twice and can't find a damn thing on it."

"There has got to be something on that tape Kelly doesn't want anybody to see." Natalie flopped back in her chair, frustrated. "Didn't you tell me that same dub disappeared once before?"

"At the time I thought I misplaced it. Now I know better." Through the phone line Natalie heard Ruth drumming the metal tabletop in Edit Bay 5. "I'll screen it one more time. Anything on your end?"

"Good news for a change. I just got off the phone with Brad Fenton, the MetroSeek CEO. I showed him my business plan, to get his feedback."

"And?"

"He had some suggestions, but—" Natalie hesitated. It was hard to say the words. Saying the words made it real and making it real was frightening. "Overall he liked it. He said he'd put me in touch with the venture capitalists who funded MetroSeek."

Ruth whistled. "Line up a few more of those guys and you might have a business to run."

"We'll see." She paused. "So what do *you* think? Am I going to launch this business myself or with a partner?"

This time Ruth hesitated. "Why don't I come to your office?"

Here it comes. Natalie sighed as she hung up the phone.

Ruth appeared a minute later, looking uncomfortable. She arranged herself on Natalie's moth-eaten beige couch and picked at some nonexistent lint in her lap. Finally she raised her eyes. "Turns out big bad Ruth may not actually be as bold as she wants everybody to think," she said quietly. "Maybe not as bold as she wants to think *herself*." She shrugged. "I'm thinking I'd like to ride this TV-news horse for as long as I can stay on. I've been doing it since the dark ages. It's what I know."

"It's what you *love*," Natalie corrected.

"That, too. Damn shame."

They were silent. Natalie was disappointed but not surprised. Ruth was a news hound from way back. It was damn near impossible to imagine her not in a conventional newsroom.

Finally Ruth broke the silence. "I am sorry, Natalie, and very flattered that you asked me."

Natalie waved a hand to quiet her, not looking up. "It's all right, Ruth. Really, I understand."

Ruth was quiet for a second. "Is this what's upsetting you? Or is something else going on?"

Natalie let her head drop back, her eyes drifting across the ceiling. She felt as drained as she ever had in her life. "There's nothing else going on, Ruth—that's the problem. I'm ten days away from my contract expiring and there's nothing else going on."

"Let me guess. You don't want to sign Scoppio's deal."

"Right."

"But you're not completely sold on the Web venture."

"Right again."

"And your agent is about to marry the Breck girl."

At that Natalie raised her head and met Ruth's eyes. "When did *you* get so smart?"

"Born that way. Anything you can do about it? Tell him how you feel, for example?"

She shook her head. "I already tried that."

"Hmm. Well, maybe I can cheer you up. Have you heard about the lawsuits?"

Natalie had barricaded herself in her office to make

phone calls, but not even solitary confinement could have prevented her from hearing about the lawsuits. The entire station was in an uproar. "Did another shoe drop?"

"Not unless you call Tony going berserk another shoe." Ruth chuckled. "When I saw him, his face was so red I thought he might have a seizure. I hear that, since he couldn't get Kelly on the phone, he went off on her agent. But now the *real* fun begins, because he's got to tell Pemberley. Maxine said he's taking a walk around the lot to work up to it."

The vision of an apoplectic Tony circumnavigating KXLA made Natalie feel marginally better. She managed a smile. "It sounds like Tony and Kelly might both blow up, even without our help."

"Maybe," Ruth agreed. "But I'd still like to lend a hand."

Tony slammed shut his office door, still struggling even after his long walk to take in the unbelievable blow of the lawsuits. Sure, he'd headed news departments that had been sued; all news directors who'd been around the block had. But never two at a time. A two-fer. Slam, bam.

And both of them justified.

He sat down at his desk and stared at the sickening details in the memo Elaine had drafted. His heart plunged to some lower lumbar region where God could never have intended it to be. Forty million smackers' worth of lawsuits, plus the legal fees, plus *Hard Line*'s fees if KXLA lost.

In his mind rose a vision of his bonus check being carried away by a great wind, generated by an Oz-like figure who bore an astonishing resemblance to Rhett Pemberley. And now, merely losing his bonus check was the best-case scenario.

Sweet Jesus. Tony rubbed his left temple, where the headache that had started in his right temple began an assault on new territory. How was he going to explain this to Pemberley? No way in hell had he authorized that video to leave the lot, let alone be aired elsewhere. On a national tabloid? After KXLA had dodged a bullet once with the Manns? Who would be so asinine?

Though that was a rhetorical question. He knew the answer. And it astonished him the trouble one piece of talent could generate.

Maybe Bjorkman knew something about it? If he did, Tony might be able to shift blame and have some semi-reasonable explanation to hand Pemberley. He punched his intercom button. "Has Bjorkman shown up yet?" Howard was late coming in because of a root canal that morning. Once he got to work his day would *really* go downhill.

"Just arrived," Maxine rasped.

"Get him in here."

Howard joined him a minute later. Tony narrowed his eyes at his managing editor. "You've been named in a lawsuit," he told him.

"Oh, my God." Howard sank into the chair in front of Tony's desk, leaning his elbows on his knees and holding his head in his hands. Tony got a great view of his spreading bald spot. "Oh, my God," Howard repeated a few more times. Finally he raised his eyes. Behind the preppy horn-rimmed frames, Tony could see that his managing editor was scared shitless. "I know it was an error in judgment, Tony, but you've got to believe me, it was consensual. And it was never tied to assignments, never once."

"Consensual," Tony repeated. *Consensual?*

"Yes!" Howard's face lit up, as if he thought Tony was getting his point-of-view. "And I never promised Kelly a damn thing. It had nothing to do with anything here, not assignments, not anything. I told her that, repeatedly."

"Told *Kelly*?"

Howard looked confused. "Of course. Her suit has no merit. I'm sure we can settle this in-house, with nobody ever knowing." His voice got wheedly. "It's a ploy to get money out of the station, don't you see? Women file sexual-harassment suits all the time, to get one thing or another. They don't want to take responsibility for what they do. It's like crying rape the morning after."

Tony sat in his news director's chair, adding up all Bjorkman's gibberish, and reached a total that made sense. *Bjorkman's been schtupping Kelly,* he realized. *That's what he thinks this is all about.*

Great. So Kelly *could* sue the station for sexual harassment, if she got sufficiently pissed off. For example, if he fired her.

A third suit—for sexual harassment, for *anything*—would kill him with Pemberley. One was bad enough. Two was damn near impossible to spin. But three led to clean out your desk and a guard will escort you off the lot.

"What do you know about *Hard Line* getting the Mann car-accident video?" he asked.

Howard got even more agitated. "Kelly again!" he said instantly. "I told her not to do it but she wouldn't listen to me. Tell Kelly she can't go on a national tabloid show? Are you kidding? Plus, she never listens to anybody. She's a real loose cannon, Tony," he added, as if that little tidbit were coming with enough warning that Tony could do something about it.

"You're fired, Howard," Tony informed his managing editor and watched his Ivy League face crumple in shock. "Clean out your desk and a guard will escort you off the lot."

It took Howard a while, but finally he wandered out of Tony's office, mumbling to himself like a homeless guy. But Tony didn't give a flyer. He had his own ass to save. He forced himself to punch his intercom button again. "Get Pemberley on the line," he ordered Maxine.

Tony had already decided to be sober yet matter-of-fact. The lawsuits weren't that big a deal, he'd tell Pemberley. The forty million was posturing. KXLA's lawyers wouldn't break a sweat.

He wiped his palms on his khakis, waiting for Maxine to buzz him back. Maybe Pemberley would be out on the golf course.

Maxine buzzed. "Pemberley's secretary on line one."

Reluctantly Tony picked up the phone. "Hold for Rhett Pemberley," the woman murmured. There was no getting out of it now. His heart rate picked up so much it made him think he should take one of his blood-pressure pills. But he didn't have a chance because then Pemberley's voice came booming over the line. "Tony, what can I do for you?"

Not fire me for the first time in my career, Tony answered silently. He cleared his throat and pulled out his most serious tone—the one he used in interviews to shmooze station owners into believing he was the best man to run their news departments. "Rhett, we have a development here to which I want to alert you." He cleared his throat again. "A local family has filed suit against the station, charging us with recklessly distributing car-accident video of their son, now deceased, without permission."

"How much?"

Great. The question he most wanted to dodge was the first one out of Pemberley's mouth. "Like everybody else in America, they think TV stations have deep pockets. Thirty million."

"But they don't have a case," Pemberley stated confidently.

Tony winced. "The video did get out of Archives—"

Pemberley's voice ratcheted up. "They *do* have a case?"

"I've fired the man responsible." That was stretching it, but no way would Tony admit Kelly's role in this. Kelly, Tony had promoted. Bjorkman, Tony had inherited. "Howard Bjorkman, the managing editor. He's gone. And with what's on the air these days, our lawyers can easily convince a jury that this material was comparatively mild."

"But the video *was* distributed without a signed release?"

"Strictly speaking, yes. But I'm confident our lawyers can get around it without any difficulty." He paused. Now came the *really* tough part. "There is a second suit as well, brought—"

"What?" Now Pemberley was yelling. "You're telling

me KXLA is being sued *twice*? What the hell are you doing out there, Scoppio?"

Tony desperately wanted this conversation to be over. "The second suit is related to the first. It's—"

"Who's it being brought by?"

Tony closed his eyes. "*Hard Line.* They—"

"We're being sued by another broadcaster? Goddammit, Scoppio, win or lose that'll cost a fortune!"

Tony heard Pemberley slam his open palm on his desk, which he knew was a mahogany monolith large enough to land a 737. He could just imagine him sitting there in his gigantic Phoenix office, the panoramic views of Camelback Mountain failing to distract him from the legal crisis in his Los Angeles newsroom. Which was run by a buffoon who would never see hide nor hair of . . .

"You can kiss that bonus good-bye, Scoppio," Pemberley declared. "Legal fees alone will eat it up."

Tony felt as if he'd been mowed down by the Cadillac DTS that now he'd never be able to buy. "Rhett," he managed, "I assure you this matter will be resolved quickly and—"

"It better be. You get us out of this mess or you're gone. The next piece of news I hear out of you had better be good." He hung up.

Tony remained in his chair, trying to make his heart stop pounding. The next news had better be good. He couldn't agree more.

"Jerry!" Natalie stood in her bathrobe grasping her kitchen phone half in delight and half in shock, something fierce clutching inside her stomach. She hadn't spoken to Jerry in the eight years since he and Miles had broken up. Why would he be calling her at this hour except for the script she'd sent him? "It's great to hear your voice," she managed. "How are you?"

He laughed, a baritone chuckle that seemed to resonate from deep within him. Jerry had always reminded her of Burl Ives: a burly, warmhearted bon vivant who also happened to be an immensely gifted writer. "I'm well and back in L.A."

Natalie sagged against the counter. "So your sabbatical in Italy is over then?"

He paused. "I don't know. That package you sent me set off, shall we say, a chain of events."

She frowned. "I agonized over whether to send you that script, Jerry. I can't tell you how appalled I am at what Miles did. It's"—she groped for the right word—"mind-boggling."

Jerry was silent. She could only imagine how betrayed he must have felt. She knew how during their lengthy partnership, Miles and Jerry had struggled jointly toward the same goal like tandem bicyclists pumping together to top a hill. Miles had ridden roughshod over that bond and for Jerry it must be not only unforgivable, but heartbreaking.

He spoke slowly. "You know, the irony is I gave the script to him myself, years ago, as a writing sample. Before we started working together." He sighed. "How did you come across it?"

She shook her head. "Jerry, I'll tell you the whole sorry story someday, but suffice it to say that Miles did to me pretty much what he did to you. Lied, cheated, and stole."

"Well, you did the right thing to send it to me. Otherwise I'd still be in Italy not knowing that a spec script I wrote was about to go on the air. And despite what you say, I can only imagine what it must've taken out of you. Miles is your husband, after all."

"My soon-to-be ex-husband." *Very* soon. Berta had told her that what was likely to be the final session for her and Miles and their attorneys was set for the next week.

"So I've heard. If I may be so bold, he never deserved you."

What to say to that? *So I was an idiot to marry him?* That much had become obvious. "Have you spoken with him?"

"No. I've tried. Numerous times. But he doesn't return my calls." He paused. "Natalie, I'm filing a grievance with the Writers Guild."

She closed her eyes. The union would judge whether plagiarism had occurred, and if it ruled in the affirmative, it would provide Jerry a tremendous boost if he filed charges in civil court.

"It's not clear what'll happen next," Jerry went on, "but please know how grateful I am. Someday I'll find a way to repay you."

"Jerry, honestly, there's no need."

"I'll be in touch." Then he hung up.

Natalie had just replaced the receiver when again the phone rang.

"It's Ruth. You awake?"

Natalie stiffened at the uncharacteristic excitement in Ruth's voice. "What is it?"

"I found it. I found the smoking gun."

"You mean on the CNN tape?"

"You won't believe it." The imperturbable Ruth sounded stunned. "I just went through it again and you will not believe what I saw this time on that goddamn tape. How fast can you get here?"

"I still have to shower, but fast." Natalie glanced at the kitchen clock. 7:12 A.M. "How's forty minutes sound?"

"Do not pass go. Come straight to Edit Bay 5."

CHAPTER TWENTY-TWO

Friday, September 27, 10:38 A.M.

"Would Natalie consider three fifty for anchoring the four o'clock and filing the health reports for the six and eleven?" BD asked.

Geoff leaned back in his ergonomically correct Dewey, Climer chair, the phone in his hand, his muscles slowly relaxing into the chair's flawless contours. At this midmorning hour sunshine spilled through the floor-to-ceiling windows, illuminating dust motes dancing in the air. In the Hollywood Hills to the east, a plume of gray smoke spiraled into the air; even from the thirty-eighth floor of his Century City tower, he could vaguely make out the wail of sirens.

BD's job offer to Natalie was slow to take root in his brain, like a plant struggling to poke its roots through hard, dry soil. At long last: an anchor option for Natalie. In Los Angeles, no less. Talk about in the nick of time; her KXLA contract expired in exactly one week. It was so out of the blue, coming after so many setbacks, it seemed unbelievable. It took him a moment or two to revert to agent mode and begin to tote up the pros and cons.

In Los Angeles, tremendous. At a network-owned station, quite good—in fact arguably preferable to the independent KXLA. But at four p.m., so out of prime time? Only a half hour a day? For less than half what Natalie was making now? Requiring daily reporting, though

Geoff knew the health beat wasn't taxing. Most of the video was archival or came off a feed; usually the only original shooting was a health-expert interview or two.

An improvement to the offer skidded across his brain, though he knew his bargaining position was painfully weak. BD knew full well that Natalie wasn't exactly swimming in offers. "How about four weeks a year of substitute anchoring on the five, six, and eleven?"

"I can do three."

"Will she be on set every night at six and eleven for a live toss to the health reports?" The more Natalie was live on set in prime time, the better, even in a reporter role.

"I can't guarantee twice a night."

"Once? I'm going to want regular on-set tosses."

"I'm willing to work out something," BD conceded.

"And how many years on the deal?"

"Three."

"No cuts?"

"You're stretching, Marner. I can't do a no-cut—you know that."

He knew that. Station management wanted to retain single-year options on anchor talent, even proven anchor talent. Although Natalie was certainly proven on KXLA, she wasn't on KNBC. It never ceased to amaze him how viewers only occasionally followed an anchor from one station to another in the same market. It was totally capricious, as so much else in television news.

A nightmare scenario rose in his imagination. "Who else do you need to get this past, Bobbi?" He could easily imagine KNBC's general manager refusing to sign "damaged goods" like Natalie Daniels.

"Everybody's signed on." BD paused. "By the way, this isn't some weird way to make amends, Geoff. I'd love to have Natalie come work here."

Clearly BD had gotten over the nervous-breakdown rumor or she wouldn't be making an offer. Geoff had figured out long ago that news directors were the most risk-averse creatures in TV news, particularly when it came to who they put in the anchor chair. That was the number one reason so many bland "personalities" ended up there.

"I take it you're still pissed at Scoppio?" he asked.

"Livid. Nobody uses me as a mouthpiece." BD paused. "But I'll tell you one thing, Marner. He'll get his."

"No, rewind it again," Natalie said.

Ruth reracked the incriminating segment of tape. The women hunched forward on Edit Bay 5's hard metal seats, peering at the monitor, the minuscule editing room chilly and silent.

"There." Ruth paused the betatape player and pointed at the left side of the screen. "That's Kelly, standing by the school. In that damn aviator jacket she always wears—see, with the stick-up collar? And that's her white tee-shirt, tighter than casing on a sausage. And when she turns her head a little, like . . . there . . . you can make out her face."

"That's her, all right." Natalie squinted at the monitor. "Keep rolling."

Ruth restarted the tape. They watched as the beam from the flashlight in Kelly's hand raked across the school windows. Immediately thereafter, gunfire erupted in a staccato burst. They lost sight of Kelly then, as the CNN cameraman snapped to and redirected his lens to cops racing forward, guns drawn. One grabbed a bull-horn to exhort the gunman to stop shooting and give himself up. Through it all, kids screamed and the lone teacher still inside the school let loose a piercing wail. Then, after another gunfire blast, something closer to silence fell, broken by intermittent childish crying and reporters behind the crime tape shouting into cell phones.

Natalie felt shell-shocked looking at the images. Finally she found her voice. "Kelly might as well have killed that child herself, Ruth. The shooting might never have happened if it weren't for her."

"Damn straight." Ruth set her jaw. "That's why I wanted you to haul ass in here to see this."

They were silent for a time.

"I swear," Ruth said, "that girl deserves the electric chair."

"It's unbelievable. I can't get over it."

"Do you think she might be criminally liable?"

"I don't know. Why in the world did she even do it?"

"I bet she was just bored." Ruth let her arm drop heavily onto the edit-bay table. "I remember her complaining about having to stay out there, while everybody else in the newsroom was begging me to let them go. I would've pulled her but Tony nixed it. He wanted Kelly on a high-profile story and that was the end of it."

"We have to show this to him. He's out sick today but this can't wait. If this gets out, it'll blow sky-high."

Ruth was suspiciously silent.

"Ruth? Don't you agree?"

She spoke slowly. "The problem is, I'm not sure he'll do anything about it. He might just blow up at us."

"No." Natalie shook her head vigorously. "For his own survival, Tony'll can her. He'll see that he can't have somebody capable of this on the anchor desk. On the staff, for that matter."

"You're sure that's not just wishful thinking? Look what he's put up with already. Why should this send him over the edge?"

"Because this is in a whole other category, Ruth. This could be *criminal.* If not for any moral reason, just imagine the liability."

"Now *that's* a language Scoppio speaks." Ruth pushed her bifocals up her nose. "Shit, I want that woman gone. But I'm just not convinced Tony'll do it. Not unless he's backed against the wall."

"There's only one way I can think of to do that."

The women stared at each other.

Slowly Ruth nodded. "The last thing Tony wants is for Pemberley to see that tape. That's our best leverage." She slapped the table. "I'll make a VHS version to hand-carry to Scoppio's house."

Natalie paced the hallway outside Edit Bay 5 while Ruth made the dub. She knew she had a huge vested interest in getting Kelly canned. How gratifying would it be if Tony Scoppio were at long last forced to admit that Natalie Daniels, thanks to her maturity and judgment, was the superior choice for the anchor desk? And if she could get the woman who'd betrayed her summarily fired?

"I like being powerful for a change," Natalie said when Ruth emerged, videocassette in hand.

Ruth grinned. "No kidding."

Tony's head reared up from the blue porcelain toilet bowl when he heard the doorbell ring. Jesus Christ, who'd have guessed his house would be like Grand Central Station on a weekday? He could barely get a moment's rest, which was sure as hell what he needed to kill whatever raging beast had gotten hold of his stomach.

He heaved himself to his feet and flushed the toilet, then cranked open the window. It was baking like only the San Fernando Valley knew how to bake but he couldn't very well leave the window shut. The bathroom reeked. He didn't know what was making him sick: eating Anna-Maria's veal parmigiana last night or having lawsuit-magnet Kelly Devlin on his air. Whatever it was had sure opened up the sluices at both ends.

He was interrupted by a knock.

"Tony?" Anna-Maria whispered through the door. "It's that Natalie Daniels from the station. With somebody named Ruth Sperry."

He ran his hands under the water, frowning. "They're both on the phone?"

"No, in the living room. They didn't want coffee."

He turned off the faucet. "They're *here*?"

What now? The last thing he needed was another KXLA catastrophe. As it was, his main female anchor got named in lawsuits like other people got parking tickets, but he couldn't fire her because she'd just turn around and sue the station for sexual harassment, thanks to that moron Bjorkman. And even though he'd just about convinced Pemberley to let him stay on as news director, he'd be SOL if anything else hit the fan.

He swallowed hard, then threw cold water on his face. When he opened the door, Anna-Maria was still standing in the hallway, wringing her hands. "All right," he told her. "I'll be right down."

His wife nodded and bustled away.

Tony stared at his reflection in the medicine-cabinet mirror. A balding, middle-aged, fat guy in gray sweats stared back—a guy who looked so sick that somebody should just put him out of his misery.

He forced himself downstairs, where Princess especially seemed to get a shock when she saw him. "Sorry for bothering you at home, Tony. It's clear you're not well." Her nose twitched, like a doe who smelled something bad in the forest. Like him, for example. "But something has come to our attention that you need to see."

Ruth held up a videotape. "Where's your VCR?"

He led them into the family room. "This better be good," he warned, but nobody seemed to hear. Ruth popped in the tape and they all watched for a while, but the dark blurry images made no sense to him. "All right," he said eventually. "Clue me in. What the hell *is* this?"

"It's that elementary school shooting from back in July," Ruth said. "This is CNN's video, which I brought in-house for *Kids in Danger.* A six-year-old boy died, remember? Kelly covered it."

Sure, he remembered. Tragic stuff, sure, but these days it happened so often that the edge had worn off. You couldn't be in TV news and not have the edge wear off. His brother told him it was like being a cop. "So?"

"So watch it again," Ruth said, and this time she replayed the tape on slo-mo and pointed to the left side of the screen. This time he saw the point. Man, did he see the point. There was a shadowy figure, and now he could tell that it was Kelly. Ruth reminded him how Kelly had groused about having to stay overnight to cover the story. And then Princess showed him how Kelly had shone a flashlight up at the windows and how right after that the shooting started.

And then the kid had died.

Tony stared at the screen, grappling with it. Was he seeing what he thought he was seeing? In all his years in TV news, he'd never run across anything like this. Then again, he'd never run across anybody like Kelly. If it was true, and it sure as shootin' looked true, then he had a gi-normous problem on his hands.

Jesus Christ.

His stomach started its preheave dance. He was done for if this tape got out. He was staring at lawsuit city. Wouldn't the dead kid's family sue, for wrongful death or something, if they saw this? Wouldn't the feds get involved? Sure as hell there'd be a mob of picketers outside the station where the "child killer" worked. Christ, if this got out, Rhett Pemberley would can his butt faster than ice melts in Phoenix in July.

Tony looked at Princess, on the couch silent as a cat, and Ruth, still standing by the VCR. The two most contentious broads in his employ now had the power to bury him with Pemberley. "Who else has seen this?" he asked.

Princess answered. "So far, only Ruth and me."

So far. "Nobody else?" He felt the need to confirm it.

This time Princess hesitated. "Not yet."

That was pretty damn clear. He had to hand it to her. What do you know? Princess *could* go for the jugular.

Then he had another thought. "Does Kelly know *you* know what's on this tape?"

Princess shook her head. "We came to you first."

Now *that* was good news. Tony paced the family room, his mind working. Maybe this thing was a blessing in disguise. *Heavy* disguise, but still. Because if he had something on Kelly, something she didn't want the world to know, he could can her ass and still keep her from filing a sexual-harassment suit. Then his Kelly problem would be solved. And he would emerge, not exactly *victorious*, but still standing.

He stopped pacing. "All right," he told them. "Kelly's gone."

Princess apparently needed clarification. "Do you mean off the anchor desk? Or fired?"

"I mean fired. But it's important how I play this, so for right now I'm just gonna tell her she's suspended." He had to get all his ducks in a row, maybe get Elaine to draft paperwork he'd make Kelly sign. "The most important thing is that nobody see that tape."

Princess was shaking her head. "I won't agree to stay mum indefinitely. The L.A.P.D. should see it."

He jabbed his finger at her from across the room. "All the cops'll do is show it to the kid's family. You might as well ask for another lawsuit."

"Tony." Princess rose from the couch. "A child lost his life. Kelly shouldn't get away with just losing her job."

Ruth popped the tape out of the VCR. "I say the first order of business is to get Kelly fired. Then we revisit what to do about the tape. Agreed, Natalie?"

Princess hemmed and hawed for a while but finally gave in, though it seemed pretty damn grudging.

Then Ruth piped up again. "So what about the show tonight?"

Tony looked at Princess, standing in his wood-paneled family room. It always came down to her, didn't it? Whatever went down. Whatever he did.

The next thing he said took a lot out of him. It was like passing a kidney stone: had to be done but hurt like hell. "As of tonight," he told her, "you're back on the anchor desk."

He stopped. Princess waited. It killed him but he had to keep going. "You've got the job back. I'll haggle with Marner over the particulars."

All she did was nod. Cool cucumber. But he'd always known that. He tried to lighten the moment. "So what do I get for my magnanimity?"

Ruth scoffed at him. "Come on, Tony. You get survival. Maybe Pemberley won't find out you handpicked a lunatic to be main anchor."

She had a point.

For the first time he saw these two broads in a whole new light. Maybe he *could* do business with them. After all, there'd been nothing to stop them from showing the tape to Pemberley first and blowing his ass from here to kingdom come. But they hadn't.

He smiled at Ruth and winked at Princess, who he'd never liked more than he did at that moment. Who, in fact, he was gonna be damn happy to have back on his anchor desk.

Too bad he hadn't known that back in June.

Kelly drove her black BMW 323i east on Sunset Boulevard like a bat out of hell, trying to do the eight miles from Bel Air to KXLA in record time. She *had* to find out if what Rico told her on the phone just now was true. No way it was, but still.

That Tony had suspended her? Without pay? Indefinitely? No way. She'd anchored the night before and he'd known about the lawsuits then, so why would he suddenly turn around and suspend her?

One thought kept wriggling into her brain and she kept trying to squish it. What if Tony found out about the CNN shootout tape? What if that bitch Natalie watched it a million times and finally saw her on it with the flashlight?

Kelly clutched the steering wheel. *God.*

The light turned red at Beverly Drive but Kelly ran it, jamming her foot down on the accelerator. A bunch of idiots in a VW convertible honked like mad but she ignored them and hurtled on through Beverly Hills and into Hollywood. The closer she got to KXLA, the more nervous she felt. There was a buttload of stuff coming down that she didn't like. Howard getting fired? That'd blown her away. But better Howard than her. And he *had* let her take that Mann accident videotape off the lot.

Kelly arrived at KXLA and rolled the Beemer up to the guard gate. The usual afternoon security guy was there but he had the bar down and was on the phone looking away and didn't raise it.

She sat and waited and wondered. Finally the guard got off the phone. Kelly honked her horn at him, since he still didn't raise the bar. But, she couldn't believe it, he shook his head no!

She lowered the window. "What do you mean, no?" she bellowed. "Lemme in!"

He didn't want to, she could tell, but he walked his skinny Hispanic ass out of the guardhouse and approached her car. "I can't do it, Miss Devlin," he told her. "I was told you've been banned from the lot. I got orders."

"What the fuck? I've been banned!" she screamed at him. "I *work* here! You've let me in a million times!" She jabbed a finger at her windshield. "Look at my pass! I've got a reserved space!"

He kept shaking his head. "No can do, Miss Devlin. I'm sorry." He held his hands up, as if there wasn't shit he could do about it. "Orders." Then he walked back into the guardhouse and closed the sliding glass door, as if she wasn't even there.

Un-fucking-believable! She wasn't gonna put up with this. She was the main female anchor at this station! She could eat this joker for lunch, then spit him out by prime time.

Kelly sat in her Beemer, fuming. But could it be that she *was* banned from the lot?

That really ticked her off. Plus it petrified her. She grabbed the Club from the passenger seat and got out of the Beemer. "Lemme in!" she yelled at the security guy, brandishing the Club and approaching the guardhouse. He looked freaked, which gave her kind of a thrill. "Lemme in or say good-bye to your windows!"

He scrunched himself against the wall and reached for the phone, as if she was a menace or something! But he still didn't raise the bar so she gave the Club a swing.

Bam! The glass windows on the little guardhouse shattered like nobody's business. The guy stood inside cowering, still on the phone, so Kelly gave it another whirl, aiming at a window closer to him. *Bam!* More glass fell on the asphalt, in tiny pieces that glittered in the sunlight. Still he didn't raise the bar!

Kelly stood there panting. He *still* wasn't gonna let her in? What was this shit? Now she didn't know what to do. Who should she call? Rico?

She ran back to grab her cell phone from the Beemer. But before she could dial, it rang. "Yeah?" she answered.

"You are a fucking maniac—you know that, Kelly?"

"Rico! I was just calling you! Do you know—"

"You were calling me *for the last time.* I just got off the phone with Scoppio and you've got two minutes to get off that lot. Do you understand me, Kelly? *Two minutes.* Before you get arrested for destroying private property. I'm not shitting you and I'm sure as hell not bailing you out."

He stopped to catch his breath and Kelly was so freaked she didn't say anything. How did Scoppio know so fast? Probably the gate guard had called him. Then Rico started talking again, and what he said next she never thought she'd hear in a million years.

"I'm not representing you anymore, Kelly. I am dumping you as a client. You're on your own now—you got that? Consider our contract severed." Then Rico hung up. On *her.*

Geoff drove the Jag at his usual breakneck pace to a destination he refused to divulge, grinning at the hostage in his passenger seat over whose eyes he'd tied a blue bandanna. This was by no means typical client treatment but it'd been a while now since Natalie Daniels had been a typical client. And he hadn't even considered giving her the good news in typical over-the-phone agent fashion.

"Where are you taking me?" Natalie demanded, but he refused to answer, judging from her smile that she was happy to play along. And why not? In extraordinary fashion, and with only one week to spare before her contract expired, she had that very day been reinstated to KXLA's anchor desk. In mere hours she would anchor for the first night in months. And she was about to find out that she had still another option.

He stopped at a red light at Hollywood and Gower and pried the lid off the box of Belgian chocolates he'd brought with him. "Open your mouth," he ordered softly, and after some initial resistance she complied. Geoff laid a truffle on her tongue. She chewed, then moaned appreciatively. "Oh, my God, that's wonderful."

He grinned. He liked this game.

"Amaretto something or other," she declared, then slapped her palms on her black trousers. "But I don't get this! Where are you taking me? Why is chocolate involved? What is this all about?"

"Didn't you forget 'how' and 'when?' " He made a right from Franklin Avenue onto Outpost Drive and headed into the Hollywood Hills. "Stop asking questions. Have another chocolate and let me drive."

She groaned but then opened her mouth to receive a roasted caramel bonbon and they continued on in amiable silence. Natalie was one of the few people with whom he could be quiet, he realized. He didn't feel a need for noise or conversation. Janet hated silence. Whenever they got in the car or the house, she immediately turned on the stereo. For background, she told him. Once they'd even picnicked on the beach and she'd insisted on bringing a portable radio. To the beach? He'd been flabbergasted. What was better to listen to than the surf?

One steep final turn and they arrived at the crest of the hill. At a small gated overlook off Mulholland Drive, not far from Runyan Canyon, he pulled off-road to park the Jag. "I'll come round to help you get out," he assured her, but first he extracted from the trunk two plastic champagne flutes and a bottle of chilled Veuve Clicquot, setting them on a rock outcropping. Only after everything was set up did he help Natalie from the car and lead her to a prime viewing spot. Swiftly he uncorked and poured the champagne, putting a full flute in her hand, the bandanna still shielding her eyes.

He was excited. It was fun doing this for this woman. She'd worked so long and so hard for this moment. No one knew that better than him. And he'd see her joy firsthand.

But as he removed the bandanna she looked more puzzled than happy.

"No, don't look at me. Look out there." He pointed with flute in hand at the magnificent vista that lay below them. Los Angeles, in all of its far-flung splendor, on this day its brilliant blues and whites unmarred by smog. "The city is at your feet. You got it back, though I never really thought you lost it." He touched his flute to hers and grinned. "I'm incredibly delighted to tell you that you have received a *second* anchor offer. From KNBC Los Angeles."

Her eyes flew open and her lips parted in a silent shriek. Geoff threw back his head and laughed. "Do you want details?"

"Yes!"

Those didn't take long to relay, and Natalie seemed to savor every word. *These are the moments that make being an agent worthwhile,* Geoff thought, watching Natalie jump up and down, spilling her champagne everywhere, *this helping make somebody*'s *dreams come true.* Trite as that sounded. Finally, he was able to help her, in a real way, after having caused her so much grief. It made him believe that, after everything, they'd still be friends.

He looked into Natalie's big blue eyes, which by now were moist with tears, and when she threw her arms about his neck and hugged him, jumping up and down so excitedly he could barely keep ahold of her, something in his heart leaped. Something wonderful. And profoundly satisfying.

Hours later, Natalie sat down at the anchor desk for *The KXLA Primetime News*, in what she still considered "her" spot across from Camera One. She had dreamed of this moment so much, had ricocheted so often between certainty that it would happen and despair that it would not, that the reality was surreal. The studio felt hot, supercharged, more starkly lit than she remembered; the crew noisy and rambunctious. Yet everything was oddly unchanged, too, as if the last painful months had never happened: her charcoal-gray swivel chair was calibrated perfectly into position, the monitors were angled to her liking, her earpiece volume was clear and strong, and a Styrofoam cup of her preferred throat-soothing lukewarm water was at her elbow.

As she stared at the cup, her eyes misted. There was one reason and one reason only that everything she needed for a perfect broadcast was in place, despite her months of absence: the crew. They'd remembered every last detail, the director and floor manager and audio technician, and wordlessly provided it. They could not have given her a more deeply felt welcome.

Adding to the evening's luster were the four dozen long-stemmed yellow roses that had arrived at the station a few hours before airtime and now held pride of place on the file cabinet next to her Emmys. It was Maxine who had carried the crystal-cut vase to her office. Natalie had turned her back on Maxine's curious eyes before ripping open the tiny white envelope to reveal a card crammed with Geoff's neat lawyerlike script, the only thing lawyerlike about him:

Congratulations! Your triumphant return to the anchor desk may be just enough to convince this cynical Aussie that truth and justice, not to mention never-say-die women, do in the end prevail.

With endless admiration,
Geoff

She'd read and reread the card before stowing it in her pencil drawer for safekeeping. *With endless admiration.* Staring at the inscription, to which Geoff had clearly given some thought, she'd found herself caught between pride and frustration. *Endless admiration.* Certainly that was a wonderful emotion to inspire, but it was also a cold emotion, an arm's-length emotion, one that reverberated more in the mind than in the heart.

She was drawn back to the present by the floor manager noisily banging his headset against Camera One. Suddenly she realized that all around her was a mob of techies and writers and producers and desk assistants and reporters and cameramen, who'd sidled in quietly through the half-open studio doors. The floor manager, who on most nights did his best to vanish beneath the bill of his Dodgers cap, cleared his throat, then met her eyes. "Natalie," he declared, his voice booming, "for everybody here, let me just say that we are so damn glad to have you back!"

The applause that followed was massive and exuberant and raucous. Actually, Natalie thought, struggling to keep the composure she was within a hairsbreadth of losing, "applause" was far too weak a word for the thunderous ovation that filled the studio. There by the massive studio doors stood Ruth, her bright blue eyes looking shockingly close to teary, flanked by the last of the real newsies, Natalie thought, the people who made it all worthwhile, the people who, like her, were the true believers. She gazed about her and did her best to memorize the scene, never to forget the faces, as if it were the last time, though of course that couldn't be.

Eventually she rose to her feet and applauded her colleagues right back, the din reaching a point where it bordered on deafening. Then she stopped clapping and bent her head. After a few whistles and bravos, the studio again grew hushed.

"You are the people who make this crazy business worth it," she said into the silence. "I thank you, and I will never, ever forget you." As she felt her composure again begin to slip, the communal strength of these people who had never once doubted her reached out to buoy and carry her through. Again she gazed around the studio she'd loved for years, the arena in which once she'd fallen but had survived to return triumphant. "Now let's put the news on the air."

OCTOBER

☆

CHAPTER TWENTY-THREE

Tuesday, October 1, 12:18 P.M.

"You're on to me." Tony did his best to smile at BD over the Nachos Grande that rose like a greaseball mountain on Las Casita's little red table. "You've taken over my favorite place to treat people to lunch."

He wanted to make nice because BD was still mad at him over that fake story he'd told her way back when about Princess. She was too much of a powerhouse to have as an enemy, but making nice was damn hard to do when BD was in the wackiest mood this side of menopause.

"You got that right, Scoppio." BD cracked him another cuckoo smile. "I *am* on to you. Another chip?" She plucked one out from the mound of melted cheddar and ground beef and sour cream and held it out to him. He didn't know what the hell he saw on her face.

"Uh, no, thanks," he told her, then looked down fast at his Coke. Did BD want to sleep with him? He got worried. Did he have to sleep with her to stop her being mad at him? No way, Jose. He'd never cheated on Anna-Maria, and he sure wasn't gonna start with BD.

"So, Tony, I want to ask your advice," she said.

He felt a rush of relief. "About what?"

"I've got a problem with a talent. She's getting a little big for her breeches. I want to cut her down to size."

He nodded. "I know the feeling."

"Just so happens I've got something on her." BD

stirred her iced tea. "Something she wouldn't want spread around. You get my drift?"

Did he ever. "Isn't it pretty obvious what you do?"

BD met his eyes. "What do you mean?"

"Well—" He shrugged. He wasn't usually this forthright but he did want to get back on BD's good side. "So tell a few people."

"You mean . . . like news directors?"

"You're worried she's gonna try to up the ante at contract time, right? So make that harder for her." And who would be better at this than BD? She could spread gossip quicker than Farmer John could lay manure.

"It's funny you should say that." BD laughed so loud people at other tables looked over.

Tony didn't usually get embarrassed, but he did this time.

"Because," she went on, "I jotted down a list of people to talk to." She pulled a piece of paper out of her monster of a purse and handed it to him.

More weirdness. "These are all the news directors in town. Minus me." He looked up at her. "Why'd you write up this list? You know these names like the back of your hand."

"You know what else I got in my purse, Scoppio?" Now her eyes were all shiny, as if she had a secret he'd never guess but would really like to know. Was BD on something, maybe?

"No," he said warily. "I don't."

This time she pulled out a tape and held it up. He took one look at the label and thought he was gonna barf.

"That's right," she chirped. Man, did she sound happy. "It's Kelly Devlin, starting a gun battle that got a little kid killed." She put the tape back in her purse. "Just FYI, I sent dubs to my favorite sources at the L.A.P.D. and Child Protective Services."

Tony felt his Burrito Grande begin a return trip up his gullet. So much for the agreement with Princess and Ruth to keep the tape on the QT. One of them had double-crossed him. And he hadn't even fired Kelly yet because Elaine hadn't finished the goddamn paperwork! But now everybody would know. Absolutely everybody.

Including a certain station owner in Phoenix, Arizona.

"Did you say, 'sent dubs?' " he croaked. "Past tense?"

"Oh"—BD waved her hand airily—"those tapes are long gone." She rose from her chair and leaned toward him over the table, a big fat grin plastered all over her face. "Because nobody spreads gossip faster than I do, Tony, now do they?"

Natalie sat at the glitzy Italian table in Dewey, Climer's glass-walled penthouse conference room, hot midday sunshine doing its best to combat the air-conditioning, and ran her damp palms down the skirt of her most formal suit, a gray pinstripe. So far her preair relaxation exercises weren't working: her heart was pounding, her stomach roiling, her throat dry. She was suspended in that tense expectant state when time gyrates between dragging and speeding forward, the seconds inexorably leading to a scene she both dreaded and heartily wished to be over.

"How you holding up?" Berta asked briskly, not bothering to raise her eyes from a manila folder labeled DANIELS, NATALIE.

"I'm fine." Natalie glanced to her right and eyed her attorney appreciatively. Other clients might find Berta Powers's no-nonsense manner off-putting, but not her. She didn't need a new best friend; she needed a fearless attorney. Especially this afternoon. "Don't worry about me. I always perform under pressure."

Berta looked up and grinned. "And you're not even a New Yorker. Do you want to go over the drill one more time?"

"No need."

"Good." Both women's eyes were suddenly drawn to a flurry of activity in Dewey, Climer's reception area, just outside the conference room's glass walls. "They're here." Berta's gaze didn't stray from the duo striding toward them. "Now remember, let *them* be the hotheads, no matter what they try to pull. Even if Miles has figured out you lifted the *Forget Maui* contract or the plagiarized script."

Natalie nodded as Miles and Johnny Bangs swaggered into the conference room. Both were so obviously pumped up they might have been boxers entering a ring. Although, as Natalie's practiced eye quickly noted, her soon-to-be ex-husband wasn't quite as cocksure as he was trying to appear.

He was dressed in his all-black workaday uniform, which as long as she'd known him he'd considered Hollywood's highest fashion statement. Its somberness was only slightly relieved by the silver threads in his sports jacket, the same shade as the growing number of streaks in his wavy dark hair. His eyes darted everywhere but into her own. And once he sat down across the wide glass table, his hands fidgeted in his lap until his attorney laid a calming hand on his arm.

He's even more nervous than I am, Natalie thought, surprised and, she had to admit, gratified. Then a disturbing notion shot through her as she watched Johnny Bangs, slickly well groomed in a navy worsted double-breasted suit and light blue tie, showily thumb through an imposing stack of documents. *But it's clear they have* something *up their sleeve. What?*

"Let's dispense with the small talk and wrap this thing up." Bangs looked across the table at Berta. "You've been dragging this out for months and I'm putting a stop to it today."

Natalie watched her attorney nonchalantly roll her eyes. "My ass, Johnny." Her tone was casual. "What you call 'dragging this thing out' is simply refusing to cave in to your client's bald-faced lie that he never signed a prenuptial agreement. But I *will* agree on one thing. We'll put a stop to it today."

"He never did sign a prenup," Bangs declared calmly. "And if he had, surely after all these months you would have produced a copy."

"We *would* have if your client hadn't stolen the only copy from their safe-deposit box," Berta retorted. "*After* lifting the key from her house under the pretext of a reconciliation."

"Oh, and did my client also pilfer Dewey, Climer's files?" Bangs threw back his head and laughed. "Come on, Berta." He paused, cocky as hell, and Natalie watched his eyes grow glittery.

He's enjoying this, she thought, and her tension ratcheted up another notch. *What does he think he's got?*

"Besides," he continued, "you should be more careful about lobbing around accusations of theft, given your own client's penchant for criminal behavior. Though I gather trespassing is her preferred transgression."

Natalie froze. To her right she heard Berta snort. "What in the world are you jabbering about now?"

Wordlessly Johnny Bangs extracted a slim document from his stack and tossed it across the glass table at Berta. It slid to a stop right in front of her, like a ballplayer sliding into base. At first Natalie could read none of the typewritten script, but as Berta moved to page two, she saw beneath the text two smudged fingerprints with her name and the date July 11 printed next to them. And beneath: *Los Angeles Police Department.*

What is this about? Natalie struggled to remain calm, though her pulse was racing. *That's my booking sheet from the day I got arrested for stalking Hope Dalmont! Why is he bringing that up?*

Berta slapped the paper. "This is old news! What's your point?"

An arrogant grin spread across Johnny Bangs's face. He looked like a predator prolonging the kill for the sheer enjoyment of his victim's panic. "Mr. Lambert's home was dusted for fingerprints a few weeks back, after he returned from taping his sitcom one evening to find evidence of a break-in."

"So his house got broken into! What does that have to do with this proceeding?"

"Quite a bit, as it turns out." Bangs continued smiling, all infuriating confidence. "You will recall, of course, your client's history of hooliganism at my client's property." He arched his brows. "The window-breaking episode, for example?"

"Oh, please," Berta scoffed. "Any woman in America would have done the same if she'd been similarly provoked. The court of public opinion would applaud Ms. Daniels for far worse."

Bangs shrugged. "Doubtful. But at any rate Mr. Lambert knew immediately that it was Ms. Daniels who'd broken into his home, for what purpose he couldn't fathom."

"What evidence could you possibly have to back up this lunatic accusation?" Berta demanded.

Bangs let the silence grow before he leaned back and casually clasped his hands in his lap. "First, perfume."

"What?" Berta laughed. "Your evidence is *perfume*?"

"It's a distinctive scent," he continued, apparently unfazed. "Mr. Lambert smelled it for a dozen years. And indeed, his initial suspicion was confirmed by Mr. Lambert's handyman, a"—he glanced down at his documents—"Dale Tritt. He swore in this deposition"—he held up a document—"that he recognized Ms. Daniels from Channel 12 and that he left her alone in Mr. Lambert's house while Mr. Lambert was at a taping. We dusted for prints and found many that matched those of Ms. Daniels, which of course have been on file with the L.A.P.D. since after her arrest." He arched his brows again. "The Hope Dalmont episode?"

"Don't make it sound so incriminating, Johnny," Berta said. "The fingerprints of all local newspeople are on file with the L.A.P.D. And if you care to recall the so-called Dalmont episode in its entirety, you'll remember that not only did Miss Dalmont *not* file charges against my client, but that she selected her to conduct an exclusive interview."

Natalie sat in frustrated silence listening to Johnny Bangs's character assassination, restraining herself from screaming out that she never would have gone into Miles's house in the first place if he hadn't lied both about the prenup and his sitcom deal and then cajoled the studio into withholding the documents, despite the subpoenas. And all in a greedy attempt to wrest whatever financial gain he could from the ruins of their marriage. Damn Miles and his attorney! And damn herself for handing them ammunition. How stupid to wear perfume! But she hadn't thought twice about it. And wasn't it just her luck that that *one* time Miles turned out to be observant?

Natalie found Bangs's laser stare focused on her. "Yes," he said, "we are all well aware of Ms. Daniels's journalistic coup in Monaco. And that charges were never filed . . . in *that* case," he added.

The conference room grew silent, the only sounds the hum of the air conditioner and the muted tones of attorneys in adjacent offices.

This is it, she thought, her mouth dry. *He's about to play his trump card.*

"What's your point?" Berta asked.

Bangs leaned back and clasped his hands in his lap, taking his sweet, infuriating time. "I cannot imagine that Ms. Daniels would like to have this latest break-in become public knowledge," he said, as though that idea had just occurred to him for the first time. "Particularly not at this sensitive juncture, when she was just reinstated to the anchor desk. *And* in negotiations to renew her contract. No doubt she strongly desires the negotiations to proceed smoothly."

Natalie looked down at her lap while her emotions were in a tumult. The threat was clear. Unless she caved in and distributed to Miles half the remaining marital property, Bangs would go to the press with the evidence of her break-in and paint her with a brush so black she could well lose the anchor job she'd just gotten back. Not to mention that BD might also withdraw her KNBC offer.

She certainly was vulnerable in that regard. It wasn't long ago that she'd gained notoriety for chasing Hope Dalmont into the Millennium Club, and swearing on-air during her earthquake remote. If there was yet another incident, who wouldn't believe she was demented? The public, not to mention television management, was only so tolerant.

Berta was silent, tapping her pen against the glass table. *Tap, tap, tap.* Finally she shook her head. "Johnny, I've always admired your chutzpah, and never more so than today. What other attorney would turn the tables to accuse his opponent of the very transgression his own client committed?" She smiled sweetly. "But I'm afraid this time your strategy will backfire."

Natalie watched as her attorney pulled from her sheaf of papers copies of the Heartbeat Studios contract and check stubs and handed them to Miles and Johnny Bangs. Natalie watched the men closely. Bangs retained his composure but Miles's face grew ashen.

Berta's tone was wry. "Mr. Lambert, I see you recognize these documents."

"Why haven't I seen these before today?" Johnny Bangs demanded. "Why were these not provided to me by the discovery closure date?"

"Didn't we include these in the packet of materials?" Berta asked mildly. "Oh, dear." She waved a dismissive hand. "It must've been an oversight."

Natalie had to restrain herself from chuckling. For all Miles and Johnny Bangs knew, Berta had gotten the documents from Heartbeat Studios in response to her repeated subpoenas. They had no way of knowing otherwise without indicating that they had maneuvered to have the studio withhold exactly this paperwork. And now they could no longer pretend that Miles had deferred his compensation.

"The point is," Berta said, "that I believe we have grounds for a compromise."

Johnny Bangs was silent for a beat. "I'm listening," he said. Natalie noted with some satisfaction that he'd lost no small degree of his earlier bravado.

"If indeed there *were* no prenuptial agreement," Berta declared, "Mr. Lambert would be required as part of the divorce settlement to give Ms. Daniels one half of this fee, i.e., one point five million dollars. He would receive from Ms. Daniels one half of the remaining marital property, or six hundred thousand dollars. In short, he would suffer a net loss of nine hundred thousand dollars.

"However," she continued, "if we did the same calculation according to the terms specified in the misplaced prenup, Mr. Lambert would receive nothing from Ms. Daniels. He would, though, retain his entire studio fee of three million dollars."

Johnny Bangs shook his head. "Why would your client agree to this? That would put *her* out nine hundred grand as well."

Berta leaned forward. "Because unlike *your* client, Counselor, Ms. Daniels will abide by the terms of the prenup that she knows exists. Despite the financial cost. In addition, and here I quote, 'I don't want any of Miles's stinking money.' End-quote."

Natalie watched the color return to her husband's face. Now he looked as if he could barely keep himself from gleefully bounding out of his chair. She didn't allow herself more than a cursory glance at Berta, for fear that if she met her attorney's eyes she'd jump up and scream, *We're winning! We're winning! They're falling into our trap!*

Johnny Bangs cleared his throat. "Allow me to confer with my client." The men put their heads together and began murmuring, Natalie nearly bursting with impatience. Finally Bangs raised his head and met Berta's eyes. "I'd say we have a deal."

Berta whipped out several copies of a one-page document. "I've taken the liberty of drafting an agreement to that effect." She rapidly handed it around. "Look it over."

Johnny Bangs's eyebrows arched. "You want us to sign it today?"

Berta shrugged. "Why not?"

Bangs grabbed the document, only a few paragraphs long. Again he conferred with Miles, who nodded, then attempted unsuccessfully to hide a smirk.

You idiot, Natalie thought. *You're so damn full of yourself you can't even tell we've got you by the short hairs.*

"We're willing to sign this," Bangs declared a few minutes later. He handed Miles a thick MontBlanc pen from his briefcase.

Natalie watched her soon-to-be ex sign with a flourish.

Berta nodded and held out her hand to her fellow attorney, who shook it quickly before the men strutted out of Dewey, Climer's sunny penthouse conference room.

"Don't let your plumage get caught in the doors," Natalie remarked dryly, still watching them through the glass conference-room wall.

Berta laughed. "You feeling rich yet?"

Natalie thought for a moment. "Not rich. Exonerated." Then she threw back her head and laughed. "Free as a bird!"

Berta grinned. "When do you think Miles will understand that he'll never get the rest of that studio fee?"

Natalie shook her head. She knew that Jerry Cohen had filed a grievance with the Writers Guild; she had no idea how long the process would take. To her knowledge, as yet Miles didn't know that his plagiarism had been uncovered.

But soon he would; soon *everybody* would, including his employers at Heartbeat Studios.

"We'll hear the explosion when he finds out, Berta." Natalie smiled. "They'll probably hear it all the way in New York."

Kelly sat cross-legged on her yellow suede sofa, still the lone piece of furniture in her living room, staring at her TV and watching other people do the news. *Still* Tony was mad at her, even though she'd sent big bouquets of red roses to both him and Rico, with long apology notes attached. That was two days ago and she hadn't heard anything yet. But on some level she wasn't really surprised. Men liked to make women wait to show how powerful they were. It was pathetic, really, because they always came around in the end.

The doorbell rang. She padded over and pulled open the door and said, "Yeah?" before she focused on who it was. Then she had to start over. "Tony!" she chirped. "What a pleasant surprise!"

"Yeah, right. Move over, I'm coming in." He barreled past her into the foyer.

It sure didn't seem as if he'd accepted her apology. "Would you care for something to drink?" she offered, trailing after him into her living room.

"I'm not here on some damn social call, Kelly." He turned around and stared at her and she got another shock, because he had an expression on his face she'd never seen before. "I only want one thing from you and that's an explanation," he said, and then he reached inside his jacket pocket and whipped out a videotape—*the CNN shootout tape!*—and Kelly thought she was gonna croak right then and there. But she couldn't, 'cause she had to save her ass.

Her brain cranked into high gear. "I know it looks pretty bad when you first see it." She tried to sound contrite. "But I gotta tell you, Tony, you wouldn't think it was so bad if you'd actually been there. Videotapes lie, you know."

"They don't lie, Kelly. They're the only thing in a goddamn TV newsroom that tells the truth."

"But the tape makes it look like I had something to do with that kid getting shot and I didn't!" She started pacing the nearly empty room, like a lawyer arguing in front of the jury. "He would've gotten shot anyhow. The gunman was nuts and somebody was gonna get hurt!"

"It had gone on for fifteen hours already and he hadn't shot anybody. Not until you spooked him with that goddamn flashlight!"

"So maybe I hurried it up a little." She kept her voice reasonable. "But it was still gonna happen—I know that."

"You don't know a damn thing, Kelly! You don't know a goddamn thing!" Now Tony was shouting at her, as loud as she'd ever heard him. And his face was all red as if he was gonna have a heart attack. It reminded her of Miles that time she'd told him she wasn't gonna give him his loan money back.

Maybe I should do now what I did then, she thought. She eyed Tony across her living room. *Wait it out. Just let him get it out of his system.*

In fact, right then he tuckered out. He shook his head

and seemed to shrink, walking away with his head down, staring at the hardwood floor. "It's my own damn fault," he mumbled, so quiet she could barely hear him. "I should've fired you long ago."

What? Now she made her voice all wheedly. "Tony, you don't want to fire me. Not really." Very slowly she got closer, as if he was a wounded animal who might attack if she made any sudden moves. "I'm exactly what you need to pump the numbers. You know what you should do? You should fire Ken and hire somebody new to be my coanchor and then we'll go gangbusters! And you know I don't cost you much." Tony wasn't saying anything so she kept on going. "Now I'm willing to go for the hundred thirty K the first year of the contract. You've already punished me by suspending me and banning me from the lot, and those are both pretty bad."

He stood there, still staring at her that weird way, but she figured she must be getting through because he wasn't arguing.

"And besides," she went on, "nobody else knows what's on that tape. We can keep it our little secret."

Then he started shaking his head. "You're a piece of work, Kelly—you know that? A real piece of work. What about those lawsuits? You want me to forget those, too? No chance. I'm firing you. Maybe I can still save myself. Here's the paperwork you gotta sign." He pulled some documents out of his other jacket pocket.

Okay. Now was *definitely* time for desperate measures. She got up real close to Tony and ran her hands lightly up his chest. "Please." She stared into his eyes and made her voice all breathy. "I can make you forget all of it, the lawsuits and everything."

But he pushed her hands away. "Don't even try that shit on me, Kelly. It won't work."

Right then she gave up trying to be nice. "I'll sue the station for sexual harassment!" she shrieked. "I'll name Bjorkman! And *you*! I'll say that's why you fired me, because I wouldn't sleep with you, you pig!"

Then he gave her another look she'd never seen before. "You do that," he said, "and my first stop is Parker

Center. With this tape in my hand." He held it up in the air. "Because I'm sure the L.A.P.D. would want to see it."

Kelly backed onto the suede couch. All of a sudden she was scared shitless. The cops might come after her? Then wouldn't everybody know? Every news director in town? She'd never get another TV job! In L.A. or anywhere!

That made her start shaking so hard she couldn't stop.

Tony held a pen up in front of her. "Sign these papers. Here, on this dotted line."

"What do they say?"

"They say you understand that you're fired. They also say you won't sue KXLA for any reason. Ever."

"You won't go to the cops?" she asked him.

He didn't say anything for a second, but then he said no, he wouldn't go to the cops. So she took the pen and signed—because what else could she do?—and he tore off a copy for her and left.

Kelly watched him go and kept shaking.

No TV job. No agent. No money.

It was everything she never wanted, and all at the same time.

It was 11:12 P.M. on Wednesday night when Natalie exited the KXLA lot and made two lefts, the second landing her on a smarmy stretch of Sunset Boulevard, heading west. She cruised swiftly, the adrenaline that had pulsed through her body while she anchored the newscast dissipated. Now she just wanted to make the right turn that led her north into the Hollywood Hills and Nichols Canyon and bed.

Just past the intersection at Gower a car careened into traffic behind her and raced up close to her tail, its headlights on high beam blinding her in the rearview mirror.

She squinted, flicking up the mirror's bottom edge to escape the glare. Then the car behind began weaving erratically, the driver honking his horn and punching up even closer to her rear bumper. Her foot pushed down on the accelerator. Why didn't he just pass her? Was it some maniac?

Her heart sped up, like the speedometer on her dash. Was it a maniac like that other guy? Years before she'd had a stalker—a felon who'd tracked her home from KXLA after lying in wait outside the lot till she drove out after the newscast. The L.A.P.D.'s threat management unit had to be brought in. Until the day he was arrested she'd been petrified.

Was it happening again now, as she drove to an empty house?

She sped through a yellow light at Cahuenga. The other car followed, close on her tail. She hit the steering wheel with the palm of her hand. Damn! It was a Porsche, she could see now. So it was a rich maniac, but a maniac nonetheless.

I can't go home and lead this guy to my front door. Nor did she want a chase through the canyons, poorly lit and steep and narrow. *I'll drive to Hollywood Division. No way will he accost me in front of a police station.* And the location was burned into her memory from her arrest for stalking Hope Dalmont. How ironic.

Abruptly she pulled into the left turning lane. But the Porsche sped up along her right side. She glanced over and looked at the driver.

Miles!

She was stunned. Miles? Had he gone mad? She glanced over again. He was motioning for her to pull over.

She didn't want to pull over. But how could she dodge him? Not only would he follow her wherever she went, he knew where she lived.

Fine. She'd pull over, here on Sunset Boulevard. Not in the dark emptiness of Nichols Canyon.

She pulled over by a closed Jack in the Box restaurant. Miles parked just behind, then emerged from his car and approached her.

She kept the engine running, the door locked, and the window closed. If he got crazy, she'd just go.

She couldn't believe it. She was afraid of her own husband.

He bent to regard her through the car window. "Hello, Natalie." His tone was as calm as if they'd casually run into each other. "I apologize for accosting you like this but I was afraid that if I called you wouldn't agree to meet me."

You got that right, she thought, but remained mute.

"Will you get out of the car to talk to me?"

"No."

"Will you at least roll down the window?"

She hesitated, then obliged, but cracked the window only slightly.

His brow furrowed in disappointment. "Fine. We can talk like this."

Now *she* was frowning. This was puzzling, this sudden reappearance of the understanding, rational Miles. Whom she hadn't seen for some time, not since . . . *My God.* Her heart began to pound. *Not since the night he seduced me to steal the prenup.* She clutched the steering wheel, thankful that a ton of steel and eight cylinders separated her from her husband. *He wants something.*

"I've been doing a great deal of thinking," he said. His face assumed a tortured expression. "Natalie, I've realized that all this has been an enormous mistake. It's killing me. I know now that my professional success is damn hollow without you."

She stared at him, incredulous.

He leaned in even closer, such sadness filling his eyes that she couldn't tear her own gaze away. "I'm saying that I'd like us to give it another try, Natalie. Our marriage. Before we make the biggest, most heartbreaking mistake of our lives."

All she could do was shake her head. It was unfathomable, what this man was capable of. He would stop at nothing. Nothing was too hypocritical, or grasping, or contemptible.

"You never cease to amaze me," she said in a low voice. He looked startled, and she realized it was because she'd segued from thinking to speaking aloud with nothing in between. "I bought your shit for a dozen years. I paid for it hook, line, and sinker. You married me because I brought home a nice big paycheck, which you were too lazy and incompetent to do yourself. What a fool I was. Not anymore." Suddenly she slapped her open palm against the window in the direction of his face and he recoiled, eyes blazing. "So what do you need now, Miles?" she yelled. "A new sugar mama, is that it? And you picked me because I performed so beautifully for a dozen years? You can just forget it!"

Miles just stared at her, until something in his face twisted. Suddenly he pushed hard against the car, rattling the chassis. What few passersby there were on Sunset Boulevard at that hour stopped and stared. "You self-centered bitch!" he shouted. "You might as well know you got what you wanted! Because I got fired! *Fired!*"

She stared at him. "The studio fired you?"

"They say I plagiarized the script!" He was standing back from the car now, still shouting at her. "They're not gonna pay me a dime! In fact, they'll probably sue me to get back what they *already* paid me! And the show won't go on the air *once* with my name on it. Not *once*! All thanks to you!" He executed a mocking bow. The people on the street were mesmerized. "It took me a while but finally I understood what else you stole when you broke into my house." He leaned so close then that his breath fogged her window. "Ransacking my private files. Isn't that just like you? You and that fucking ex-partner of mine!"

"No, Miles." She was shaking her head violently, her entire body trembling with anger. "Not thanks to me. Or to Jerry. It was *you* who stole Jerry's work. You alone. Because you are a talentless hack who has to ride somebody else's coattails to make it around the block. So don't you *dare* blame me or anybody else for getting fired! You did that all by yourself."

"You need to see me brought down, don't you?" He jabbed at his chest, his voice rising. "You can't stand it! You can't stand to have me do well."

"You're delusional." She'd had enough, and she was frightened. She turned the key in the ignition and the engine leaped to life. "I'm leaving."

"You're sleeping with him, aren't you? Jerry?" He leered at her crazily through the window. "*That's* what this is all about! That's why he filed with the Guild and went crawling back to Heartbeat!"

"Don't you even *speak* to me about sleeping with somebody else!" she screamed. She could feel her control slip away from her like a car on an icy road. "Not after you *fucked* Kelly Devlin *under our own roof* while we were married! You didn't think I knew about that, did you, you bastard?"

Shock registered on his face, which gave her a jolt of pleasure.

"You did a good job of bleeding me dry, living off my money, sleeping with who knows who, stealing our prenup." She could barely speak for the rage flowing through her. "You are a despicable human being, Miles Lambert. I want you the hell out of my life. I wish to God I'd had the sense to kick you out years ago." Then she jammed her foot down on the accelerator and the Mercedes shot forward. She didn't care if she ran over him or not.

When she looked in the rearview mirror, still shaking, Miles had dwindled into a distant speck, too small and impotent to hurt her anymore.

Tony paced Pemberley's office, not sure whether to sit, where to sit if he did, what to do with his hands. He felt like shit. He looked like shit. And he was pretty sure that very soon, shit was not only gonna fly but land on his head.

Because there could be no good reason for Pemberley to have chosen this morning to summon him to Sunshine Broadcasting headquarters on a next-plane basis. None. Just when Tony was starting to think maybe, *maybe*, he'd squirm out of this mess, Maxine informed him that he was wanted in Phoenix ASAP. Pronto. *Yesterday*.

"You're here." Pemberley's voice, which sounded none too happy, boomed from the doorway. Tony's insides rearranged themselves, much as they had during the turbulent flight, only worse.

Pemberley walked behind his shuffleboard court of a desk and scowled at him. He was backlit in the floor-to-ceiling windows and looked like a silver-haired Darth Vader. "Scoppio, I've never been more wrong about a man than I've been about you."

Tony cleared his throat. "I—"

"When I hired you, I thought there was a better-than-even chance you'd be the best news director I ever had, in all my years at Sunshine. I expected to be handing over your bonus within three months of your start date. You came with the most impressive credentials that had ever crossed my desk. You were a hard-ass, but in my book that's a plus."

"Rhett—"

"But in the ensuing months, not only did you fail to get the prime-time newscast to number one and keep it there, you also failed to get the news department out of the red. You demoted a well-respected veteran anchor for an inexperienced no name who in no time at all not only got KXLA slapped with two lawsuits but got a six-year-old killed! And *then* you kept her on staff!" Gone was Pemberley's logical voice, replaced by a roar that in southern California would have accompanied a seismic event.

Also gone was whatever shred of calm Tony still possessed. *Jesus, Mary, and Joseph,* he thought, seeing his career flash before his eyes, *Pemberley knows about the CNN tape. Thanks, BD. Or maybe Princess? Or Ruth?* He realized, suddenly, that he had a few enemies.

"The lawsuits I might have gotten past, because of my confidence in you," Pemberley ranted on. "But this flashlight . . . *monstrosity*!" He slapped his open palm on his desk. "Never!" Then he pointed his finger at Tony like an accuser in the Salem witch trials. "You lied to me and that I will not tolerate."

Tony's mind raced. He'd lied? He'd withheld, sure, but not even Catholics considered that a sin. And in the TV-news world, it was standard procedure. Before breakfast.

"You told me," Pemberley continued, enunciating every

syllable like he was in the national spelling bee, "that Howard Bjorkman was to blame for that damnable car-accident videotape getting off the lot. Well, I've spoken to Howard Bjorkman."

Shit! Tony felt like an ant in the midday sun, cornered by a kid with a magnifying glass and a mean streak.

"Oh, yes." Pemberley nodded. "You think that because I'm hands-off, I don't know what's going on? Wrong!" he roared. "I know *exactly* what's going on! And so I know that you tried to weasel out of your responsibility by shifting blame onto your managing editor. Instead of where it belonged, on that menace of a female you promoted to your flagship newscast. What kind of management is that? How do you expect me to stand for that?"

Tony hadn't the slightest idea.

"What you did to Howard Bjorkman," Pemberley announced, "I am now doing to you. You're fired. Effective immediately. But I will not dodge my responsibility for hiring you, which I now consider the single greatest mistake of my career. And I will gladly describe it as such to anyone who asks. Consider yourself blackballed, Scoppio. Now get your sorry ass out of here."

And Pemberley sat down at his corporate throne, leaving Tony to slink out of Sunshine headquarters into the unrelenting Phoenix sun.

CHAPTER TWENTY-FOUR

Friday, October 4, 6:16 A.M.

Kelly tore her eyes away from *The Early News* on KYYR to glare out her front window at the mob of reporters camped on her lawn. What must her neighbors think about *this*? A row of ENG trucks nearly blocked the street, their masts high in the air, probably sending out enough radiation to give cancer to everybody in Bel Air. They were tramping down the lawns and leaving trash everywhere and it was a goddamn mess! She'd call the cops, except she didn't want anything to do with them, either.

These media people had a helluva nerve using *her* to beef up their newscasts. And that bastard Tony Scoppio! So much for his promise not to call the cops about the tape. Kelly grabbed the TV remote and jabbed the volume button. On KYYR, that bitch Mindy Lee was reporting:

"At this hour, Devlin is closeted inside this Bel Air home, refusing to answer reporters' questions about her role in July's tragic shooting death of six-year-old Jimmy Taylor. The L.A.P.D. is reviewing the videotape that captured Devlin's actions that night, though experts say criminal charges probably will not be filed against her. But little Jimmy's mother says she's consulting an attorney about a possible wrongful-death suit. 'I'm not going to let that reporter

get away with this! I can't get my Jimmy back but I can sue!' "

Kelly watched the TV screen as the kid's mother pumped her fist. That truly pissed her off. *Another* lawsuit? What did that make, three? Was this the new American way to make money or what? At least it looked like criminal charges might go away, so she wouldn't have to rot in jail.

Then Mindy Lee cut away from the mother's sound bite to live pictures of picketers in front of KXLA. Kelly couldn't believe the nerve of those lowlifes, either. Didn't these people have jobs?

"The victim's family is receiving a lot of support from child's rights organizations, who vow to raise money for any legal action she might take. They're picketing KXLA and organizing an advertiser boycott, even though both Devlin and News Director Tony Scoppio have been fired."

Kelly let out a whoop. Now *that* was good news! He deserved it, the double-crossing prick! But at that moment Kelly happened to focus on one of the picketer's signs and it felt like her blood suddenly ran cold. CHILD KILLER! it read, in dark red marker made to look like blood, with a drawing of *her* using a gun to shoot a kid!

She gaped at the TV. This was outrageous! She had half a mind to run outside and give a statement to those frigging reporters. But just as she was thinking about it, her phone rang.

Again! Kelly ran into the kitchen to stare at the bright red message counter on her answering machine. Forty-four messages. They were all from reporters wanting a comment, print *and* radio *and* TV. So far she hadn't spoken to anybody but maybe now that all these crazy accusations were flying around she should. She wasn't sure. It was too bad Rico had dumped her because otherwise she could ask him. But maybe all this publicity would make him want her back, which would be good because she really did want to get back on the air. So long as she was back on the air, everything else would work out.

She couldn't help but be nervous as she listened to her answering-machine announcement finish. What if the cops had changed their mind and were calling to see if she was home before they came to cart her away? A male voice came on and she held her breath.

"Kelly, this is Bru Constantine from Final Copy.*"*

She let out a relieved breath. Another tabloid TV show calling for a comment. Actually, not bad. *Final Copy* was *Hard Line*'s biggest rival. So that was pretty cool.

"We know you're preoccupied right now, but some people here want to talk to you about a reporter opening. We think you might be perfect for it. Please call at your earliest—"

Kelly missed the rest of the message because she was hollering so loud. *Final Copy*! Take that, *Hard Line*! She slammed down her fist on the limestone counter. Yes! It was like everybody said. All publicity was good publicity. Hell, maybe eventually she could even get her own talk show out of this! Didn't Joey Buttafuoco get one? And he had nothing on her!

She ran to the fridge for a bottle of champagne. So what if it wasn't even seven a.m.? Kelly Devlin had something to celebrate.

10:46 A.M. Natalie looked up from her business plan and drummed her fingers on her desk. Should she postpone Jerry Cohen? He'd asked to come by the station and said he'd be there by ten-thirty, but there was still no sign of him.

And Geoff's wedding was at noon. She didn't want to be late. Actually she didn't want to *go*, but felt she had to. She'd said she would, RSVP'ed in the affirmative, checked her preference for salmon over steak at the reception, so there you go.

Plus, she had to put on a good show. Her pride demanded it.

Restlessly she rose to pace her little yellow office. Maybe she should just skip the ceremony and do the reception bit. Participate in the eating and the drinking and bypass the vowing and the kissing.

She stopped dead. Right. Like there wouldn't be kissing at the reception. There would be scads of it, only she would be a witness and not a participant.

Her phone rang. She raced back to her desk. It was the gate guard, shouting over the Kelly picketers to ask if a Jerry Cohen should be let in. "Yes, I'm expecting him," Natalie yelled back.

If she kept Jerry to half an hour, she calculated as she replaced the receiver, she could still get to the church before it got embarrassingly late. She didn't want to put in an appearance at some critical moment, à la Dustin Hoffman in *The Graduate*. She'd just pulled out her Thomas guide to map the fastest route when Ruth appeared in her doorway, glowing in a seafoam-green suit. Natalie had to smile. "Feeling better with Tony and Kelly gone?"

Ruth grinned and sat down on Natalie's battered office sofa. "Gotta say it's a nice change."

"I'm still in shock."

"Maxine told me Scoppio cleaned out his office in the middle of the night, to make sure nobody would be around."

"Can't say I blame him. Funny." She shook her head. "I was just starting to think we could coexist and now he's gone." She winced, worry clutching in her gut as a horrible new possibility occurred to her. "And who knows who we'll get next? Maybe somebody even *worse* than Scoppio."

A new news director who may not like me. It could happen all over again, just like Geoff said about Tony back in June. "Tony's new to KXLA and wants to make his mark. And the easiest way to do that is to change who's on the air . . ."

"Pemberley's here on the lot, apparently," Ruth went on, pulling Natalie back into the present. "And Elaine says the station probably will get sued because of Kelly starting the shootout. By the boy's family. Don't quote me but I say fine. They deserve whatever they can get and it still won't bring their kid back." A look of disgust crossed Ruth's face. "And chances are Kelly'll slime out of criminal charges."

"You're kidding! How?"

"Because there's no proof she willfully endangered lives. She was negligent, and should've known, but that's not enough."

"That's a damn shame." Then Natalie narrowed her eyes at Ruth. "Do you know how that CNN tape got out in the first place?"

Ruth looked away. "Seems BD got her hands on it."

"BD? How in the world did she get it?" Natalie eyed her producer closely. "Ruth? How did she get it?"

Finally Ruth met her eyes, then shrugged. "The more I thought about it, the more I thought Kelly should be held responsible. And there was no way in hell Tony would ever let that tape see the light of day. Then BD and I happened to go out for drinks, and one topic led to another, and there you go." Then Ruth pushed her bifocals up her nose and gave Natalie her own appraising stare. "By the way, *I* learned a little something in that conversation, too."

Now Natalie looked away. "You mean about her offer."

"So are you planning to take it? Or re-sign here? In other words, am I going to lose my anchor?"

Natalie rose restlessly from the couch's arm. "I know my contract expires today. And I know I should have already decided. But I haven't. And there's the Web venture to consider, too."

"So you need more time to think. Well, say you'll anchor next week, at least."

"I'd love to."

Ruth nodded and again Natalie felt herself under the microscope of Ruth's gaze. "Correct me if I'm wrong,

Ms. Daniels," Ruth went on, "but you're mighty dolled up for ten hours before airtime."

Natalie scoffed. "This old thing?"

"That old thing is an Armani—am I right?"

She was surprised. "Since when can you tell one designer from another?"

"One of my hidden talents. Along with my astonishing ability to remember dates and names. And if memory serves, today that dashing Aussie agent of yours is tying the knot with the Breck girl."

Natalie was silent.

Ruth persisted. "So the outfit leads me to believe you're attending the nuptials?"

"I am."

"Well, *this* one'll be worth crying over. Tell you what. Let's do drinks and dinner after the newscast. My treat. At Cicada, where they still serve at that hour."

Natalie was touched. "Ruth, you don't want to eat dinner that late." She paused. Ruth was eyeing her steadily. "I know what you're doing, and I appreciate it. But I'll be fine. Really."

"I know you will. But *I* want to eat at Cicada at eleven, with or without you. So are you in?"

"Cicada's great." Jerry Cohen strolled into Natalie's office and halted in front of Ruth. "The lady knows her restaurants."

"I know their *hours.*" Ruth rose from the couch and extended her hand. "Ruth Sperry."

Jerry grasped her hand. "Jerry Cohen."

Natalie watched the exchange, thinking Jerry looked more Burl Ives than ever. Hale and prosperous, his closely cropped beard mostly white, his figure under his navy sport jacket full but not heavy.

She took the opening to glance at her watch. 11:06. Again she felt a rush of anxiety.

Ruth was being her usual outgoing self. "Jerry Cohen? As in the renowned sitcom producer?"

He bowed his head, laying a hand over his polo-shirted chest. "You honor me."

"I *describe* you, from what I hear from Natalie here."

Jerry didn't even glance at Natalie. "What do you do here, Ruth?"

"I produce our best news show."

He threw back his head and laughed. "Somehow that doesn't surprise me! Someday I hope you'll tell me all about it." He paused. "I'm sure I'd find it fascinating."

Now neither of them seemed to remember that Natalie was in the room. She cleared her throat.

Jerry came sufficiently out of his daze to approach Natalie. "You look fantastic." He kissed her on both cheeks, European style.

"As do you."

"Excuse me," Ruth interrupted. "Great to meet you, Jerry, but I have to get back to the salt mines." She exited, Jerry staring after her retreating back. Then he glanced at the monitor mounted high on the wall above the door and asked, in a poor imitation of casual interest, "So is Ruth married?"

"No." Natalie laughed. "I take it *you're* minus a wife at the moment?"

"Your mother hen is showing, Natalie." He winked. "You can rest assured that both prior specimens have gone bye-bye."

"The way you say it I guess that's good news."

"Well, I've gone the starlet route a few times now and am happy to report I'm finally over it. Finally, by age fifty." He grinned. "So will you put in a good word for me with Ruth tonight?"

"I'll do you one better. Why don't you stand in for me at Cicada?" Natalie knew perfectly well she wouldn't feel like socializing that evening, not even with Ruth.

Jerry grinned, clearly delighted. "I'd love to, thank you."

Natalie motioned to the couch and they both sat down. "What can I do for you, Jerry?"

"You can take this." He extracted a business-size envelope from his inside jacket pocket and held it out.

"What is it?"

"Open it up and you'll see."

She did and instantly forgot everything else. Because

inside was a check, made out to her, in the amount of . . . *"One point five million dollars?"*

Jerry nodded. "I've done a deal with Heartbeat Studios. They want me to take over as *Forget Maui*'s executive producer. That's half the fee."

She was flabbergasted. "But I don't understand."

"Natalie, I'd be receiving no fee at all if it weren't for you. I was so immersed in Tuscan vineyards and writing my screenplay and playing the expatriate American that I had no idea what was going on back here. Thanks to you, I found out. When I said I wanted to repay you, I meant it. I was thinking maybe you have a favorite charity you'd like to donate it to."

"But, Jerry, *you* could donate this money in your own name." She forced herself to hold the check out to him. "It's unbelievably generous but I simply can't take it. It's too . . . enormous."

But Jerry raised his hands in the air. "I want you to have it, Natalie. Really. I insist."

Reluctantly, she lowered her eyes and gazed at the check. She'd never seen such a number arrayed on a check before. It looked fake.

But it wasn't. It was astonishingly real. An idea wormed its way into her brain. *Why not put it into the Web venture? Make Jerry an investor*? *It would get you started, and who knows? Someday you might be able to repay him ten times over . . .*

"That's settled, then." Jerry smiled and rose to his feet.

"Jerry, I don't know how to—"

He shook his head. "I should be thanking *you*."

"I'll walk you out," she offered lamely when her phone rang. "Hold on a second." She crossed over to her desk and picked up the receiver. "Natalie Daniels."

"Good, I caught you."

She frowned, caught off guard. "Rhett?"

"Have a moment to chat?"

"Uh, sure." She glanced at her watch. 11:22.

"Meet me in the news director's office," he said, then hung up.

* * *

Tony missed all the monitors he used to have at KXLA. At home he had one TV. *One*. A stinking twenty-eight-inch in his family room. How could he do any serious news watching with *that*? And serious news watching he had to do, because Kelly Devlin, who he'd been stupid enough to let ruin his life, was on every newscast in town. He half expected her to make the networks by dinner.

He sat in his La-Z-Boy across from the TV, the room as dark as he could make it, even though it was noon and Valley life was going on all around him. That was what he hated. Even the cheery little rays of sunshine that sneaked in around the curtains were annoying. He wanted to be closed off. He wanted it to be dark. He wanted to be alone.

Twelve noon exactly. For a change from local news, he switched to *CNN Headline News*.

They had a good-looking woman anchor. Young. Read PrompTer well. "But you should be doing the Charlotte refinery fire as the top story!" he yelled at her. Bad producing, but that wasn't her fault. He relented, thinking maybe he should write down her name for future reference, but then he remembered. Why bother? He couldn't hire her. He'd been fired himself, after only six months on the job. For the first time since he was thirteen years old and worked after school and on weekends in his old man's shoe repair shop, he was unemployed.

Maybe that was what he'd end up doing, now that his name was mud in TV news. He could smell the polish even now. He felt his stomach turn.

Then the phone rang. "I'll get it," Anna-Maria called out. She was acting as if she was scared to be with him. Her own husband.

He closed his eyes. He'd screwed up big-time for Anna-Maria. No Cadillac now. Sure, they could hold on to the Hondas, and they had money socked away for retirement and the kids' college, but he'd wanted to give her life's real luxuries.

She came back looking puzzled and holding out the cordless phone. "It's Gino Carlutti."

He frowned. His old GM from WNNC in Syracuse, where he'd gotten his start? Calling him at home? Did Gino know he'd been canned? Did *everybody*? He took the phone, girding himself. "Gino!" he boomed. "How's it hanging?"

"Like a *gavone*, my friend." Carlutti chuckled, then hesitated. "You're sounding well."

"You're fishing, Gino."

"Can you blame me, when I hear that the best news director in the goddamn business is on the beach because of some cockamamie screwup?"

Tony's heart leaped. Gino didn't believe the stories? Which were true, of course, but still. "What're you saying to me, Gino?"

"I'm saying I lost my news director two weeks ago. Guy up and left for a job in Minneapolis. No warning. Now I know you're in the big time and Syracuse might look like small potatoes to you, but hey!" Gino laughed again. Tony loved Gino like a brother. "Would you and Anna-Maria consider your old stomping grounds for, what do they call it these days, lifestyle reasons?"

Would Tony *consider* it? Despite how tiny the Syracuse market was, despite the fact that it'd be like starting out all over again, despite how he'd probably have a heart attack shoveling snow, he had to stop himself from grabbing Gino's offer right then and there. How many offers was he gonna get, after all? Tony Scoppio was a marked man! Only a friend would hire him. And he didn't have many friends in TV news. He'd never bothered to make them. His strategy had been to kick ass and take names.

"I've got to tell you, Gino, you're not the first person to call," he lied. "But you *are* one of my good buds from way back."

"So for old times' sake you'll look at an offer? Lemme fax it over to you. What's the number there?"

Tony gave Gino his home fax number and they hung up. He hoisted himself out of the La-Z-Boy and trundled toward the kitchen. "Anna-Maria!" he yelled. "How about Syracuse? You like Syracuse?"

* * *

Rhett Pemberley rose from behind Tony's desk the moment Natalie entered the news director's office. "Come in. Good to see you." He shut the door and waved her toward the lone chair in front of Tony's desk.

None of this is Tony's anymore, she had to remind herself. The office had an entirely different aura now that Tony had cleared out his junk and the cleaning crew had given it a good once-over. No more yellowing newspapers or coffee-stained cups or greasy takeout. No more blinds pulled down over the windows that overlooked the newsroom. No more news blasting from all six monitors. Not to mention that the immaculate Rhett Pemberley, reclaiming the chair behind the desk, cut quite a different figure than Tony Scoppio. The only similarity between Before and After was the teetering stacks of résumé reels. *Tony may be out but my competition's still here,* she thought, *and they're not going anywhere.*

"I'll get right to the point." Rhett leaned forward, interlocking his fingers. "I've always admired you, Natalie. Over the years you've contributed a great deal to this station and been a valuable asset to Sunshine. That said, KXLA is in serious trouble and I have to take strong action to salvage it."

Natalie stared at him, every inch the cool, calculating executive, and felt as if her heart skipped a beat. The fates, cruel, cruel fates, were throwing her back in time, to that horrible June day when Tony said he wasn't going to renew her. *I cannot believe this. Now* Pemberley*'s going to fire me. I've been back on the anchor desk one goddamn week and I'm getting blasted out again!*

Somehow, *she* wanted to be the one to walk out on KXLA. Even though she was considering leaving either to start the Web venture or cross the street to KNBC, *she* wanted to step out on her own, not have them—*again!*—do the pushing.

Rhett began to tick off items on his fingers. "We've had three high-profile firings, of news director, main anchor, and managing editor. We're losing at ten o'clock. The news department is in the red. Two lawsuits are pending against us. Children's rights groups are organizing an advertiser boycott. Morale is rock-bottom. And our reputation is shot."

Amazingly, all that was true. But none of it was her fault! "Rhett," she began, "I . . ."

He slapped open a manila folder. "Today is the final day of your personal-service contract," he went on. "Is that correct?"

She shook her head. "It is, but . . ."

"Then today is the perfect time for you to make a new start." He locked her gaze, and then, slowly, he smiled, revealing a set of perfect white teeth. "How about taking over as news director?"

She gave an awkward laugh. No way could she have heard him right. "I don't understand."

"What's not to understand? I'm offering you the news director job." He came out from behind the desk and perched on its right front corner. "Natalie, it makes perfect sense. You know the station inside out, you have the respect of the staff, and you have solid news judgment. Moreover, you have the kind of character and integrity I want to see in this position. Why is it so surprising?"

Why indeed? Natalie fell back in her chair and wondered. Maybe because she'd never held the job before, in any station anywhere, let alone in the second-largest TV market in the country. Maybe because, thanks to Tony Scoppio, lots of TV people nationwide thought she was mentally unstable. Maybe because she'd spent the last eighteen years trying to make news directors happy and had never dreamed of being the one in the power seat herself.

But did she think she was up to the job? Yes, Natalie realized, surprised. Yes. As a matter of fact, she thought she'd make a damn fine news director.

"Of course," Rhett was saying, "with all these hurdles to get over, the job is no walk in the park. Nor does the salary compare to what you earn as an anchor. I'm prepared to offer a three-year deal at two hundred the first year, two fifteen the second, and two twenty-five the third. But Sunshine does have an attractive stock option . . ."

Natalie tuned out, completely flummoxed. This was *so* far out of left field, it might as well be coming from another ballpark. She had never in her life considered going the management route in television. She'd have to give up being on the air, but being a news director certainly had compensations.

Power, for one. Both editorial and over personnel. And experience was genuinely valued. True, news directors did face some of the same risks as anchors—station owners were always on the lookout for the latest news director star, too—but it wasn't *quite* as capricious.

Rhett was still talking. ". . . at Sunshine. A few years down the road, you might be interested in coming out to Phoenix. We could use a woman of your caliber in Sunshine management. Who knows? Maybe it would make sense for you to do a midcareer executive program, at Harvard Business School, for example." He paused. "What do you say?"

She took a deep breath. *What a great feeling. In demand, able to say yes or no, and he's waiting for my answer.* She rose and paced the office, staring down at the woven gray carpet. "I say I'm very flattered, Rhett, and certainly interested, but I need time to think."

"Certainly. Of course." He rose and extended his hand, then held on to hers and covered it with his own. "If you'd rather stay on the anchor desk, Natalie, that's an option, too. But I truly believe the best next step for you is the news-director role."

"I will think about it."

"If you have any questions, call me. Anytime."

She nodded and walked out, her head high and her heart thumping. It wasn't until she was leaping up the stairs two at a time to grab her purse out of her office and dash off to Geoff's wedding—so much for not making an embarrassingly late entrance; it had started ten minutes ago—that she realized what a rich turnaround Rhett's offer presented.

Not only did Tony Scoppio lose his job—Natalie Daniels found it.

Geoff stood before the mirror in the west anteroom at St. Jude Episcopal Church in Pacific Palisades and adjusted his bow tie one more time.

His brother, Russell, also in black tie, watched from across the tiny room, bewilderment on his face. "It hasn't moved in the last two minutes, mate."

Geoff dropped his arms to his sides. No, the tie hadn't moved. Nothing had. Nothing had changed. Except the position of the hands on the loudly ticking clock set on the musty room's mantel.

A knock sounded on the door, which then opened a crack. St. Jude's senior minister poked his head inside, his expression grim.

"Just a bit longer," Russell said, and the minister slid away, looking unconvinced. Russell raked his fingers through his dark hair and cleared his throat. "Quarter after now, mate."

Geoff noted the discomfort in his younger brother's voice. Naturally. Several thick doors and a few dozen yards away, four hundred well-dressed guests were arranged in pews. From noon until ten after, they'd been quiet. But now, five minutes later, they were starting to get restless. Geoff sensed their consternation more than he heard it. The questions no doubt racing through their collective mind were also making tracks across his own. *What's the problem here? Is this going to happen or not?*

"The problem," Geoff muttered to himself, "is that for the first time in my life I dread the future."

Russell came a few steps closer, his head cocked. "What's that? Didn't quite hear you."

Geoff regarded his brother. "Did you feel like that when you got married? Like the best was behind you?"

"Oh, no, mate." Russell shook his head vigorously. "Just the opposite. Couldn't believe my luck, really."

Geoff grunted. Just what he suspected. Not all grooms felt the way he did. It wasn't just a function of the moment. He raised his eyes to stare again at his reflection and had another first-time sensation. He was looking at a bumbling fool.

How had he ever let this get so far? Geoff had always considered himself a competent man. Other men missed the mark, made fatal life-killing decisions, but never he.

I could always marry her and see how it goes, he reminded his reflection, but was immediately disgusted. Cowardly strategy, that. In fact, just the kind of strategy he had been employing.

Just the kind that had gotten him so far into this mess.

Geoff paced the tiny anteroom's worn crimson carpet. Back and forth. Back and forth.

He knew what his gut was telling him. But sometimes, he reminded himself, he ignored his gut, if the pain was worth the prize. But what was the prize here? And what was the penalty?

Finally he raised his head and met his brother's eyes. "Do a favor for me?"

Russell looked relieved. Action at last. "Anything, mate."

"I need to talk to Janet." He needed clarity, and the only way to get it, taboo though it might be at this moment in time, was from his fiancée. "Do you know how to get to her without running into a mob?"

Russell thought briefly; then his dark eyes lit up. "Yes, I do."

Geoff nodded. "Lead the way."

Natalie sat in the rear of St. Jude's Episcopal Church, squeezed into the last free space the pew afforded next to the central aisle, the only spot she could locate in her superlate arrival. Behind her sat a young Australian mother with a squalling infant; to her right was a middle-aged American couple who couldn't stop sniping at each other.

But amazingly, late as she was, she hadn't missed a thing. The wedding was supposed to have started fifty minutes ago and still nothing.

"Something's wrong," she heard the female half of the unhappy couple hiss.

"Nothing's wrong." The woman's husband was dismissive, which seemed habitual. "The girl's taking her sweet time. He might as well get used to it."

He's right, Natalie told herself, though she felt a guilty excitement at the notion that something might be amiss. Immediately she forced herself to banish it. Janet was the primping kind, the not-used-to-deadlines kind—it was that simple.

She glanced around. Geoff's side of the aisle could have passed for a TV-news convention. She locked glances with Rebecca Himada from Channel 6, who was a young Japanese-American morning anchor and another of Geoff's clients. She was still in studio makeup and the pink suit she'd worn on air. Rebecca rolled her eyes in a "What in the world's going on?" expression but Natalie just shrugged as if to say, "Nothing at all." Rebecca next mouthed, "I'm hungry!" and Natalie smiled in commiseration.

The infant behind Natalie set up another high-pitched wail, its mother attempting futilely to shush it. "Should've left it at home," the man to Natalie's right remarked, loud enough for everyone around to hear. Titters erupted. More people stood to mill about.

Natalie recrossed her cramped legs, a difficult trick with the kneeler down, then kicked off her ivory-colored pumps, no more comfortable now than when she'd worn them for the Hope Dalmont interview. Even her panty hose hurt, somehow making her thighs feel like sausages squished inside too-small casing. Maybe it was a blessing in disguise, distracting her at least temporarily from the horror she was about to witness.

How could Geoff go ahead with this? Weren't those serious doubts she'd heard him express that Saturday afternoon at her house? Maybe he was ignoring whatever doubts he had. That would be disillusioning. *Look on the bright side,* she told herself. *If he's a coward you don't want him.*

Behind her the infant's wail escalated into a full-out scream. "Let's get this show on the road!" the man to Natalie's right declared, making zero attempt to be quiet, and people began chuckling.

The troops are getting restless. Again she glanced at her wristwatch: 12:53.

Then a commotion erupted to her left, in the central aisle, and Natalie glanced sideways to see Geoff, at that very moment, appear with his brother at the rear of the church. He stood not two feet away, in black tie, looking strong and sure. A sort of wave rippled through the crowd, prompting people to scamper helter-skelter back to their seats.

Natalie felt a crushing disappointment, so piercing as to be almost physically painful. *It's going forward. That was just a delay.* Without warning her heart sank from its usual position to some black hole where hopes she didn't even know she had got dashed into oblivion.

She clutched her ivory silk purse, her heart pounding. Geoff and his brother began to walk up the aisle.

Unthinking, Natalie suddenly stood up. *I can't do this. I thought I could but I can't.* She jammed her feet back into her pumps and exited the pew, suddenly desperate to get out of the church before something else happened.

Then something else did, which arrested her progress. Behind her, just as she crossed the church's threshold, just as the organist struck up the wedding march, she heard Geoff's voice call out loudly, "Organist, please stop the music. I have an announcement."

Funny how fast people can quiet down when they want to. Geoff gazed at the sea of expectant faces turned in his direction. Nothing like a bit of high drama.

As he gathered his will, a few faces popped up in the crowd. His mother, whose smile startled him momentarily. His Aussie surfing buddy Ian, who'd hosted the bachelor party, looking puzzled. Seamus Dewey, the firm's senior partner. Scowling.

His gaze continued to travel. Involuntarily, he searched. *Natalie.* Then he spied her and his eyes ceased roving. For some reason she was standing in the church's foyer, by the still-open doors leading to the outside. She was staring right at him. Their eyes met. For a moment, the several hundred people around them receded into a kind of unimportant blur.

Then Russell cleared his throat and Geoff was forced to tear his gaze away. The church was absolutely still.

He gathered his forces. "There is no easy way for me to put this," he began, "so here among family and friends, I will just put it straight. There will be no wedding today."

A few gasps, a low murmur.

Geoff continued. "Janet, a lovely woman for whom all of us have the utmost love and respect, does not wish to go forward."

Louder gasps. He paused, his mind working. Interesting that that little tidbit was greeted with such surprise. He used the shock wave to look again at Natalie, but this time what he saw unnerved him. Now she looked grief-stricken.

But he had to finish. "While the choice is hers, the fault is mine. I will always hold Janet in the highest regard for her courage in doing what was right even at this most difficult moment. Please accept our most sincere apologies for any inconvenience we caused you today. And thank you for your understanding."

He bowed his head and retreated a few steps. Russell thumped him twice on the back. "Good show, mate."

Was it? "It would have been a far better show never to have gotten this far," he muttered.

He raised his head to look again for Natalie.

But the space where she had stood was empty. She was gone.

CHAPTER TWENTY-FIVE

Saturday, October 5, 5:52 A.M.

Grateful for the dawn, Natalie threw back the duvet and rose from bed. Swiftly, anxious to leave the house, she donned shorts, a tee-shirt, and running shoes, and embarked on the three-quarter-mile hike to the overlook at Runyan Canyon. Only the diehard walkers were out at this hour. Already the air was warm, with the sure promise of heat.

Natalie maintained a rapid pace, running shoes crunching on the gravel that lined Mulholland. She thought back to the prior afternoon, most of which was a blur. She'd returned to the station after Geoff's aborted wedding and somehow filled the eight hours until airtime with editing the newscast script and fending off Ruth's questions. Then she'd anchored the show and driven home, bypassing Cicada, where she imagined Ruth in a dither of both irritation and pleasure to find herself alone sharing a late meal with Jerry Cohen.

Natalie hadn't allowed herself to think much about Geoff, in part because it seemed dangerous territory. And in part because her own life was in such a muddle.

She arrived at Runyan Canyon, then after another ten minutes of hiking sank down on the run-down bench that overlooked the L.A. basin. The city shimmered below, white and blue and blurry in the rising heat.

If I start the Web business, Natalie thought, *I'll be getting up every day at dawn. I'll be living on Internet time.*

For the first time in all her forty years, she would be creating something totally new. Truly putting her own stamp on something.

I just wish I had more confidence that it would work.

That was one of the big problems. The other was that she would be leaving TV. Forget about giving up airtime—that would be tough enough. She would also be giving up the whole crazy, cockamamie world of television news, which she'd never stopped loving.

It must be like having a child, she thought. *You just adore it, no matter how infuriating it can be.*

And once she was out, she'd be out forever. It was too competitive a business to allow second chances.

Natalie rearranged herself on the bench and thought about everything she'd done in eighteen years of television news. Reporting and anchoring. Mornings, midday, and prime time. Domestic and foreign. Live and to tape. Ad-lib and scripted. Earthquakes, mudslides, riots, trials, elections, wildfires, wars, executions, and in between vanilla days during which nothing much newsworthy happened at all.

I don't want to give it up. I'm not ready. Bottom line.

Maybe that meant she was weak. Natalie threw back her head and stared at the blue, blue California sky. She had always secretly thought Evie was weak in this regard, being forced to leave TV and never really getting over it. But then again, she hadn't really understood Evie until she herself had stood in the same spot.

Was the news director job the answer? It was the one way both to stay in TV news and yet branch out in a new direction. But yes, there too she would pay a price.

Natalie rose restlessly to head back home. The overlook was crowded now, with hikers and runners and dogs out for their first walk of the day. She began the uphill hike. What would it be like to give up airtime, now and forever? Natalie waited to have an appalled reaction, yet none was forthcoming. What she most felt was adrenaline coursing through her veins, and it was at the prospect of running a newsroom. *The best next step for you,* Rhett Pemberley had said.

Natalie grinned and wiped her brow. *Maybe so. Maybe all along it's been the business I love, not the airtime.*

Damn good time to find that out, too, and none too soon.

She had a strong sense, as she neared the home she had shared for a decade with a man who was now long gone, of life running its course. One thread ends; another begins. Life moves on. Different. In some ways better, in others worse.

She was so deep in thought, she didn't notice until she was mere feet away the man who awaited her at her front door. He rose from the stoop, dressed like her in shorts and a tee-shirt, and her heart lurched.

"Morning, Nats." Geoff smiled thinly. He was unshaven and looked as if he'd just tumbled out of bed. Or perhaps never been in it. "I thought maybe you'd gone for a walk."

She felt a bit on guard. "I had a restless night."

He nodded as if he understood the feeling. "I left the house early, too. Then I found myself headed here."

She nodded, pleased though still wary. "How do you feel?"

"Shell-shocked." Almost imperceptibly he shook his head. "I bungled everything."

She held her breath. "What do you mean?"

He continued as if he hadn't heard her. "I did the right thing, finally, but it was still unbelievably difficult."

"You mean you think *Janet* did the right thing?"

He raised his head, a frown creasing his brow. "Janet didn't call off the wedding."

Natalie felt the seed of an excitement. "She didn't?"

"I did."

The seed sent out a hopeful shoot. "But that's not what you said at the church." She realized she was being insistent, but she wouldn't let herself believe until it was absolutely, positively clear.

"No." He shook his head. "Because the last thing I wanted, on top of everything else, was for her to look jilted."

"Ah." Now it was clear. "Ah," she repeated. She regarded him with fresh eyes. "That was very considerate."

"It was the least I could do. I put her through hell." He met her eyes. "You, too."

She waited, barely breathing.

He shook his head. "Natalie, I don't know how to explain what I've been doing the last few months. I have been so completely fucked up and I have sent you a million mixed signals." He looked away from her and scuffed his Topsider along the stone walkway. "I don't know. Somehow I got caught up in all these things I thought I should be doing. I thought I *should* get married. Then I decided I needed X, Y, and Z in a wife. Then I decided Janet fit the bill." He threw back his head and stared at the sky. "It took me a long time to realize I was living my life according to some crazy set of rules I didn't even believe in. But by that point, I didn't know how to stop it. Since when have I done that? It's nonsensical." He lowered his head and met Natalie's eyes. "Does this make any sense at all?"

"Some." She smiled but he remained somber.

"Let me tell you the one thing that does make sense." He stared at her and the stillness of his gaze made her heart stop. "Giving us a real shot. Not some half-assed, now on, now off kind of shot, but the real thing." He paused. "You know, Nats, you're a big part of the reason I did what I did yesterday."

She made her voice light, though her heart dangled on his answer. "You're sure this time?"

He moved a step closer, his face serious. "Absolutely sure. And believe me, despite my performance in recent months, I am capable of knowing what I want."

She watched him. What to believe? How not to believe Geoff? "I may be a fool," she told him, though she didn't really think she was. "But I do believe you."

"There's only one fool here, Natalie." He shook his head, a grimace twisting his features. "The man who didn't see what was right in front of him."

The canyon was silent, as it had a funny way of being when Natalie's life was turning on a dime. She watched as Geoff came a few steps closer, then stopped and grinned that long slow beguiling grin with the tiniest hint of mischief.

"Guess I haven't lost all my charm," he said.

"No." She grinned back. "Guess you haven't."

He walked the last few steps along the stone pathway and very softly, very slowly bundled her into his arms. His voice came in a whisper that answered a deep call in her own soul. "Would you believe me if I told you I love you, Nats?"

How not to believe Geoff? Especially when he kissed her, there in front of the house where she'd lived ten years of her life, some happy, some sad, all a struggle somehow, but leading her still standing to this place in time.

It felt like an eternity before she pulled away. "Is it too hot to build a bonfire?" she asked.

He laughed. "Why in the world would you want to do that?"

"Because I've got some letters I want to burn. In boxes in the study closet." She edged past him to unlock the front door. "It's a long story but kind of the anchor equivalent of throwing crutches off a cliff."

Natalie led him into the house. "And you know what else? We have to find a really good charity. Because I've got a million and a half bucks I've got to donate."

But before she could make it to the study Geoff again pulled her into his arms and smothered her in yet another kiss. Not an agent kiss, not anything remotely resembling a peck-on-the-cheek kiss, but a let's-get-started kiss. One that even in hardened, love-tired Los Angeles had a better-than-even shot of producing a happy finish.

Acknowledgments

Falling Star is a grown-up version of the stories I scrawled as a child on the big white pads of paper my father brought home from his office. In those days I cut up the pages, stapled them together, dreamed up a title, and drew the cover. The grown-up process isn't so very different, save for the fact that I have been blessed throughout with a great deal of help.

I first thank my parents, Helene and John Koricke, who provided a warm and loving springboard for Debbie, Jonathan, and me, and made it quite clear that, what we could dream, we could do.

I thank my critique partners, dear friends and generous souls all: Tracie Donnell, whose talents blind whether she wields a chef's tools or an editor's pen; Danielle Girard, scare-you-so-you-can't-sleep thriller author; Sarah Manyika, inspired essayist and budding novelist; and Ciji Ware, superlative veteran novelist, fellow news hen, and tireless advocate. Were it not for these women, *Falling Star* might well have plunged to earth with a thud.

I thank L.A. screenwriter and great pal Bill Fuller, whose insight into plot, character, and the machinations of Hollywood is best discussed over chardonnay in the Jacuzzi.

Many thanks to writer Catherine Walters, who helped keep me on the right path during those daunting early months when this manuscript first took shape; and Chicago divorce attorney Bonnie L. Alexander, who not only provided expert advice but double-checked pages.

I will be forever grateful to my agent, Maureen Walters, whose wisdom, support, and guidance paved the way for this fledgling author. And I thank my publisher, Kara Welsh, and Berkley/NAL president, Leslie Gelbman, who solved the title riddle and gave this book a happy summer home.

How can I thank my editors enough? Audrey LaFehr and Jennifer Jahner transformed a manuscript into a book, indeed a far better book than the one they first read. Their passion, commitment, and enthusiasm made my lifelong dream come true, and I am deeply thankful.

Last, I thank my husband, Jed, who didn't even flinch when I floated the cockamamie notion of abandoning my L.A. anchor job to write novels. His boundless support, confidence, help, and encouragement gave wings to this venture and validated my belief that a wise woman waits for the right man. I waited so long I found a treasure.

Alicia Maldonado exited the Monterey County district attorney's office into the high-ceilinged, red-tiled entry hall of the courthouse, nearly empty on a Saturday afternoon. Her arms full of case documents, she let the D.A. office's heavy glass door slam shut behind her and strode toward the stairs that would carry her to the third floor and the superior courts, where prosecutors like her spun tales of true crime to persuade juries to render just punishment. Which worked most of the time but, as Alicia knew all too well, not always.

Three in the afternoon and outside the courthouse it was chilly and overcast, December wind whipping down the streets carrying with it the unmistakable whiff of manure that indicated farmwork was close at hand. To the east rose the Gabilan Mountains, the Santa Lucias to the west—two formidable ranges that stood sentry over California's Salinas Valley, trapping heat in summer and cold in winter and farm smells year round. Sometimes the Valley was a beautiful place, Alicia knew, especially in spring when the rich soil gave birth to seemingly endless fields of blue-white lupins and wildly cheerful orange and gold California poppies. But Salinas itself, the county's little capital seat, wasn't exactly picture-postcard. It was too dull, too dusty and flat, too much a throwback to the 1940s. And as a street-corner Salvation Army Santa rang his bell trying in vain to improve his take, it was too poor to do much about it.

Inside the courthouse, Alicia mounted the last flight

of stairs and hit the third-floor landing, where a Charlie Brown Christmas tree strung with multicolored lights held rather pathetic pride of place. She met the eyes of Lionel Watkins, a burly black janitor who was as much a courthouse fixture as she was and had been for so long he was nearing retirement. He paused in his mopping to shake his head and chuckle when he saw her. "You at it again? And on a Saturday?"

"Will you let me in?"

"Honey, don't I always? Even against my better judgment." He leaned his mop handle against a lime-green wall, a discount color found only in county buildings and V.A. hospitals, and without waiting for further instruction made for Superior Court Three, Alicia's good-luck courtroom and hence invariably used for rehearsal. "You always win," he said without looking back at the woman trailing him. "I don't get why you bother to practice."

"I win *because* I practice."

"You win because you's good." They arrived at the courtroom door. On the opposite wall hung a primitive hand-lettered sign: ONLY FOUR MORE SHOPLIFTING DAYS UNTIL CHRISTMAS. Apparently the sign had been hung on Tuesday, since numbers eight through five were crossed out. Lionel selected a key from a massive ring and poked it at the lock. "At least Judge Perkins is long gone on his Christmas vacation." He swung the door open and gave her a quizzical look. "So when *you* gonna run for judge again? Third time's the charm, they say."

Annoyance flashed through her, cold and fast. "I have no idea," she snapped and pushed past him into the darkened courtroom. He raised the overhead lights, chasing the shadows from the jury box, which even empty seemed strangely watchful. Alicia turned back around and forced her voice to soften. "Thanks, Lionel. What'll I do when you get your pension?"

He chuckled. "Find some other soft touch." Then he was gone, the tall oak door clicking softly shut behind him.

Alicia dumped the file for case number 02-987 on the

prosecution table, then loosed her dark wavy hair from its plastic butterfly clip and gathered it up again atop her head, a neatening ritual she went through the dozen times a day that she stopped one task and began another. She shed the black jacket she wore over her jeans and white cotton turtleneck, the jacket getting that telltale shiny veneer that came from age and too many dry cleanings. That was a worry: clothes were expensive and her budget beyond shot.

She chuckled without humor. She could barely afford to maintain a decent wardrobe. How in the world was she supposed to pay for a campaign? Especially now, when nobody would put up a dime for a woman considered damaged goods?

Oh, she'd had her Golden Girl period, when some of the top people in her party thought she was the next great Latina hope. She knew what they said about her: well-spoken, beautiful star prosecutor, pulled herself up by her bootstraps, desperate to win political office to do a good turn for the forgotten many who, like her, came from the wrong side of the tracks. It was P.C. to the max and a great story, or at least it had been until she lost. Twice. Then the bloom was off the rose. And off her.

She threw back her head and gazed at the huge wall-mounted medallion of the Great State of California. It baffled her to no end how she'd managed to go from promising to stalled in the blink of an eye. Now she was a thirty-five-year-old shopworn specimen with no man in sight, at least none she wanted. That sure was a prescription for a Merry Christmas and a Happy New Year.

Enough already! Get over yourself and practice the damn opening statement. "You're right," she muttered. Before she knew it, it would be Monday, nine in the morning, and she'd have to go to work persuading the jury to convict. She dug into her pile of papers for the yellow legal pad on which she'd scrawled her notes. But it wasn't there.

Damn, she'd left it on her desk. That was easy to do, because there was so much crap piled up on it. She made tracks out of the courtroom and back down to the D.A.'s office, where she punched in the numbers on the door's code pad to buzz herself in.

She was partway down the narrow cubicle-lined corridor to her office when she realized that the main phone line kept ringing. It would ring, get picked up by voice mail, and ring again. Over and over. Somebody wanted to reach somebody, badly.

She marched back to the receptionist's desk and picked up the line. "Monterey County district attorney."

"It's Bucky Sheridan." One of Carmel P.D.'s veteran beat cops but not the brightest bulb. "Who's this?"

"Alicia. What's up?"

"I gotta talk to Penrose."

She had to laugh. As if D.A. Kip Penrose was ever in the office on a Saturday. He was barely there on weekdays. "Bucky, you're not going to find Penrose here. Try him on his cell."

"I have. All I get is his voice mail."

"Well, he's probably got it turned off." That was standard procedure, too. "Anyway, what's so desperate? What do you need?"

Silence. Then, "We got a situation here, Alicia."

She frowned. It was at that moment she realized Bucky didn't sound like his usual potbellied, aw-shucks self. "What do you mean, a situation?"

"I'm at Daniel Gaines' house. On Scenic, in Carmel."

"*The* Daniel Gaines?" Something niggled uncomfortably in her gut. "The Daniel Gaines who just announced he's running for governor?"

"He's not running for anything anymore." By now Bucky was panting. "He's dead."

Alicia shivered, staring out the floor-to-ceiling windows of the enormous steel-and-glass structure that Daniel Gaines had called home. They overlooked Carmel Bay and the Point, one of the most exquisite vistas money can buy, a sweep of sea and sand that all day long had been overhung with gloom as if to reflect the horror that had transpired.

What Bucky had told her—she couldn't get out of her

mind. What a horrible way for a man to die. How grotesque, how *primitive.* She knew she shouldn't leap to conclusions, yet one was so very obvious. Still, she had to wait and see what the evidence revealed.

She glanced down at the checklist in her hand, scrawled on the yellow legal pad that also held her notes for Monday's opening statement, whose importance was now dwindling into near nothingness. The top page had no heading but she might as well have written: HOW TO WREST CONTROL OF THE GAINES CASE AND JUMP-START YOUR LIFE by Alicia Maldonado.

In a small-time D.A.'s office like Monterey County's, there was a kind of finders keepers rule regarding the best cases. When something high-profile happened, which almost never did, a prosecutor who got to the scene first could lay claim. It was ambulance chasing, county-style, about the only way a prosecutor could advance her career.

Well, she got there first. She could lay claim. Besides, she'd won more cases than any other prosecutor. *Penrose has to assign me this case,* she told herself. *I'm the best he's got.*

And the bottom line was, this was big-time. Murders didn't happen in Carmel-by-the-Sea. But now one had, and of a gubernatorial candidate, no less. It could make or break the lawyer who prosecuted the case, depending on whether or not she screwed up. That explained the sick, nervous feeling in Alicia's stomach.

She forced her attention back to her list, the only thing that afternoon anchoring her to a sane reality. Item One: *Get the DOJ criminalists.* Done. They were in the house collecting evidence. *Get Niebaum.* Done. The pathologist was bent over what they had all begun to call "the body." *Get Penrose.* Done, unfortunately, because she had to. He was on his way. *Call the Gaines campaign.* Done, with a promise to call again when she had more info.

Her cell rang. She flipped it open. "Maldonado."

"Alicia, it's Rocco."

Great. Rocco Messina, the second-winningest prosecu-